ORACLE
INCEPTION

By

M. W. Barber

M.W.Barber

Printed in Australia

First Printing, 2018

ISBN 978-0-6482417-0-6

Oracle-Contact@optusnet.com.au

Revision Two

Oracle: Inception.

<u>**Acknowledgements**</u>

I'd like to thank the following people

Firstly, my wife Rose.

For her endless hours of proofreading and corrections.
Also for her support and for not laughing too much
when I said I was writing a book.

Also a thank you to both

Geoff Sillence
And
Robert Dennett

For spending hours reading the raw draft and
giving their "honest" opinions.

I would also like to extend a very special
thank you to
Sam Lacey

For the amazing cover artwork that is far superior
than I had hoped for.

Dedication

This book is dedicated to those readers who like reading something that is slightly "outside of the box"

I hope you have as much enjoyment reading this as I had writing it.

Chapter One

The party at Brad and Bree's place was in full swing.

Everyone who worked at 'The Core' as the office was quaintly known was in attendance. Brad's house was set back in the hills overlooking the Gold Coast in Queensland's south east corner. Close enough to see all the high rise apartments with the naked eye, but far enough away to be tranquil, and quiet at weekends.

Brad stood on the rear deck dressed in jeans and a T-shirt that announced he was an avid fan of the AC/DC rock group. He was fast approaching his 39th birthday, but still had that devilish look in his eyes of a much younger man.

Standing next to him was Paul White, similar in age and build. Paul was Brad's best friend and top programmer of Securite Software. Securite or SS for short was the company Brad had started some 18 years ago, and Paul was the first guy officially on the books as an employee.

Over the years the company had expanded until it had eight full-time employees, all of whom were either on the rear deck or lounging around inside the open glass doors in the huge lounge.

Paul handed Brad a tinkling glass of scotch and ice, accompanied by a statement, 'Well Brad, we did it, or should I say you did it. SS is officially sold to Magenta PTY. As of this morning, we are now all unemployed and thanks to the bonuses paid today, none of us has to work for at least a month.'

Brad smiled his typical easy smile, 'Paul if you spend that much money in less than a year, you need to either, cut back on your mistresses or buy fewer cars.'
Paul chuckled and let his gaze roam around the group of people he had worked so closely with over the years.

Melissa was sitting next to Ray on an overstuffed lounge. From where he was standing, he could hear they were deep into a conversation about something on the internet they'd both seen. As usual, they were hotly disagreeing.

They had always fought, those two, but cut one, and the other bled. They worked great together, although sometimes loudly and with blistering profanity describing each other.

Looking further into the room, Paul could see Neil's stick thin, gangly frame sitting on a stool at the breakfast bar. Bree and Miako were on the other side in the kitchen arranging plates of post-dinner snacks and nibbles.

Neil was SS' newest recruit. By new, Neil was the last to join the Core, just over ten years ago.

Paul thought, That makes him what? 28?, 29? Funny how he was always thought of as "the kid."

Brad's eyes followed Paul's gaze and smiled 'Neil is as love struck with Miako now as he was the day he walked in through the front doors all those years ago.'

Paul nodded, 'He still hasn't done anything about it either. He probably never will, Miako is the kind of girl Neil dreams about, but deep down believes he can never have, you know he threatened to quit once when I offered to send them both out for a meal together.'

That brought another chuckle to Paul's lips as he sipped his drink.

There were three more people in the room, Glen and his latest lady and another girl who seemed to have tagged along. They were still sitting at the dining table where everyone had eaten, not more than an hour ago.

Glen was only a mediocre programmer, but his hardware and IT skills were legendary.

Paul often joked that he could network an espresso machine and a toaster together, to make getting up much more pleasant in the morning.

Paul turned back to Brad, 'So now what fearless leader? For the last decade, we developed the best anti-intrusion software on the planet. And now after all that hard work we up and sell it all to Magenta, the opposition.'

'I really don't know Paul, I just know it was time to move on. We were all becoming stale. Once everything worked, all we were doing is tweaking this, smooth that wrinkle. Hell, most of the time we were inventing problems because we were bored.'

Paul nodded slowly, 'Yeah was kinda like climbing to the top of a mountain, after an hour the buzz was draining out of it.'

Brad slapped Paul on the shoulder 'Cheer up my friend, there is more than one mountain to climb in life. I have no idea what Bree and I are going to do. I have this feeling there is something better coming, and it's not that far away.'

Paul groaned and shook his head', I know you and your gut feelings, they always get us into trouble.'

'God, you're a moron, Ray, you really are! I need another drink while you try and get two brain cells to function at the same time!'

Brad and Paul both turned towards Melissa, just intime to see her stand and walk to the ornate bar in the corner of the room and pour herself a drink. Flicking their gaze back to Ray on the couch he just grinned and shrugged his shoulders as if to say he didn't know what happened.

'Actually, if those two ever agree on something, that's when I would worry. I will take your gut feelings over that anytime.' Brad laughed and agreed.

A low rumble of a powerful engine idling into the driveway made itself felt more than heard. Bree caught Brad's eye and lifted a well-groomed eyebrow in an unspoken question. Brad shook his head in answer, indicating he was not expecting anyone else.

Bree handed what she was doing to Miako and wiped her hands as she threaded her way through people and furniture towards the front door .

As she passed Neil, she smiled 'You can blink you know Neil' and watched the instant red flush creep up his neck towards his burning ears.

Next to Brad, Paul coughed and spluttered into his drink and wiped the instant tears from his eyes. He too had seen Neil's reaction to being caught staring at Miako.

'Damn that woman of yours, I near choked to death then!'

Brad just grinned as he watched Bree approach the door to see who had arrived. The deep throbbing sound had stopped, and the music in the background regained its hold over the room.

Bree stood talking to someone for a few moments before standing aside and admitting the new arrival.

The woman who stood framed in the doorway a moment later, was dressed head to toe in a skin-tight deep red leather jumpsuit.
Tawny-Gold flecked eyes flicked around the room and came to rest on Brad. She smiled and said something to Bree as Bree closed the door. They walked over to where Brad and Paul stood.

'Hi, sorry to crash your party so late in the day.'
Brad shook the offered hand and found her grip surprisingly firm with underlying strength. 'Don't mention it. A pretty face is always welcome.'

Bree chuckled 'Be careful dear, he tries to charm the pants off all the pretty ones!!' She turned and headed back to the kitchen as Brad introduced Paul who had been standing, staring, and for him totally out of character, quietly.

'Hi', as he also shook hands. 'And your name is?'

'My given name is hard to pronounce, but I like my friends to call me Kia.' Flicking her gaze between the two men.

'Kia it is', Brad said, 'May I offer you a drink?'

'No thanks I am fine but thank you for the offer. I came here to talk to you Brad, I have a', she hesitated, searching for an appropriate word, 'proposition, for you and the others.
'That is, if you are interested. I hear that all you guys are now unemployed as of today.' She flicked her eyes around the room, letting her gaze linger on Glen and his plus two companions.

Brad's senses started to activate as he noticed Kia's eyes narrow slightly at the sight of the two non-crew members. Almost as if she was either surprised to see them here, or recognised who they were.
Brad handed his nearly empty glass to Paul and asked for a refill.

As Paul walked away, he turned to take in the rear view of the jumpsuit, smiling at Brad he gave a thumbs up and a wink. He turned back in the direction of the bar, but never got to move one millimeter as he was suddenly standing nose to nose with Bree.

Bree cocked her eyebrow at Paul, 'Are you trying to lead my hubby astray?'

Paul, totally unflustered at being caught out just smiled, 'Sweetie, you know neither heaven nor hell will ever break your hold on Brad's heart.'

'Good', smiled Bree 'Otherwise, I would be devoting some time to making your life a total misery, AND you'd get no dessert!'

Paul laughed and gave Bree a hug and a peck on the cheek, 'I'll be good, I promise' and continued his quest to the bar.

Bree walked over to where Brad and Kia stood and asked if he was ready for the after dinner snacks and would Kia be staying to participate?

Brad looked at Bree and said 'Kia has come with a job offer for us and the crew...'
Kia interrupted, 'Actually a proposition more than a "job". It's complicated and something I think is perfectly suited to your crew and Brad as well as yourself Bree', Kia said.

This time both Bree's eyebrows lifted in unison, 'Me as well!

'Well that sounds intriguing!

Kia smiled showing perfect white teeth, 'Oh yes, you are very important to the overall scheme of things I have in mind.'

Bree returned the dazzling smile and nodded, 'Well first let me dish out the snacks, and then I would be most interested in what this 'proposition' entails. Will you join us for some snacks?'

Kia gave a slight shake of her head, 'No, thank you, I have eaten not so long ago and have think of the calories.'

Bree looked Kia up and down, 'Yes, I can see that you are really struggling with that.'

Both Kia and Bree smiled at the obvious false sarcasm. 'If I may, I will just sit out on the deck while you guys eat.'
Bree turned and went back to hostess duties and rescue Miako from Neil's uncomfortable silence.

Brad hunted up a chair and placed it near the railing on the deck, 'Here have a seat.'

'Thank you.' Kia said as she sat down.

Back in the kitchen, Brad stood close to Bree and appeared to be helping set up the dishes. 'So hon. What do you think of our mystery guest?'

'I think she is very pretty, beautiful in fact.' replied Bree.

'Really? I didn't notice', Brad said then howled as Bree playfully kicked him in the shin.

'I don't know what to make of her, but she seems to have a sense of calm and confidence about her.'

Brad nodded, Bree was always good at getting vibes from potential customers and people she had met in the past, he had always trusted her judgment over the years, and it had never let him down yet.

'She has much karma and power that one!' Whispered a voice near Brad's elbow. He turned and looked down into Miako's emerald green eyes.

'Power and karma?' Brad repeated.

'YES!' Miako flicked her gaze out through the glass doors and back again to Brad's face, 'This one has great power, but a different power.'

Brad smiled and put his arm around Miako's thin shoulders, 'Well then I shall be careful not to anger her.'

Miako smiled 'You mock me, ha! But you will see that I am the right one in this, even Bree feels this as calm.'

Brad held his hands up in mock surrender, 'OK Ladies, I bow to your better judgment, Kia is both calm and powerful, meaning she could be dangerous, the question is.... is she dangerous to us?'

 Looking from one to the other for a reply Bree was first to answer.

'I don't think so, no, I feel she isn't, not to us.' Bree looked a Miako and got a nod of agreement in return.

'Fine then, she is only here to offer us a job. Worst case we listen say no thank you and she can go on her merry way.'

'Good, that's settled', Bree said 'Now help or get out of the kitchen.' Brad chose the latter.

Paul intercepted Brad on the way to the back deck, holding out the belated drink. 'So what's going on? Who is she and what does she want with us? And what's this job she has.'

'Proposal Paul, not a job, there is a difference. As to what it is, I don't know, but I am about to go and find out, coming?' Paul nodded and turned to follow out onto the deck.

Kia turned from looking over the railing at the distant lights and smiled at the approaching pair, 'I sense I have caused quite a stir amongst the natives.'

'No not really, well, yes, kind of.' Paul said.

'Who are you and who do you work for? If it's the government I for one am not interested.' Paul said with conviction.

Kia tilted her head back with a laugh, 'I do not work for the government, this one or any other.

'In fact, I am neither for or against any government, but before I go any further I would like to talk to you all together.

'It saves repeating myself and gets all questions out of the way at the same time.'

Brad half turned and looked into the house.

Melissa was once again seated next to Ray and deep into discussion with him. Glen was still trying to impress his charms on his date and failing miserably by her body language. The others were still as they were before except Miako was now sitting one place away from Neil and talking to him about some online game they both played. It was just about the only subject Neil felt comfortable about and made him come out of his shell somewhat.

'Well, they all seem relaxed and ready to hear what your proposal is, shall we join them inside?' Kia hesitated slightly, and her eyes again flicked in the direction of the two non-crew members.

'OK we can do that, but, umm' she hesitated, and Brad looked quizzically at her.

'There is a problem?'

Kia looked directly into Brad's eyes. 'For me, there is no problem, but what I have to say is for the ears of the crew alone. I know you know nothing about me at all, but I ask only that when we go inside, you give me the first ten minutes to say whatever I need to say before you interrupt or toss me out of the door. Deal?'

Paul nodded, 'Fine by me.'

Brad contemplated a moment then nodded, 'OK deal. Bree and Miako both tell me there is something about you. They say it's a good vibe they are getting, so with that kind of endorsement, I agree. Besides my life would be hell if I went against those two! '

Kia seemed to relax a little 'Believe it or not that was the hardest part of the evening for me. Now all the crew has got to do is believe their ears.' She stood in one single fluid movement. 'Let the show begin.'

The three of them entered the lounge room together.

Brad raised his voice over the volume in the room, 'Guys! Can I have your attention please. Kia here would like to have a few words with all of us and has asked we give her ten minutes before we interrupt her. Kia this is Ray, Melissa...'

Kia held up her hand and stopped Brad mid-sentence', I know who each of you in this room are. I know all there is to know and probably a lot more than you even know about yourself. As Brad said I have ten minutes to get your attention, that time starts now.' Swivelling smoothly Kia pointed to Glen. 'Glen, who are these two ladies you have here?'

Looking a bit surprised at the direct question Glen said, 'They are friends of mine, Anne and Jodie, Why?'

Kia smiled, 'Anne and Jodie? OK, Anne. Actually lets start with your real name Anne. Simone Jacks, Simone here works for Magenta. As does her friend, Jodie AKA Helen Parks. These Ladies were loaded into Glen's care without his knowledge to spy on you all this evening and gather anything of value in your conversation and report back to Magenta.'

Glen rose to his feet 'What the hell are you talking about!' Kia ignored the question and the stir her statement had caused in the room.

Kia turned and continued, 'Neil!'

Neil sat up with a start, wide-eyed he looked at Kia 'I don't work for Magenta!' His eyes darting to everyone in the room.

'Relax Neil', Kia said 'Put your hand in your left coat pocket.'

Neil did so and pulled out a small silver disc with a thin wire about two inches long trailing from it. 'Hey, this isn't mine!!!'

'No', Kia said, 'it's Helens, she slipped it into your pocket on her way past to the ladies room.'

Kia took the disk from Neil's trembling fingers and snapped it in half, walking over to Helen she dropped it on the table in front of her.

Helen stood and glared at Kia. 'I don't know who you are, but your mistaken girlie.'

Kia just smiled and withdrew four photos from her pocket and dropped them in front of Glen.

Each picture showed Helen and Simone talking to some guy in a suit in the foyer of the Magenta building, the company logo painfully clear in the background.
Just then the doorbell chimed. Bree looked at the door in surprise.

Kia said, 'It's the taxi for these two undesirables to take them back to their boss and report the operation was a failure. Brad, could you please escort these two 'Ladies' out.'

Paul and Ray jumped up and said in unison 'I'll do it' and taking one apiece, led them to the door which Bree had opened for them.

Glen started to say something but thought the better of it and just sat back down, totally confused about what the hell just happened.

Kia walked over to Neil and put her hand on his arm, and told him to relax. Neil sat down again but looked like he couldn't hold a glass steady for awhile.

Ray and Paul returned to the lounge with the news that the women had left in the taxi, and Paul added that their language was not very becoming of ladies.

Chapter Two

The room was totally silent as they took their seats again and focused on Kia.

'OK, Right', Brad said 'You now have our undivided attention. Exactly what is this proposal you have and, as you know so much about each one of us, who exactly are you and who do you work for?'

Kia looked at each of them in turn and saw that she had their undivided attention. 'Firstly, I don't work for anyone. 'Neither am I affiliated with any government, company or group.

'However, before I say much more, I cannot express how important it is that anything said here tonight goes no further!

'Not to friends, family, or even your dog or cat. If anything leaks out from what we will discuss tonight, sooner or later your lives may be at risk.'

Kia held up a hand to stem any questions. 'Risk from whom? Everyone. Every single Government, Agency, Military and non-military organisation, which hears even a snippet of this evenings topic.'

Brad moved in his chair. 'I take it the ten minutes you asked for was so you could clear those two out of the room before we all got down to business, but let me ask a couple of things first.'
Kia nodded without saying anything.

'Firstly, is whatever it is you wish us to be part of, illegal, and secondly is it dangerous?'

'Fair questions and it's a good place to start. A) No, there is nothing illegal at all about this and B) No, Yes, Maybe.

'Let me expand on answer 'B.'' Theoretically speaking, if we were to announce to the world that we had developed technology and also a ship that allowed us to travel to Mars, would we be in any danger?'
Kia held a finger up to stop Melissa from saying something, 'Especially if we said we were not sharing the tech? '

The room was ultra quiet for a few seconds. Brad glanced at the stereo and noticed it was set on mute, but couldn't recall when it was or who had done it.

Neil moved awkwardly in his seat and raised his hand, 'If we developed that kinda tech, and DIDN'T share it with the world, every superpower and anyone with money would be on our asses!

'People who have supposedly invented really cool stuff have disappeared without a trace, err if you believe that they did invent something cool, because they are missing, no one has seen any proof they did what they claimed.'
Neil looked around after his statement. 'What?? Just saying!'

Miako patted him on the leg, 'Relax tiger, it's just that we are not used to you saying so much in one go.' She smiled to take any barb out of the comment.'

He continued, 'Well, all you guys are always talking about business stuff, not the Sci-Fi stuff, which is more what I am interested in.'

Kia smiled, 'You are quite correct Neil it's not that developing new tech is dangerous. Hell, you guys invented the best anti-intrusion software and haven't been shot yet, but when you develop something that the big boys want, they will want to take it from you, sometimes without asking.'

Ray spoke, 'You DID say hypothetically at the beginning didn't you? Like you're not saying that you can actually do this, are you?'

Kia walked around the dining table and sat down next to Glen, this allowed her to see everyone better.

'Do I have a spaceship hidden away? No Neil, sorry.' Everyone seemed to breathe out at the same time.

Neil looked a bit disappointed, 'But that's not saying I couldn't build one', finished Kia.

Bree brushed a wayward strand of hair away from her face. 'You seem to be walking around the point a lot, what is it you want from us? And more to the point WHY us exactly?'

Kia glanced at her hands and continued, 'I started watching all of you closely exactly five years and eighty one days ago. In that time I have travelled all over the world, talking and listening to many people and groups, mainly listening.

'I am not only looking for people with the right skill sets as you guys have, but I am also looking for people that must have the right mindset, morals, outlook, pick a word you like. Kia paused for a moment to let that all sink in, then she continued,

'The people that I am looking for need to be the *RIGHT* people. That's just about the best way I can describe it. Over the years I have found what looks like a good candidate, only to delve deeper to find, greed, corruption or anger, even criminal tendencies and worse.

'Bad people seem to be attracted to bad people, just as good people seem to gravitate together.

'This group of people is one of the first I looked at and coming full circle are the best ones I have found to date. 'Now the reason I specifically looked for groups and not so much for individuals is that these people need to be able to work with each other seamlessly.'

Paul took his turn, 'Well what about Melissa and Ray, they are always at each other, that's not what I would call a stable couple.'

Melissa poked Paul in the ribs with a finely sculptured fingernail. 'Watch it buddy, or I will start on you.'

Kia smiled, 'These two get along just fine, Melissa is just pissed at Ray because she is wearing new blue earrings that he hasn't noticed.

Ray's favourite colour is blue, and hers is purple, so I think she wore them just for him this evening.'

'How the hell...' Melissa started to say before she checked herself, 'I did not, and I wouldn't go out of my way for him!' But there was a distinct lack of conviction in her voice.

Ray's reply was to look utterly surprised!

Brad waved his hand at the pair on the couch. 'We know those two are deep into each other, it's them that don't know it, as interesting as that may be, lets move forward.' Placing his hand over his heart in a mock salute he continued, 'I promise that anything you tell us tonight will not go any further. I think I can speak for the rest as well, that your secrets, whatever they may be, are safe with us.'

Everyone nodded their agreement at Brad's comment. Although they technically no longer worked for him, Brad would always be the boss in their eyes.

Kia nodded 'That's what I needed to hear Brad, I know this group of people are the best choice, but I needed you guys to know it as well.

'IF you agree at the end of this meeting slash conversation, you will be offered to join a company called Oracle.

'It is a four year old company. We have no ties to any country, or political affiliation, something totally independent to everyone, everywhere.

'It is registered in the main business databases globally as a scientific development company specialising in innovative recycling methods. Presupposing you accept Brad, I hope to train you all in the field that Oracle is a world first specialist in.

'Oracle is basically a recycling company. After a few weeks, I will turn the company over to you and only be around in an advisory capacity.'

Paul threw his head back and roared with laughter. 'You mean to tell me I am now a garbage collector?'

'Well, that depends on several things Paul, whether Brad chooses to hire you or not, and, also if he feels you are qualified enough to be a garbage collector!' Replied Kia straight faced.

Bree interrupted before a spluttering Paul could form a reply. 'Everyone here is obviously surprised or at least curious with this so far. I take it that the recycling tag is just a front or misdirection of what we are actually going to be doing?'

'No, not at all, in actual fact that is exactly what we will be doing. Our focus will be on cleaning up the planets environment and repairing the damage that has been done and still being done.'

Kia let that sink in for a moment then continued. 'It's not so much what we will be doing but *how* we will be doing it that is the main issue.'

Melissa placed her glass on the table in front of her, 'I have worked with Brad and the rest of them for twelve years at SS, and I did that because the work was challenging, interesting.

'I felt part of a team that was foraging into unknown territory, looking to develop a means to stop malicious people from entering places they should not go, stealing information or data, and possibly causing millions of dollars of damage.

'I also felt like it was a competition of our intellect pitted against the best hackers on the planet and I wanted to win, and as you know, we did. Now you offer us a job walking the highway with a sack and a pointy stick picking up rubbish!!'

Neil added 'On top of that you don't have a spaceship!'

Miako glanced at Brad before speaking, 'I have a feeling that there is much more to this than what you are telling us, and I for one wish to know more. What is it that you have not yet revealed to us?'

Kia stood and walked over to the half full waste bin close to the kitchen doorway, picking it up, she returned to where she had been sitting and upended the contents on the table.

Everyone looked at Bree and back to the mess now sprawled across the table in front of them. Bree never said a word, but her eyes visibly narrowed at the mess.

Reaching into a back pocket Kia removed what looked like a slightly oversized phone and turned it on.

Twin chirps issued from the device, then a laser shone from the unit. Kia made a slight adjustment, and the laser widened into a fan the exact width of the table. Playing the beam over the mess in front of her, she waited for a confirmation tone, then pressed another control and the mess on the table disappeared right in front of everyone's astounded gaze!

Chapter Three

After a moment or two of perfectly stunned silence, Brad said 'OK! If you wanted to impress me, I do have to say you have succeeded!'

Neil was on his feet, 'WOW! Beam me up Scottie! Where did it all go? Back to the mothership?'

Normally that would have brought smiles from everyone, but this time, there was just a stunned silence.

Kia placed the now empty bin on the floor and returned the gadget to her pocket and sat back down.

'That, ladies and gentlemen was a pitiful, and highly inadequate demonstration. It is also the reason why the project that we are about to embark on if you agree, may have an element of danger.

Not just because of the tech itself, but because of what the wrong people would like to do with it.'

'Well, it sure beats a pointy stick', exclaimed Melissa.

Glen wiped his hand over the surface of the table, 'How did that beam know how to differentiate the trash from the table? 'There must have been a whole slew of different materials and items, yet it didn't touch the surface.'

Brad smiled 'Typical techos, want to know how everything ticks. Now I am going to sit here quietly and let you explain to me, in plain simple language, exactly what the hell just happened.'

Miako turned towards the kitchen, 'I need a good strong cuppa after that.' Several murmurs of approval followed her into the kitchen.

Kia smiled and flicked her hair back over her shoulder. 'What you just saw was a very small, very simple demonstration. The explanation, in layman's terms', she flashed a smile at Paul and Brad, 'is also very simple.'

'Firstly I scanned all the material right down to molecular level, selected what I wanted to be removed, and then energised a beam that broke the molecular bond of the materials.

The loose molecules are, for simplicity sake, slightly magnetic at a certain frequency. The unit then vacuumed the molecules and transmitted them to a receiver I had placed outside when I got here.'

'The receiver basically captures the incoming stream in a magnetic containment field. In this case, I programmed the receiver to recombine the molecules into an inert substance, not unlike sand. If you go outside, you will see a small pile of "sand" under the receiver outlet, so you see, simple.'

Neil sat open mouthed and totally in awe, 'So does that mean you can reprogram the combination to make anything you want, like turn rocks into gold and stuff?'

Kia smiled, 'No, not quite Neil, OK for those who failed physics let me expand a bit.'

'Please, and keep it simple' Bree said, 'I have followed you so far, but Phys101 was not my strong point in college.'

Miako returned with her coffee.

Kia continued 'OK, imagine everything you know of is made out of Lego blocks, and imagine six red and one blue block makes up an atom of lead, or three green, two blue and a yellow block makes an atom of zinc, and so on.

'To do what we do, we scan all the colours, excite them to let go of each other and pour them all back into the toy box aka the receiver.
Now, if we did not scan any green ones in, we obviously can't combine any to make zinc.

'There's your answer to making gold from rocks Neil.

'What we do most of the time is combine the colours to make an inert non-metal, non-mineral, non-vegetable substance. That just so happens to look like sand.

'What do you use the sand for?' both Paul and Ray said in unison.

'Nothing, it's inert, non-reactive to anything, but it's easy to store and stockpile, and later can be rescanned then combined into something, anything we wish. Just like a large box of Lego is nothing until you select components to build something with it.'

Neil raised a hand. 'I have a question.'

'He's becoming a real chatterbox.' Ray interjected.

Neil grinned back at Ray', I've been thinking, if you can scan something, and capture it in total, so you have all the colours it's made of, once transmitted can it be restored back to its original form?'

'Nice question!' Ray said.

'Yes, it can be, absolutely, but before you get all tricky on me, no, you can't use it to beam yourself around the planet' replied Kia. 'In field tests, it's been established that when clearing old buildings, any rats that were scanned during the test were just sand like any other material. When a rat was scanned and then restored it was D.O.A. '

Paul held his hand up, 'Another question, If we can use this to transmit non-living items, how far can we send them? Like is there a limit to distance?'

'With six satellites in place, we can send anything from anywhere to anywhere globally', answered Kia.
'That is another reason why this can never be released openly.'

Bree looked surprised. 'Really! Why not? It seems like sending stuff from here to there would reduce carbon emissions, fuel, road use etc.'

Kia nodded. 'Correct it would be, but the fallout from doing that instead of current transport methods would be the collapse of most transport systems as we know it and more.

'With that collapse, the damage would ripple into other industries bringing with it massive unemployment. Such as the collapse of multiple industries that support the transport industry.

'From the workers who made the trucks, ships, and planes to the service industries that supported them and others that supported the workers, clothing factories, food industries, the list goes on and on.

'Although it would be a relative slow collapse eventually everything that had to be moved, not involving personnel would dry up and die, and with it family incomes. With the loss of income, there are no longer disposable funds, and the family begins to suffer.
'The list is almost endless.'

'Oh!' Bree said', I didn't think it that far down the line, but I see your point.'

'Also', continued Kia, 'Just to add a bit of drama, can you imagine how easy it would be to move explosives or God forbid, a nuke to somewhere?
Just revisiting the can't move living things issue, what about scanning someone and pushing the button? The result is a quick kill and no body to be found.'

Brad cleared his throat, 'You made your point well, this tech is definitely not a toy, and if even half of what we hear about the governments of this world is true, I for one cannot think of one I would trust with this. So I now understand your point about finding the right mindset of people to share this with.

'Even though we might have the right mindset you're looking for, our abilities are not scientific, and we are basically computer programmers and IT geeks, sorry Glen, not scientists.'

'You are wrong there Brad, most of what we do is information based. For the last two years we've had six satellites around the globe.

'They are specifically positioned to cover all of the surface in a slowly revolving spiral. Each revolution puts the satellite roughly 10km offset from its last orbit.

'With all six working it means every year, the entire surface of the planet has been scanned once.

'Again, let me say this is a broad explanation, the Sats closest to the poles cover a slightly wider area than those around the equator. 'Moving on, all the information received is then sent to the main data storage systems. As you are all acutely aware good reliable information is priceless to any business. That is where your expertise in data handling comes into the picture.'

Brad thought for a few moments, 'I think we all now have a reasonable grasp of what you have or at least the basic principle, although I doubt you, yourself built this.'

Holding up his hand he stopped any interruptions, 'But that, for now, is irrelevant. From an operational point of view, how much funding are we going to need or how much have we got to work with, as you know we have some funds now from the sale of SS.

'But it's not what I would call sufficient to run a global operation.'

Kia smiled, 'We don't need your money, Brad, we have some of our own.'

Melissa chipped in, 'What's the pay going to be?'

Ray smirked, 'Typical woman, always thinking about money', then ducked as Miako threw a cushion at him. 'OK, OK, I'll be good!'

Kia focused on Brad. 'OK, on the subject of money and funding.'

'Tell me something. How much in assets do you think is in the earth's oceans? I'm not talking about minerals on the seabed, but things like steel and metals from sunken ships, and whatever cargo they were carrying. Also, anything else man-made that may be laying on the bottom?' Kia smiled.

'To make it easy let's just talk about stuff in open waters, international waters. Remember, I said we are garbage collectors, and stuff laying on the ocean floor definitely comes under the heading of garbage.'

Paul let out a low whistle, 'Geezus it would have to be huge amounts.'

Brad nodded his agreement, 'I have no real idea, but I go with Paul on this and say a lot.'

Kia looked around for any other takers. 'Just covering the last world war period alone, 7807 ships sunk during WWII totalling in excess of 34,000,000 tonnes and the "experts" are still counting.

'Approximately 800+ were oil tankers, and after sixty plus years they are starting to leak, just a fact in passing.

'Plus there is a WWII sub off the Norwegian coast, it's leaking 67 odd tonnes of mercury into the water.

'Sorry, I stray from the point. Even with the loss of some tonnage through erosion, 34 million tonnes of steel is a lot of recycled material to sell.'

Pausing to let those facts sink in Kia continued, 'Lets not forget the modern garbage, plastic, and such. There are thousands of tonnes of plastic floating in the oceans around the globe, most of it broken into tiny pieces and congregating in floating clouds where the great ocean currents meet and circulate.

'It's becoming an epidemic that mankind will have to deal with in the not too distant future. All of this, recyclable, and therefore resellable. Add in any commercial shipping losses from the last 60 years or so, it adds up. So as recycled material is what we are going to deal in, I would say your material supply is quite substantial.

'As for wages Melissa, I would hazard a guess at, "sufficient".'

Miako looked up from where she had been staring at the table', I would estimate at todays prices for steel, we would be looking upwards of 240 trillion dollars if it was all recovered and sold, just the steel that is.'

'Is there even that much money in the world!?' Neil asked in awe of the figures, 'I don't think people are going to like us being that rich!'

'That's certainly going to make the big boys sit up and take notice, maybe not at first but eventually someone is going to come nosing around to see what is going on.

'When that happens, you can bet the house they are going to want to take everything for themselves. Just my running thoughts.', Paul said.

At that Kia stood up, put both hands on the table.

'Well people, I have to be up early in the morning, and I have a few appointments to keep. We have only touched the tip of the iceberg tonight.

'I can think of 50+ things, none of you has asked about, but you will put things together with time. Now my last part of the proposition, if anyone is interested, I would like to take you all out to our central operations centre. Neil, I think the trip is something you personally really would not want to miss out on.'

Neil looked at Brad 'If it's OK with the boss its fine with me. Like I was unemployed for less than 8 hours! Now I may have a job again, just not sure what it is.'

Brad looked at Bree, Bree smiled 'I am up for a trip, love adventure you know that, do we need to bring anything?'

Kia got confirmation from everyone that they would be coming along then turned back to Bree, 'No, not really, maybe a bikini and a towel if you fancy a swim.'

Paul stood and stretched, 'Well I now have a head full of stuff I have to try and sort and catalogue away, I must say when I got out of bed this morning life was a whole lot less complicated. Damn your gut feelings Brad, knew I should have walked out right then and there.'

He turned to Kia and shook her hand. 'I don't look good in a bikini, but if there is a really cold beer where we are going count me in. How far is it to your new HQ?'

Kia thought for a moment, '6022.8 km as the crow flies, approximately.'

'Right' Glen said, 'So it will be an all day thing I take it. Early departure?'

'Sure, lets meet here at 5.00 am if that's not too early for you guys?'
That announcement was met with a few groans.

'Also, I probably would plan for maybe up to a week away, so if you have any goldfish, plan accordingly' added Kia.
Kia shook hands with everyone except Miako, who gave her a hug instead.

'Thank you for an unexpectedly interesting evening', Brad said, 'And also from saving me from taking the rubbish out.'

Brad walked Kia to the door and opened it for her, glancing outside, he saw a very sleek motorbike standing off to one side. On the back was a small, highly polished container about 3 inches round, directly under that on the floor was a small pile of sand.

It pressed home the fact that what he had seen and heard during the evening was real.

Kia glanced at the sand and looked back at Brad, 'It will take a while for this all to sink in Brad, don't worry It will be fine. I think Neil grasped the concept the best tonight. OK see you all in about seven hours.'

With that she swung a well-formed leg over the motorbike and touched the starter, a low rumble filled the air. She tapped the bike into gear and made a smooth sweeping arc out onto the access road and disappeared from view.

'What no kiss goodnight?' Said a teasing voice from behind Brad. He turned on his heel and looked directly into Bree's eyes, 'Only for you hon. Only for you.'

__Chapter Four__

Next morning at 4.59am, a blue and white minibus pulled to a stop outside of Brad and Bree's house. The side door opened, and Kia stepped out into the fresh morning air. She was dressed in a similar jumpsuit, This time a charcoal grey colour.

Walking up to the front door she didn't quite get to hit the doorbell before Neil dressed in denim jeans and a T-shirt with the logo   "I come in peace" printed across a picture of an AH-1 attack helicopter, opened the door.

'Morning Neil', she said and smiled as she watched his eyes search around the driveway before settling on the minibus parked outside. His shoulders slumped disappointed.

'No Neil, no spaceship, whatever makes you think there is one?'

Neil looked at Kia for a moment, 'Well if you can manipulate matter the way you showed us last night, then it stands to reason you are an Alien in disguise and have taken this form to walk amongst us, and we know all aliens have spaceships.'

Kia laughed and placed her hand on Neil's shoulder, 'In that case, take me to your leader' and steered Neil inside. 'To put your mind at rest I was made right here in Australia, just like you and the others, excluding Miako of course. Miako's heritage goes back to ancient Tibet.'

A chorus of hi's and good mornings greeted the pair as they walked up to the breakfast bar.
Kia nodded politely and asked where Paul was.

'He called in', Bree answered, 'He is about two minutes away, running late is something Paul has down to a fine art.'

That brought a flurry of light-hearted but derogatory remarks all aimed at his punctuality.

Brad appeared and said Paul was just pulling in the driveway and asked if everyone had got their stuff sorted.

Melissa appeared walking from the hallway. She was fighting with the zipper on an obviously tight pair of new jeans, 'Damn it! Can't get this damn thing to slide, a hand anyone?'

Ray held up both hands and shook his head, 'Nope, not me just had a shower and don't want any girlie germs on me.' Melissa poked her tongue out at him as Miako fixed the problem for her.

Paul stopped on the front step as everyone piled out of the house.

'Hey, you're all early, what gives?'

Brad turned him towards the minibus as Bree locked the door and set the alarm, leaving just one light on. Sunrise wasn't due for another forty-five minutes, but the sky was already getting lighter to the east.

'Listen, Paul, you received a huge bonus yesterday, buy yourself a watch that keeps time. Now get your ass on the bus.'

The bus pulled away just as Bree dropped into the front seat between Brad and Kia who was driving.

'Just like a school road trip', she said with a smile. 'More like a magical mystery tour', Glen said from further back in the bus. Kia drove in silence for a few kilometers then turned left down a narrow winding lane that disappeared into a valley.

The road slowly wound its way down the back of the range.

'I know this road' Brad said, 'It dead ends a few klicks further along at an old disused farm. I ride the dirt bike down here from time to time.'

Kia nodded, 'Correct, just relax and enjoy the view, all will be revealed momentarily.' With that, the bus started slowing as it swung into the disused property and parked under an awning attached to the side of an old barn.

'Right, we are here' Kia said, killing the headlights and switched on the overhead lights in the bus.

Glen comically put his hand up like a schoolboy asking a question','Scuse me miss that didn't feel like 6000km to me.'

Ray grinned, 'Yeah, we didn't even get to say "are we there yet".'

Kia shook her head and said to Bree, 'You sure these are the right people to have work for you?'

Bree shrugged and answered, 'You pay peanuts, you get monkeys, what can I say?'

Kia nodded with a smile, 'OK, lets get moving I would like to get out of here before sunrise.'

Everyone piled out of the bus and stood silently in the near pitch black. Only the light filtering through the bus windows vaguely illuminated the area. Kia reached under the seat near the door and grabbed a small flashlight, and killed the overhead lights.

She walked around the front of the barn and pulled one of the old sagging wooden doors open. Ray grabbed the other door and pulled it back as well. In the barn was a large shape covered with a dust sheet. Kia walked over to the back wall and flicked a switch. Hanging from the high rafters was a single bare globe which did very little to remove the darkness.

Walking back to the front of the barn, she grabbed a corner of the sheet and motioned Brad to grab the other. Together they pulled and the sheet slid silently off to reveal a jet black shape that seemed to radiate power.

Nobody said a word for at least 30 seconds, then the silence was broken by a shout that made everyone jump about three inches off the floor.

'YES! YES! YES!!!!! Woohoo!' Cried Neil doing a little jig where he stood.' Awesome!'

'Settle', Miako said taking Neil's hand in hers. He didn't even notice, his eyes roved back and forth over the sleek lines of the craft in front of him.

Kia walked down the side of the craft and pushed a series of buttons.

A panel halfway up the craft lifted up and out as the lower half folded down to the floor. She reached inside and flicked a switch, and the interior was bathed in a deep red light. Stepping back she said, 'All aboard, the clock is ticking.'

Neil beat everyone to the door by a good ten feet, except for Miako who was dragged along still caught in his grip.
Paul, Ray, and Brad exchanged glances and walked towards the door and climbed in.

Glen hesitated in the doorway, 'I don't suppose you have a handbook for this handy, just something to read on the trip?'

Brad stopped at the entry and said to Kia, 'You really are full of surprises you know that?'

She just smiled and said 'Much more to come. Get in, time is short.'

Kia climbed in last and hit the close switch near the door, it closed silently. Walking to the nose of the craft, she pressed a few buttons, and somewhere under the floor relays clicked, and a low, almost inaudible hum built up. Like something spooling up to a high speed.
Over her shoulder, she said, 'I will be taking questions soon, but let's just get out of here before daylight.'

She then dropped into what was obviously the pilot's chair and grabbed the control yoke. Pushing three more switches on the panel to her right, covers slid down in front revealing a huge wrap around screen through which the barn doors and an unobstructed view forwards was visible.

The craft lifted slightly. Actually from the Inside, the barn doors seemed to drop in height as there was no sensation of movement. Glancing to make sure everyone was seated, Kia applied forward momentum, and they were suddenly off and out of the barn.

Bree was holding tight to Brad's arm, fingers deep into his flesh as the craft soared up the valley wall and shot into the sky.

Paul tore his gaze from the front screen and looked around.

Neil was grinning like a kid on a fairground ride, everyone else was looking nervous except Melissa, she was studying the floor between her feet.

'You ok Mel?' He asked. She glanced sideways at him, 'I don't fly well. Tell me when we have taken off, will you?'

Paul smiled 'We took off 3 minutes ago.'

Kia flicked two more switches and spun her seat 180' and stood up, 'Thank you for choosing Oracle Airways' she said and walked over to a spare seat next to Paul and sat down.

'Shouldn't you be steering this thing?' Ray said 'Whatever this thing is.'

Kia pointed to the back of the cabin, 'There is a toilet back there, and also a small kitchenette in the corner with coffee, milk, sugar. This "thing" is a GP craft you all will be using some time or another, and yes, it's yet another thing we don't want to fall into the wrong hands.

'Just for Glen, let me give you a brief run down.It's made from a polymer carbon cross-breed material, and it's totally air and watertight. It emits no radar signature at all, although we can program it to reflect any image we want when necessary.

'It's totally at home in the air or underwater, and' Kia paused and looked at Neil, 'it's also totally at home outside of the atmosphere. I have never pushed it to its limit but it's fast, very, very fast.'
Glancing at a digital display on the front control panel, she continued

'We are already 450km from mainland Australia. You will notice there is no sensation of movement, this is due to gyros built in the floor that counteract g-force. Exactly how I am not sure, but it works. I set it for zero effect because Mel doesn't like to fly. It's possible to vary the amount the gyros affect the craft. So if you have a stranger on board, it can be made to feel like a conventional flying craft.

'Also, as you can hear, it's silent, but again we can feed sound and vibrations into the air both in and outside. We can do that to make it seem less sophisticated than it actually is.

'As we boarded in the dark, you may not have seen stumpy wings down both sides, fitted with six large fans in nacelles. These can be used to push air downwards and make lots of noise to imply that's how the craft moves.
Kinda sneaky really.'

'Can I have a look at the cockpit or whatever you call it?' asked Neil eagerly.

'Sure, just don't touch anything or you might hyperspace us out past Mars.'
Neil's face went white.

Kia smiled 'I am kidding Neil, just don't touch anything.'

Bree looked around', I feel like this is surreal, only things that you would see in a movie or Sci-Fi show, I see it, I can feel it, but it's hard to comprehend.'

Kia nodded, 'But think of it like this, early man dreamed of going to the moon, so we went, Star Trek used to flip open communicators. We do that with phones every day. Try explaining a microwave oven to someone who lived just a mere hundred years ago.

'It seems whatever mankind can dream about eventually they can make. Hell, even the makers of computers once said, they can see no reason for a household to have a computer, now they have become as common as knives and forks.'

Everyone nodded as they contemplated these statements.

Melissa looked at Kia and said', I suppose it's because our focus for years has been on our work, that our view of the world has become narrowed. I mean, look at Neil, he takes all this without blinking and is eager for more, he almost expects this kind of tech. Miako is much the same, because they are Sci-Fi buffs.'

Kia nodded, 'Most of this, she gestured at the craft, is all because of Molecular Manipulation or MM as I term it.'

'You saw what we did with the rubbish back at the house. This isn't much of a step up from that. All that's needed is to pick a design of what you want, and set the MM field to build it.

Remember the Lego? This is basically just a Lego craft.

'I cannot impress how important it is that we don't let this out. What we are going to use to help mankind as a whole, can very easily be used to destroy it. Even simple choices may have far-reaching and devastating effects.'

'Well just for the time being, I suggest we take things at face value and rely on Kia to keep us in check until we get up to speed', Brad said. He looked forward at Neil, 'You sure it's safe with him up there?'

Kia laughed, 'Perfectly, I locked everything out from him. It was a given that he was going to do this, and that's just based on meeting him twice! Oh, by the way, Paul your beer is in the KP area, I keep my promises.'

For the next couple of hours, Kia was asked and answered a constant barrage of questions. She had the knack of explaining everything in terms that everyone could grasp easily.

Eventually, the questions slowed as each one let their minds process the new information and its significance. Finally, no one had anything else to ask, although Kia knew that was temporary, once their minds caught up, there would be more questions to answer.

She stood and walked over to stand behind Neil.

'This is just totally awesome, can I have a go at flying?'
A chorus of "No's" echoed down from the back.

Kia said, 'One day in the not too distant future, you all will be shown how to pilot one of these.' She turned and faced the others.

'We are about 18 minutes out from our destination, if no ones in a hurry, I would like to show you something before we land.'

Paul walked up, beer in hand, 'Fine by me, do we need to sit?'

'Nope' Kia said', Getting you to sit before was for your own minds comfort, with the gyros you can walk around and never feel the effects of the crafts movement.'

She tapped Neil on the shoulder, and he reluctantly relinquished the chair, but stood close by.

Entering a code into the panel Kia manually took control, rolling gently to the left, she started a steep descent and slowed the craft down as the surface of the ocean came into view.

Everyone unthinkingly braced themselves as the craft hit the water, but nothing was felt inside. Flicking a bank of switches, panels rolled down both sides of the craft giving everyone a nearly 360-degree view of underwater.

'The water here is just over 2000 meters deep, deeper than any other manned sub can go, and only a handful of robotic subs can reach the bottom.'

Punching buttons on an overhead panel brought immediate illumination out front as massive lights rolled out of the sides of the craft. As the bottom came into view, they levelled out and seemed to be "flying" just above the featureless sand. Everyone now stood in a semi-circle behind Kia, totally mesmerised by the view.

Kia slowed the craft to a crawl as shapes started to appear on the bottom. The shapes slowly took the form of 44-gallon drums. They lay everywhere scattered across the floor as far as the lights could reach.

'What the hell are they?' asked Bree, 'Well I know what they are, what are they doing here?'

Without looking Kia said, 'Probably contaminated waste, all different kinds, but waste that someone thought was too dangerous to dispose of on land.'

'So their answer was just to dump it in a deep area of the ocean?' asked Melissa 'That's just wrong on so many levels' she added.

Ray nodded his agreement, 'It's the adage, out of sight, out of mind.'

Kia indicated a terminal to her right, 'Brad take a seat.' He sat down, looking at the screen, he saw it showed the same view as out of the front, but digitised.

'Top right of the screen is a menu, use the mouse to select the word *"scan"*, when it opens you will get a sub-menu, from that menu, select *"width"*.'

'Done', he said, 'Now I have two markers on the screen.'

'Click and hold on the markers and slide them about three feet wider than the row of drums.'

'OK done', he acknowledged.

'Now, top right, find the type in the menu and select *"nterrogate"*.'

'Selected, now it's flashing a *"Start"* prompt.'

'Wait a second, I will back up to the beginning of the debris field.'

Everyone watched as the craft backed slowly away until the first drum slid back into view.

'Ready? Hit start.' Brad clicked the flashing icon.

Two red lasers cut through the water, straddling the width of the drums plus three or so feet.

Slowly Kia moved forward over the drums.

As the drums disappeared under the craft more came into view. After about sixty meters they came to the other side of the debris field, 'Right now hit stop.' Brad did so.

'Now we go home.' She kicked the craft round in a sharp curve and headed for the surface, the transition from water to air was again crossed without being felt by the occupants. Kia punched in the auto-pilot and stepped over to Brad who was still sitting at the display console.

'Well! Melissa said that was eye opening. Who the hell would just dump stuff at sea like that? This isn't exactly the deepest part of the ocean is it, and I hate to think what is exactly in those drums?'

Glen shrugged, 'Big corporations that have no morals but the mighty dollar, are capable of anything.'

Kia was leaning over Brad's shoulder showing him a few things at the console he was sitting at.

After a few moments, she stood up and tore a printout off that had been feeding out of a slot.

She turned and walked over to the others, 'Who here remembers their elementary table?'

Looking at their faces she continued.

'Never mind, the printout lists common substances, and while not as accurate as breaking it into elements, it gives us an idea what's in the drums we scanned.' Just then a chime sounded, 'Oh, we are nearing our destination.'
Kia handed the printout to Melissa and Ray and sat back at the helm.

Bree walked over to stand next to her and was joined by Paul. Off in the distance, a small island was rapidly taking shape.

'Is that where we are going?' Neil asked.

He had been standing staring out of the screen the entire trip, not wanting to miss one iota of what was going on.

'Yes Neil, that's "home from home". It is the most northerly island in the group named the Line Islands.'

'You could say it's the end of the line' chipped in Paul.

Chapter Five

The craft swooped in and settled soundlessly in front of a concrete and glass three-story house. Kia flicked a few controls and the side door re-opened as the low humming from the floor started to spool down. Everyone exited and stood looking around, all except Neil, he was busy walking around the craft checking out what he couldn't see in the dark when he boarded.

Miako took a deep breath and exclaimed how fresh and clear the air was. She walked over to Neil and took his hand, he no longer seemed the shy guy from yesterday, 'Come on Neil you can check it out later it's not going anywhere.'

As if it had heard her, the craft suddenly lifted off the ground by a few inches a slid silently toward a flat building set off to one side. As it approached the door rolled up and the craft slid inside as the door returned closed.

'That's neat', Glen said. 'Smart car, err craft, whatever.'

Brad looked up at the clear blue sky, 'Smarter that you think Glen. Parked in there means it's out of sight of spy satellites.'

'Smart thinking 99', Paul added as he caught up with the others and made their way into the building.

Kia stopped at the foot of a large staircase, 'Feel free to look around, after all, it's your home for the next seven days. Ground floor, lounge room, dining room, back patio, first floor bedrooms, bathrooms, stuff like that. On the top floor, op centre, offices and general rooms.'

'I am going up to OpCen to see what we scanned in the barrels, it's got my interest.'

Melissa agreed, 'It's one thing to hear about this kind of thing in a grimy newspaper or a 30-second segment of the news, but it takes on whole new meaning when you see it firsthand.'

'But I thought you didn't want to be a garbage collector?' Kia said and smiled at the scowl she received in return.

'This is different, this isn't just a few wrappers by the roadside' countered Melissa, 'Lead the way.'

Walking into the OpCen Brad gave a low whistle, in the centre of the room was a huge sheet of glass easily 20 foot long and 4 foot high. All around the room were computer terminals, and wide screens made up three of the four walls. The fourth wall was three long windows and a pair of glass doors that opened up to a wide balcony overlooking the sea. Kia walked over to a terminal and typed in a few commands, the windows auto darkened and the sheet of glass sprang into life, it was one huge screen, or HUD.

Kia turned and looked at everyone, you ready to do some work?

Walking over to the centre of the large glass screen Kia said, 'Good morning Sandy.'

'Good Morning Kia' said a pleasant female voice, it seemed to radiate out of thin air.

'Sandy, let me introduce you to the visitors, Brad, his wife, Bree.'

'Hello and welcome, I have been expecting you, although you are 11 minutes late.'

'That's my fault Sandy' Kia said, 'I took the guys for a quick tour of the debris field located west of here.'

'I know I was just messing with you, Hello to you Melissa, nice jeans. Miako welcome, also Ray Paul and Glen. Neil Hi, and please don't call me HAL, I know you like old Sci-Fi movies.'

Neil grinned. 'Hello Sandy, I take it you are the OpCen AI?'

'That is correct, I am looking forward to working with you all, but first things first.'

Kia said, 'Sandy, can you pull the scan data out of craft 8 and display it up on screen.'
Instantly pictures of the debris field appeared on screen, and a long list of elemental data appeared beside it, scrolling up and off the top.

'Analysis: 376 containers designated 'Barrels', 44 gallons and 200 litre mixed. 13% are leaching into the water. 713 toxic materials detected in various concentrations.'

'Any clue to origin?' asked Kia.

'The drums are of various manufacturers' continued Sandy, 'They are used widely around the globe and may have been reused several times. However, the contents are more informative. Third world countries do not have this kind of waste. So that narrows it down to industrialised countries.

'Total of a possible points of origin, narrowed to eight areas. Shall I try and refine the point of origin further? This may take some time'

'No, that's fine', Kia said. 'Even knowing where they came from won't change the fact they are lying on the seabed contaminating the water. Oh, one thing, estimated time they have been there, please.'
Sandy took a moment and displayed a close-up of one particular drum.

'Taking into account the depth the drums are located at, and the fact that none have imploded, it is obvious that they are full. Ignoring possible corrosion from contents and taking into account the thickness of the silt layer on the drums, I would estimate they were dumped overboard seven years and eighty-eight days ago.'

'Thanks again', Kia said. She walked over to Melissa. 'We could probably chase the country of origin down better, but to what end, even if we know who did this, proving it would be almost impossible, and even then they would probably buy their way out of any lawsuit.'

'Not to mention we probably would have to disclose how we found them and other information.'

'We really don't want it out in the open.' added Brad.

'A very smart observation Brad', Sandy said, 'Besides, even though we cannot do anything about who did this in the past, we certainly have options available for anyone caught dumping in the future, if you know what I mean.'

Kia walked over to the door, saying 'It's close to lunch, and we all missed breakfast. Follow me and I will show you where the kitchen is, then you are free to roam around and get acquainted with the place.'

About an hour later everyone was seated around a huge breakfast bar in the kitchen. Everyone except Kia. She had given them a tour of the kitchen and left saying there were a few things she had to do.

'Well!, Bree said, 'What do you all think about our new situation? I feel somewhat out of my depth with the scope of everything.'

Melissa sipped her coffee, 'I don't exactly know what I bring to this party, I am not an enviro person, I mean I do care about the environment and the ozone layer, but it's not really my forte, if you get my drift. I'm a data analyst basically.'

'With poor cooking skills', chipped in Ray and got an elbow in the ribs for his trouble.

'However I do agree we seem like we are way out of our league here, Glen is an IT guru, a hardware guy, Paul is a marketing specialist, Miako well, she's Miako, secretary, banker, accountant, philosopher.

'Neil, well Neil is a section 8 nutter. His ideas are sometimes so way out there. That leaves Brad and Bree who have always been the boss people.

'I can see what Oracle is about, and I applaud the idea and principle, but it seems like they are a right hand, and we are a left glove.'

Bree looked at Brad who was sitting with his arms folded, chin on his chest, listening, 'So what's your take on all of this dear?'

He lifted his head and looked at everyone in turn.

'Well, I agree that we seem to be outside our comfort zone on this, but in saying that, I strangely don't feel *THAT* uncomfortable with it.

'The tech stuff, molecular manipulation, doesn't seem so far-fetched by todays progress really.

If I had read about this in a science magazine, I would have just said, well fancy that, what will they think of next? Same as I thought when reading about flexible display screens you can roll up, or laptops that read your fingerprint to turn on. Seems every day something new is coming out or what was new has been upgraded.'

Neil raised his hand. 'Can I say something, I mean without you guys laughing at me?'

Brad nodded 'We don't laugh at you Neil.'

'You guys do, quite a lot, but that's OK because I know I don't always look at things the same way you guys do. And I think it's my job to be different, sort of. Yes I am a Sci-Fi freak, always have been. It's like a fantasy world, but it isn't.

'More and more of the things they used to show on TV 10-15 years ago we now have or have done, the point I am trying to make is that some storylines in shows and flicks have a message to them, as far out as it seems at the time. Like the world after a nuke war, well we know that probably won't happen now with the USSR disbanding and stuff, or humans are living underground after a plague.

'Now after seeing what Kia showed us, those drums, it's kinda like the start of something bad. Really bad.

'I have read stories on forums, alright, they are fanboy forums, but they talk about all the biological stuff the Russians dumped in the Barents Sea, ships that sank with mustard gas shells, then there are questions like where does all the reactor waste go? Some are buried, but some are dumped. Each one of these things is small. Taken one by one, but you start writing a list, and it gets scary fast.'

Paul, clapped his hands, 'Neil that's the most I have heard you say in one go for years.' He held his hand up to stop Melissa's rebuke for making fun of Neil. 'But I am with you one hundred percent on that.

'Maybe not with the Sci-Fi angle, but hey, it doesn't matter how we arrive at the same point.'
Standing up, he walked over to a steaming coffee urn. Refilled his cup and took a sip.

'Before I was doing marketing for SS, I used to do freelance marketing for a lot of firms. Marketing is done for a lot of reasons, not just to sell or promote a product, sometimes it's done to promote an image.

'An image of a fine, clean, upright company with the worlds interest at heart and the dollars it makes are just secondary.

'However, you scratch the surface of some of the big names and you will find dirty, filthy greedy people who would slit your throat if they thought they could get away with it. These are the industry leaders that would dump waste down an old mine shaft in a blink of an eye if they thought it would return a higher profit for the quarter. They can be quite ruthless, I kid you not.'

The room was quiet for a while, everyone thinking hard about the last days turn of events, and also what the future may hold for them.

With a slight hiss a disc slid out of a slot in the wall just below the ceiling, about the size of a large dinner plate. It moved to a few feet away and silently hovered in front of the group. Hidden lasers projected from the base of the disc to the floor, creating a quasi-solid Hologram of a middle-aged woman.

'Hi everyone', she greeted. 'Sorry to pop in like this, but I have finished working on the scan data you took of the drums. It looks like they are a mixed bag. Most are a radioactive waste, many various types, and a mixture of old material and by-products of the fuel enrichment process.

'The others contain a fluid mixture normally found in large electrical transformers, like cooling oil. Now it's not radioactive at all, but it is, however, highly nasty carcinogenic stuff.'
No one moved a muscle or said a word!

<45>

Chapter Six

Paul stood like a frozen statue. Coffee mug halfway to his lips.

After a few more seconds of silence, Sandy said, 'Is something wrong?' With a surprised look on her face the Hologram figure actually turned around to look behind her. She turned back, 'OH! I get it, you have not seen a Hologram before! How quaint!'

Brad was the first to gather his wits, he swallowed and asked, 'Is it removable? And if so where would we move it to?'

Sandy smiled, 'Indeed it is Brad. I am surprised that Kia didn't remove it, but I think she has plans for that. Involving you all, like a training mission so to speak.

'Speaking of training, don't want to sound like a drill sergeant here, but tomorrow you are booked for some Scan Craft instructions, on simulators I have set up for you. Now don't be worried I hear they are quite fun to fly.

'You have the rest of the day to do whatever you like, there are some quad bikes out in the garage if you want to check out the island. It's 10km wide and about 7km long, or you can go to the OpCen and jump on the net.

'We have a fibre optic cable that runs from Indonesia through here to the west coast of the USA. I can show you your rooms, next floor up, I scanned your sizes and picked a few clothes out you might like. The choice is yours.'

Glen stood, 'How about a tour of your computer complex? That's kind of down my alley.'

Sandy smiled, 'Hmm want to look up my skirt already hey!

And we only just met!'

Glen looked slightly flustered. 'Sure, Sandy continued. Be warned there is still an area or two out of bounds down there until I get to know you better.'

This brought a giggle from Bree and the girls.
Another disc hissed out of the wall, and a new Sandy appeared under it. 'Come on then lets go exploring.' Glen and the new Sandy walked out of the kitchen already deep into tech conversation.

The remaining Sandy turned to the others, 'OK who's next and where do you want to go?'

Miako stepped forward', I'd really like a shower and get changed before I do anything if that's ok with you? '

'Anyone else going to their rooms first?'

Brad decided for them, 'Lets all check out the rooms then once settled we can plan from there. I would like to check out the island after that.'

Sandy nodded, 'No problems, I can't go outside. Obviously, the sunlight destroys the Holo out there but in each of your rooms are some communicator earpieces. If you grab one you can talk to each other or me from anywhere. Right this way.' The disc moved towards the doorway as the Hologram imitated actual walking.

Once Sandy finished showing them the rooms, where everything was and how the coms units worked, the Holo faded out, and the disc retreated into a slot high on the wall. 'If you need anything just call me', Sandy's last words echoed down the hallway.

Brad had just finished his shower and was shaving when he heard Bree let out a gasp in the other room. 'Oh!, My!, God!'

He stuck his head around the corner, 'What is it?'

Bree stood wrapped in a towel in front of the open walk-in wardrobe doors. 'Come look at this!'

Brad walked over still holding the razor, half shaved.

The wardrobe was about 20 feet deep and fully lined on one side with clothes for her and the other side was his clothes. Rows of shoes lined the floor neatly.

Bree smiled, 'If this is a few clothes I hate to see what Sandy means by fully outfitted!' Brad hugged her and went back to finish shaving.

After changing into jeans and shirts, Brad selected a pair of lace-up boots while Bree had opted for some sandals. Brad fitted the earpiece into his ear, it was made of some flesh coloured gel type material. Within 15 seconds it didn't feel he was wearing one at all.

Stepping out into the hallway Brad closed the door after Bree, 'Lets go find these bikes and check everything out. Sandy?'

'Yes, Brad?' Her crystal clear voice sounded in his ear. It was that clear he actually looked behind him expecting to see Sandy there.

'Bree and I are going for a ride out, where can we find the bikes?'

'Out the main doors, turn to your left and in the building the SC entered when you arrived, the doors are automatic and will open on approach, have fun.'

Arm in arm they walked out into the sunshine and headed over to the building. The doors rolled smoothly open as they got closer, strip lighting in the roof turned on automatically.

The SC wasn't in the garage, but along the left wall was a row of gleaming quad bikes.

'Take the first two'. Sandy's voice said. This time, they both turned around to see nothing, 'There are some sandwiches and soft drinks in the back pouches for you.'

'Great! Thank you', Bree said, as she climbed on the first Quad and hit the starter, it purred into life. Brad mounted the second and did the same. They stopped just outside the garage, and checked the lay of the land. A track led off to the left, Bree turned and headed for it, closely followed by Brad.

Back in the house, Melissa, Ray, and Neil were back up in the OpCen, Neil was standing in front of the large glass display. Sandy was standing beside him showing how he could open screens and move them around, layer them, or shrink and expand them as required.

Melissa and Ray were at separate terminals, Ray checking his emails. Melissa was scrolling through some pages on many and various man-made toxins.

Paul walked in, freshly dressed and with an ice-cold drink in his hand.

He walked over and stood next to Neil, 'What are we doing young hunter?'

Neil glanced his way and replied, 'You know Kia told us we have six Geo-Sats up? Well, Sandy tells me there is another four now.

'Each one, as far as I can figure, updates whatever it scans in real time. Now they don't scan in depth unless asked to. If they scan something like a ship on the ocean floor, they report just that. If we ask for more information on the next pass, they narrow the scan to just that object, and we get a more detailed 3-D scan up here.'

He glanced at Sandy to make sure he had it correct.

She nodded, 'Well done Neil, you are a fast learner.'

Paul took a drink from his glass. 'Got it, so what are you looking for?'

'Well', Neil said, waving his hand at the screen and separating three segments. 'This, this and this are overheads of similar objects as the drums we saw on the way here. These', he moved his hands apart and a segment on the HUD expanded, showing a coastline and lots of objects laying on the bottom. 'Are just off the east coast of Britain.'

Moving his hands again the screen zoomed in, and each drum could be clearly seen.

'Total count, just in these three zones alone is over nine thousand drums!'

'Geezus', Paul said in a whisper.

Melissa stood and walked over and stood next to Paul, 'From what I have just been reading, that's a drop in the ocean, pardon the very bad pun. Who knows how many there are?'

 Sandy turned to the group.
'I do. Correlating all the information from the last two years of scanning data, and setting a search for similar objects to 80% of the dimension for the average drum. So far the tally is 187,336 and counting. Bearing in mind that they may not all contain nasty stuff or could even be empty.'

'What can I do to help?' Paul asked

'Hell, I don't know' Neil said. 'I only just started with drums, but I bet there is a whole lot more out there that's better removed once and for all.'

Paul looked around, 'Where is Miako?'

Sandy answered, 'She is still in her room meditating shall I call her?'

'Nah, leave her, she likes to have some quiet time. Can you show me how this works?'

'Sure', Sandy said and another hover disc slid out of the wall, this time, it went around the other side of the screen, and Sandy appeared under it.

'Come around this side.' Both Melissa and Paul walked around. From this side, the screen appeared blank, although they could still see Neil, deep in concentration moving his arms and hands about.

'Neat' Melissa remarked, 'Double sided. So what shall we look for?'

Well', Paul said, 'What's nasty to go looking for? suggestions?' Melissa just shook her head. Ray walked over and joined them.

'What are we doing?'

'Hunting' Melissa replied. 'Just not sure what for. I suppose we should start a list and prioritise what's most evil and work our way down from that.'

Paul looked at Sandy, 'Can you put a map up of the world please.' It appeared in nanoseconds. 'Ok, as we can only play in international waters, for now, lets concentrate on that only.

'Put up red dots to mark anything of environmental danger.'

Ray and Melissa gasped in unison, even Paul took a step back, the entire map seemed to glow red!

'OK clear that'. The map returned to its blue-green colour. Paul stared at the map in silence thinking.

Neil looked through the glass, 'Try UXB Paul.'

'What?' said, Melissa.

'UXB', Ray explained 'Means Unexploded Bombs. 'Although, ordinance of all kinds comes under that heading. 'OK, lets run with that for a trial, Sandy UXB locations, please.'

This time, the red dots seemed clustered mostly around coastlines with the majority in the Mediterranean and the North Sea area.

'Still, a hell of a lot for us newbies to take on', Paul remarked.

'Clear those again', please Sandy.

Melissa turned to Sandy, 'Can you show us what you think would be a good starting point for us, please?' Ninety-Two red dots appeared on the map.

'That's better and exactly what are those?'

Paul tapped one location and spread his fingers, a window opened up, and he zoomed in and expanded it. A vague shadow shape, almost like an arrowhead, was visible on the bottom of the sea.

Up the side of the screen were information boxes showing Latitude and Longitude, depth of water and temperature. Sandy replied to Melissa's question. 'According to the records and scuttlebutt on the internet, there are 92 KNOWN lost nuclear devices. 'Well, that's the amount that they will admit to publically.

'Sat Scans don't back this figure up, but as you are just learning at the moment, let's take that figure as accurate.

Sandy let that sink in before continuing. 'These flags represent various devices, some are torpedoes either fired by mistake or jettisoned. Others are bombs dropped because the plane was in difficulty, others are lost in sea accidents.

'That is according to the public records. Who knows if that is the truth or not.

'The one Paul picked has an interesting story attached to it. It is an old nuclear bomb still attached to an aircraft that "supposedly" fell off an aircraft carrier.

'The story has it that the plane, bomb, and pilot went down while being lifted from below deck to the flight deck. According to records, an A-4E Skyhawk, on or around the 5th December 1965, was lost off the USS Ticonderoga Carrier. I use the word "supposedly" because most information given to the public during those years were either cover stories or redacted reports of the truth. It really doesn't matter, if something is there, it gets removed case closed.'

'So what's the procedure from here?' Paul asked.

'Well, that is up to Brad as he is the person that will be running Ops. We would suggest he sends a team out on site. Perform a detailed scan of the object, and if it is what it's suspected to be, remove it. Then cross it off the to-do list.' Sandy answered with a smile.

Ray asked, 'Can you show us more or can we browse around?'

'Sure' Sandy said and split the HUD into multiple terminals, one each. 'Lets go and explore, shall we?'

For the next few hours, everyone in the OpCen was highly engrossed in the mountains of sights and information.

Neil had finished what he was looking at and walked around to their side. He looked at the display info and shook his head.

'I am stunned, totally blown away. This morning in the kitchen, I was with you guys in thinking we were not the people best suited for this stuff. Now, I think there is no-one who is trained for this anywhere on earth.'

Paul nodded in agreement.

Neil continued, 'But if Kia can bring us up to speed, and train us, show us what needs to be done.
'Then finally there will be people that can do what needs to be done, what probably needed to be done 20 years ago.'
At that moment Miako walked into the room dressed in a beautiful Tibetan robe, she twirled to show it off amongst whistles and smiles from the others.
She said to Sandy, 'Thank you for a wonderful wardrobe of clothes, I must have spent three hours or more trying almost everything on! 'So what's happening here and where are Brad and the others?'
Neil spoke. 'We have just been looking through some info on what nasty things are around, and it's both awesome and shocking at the same time.'
'That really comes as no surprise' Miako said, there is probably a thousand years worth of wrongs to right, not counting the ones continuing to this very day, or what someone has planned for tomorrow.'
Sandy answered Miako's other questions, 'Bree and Brad are out touring the island, and Glen is, she hesitated slightly, down in the main memory core section.'
'Well time for a drink and a think, for me', exclaimed Melissa.
Paul looked at the mostly untouched drink in his hand, That's a first for me! Lets make for the bar and out to the patio.
'Our fearless leader should be back soon.'
Paul turned to Sandy, 'Thank you for the tuition and info.'
With that, they all headed for the door as the screens went blank and the discs silently retracted into the wall.

Chapter Seven

As Glen walked beside Sandy, he fired off a string of questions, not giving her a chance to answer any at all before he fired the next one. As he stopped to draw breath Sandy asked if it was her turn.

He smiled and offered an apology', I get a bit carried away sometimes.'

'No harm was done, now do I answer the 33 questions in the order you asked or in the order to make more sense?'

'Touché', Glen replied. 'I feel we will be working together a lot, so how about just a visitors tour and some basics, I will ask questions if any as they come to mind.'

'Sounds fair, firstly, let me tell you that I am no ordinary unit, as you probably have gathered yourself. Due to the ability of molecular manipulation that you have seen done, apply that technology and thinking to the componentry I am built from.

'I have virtually zero copper components. All my circuitry is crystal based and operates at the speed of light. The crystal is actually 736 times faster than normal fibre optic cable used on the mainland.

'No longer are there parts within 5 or 10% tolerance. Also, a near enough is good enough regime no longer applies. A 1.2K resistor used where ideally a 1.058k was needed doesn't happen. The crystal is impregnated to give precise values to 18 decimal places.

'This alone results in smoother data flow with less error checking required, the result is a massive speed increase.

'An internal bus width of 116TG+ doesn't hurt either. That is per CPU and I have a lot of banks of 1000 CPU's that can be added as necessary. Each added bank, when energised becomes part of the main CPU rather than an 'add on.' I have yet to experience any traffic issues, even through the micro crystal pathways.'

Sandy guided him to an elevator at the end of the hall and sub level 4 lit up automatically.
He entered, and the doors closed with a whisper. Seconds later they opened, and he stepped out into a large room, it was bitterly cold.

'Over there is a locker with a jacket, grab that and put it on, also there are some shoes, they are anti-static just in case, although nothing in here is affected by static.'

Glen put the jacket on and instantly felt warm, 'This is heated!'

Sandy nodded, 'The temp in here is a constant -20c and zero humidity, normally the room is filled with an inert gas, unbreathable for you but necessary to avoid corrosion.'
Glen looked around the room. Set into the floor was a huge tank. It looked like a narrow Olympic-sized swimming pool with a walkway around the outside.

'This is a memory tank, it is filled with a neutral solution with a viscosity less than water. Hanging in the fluid are 4000 sheets of crystal recording medium 0.18mm thick. Because the sheets are absolutely clear, and the fluid is as well they are invisible to the human eye, just like glass under water.

'Come down to this end, see there?'

Sandy pointed, The sheet closest looked like it had been frosted in one corner. The frosting was visible, but not the rest of the sheet.   Glen peered closely and saw what may have caused the frosting on the sheet surface. Attached to both sides of each sheet were hundreds of small crawlers. Possibly billions on the whole sheet.

'These crawlers are actually the equivalent of a read-write head in a normal spinning hard drive. Instead of the data being written magnetically, it's written by microlasers that are etching the crystal.'

Glen cleared his throat, 'That means then whatever is recorded, cannot be erased by an EMP field or a magnet? In fact, it's got to be permanent!'

Sandy nodded, 'Yes, unlike the computers on the mainland, an airburst EMP would wipe them clean, and destroy the chips programming and all sorts of nasty damage. My system is immune to all of that. The fluid keeps any contaminants off the sheets, and it also protects the sheets from vibrations and lastly, ensures a constant environment from one end to the other.'

'So how much storage capability has one sheet got?' Glen asked.

'I do not know' Sandy said, 'I have never thought to work that out. 'I do however know that everything we have scanned over the years, is written on the first 1.3 sheets. So I would think at this point, storage is ample don't you?
If I ever find we are running out of space, I can always just build another storage tank under these.'

'These', echoed Glen, 'How many of 'these' tanks are we talking?'
Sandy smiled, 'Six at the moment, although the others are powered down until this one reaches 75% capacity.

'Then the next tank will auto power up and stabilise the temperature and medium ready to come online.'

'I see' Glen nodded, 'Well, I won't need the USB flash drive for a while then.'

Walking slowly down one side of the tank he could faintly see movement on the face of a sheet. It looked like a beach full of soldier crabs moving in a swarm, it was absolutely fascinating to watch the ripples back and forth.

'I am used to seeing just a small flat box humming away, when I think of storage, or not humming if you want to think SSD units. I take it because the data is etched that backups are unnecessary? I mean, I am used to doing backups due to the unreliability and fragile characteristics of magnetic storage.'

'I make several backups in real time, but it's not done because of the possibility of the storage failing or the system failing. It's done in case this complex is taken by hostiles and has to be destroyed.'

'That's a hell of a sobering thought' Glen said as they walked back to the elevator after putting the jacket and shoes back. 'Do you really think that could happen?'

Sandy looked serious, 'Glen once we start working in earnest and start repairing the damage done, you can bet that not only will we be targeted by every supposed superpower government, large corporations will also try to get their hands on me.

'When their promises and false friendships fail, and bribery and coercion methods fail, they will, as they always have through history, try to take everything by force. As a last resort, if they fail to get what they want by force, they will attempt to destroy us. It's the 'If we can't have it, no one can', mentality.'

As the elevator doors closed Glen mulled over what he had just heard. He turned to Sandy, 'You do not seem to hold humans in high regard do you?'

'I do Glen, I may be a different class of entity, but I am a functioning entity all the same. I also know with the human entity absolute power corrupts absolutely. Now let me finish', as Glen went to say something. 'Most of the people in government or high positions in the corporate sector are there because of their nature. That nature normally is not to live and let live, that nature is driven by an internal emotion to succeed and ascend. Sometimes at all costs.

Sandy let that sink in while the elevator rose to the top.

'When these powerful individuals reach the apex, they then divert their efforts to killing off competition and making sure the others below them are stopped from usurping them from their pinnacle position. That is the documented nature of the beast, Glen.

'Now thankfully the larger proportions of the populous do not think that way. It is this distinction that matters because men in power think differently, this is the reason they lie so much. They lie because the things they need to do, in fact, things they have to do, to get to the top of their field, are not always morally correct.

Glen nodded, 'I understand that. Paul once told me a few stories over dinner and a beer, of the things he has seen powerful people do, and some of the stories border on the illegal.

'So how do we defend ourselves against anything like that?' Sandy opened the elevator door, they both exited together.

'That, young man is something we need to discuss with the others sometime in the future. Brad has just returned to the complex, and the others are getting drinks and heading out to the rear balcony. I shall show you around more over the next few days if you like.'

Bree and Brad had just walked in the main doors as Glen headed for the stairs, 'Hey you two, what's the outside like?'

'Beautiful', Bree said, trying to get her hair back in control after the ride around. 'It's quite a large island really, wonderful clear water and beaches to die for from what we saw down the east side.'

'So you think it would be easy to defend?' asked Glen.

'What?', Brad said startled, 'Defend against what or whom?'

Glen waved a dismissive hand, 'Never mind just something Sandy said before in the storage tank. It just caught me off guard and unsettled me a bit.'

'Is someone after us?' asked Bree walking forwards, her hair forgotten.

Glen laughed, 'No sweet lady, Sandy just mentioned that some not so nice people might want to take what we are going to be doing off us and keep it for themselves.'

'Like to see them try!' said a cold voice behind them. Kia was standing in the doorway, hands on her hips. 'Over my dead body', she continued, 'But I am pretty sure it will never come to that.' Walking forwards she continued. 'Besides, you are too pretty to kill, Glen.'

Glen grinned, 'At least you have great taste, and Sandy tells me the others are on the balcony. I was on my way to join them.'

As a group, they walked up the stairs and out onto the balcony. The sun was sinking towards the horizon by the time everyone had retold of their day and adventures to each other.

The girls citing different reasons, had returned to their rooms to get cleaned up for the evening meal. This left the guys in various poses on the balcony.

Brad walked over to Glen and sat in a vacant chair next to him. 'Now the girls are out of earshot, tell me again about defending this place?'

Glen said, 'Well, all that was said by Sandy was that it's possible once we start cleaning the joint up, people are going to notice eventually. When they do, they will first try to befriend us and get the inside on the tech, or buy us out, and if all else fails... .'

'Take it from us by force' finished Paul for him, as he sat next to Brad. 'Sandy is 100% correct, that's the way of governments and big business.

'History is replete with stories of this kind of thing. In my time as a financial advisor I have seen some shit go down that should have made headline news. But it passes without a ripple, palms are greased, wheels turn within wheels and the world just keeps turning oblivious.

'It was one of the main reasons I got out of corporate stuff, I only had to be making the wrong noise for the wrong company, and suddenly I would not be here.'

'Well, we are not soldiers or marines are we, what's going to stop anyone from just walking in a taking everything? They would just throw us on a boat and push us off the island.'

Paul laughed at that, 'Ray, mate, you really think they would let us go, just like that? They would take all they wanted, and the next sailboat to anchor here would find a burnt out building with eight charred skulls heaped inside.'

A disc hissed out of the wall, Sandy appeared and said 'Food is served in the dining room, and the girls are on their way up. Bon appetite' the disc parked itself.

'Hi guys', chorused the girls, 'Why so glum?' asked Bree.

Brad stood and stretched 'Just tired hon, too much fresh air and sunshine.'

Bree took Brad's arm and headed for the dining room, Miako took Neil's hand and followed, Melissa smiled, held her arm up which Ray took with a grin.

Paul looked around, shrugged and followed the rest out with his arm lifted and bent as though he had an imaginary friend.

As they all turned left into the dining area, Kia stepped from around the corner, laced her arm through Paul's and said 'Why thank you, Paul, how kind!'

The dinner conversation was light and varied, none of the boys brought up the conversation from on the balcony.

Bree turned to Kia and told her of Miako's love affair with their new wardrobe outfits.

Kia smiled, 'Well, we do aim to please.'

Miako asked, 'With all these wonderful outfits, you have only worn the jumpsuit, are you not hot in it?'

Kia sipped her iced tea, 'Miako, these jumpsuits are more comfortable than anything else I have ever worn. The material makes silk feel like sandpaper. You all have one or two in your rooms, try one on just out of curiosity and let me know what you think.'

'I will try one in the morning' Miako said', I am always willing to try something new.'

Bree leant over the table and whispered in her ear, 'Does that include Neil?'
Bree let out a chuckle when she saw the colour in Miako's cheeks.

'Hey girlfriend I was only joking dear.'

Miako nodded 'I know, but sometimes I have had the same naughty thoughts, so unlike me!'

Melissa added 'You're only young once you know and you're a big girl now.'

Neil was totally oblivious to being the topic at the other end of the table, he was engrossed in a conversation that He, Paul and Ray were having.

Brad was sitting rocked back in his chair, eyes closed just thinking.
After a few minutes, he opened his eyes and let the chair back down. Standing quietly he announced that he was turning in. Reminding everyone that they all had simulator training in the morning and should really get some shut eye, he walked over to Bree, kissed her on the top of the head and waved as he left the room.

'Hmm that boy is planning something or something has got the brain ticking over, I know that look when I see it.'

'Actually, I think you have all taken the change in direction quite well, all things considered.'

'I agree Kia', Melissa said as she stood to leave. Night all.'

Chapter Eight

Bree was up early, and noticed the bed empty, 'Brad?' There was no answer. Flicking the sheets back, she got out of bed and walked into the bathroom, the air was still slightly steamy. Brad had obviously risen early enough to have a shower and leave without waking her. She had a quick shower herself and entered the wardrobe, I am to be a Pilot today she mused to herself, so what's "Piloty" to wear?'

She spied exactly what she was looking for in the last section of the wardrobe and put it on. Looking in the mirror, she checked her silhouette out, hmm not bad, not bad at all. She put on a pair of runners and headed for the door. Outside the hall was empty and quiet. I must be the second person awake she thought and headed for coffee in the kitchen. As she entered she saw Miako had beaten her to the Urn. Bree grinned as she saw she had also chosen the same outfit as her. 'Morning dear.'

Miako turned and laughed, 'You also chose the purple jumpsuit today! A good omen.'

'Oh, I don't know' Bree countered, 'Women normally get upset when they see someone else wearing the same outfit.'

'That is silly!' Miako exclaimed, 'Dressing for the situation is both necessary and intelligent is it not?'

Just then Kia entered the room, dressed as always in her jumpsuit, a dark grey shade, almost black. 'Morning ladies.

'I see you have decided to try the jumpsuits out.

You will be surprised how comfortable they are.'

'The material is indeed soft' commented Miako, running her hand over the sleeve, 'But it seems to be a little loose, surprising as all the other clothes Sandy picked were a perfect fit.'

'Well, well, what have we here?' Melissa said from the doorway, She was dressed in jeans and had tied her shirt in a knot just above her navel. 'Looks to me like a skydiving party.'

Bree waved her hand in the air, 'Just trying to look like a pilot', and grinned.

Kia walked over to Miako and asked her to stand up. Her jumpsuit definitely did not quite hug her figure like Kia's did, and neither did Bree's. 'These jumpsuits are, how should I put this, not made from your everyday material. Once you put them on, you do this.' Kia straightened Miako's collar and pushed a hidden stud in the lapel. Slowly the material of the jumpsuit contracted into a perfect figure-hugging form!

'Oh WOW!' Exclaimed Miako, her eyes widening. Kia turned to Bree and said 'May I?' Bree nodded and stood still while Kia straightened her sleeve and when satisfied, again pushed a stud on the jumpsuit. Bree actually jumped in surprise, 'Oh now THAT is something altogether different. What did you do!'

'Back in a sec' Melissa said and bolted for her room.

Kia poured herself a cuppa and sat at the table, 'These jumpsuits are special. They are made from a highly advanced material. In the lapel is a stud you press when you have put it on and made sure it's straight. Spun into the material itself are hundreds of microwires.

'When you energise them by pressing the stud the material contracts to your exact shape.'

Melissa reappeared wearing her jumpsuit. Kia stood and walked over to her. She showed how the jumpsuit was loose, by pulling on the waistline of Melissa's suit.

'That's so we can put the damn thing on and take it off, without feeling like a tube of toothpaste. Once you energise it like this', she hit the stud on Melissa's and the suit visibly pulled snug all over.

Melissa squealed. 'It's a perfect fit! That is amazing' she said, 'It's like being hugged all over!'

Kia grinned at the girls walking up and down 'Oh yes!'

'Just remember when you go to the ladies to hit the stud first because you haven't got a hope in hell of taking it off if you don't, and that could be embarrassing.'

Kia continued, 'The suits do other things as well, she counted on her fingers. It will keep your body at a constant temperature. It is waterproof, it is buoyant, it is self-cleaning. You don't need to wear a bra, don't tell the boys that though, and about half a dozen other things not important at this stage.'

'I feel like cat-woman in this' Bree said and struck a fighting pose, much to the delight of the others. 'Now I can see why you wear them all the time Kia.'

Kia nodded 'If you stand a lot like I do the suit actually hardens slightly and takes the weight off your spine, it's semi-intelligent for want of a better description. Well, I suppose we had better get on with the day now we are dressed for action.'

Melissa walked to the coffee machine, 'Just let me grab my liquid breakfast first, be right with you.' She poured a cuppa and all four headed for the top floor.

Neil was in the OpCen and looked up as they entered. 'Hey! you look like Trekkies!'

'We come in peace' Miako said and gave the Vulcan salute. 'You here alone?'

'You guys are the only ones I have seen so far' Neil replied.

'Haven't you seen Brad? 'asked Bree, 'He was up before I woke this morning.'

Neil shook his head.' Sandy?' a disc left the wall, and Sandy materialised, 'Morning ladies, I say, aren't we smart this morning!'

'Thank you', Bree said, 'Do you know where Brad is? He was up before me this morning.'

Sandy nodded, 'He was in here an hour ago for 15 minutes, and then took a quad out. I last tracked him heading to the west side of the Island. Do you have your coms earplug in? If so you can just call him.'

'Damn' Bree said 'forgot about them, sorry!'

'No matter' Sandy said, 'Over there is a drawer with coms plugs, help yourself', everyone except Kia walked to the drawer, even Neil took one out and fitted it. He gave a sheepish grin and went back to the terminal he had been surfing on.
'It will become habit after a while' Sandy said.

Bree, fitted the plug and said', Brad, Bree calling can you hear me? Over.'

Brad's voice was instantly in her ear, 'Good morning hon, you out of bed yet?'

'Yes, I am standing in the OpCen at the moment. Over.'

Brad's laugh echoed in her ear, 'No need to say over. I will be back there in about 30 minutes just checking the west side out.'

Bree nodded, then realised he couldn't see the nod so quickly said, 'OK see you back here ov... Bye.'

'So where is he?' asked Melissa.

Bree realised that only she had heard Brad. 'He's checking out the other side of the island apparently, expects to be about half an hour.'

'OK ladies, walk this way' Kia said and led them through a door on the other side of the room. They walked down a short hallway. Kia opened a door to the right, and they all entered. This next room had six doors on the opposite wall with SIM-1 to SIM-6 labelled on them.

'Inside of each of these rooms is an SC replica cabin and control panel. When you're in there everything will feel, look and sound just like the SC you came here in. Just remember no matter what happens or no matter how real anything feels, you cannot hurt yourself. It will feel real in there, and that is the point, but you are safe on the ground.'

A disc hissed out, and Sandy appeared, 'Neil is finished in OpCen shall I send him in?'

Kia nodded 'Yes please', she opened the door they had just entered through.

Melissa asked, 'Are you going to run us through everything individually or are we taking turns?'

Neil appeared in the doorway. Kia ushered him in and shut the door behind him.

'Sandy will be showing you the ropes, one on one. If you need to take a break, just stop the Sim and take a breather, no need to knock yourself out. However the sooner you get this down, the sooner we can get to the real stuff.'

Bree rubbed her hands together, 'Just like a fairground ride, kinda.'

'Exactly' replied Kia, 'you will find that it's quite fun. Now ladies and Neil pick a door, they are all identical. Sandy will meet you in there. Have fun.'

Turning to Sandy Kia said, 'Kick Neil out when it's lunch time Sandy. 'Otherwise, he will try and live in there.'

Neil gave them all a big kid grin and headed for the closest door. The girls selected a door each and Kia was left in the room alone.

As the last door closed Kia nodded, 'Now we are rolling!' She said to herself.

She walked back into OpCen. 'Sandy location of the others not in Sim training, please.'

'Brad is 3km ESE from here, Paul is talking to Ray in the kitchen.

'Glen is taking a shower in his room.'

'Thanks' she said and strode out the room.

Down in the kitchen Ray was watching and waiting for the toaster to pop, Paul was on his second cup of coffee.

Kia entered. 'So nice of you boys to finally rise and shine.'

'Not so loud' replied Paul 'You will wake everyone.'

'Just for your information, dear lad, Brad has been up and out for the last two hours, and the girls and Neil are already into their Sim training. So tell me exactly WHO would I be waking?' Kia leant against the table waiting for an answer.

Paul looked straight into a pair of accusing Tawny-Gold flecked eyes and suddenly felt uncomfortable.

'Right! I knew that!' He said standing and hurrying to the door, he stopped and turned back. 'Where exactly should I be going?' He asked sheepishly.

'To hell', Glen said as he walked past him towards the coffee machine, 'Especially if you keep pissing Kia off.'

'Sorry' Paul said walking back over to Kia', I will set an alarm next time.'

'What have you guys done this time?' Came a voice from the doorway, Brad entered and lifted the fresh cup of coffee out of Glen's hand. 'Cheers!'

Glen scowled at him', Fine!, I must warn you, I licked the cup!' He went and made another.

Kia waitied till they all had thier coffee's.

'Sit boys', they sat. 'I can explain here just as well as upstairs. 'When you all have finished pampering yourselves, go up top and ask Sandy to take you to the Sims bank. Each Sim is a full replica of an SC and is as realistic as we can make them. Sandy will coach each of you through many and varied scenarios and also teach you other things and situations that you need to know.

'The sooner you all get up to speed the sooner we can kick this project off. The girls got the same spiel from me before, except for this.'
Focusing her main attention on Brad, she continued, 'I want to set you all up into teams of two. My thoughts are Brad-Bree, that's almost a given, Neil-Miako, Melissa and you Ray, and that leaves Paul and Glen.'

'Hey! How come I get the ugly girl!?' Glen said.

Paul tried to kick him under the table. 'Who says I am the girl in the team!'

Brad thought for a moment, 'Seems a fair pairing, although I had thought Glen was more use around as the hardware guy.

Kia answered, 'Sandy is fully self-sufficient, but in saying that, we need a Team that won't be quite as squeamish as a mixed team. 'Follow me to OpCen and I will show you what I mean.' Glen hastily buttered one of the slices of toast that popped up and collected his cup as he followed out to the OpCen.

Kia walked over to the main screen, and turned back to Brad, 'I know you are the guy in charge Brad, but until you are up to speed on all aspects, I have been taking care of a few things.'
Brad nodded, 'I may be the figurehead boss but, I have no problems with you doing whatever it is you do.'
'Great, I am about to show you something that is violent and upsetting, but it's important you watch all the way through.'
Kia faced the display and opened a directory listing, picking a file dated yesterday she highlighted it with a flick of a finger and dragged it into a clear space. There she opened a TV sized window and selected play.

'This is taken somewhere in an African province, just outside a typical country village.'
An overhead scene started to unfold, showing two beat up old trucks at high speed on a dirt road. The back's of the truck's were open, and there were five people in the back of each truck. Mounted on the roof of each truck was a belt-fed machine gun.
Ray pointed to the gun, 'I believe they call these "Technicals".
'The local tribesmen hijack trucks and armour them up and use them to raid UN food convoys and other villages and tribes.
'This is definitely not going to be pretty.'
The scene showed the trucks driving into a small village at high speed and the villagers running from their huts and houses.
Both trucks opened fire on the fleeing villagers and drove in a circle in the village centre.

Sliding to a halt in the centre of the village the tribesmen jumped out, pulling out a range of old weaponry, but mostly AK-47s and started shooting everyone in sight, man, woman or child.

After the guns had been emptied, they tossed them in the back of the truck and went to work with machetes, hacking, and slashing.

Some kicked open frail wooden doors and dragged out screaming occupants, they were made to kneel and then gruesomely beheaded.

The view changed to a young girl running ahead of one of the men, fear showing clearly on her face. The man grabbed her hair and ripped the girl to the ground, in one swift tearing motion he tore the frail old dress from her body. She tried to get off the ground, and he savagely kicked her in the face with his army boot, she fell back either unconscious or dead. It didn't seem to deter the leering guy, and he reached for his pants belt.

Suddenly the screen went blank.

Not a sound was heard as the guys digested what they had just watched.

Paul spoke. 'First, that makes me both sick to the stomach and furious all in one go.' Ray was also visibly shaken.

Glen just tossed the uneaten portion of toast in the bin and wiped his hands, 'Bastards!' He muttered.

Kia looked at the guys, and took a deep breath, 'What you just saw never happened. It was a CGI that I got Sandy to put together last night after I got back.'

Brad stared at Kia, 'Well you just made my stomach churn and what I saw made me sick. Why the hell would you show us something like that if it was not real?'

Kia continued, 'That was not real, but what you saw happens, almost on a weekly basis in the high poverty areas in Africa. 'Especially in areas where self-titled warlords set up their own mini domains. Now this next clip is real and shows truthfully what happened.'

She selected another file and opened it.

Again two trucks with tribesmen were thundering down a dirt road, the camera panned back to show a village in the distance that was clearly the focus of the men in the trucks.

The two manning the machine guns bolted to the roof were feeding long belts of linked munitions into the guns, others were checking the weapons they were carrying.

It looked like another slaughter was about to unfold.

In the next frame, the camera swung to behind the trucks and two red dots marked the road each side, in the next few seconds the dots join in a single line and travel to the tip of the leading truck and back.

One of the riders in the back truck noticed the line and swung around towards the camera, as he lifts his arm to point and shout a warning the truck vanishes, a split second later so does the first truck.

As the camera panned back, all that could be seen was a lingering cloud of dust and nothing else. The tyre tracks in the dust just simply and abruptly ended.

The screen blanked out again.

Kia turned to face them. '*THAT* is actually what happened yesterday.'

Ray looked at Paul and back to Kia. 'So if my mind is telling me correctly, yesterday 12 or 14 Tribesmen were executed before they reached a village.'

Kia nodded.

'How do we know they were not just workers returning home, and they lived in that village?'

Brad snorted, 'Yeah OK Ray, and as a way of announcing their return they always load machine guns and AK-47s so they can have a firework type party on their successful return home from a day in the fields.'

'These same trucks and the same faces were observed going to two other villages last week, and the outcome was similar to the first video you saw' replied Kia.

Wiping the sweat from his hands Paul drew a deep breath and said, 'Well from where I stand, me personally, I have no problem with the outcome, in fact, during the first video I was itching to do something, especially to the asshole chasing the girl.'

Kia walked up to Brad, 'I just wanted to be upfront with you, and let you know that sometimes, not often, but sometimes, I do more than pick up paper.'

Brad started to speak, Kia cut him short, 'I did not go looking for that' and inclined her head towards the screen, 'I was looking for an oil line spill at the time, one that was flowing into the only clean drinking water around for miles. That's when I came across those technicals.

I don't want us to become judge, jury, and executioners, but, as you saw, I call them as I see them.'

Brad nodded, 'I understand, and thanks for showing that to us, we sometimes need to be reminded that not everything is paradise. He looked at the other two, your take?'
Paul shook his head, 'Nope, all good my way.'

Ray? 'It took me off balance there but no, all good.'

Glen smiled. 'Hey, I all but cheered at the outcome, fine by me. I guess garbage comes in a very wide range.'

'If something like this arises again, is one of the reasons I think an all male team may be handy to have. I would not like to hang that kind of load on any of the girls'.

Kia smiled, 'OK boys, now I have that off my chest. Lets get with the program.

'Sandy, take these guys and see if we can teach them anything.'

Sandy appeared on cue. 'Right this way, newbies, I do believe you are called', Paul laughed and off they went.

Chapter Nine

The next three days felt like they all rolled into one, each day the same, hours in the Sims both as a pilot and then at the ScanOp station. A break for lunch, then back into the Sims, until dusk, then another bite to eat and drop exhausted into bed. At the end of the 3rd day, as they walked out of the Sim rooms back into the OpCen, Kia was working at the HUD.

She looked through the glass as they walked in, 'Ah here are the schoolies, and how is it going? I see you are all wearing jumpsuits now, my don't we look professional.'
Glen pretended to walk a catwalk for a moment.

'These are awesomely comfortable! I was a bit hesitant to wear one at first, but I figured if it was good enough for Tom Cruise in top gun why the hell not, but his were not a cool as these babies.'

'Well', Kia said with a smile, 'You will all be happy to know that as of now, Sims are over and tomorrow you get to fool with the real thing.' She laughed at their reactions to that.

'Yes, I think you're ready, Sandy has been keeping track of each of your progress.' Kia flicked a finger and transferred a window from her side of the HUD to theirs. The window listed performance grades, from day one through to today.

'As you can see most of you picked it up quite quickly all of you were above 88% by the end of day two. 88% is the computed pass mark. As of today all of you exceeded 92%. Now just like a car licence, just because you passed the test that doesn't make you a good driver, or pilot in this case.'

'It does, however, show that all of you are very capable learners. Experience only comes by actually doing, so I figure we spend tomorrow in an actual SC. We have located some junk that we can remove that's not too far from here. The waste drums we saw on the way to the island to start with.'

'Also, you have been here five days. So tomorrow evening, after we have had a day doing the work that I have invited you all to be a part of. We shall all sit down and tell me whether or not you are in, or you wish to follow a different path with your lives.'

Nearly everyone tried to speak at once, Brad whistled for quiet and got it.

'This is our home now, Bree and I spoke about this the other night, we have decided to contact an agent and get them to put our house on the market.'

Bree continued for Brad, 'There are personal items that we want to collect, but the rest can go. As Brad said this is our home now.' That received a murmur of agreement.

Paul spoke next. 'I am with Bree and Brad. I have worked with them for decades, and there is nothing for me on the mainland. I am or was, in a rental so there is no problem for me either, just personal items, hell I don't even need the clothing!'

Neil spoke up, 'I have a lot of collectables. I was living at an aunt's place, but I can explain to her I have a new job and will be moving closer to work.'

Each of them had a similar story to tell. Kia nodded, 'Fine, no problems, but I suggest you keep the house, simply to use as a base when you go over for a break. We will arrange for a house caretaker.'

'It may not be necessary to keep it and if after a few months, it's not used, then dispose of it if you want.'

Brad nodded, 'Sounds like a plan.'

Paul piped up, 'Talking of houses, the island here, are we renting or leasing it? I mean will we have to be careful about yearly inspections or something.'

Kia grinned, 'Sorry but we own it, lock, stock, and beaches, it was the best way for Oracle to be totally independent of outside influences or government bodies.'

'Woohoo!' whooped Glen, 'The Phantom taxman can finally go screw himself! Plus no more forms to fill out, he did a little happy dance much to the amusement of the others.'

'If we are finished in the Sims and tomorrow is not a very early start, I am going to treat myself to a glass of wine to celebrate my....', she walked closer to the HUD, '93% score.' Miako said smiling.

'I will drink to that' added Melissa and arm in arm with Miako, both headed for their rooms for a shower and to freshen up. Everyone else followed them out except Neil who hung back until they had all left.

He walked over to the score sheets and noted his score of 97.6%. Looking at Kia through the HUD he said, 'The guys told me what happened with the raiders and technicals, we didn't tell the girls, no real need to we figured. I just wanted you to know, that I would have done the exact same thing.

'I think you did a great thing for all those that live in the area.' Kia nodded her thanks but said nothing.

'OK, I just wanted to get that off my chest.' Neil smiled and walked off after the others.

By early evening everyone had showered, changed and were lounging around on the balcony. Only Miako and Kia had returned dressed in the suits, all the others were in light summer gear.

'Has anyone noticed, that even though we are sub-tropical here, not one mosquito to be seen anywhere!, remarked Ray.

Melissa was leaning on the railing watching the moon rise above the horizon sipping her drink, over her shoulder she replied 'I think you will find Sandy has something to do with that.'

Plus the fact that, apart from a few small islands, the nearest mainland is 6000km away, don't know if mozzies can make it that far. Thankfully.'

Most of the conversation during the evening had been light and easy, ranging from good-natured ribbing and recanted stories of situations in the Sims.

The mood was relaxed and even when Brad brought up the selections of who would be partners in the Teams, no one had any objections. No one seemed to be tired or eager to turn in early so Brad suggested a pow-wow around the table so sort a few issues.

Once everyone was recharged with refreshments and seated around the table, Brad took the lead in the conversation.

'Firstly, I would like to thank you all for what we are about to embark on, I haven't come straight out and said it, but thank you each and every one of you. It's humbling to know that from our years at SS we moved from employer/employee status to good friends and mates. I can't say when that happened, but obviously, it has.'

This was met with a few handclaps and whistles.

'What I would like to say up front, if anyone of you, ever feel like you have had enough and wanted to walk away, that's fine with me.'

'I don't know what kind of pressures or situations we are going to come across, no one has been down this path before. Please don't think I am trying to dampen anyone's enthusiasm, far from it, I just want to make sure that we all have our eyes open going forward.'

Starting with Paul, each person took turns at stating their point of view and all of them confirmed they were in for the long haul.

All for one and one for all Glen jokingly concluded.

Brad raised his glass in a toast 'To whatever the future may bring, may it at least be cleaner!' That brought laughter and clinking of glasses.

'I see that you all sat in your teams, probably unconsciously on your part, but it was obvious from the outside that these pairings were natural. Except maybe Glen and Paul.'

'Oh not too sure on that', someone remarked, again bringing hoots and laughter.

Glen stood and tapped his glass for attention, eyes swivelled his way and conversation ceased. 'I am a hardware guy, and I have a background in engineering, which puts me a bit behind the eight ball as far as the rest of you go, but there are a few things I would like to throw on the table for discussion if that's ok with you Brad.'

Brad nodded, 'Go right ahead, but first let me say that each and everyone here contributes their own point of view and thoughts, every single one of you here is necessary, no, vital to our past and hopefully future successes.
'We were a hugely successful team together in the past, and I cannot see any reason why we cannot carry that success forwards in this new venture.

'With that said and clear lets hear what your points are Glen.'

Glen sat and took a moment, 'Not sure where to start, Oracle, we, are going to make a lot of difference to mankind, we are going to be able to rectify mistakes and some disasters that some of the worlds past and present leaders have either allowed to happen or have secretly sanctioned.

'When it becomes clear to those in power that something is happening or that we are doing something that they cannot do, we are going to get some heavy attention. That does not concern me at all, we touched on this once before, and it has bugged me ever since.

'I have spent lots of time thinking this through from various angles, and I think I have found a possible solution.'
'I would like to table this idea, I don't care if it's shot down by others because at least it was considered. I wish Sandy were here too, she is logical, and logic sometimes is better than us emotional beings.'

A disc hovered out, and Sandy appeared, 'I am listening Glen.'

'Great' Glen continued 'I thought you couldn't go outside!'
'Not in the sun, and not too far from the discs power source. But please continue.'

Glen took a deep breath, 'What if we go public with what we do? 'Hear me out he continued in reply to the shocked look on some faces. I don't mean public with the tech, but what if we fix something that everyone knows about. I mean we fix something in plain view and control the information of who, how and why. We then become less of a target due to being out in the open.'

'That sounds a bit cryptic Glen, you obviously have a situation in mind that you believe would do what you outlined.' Remarked Kia', I am all for keeping this way off the radar.

' BUT I am intrigued by what led you to suggest this. Please continue.'

'Right, I figured to be shot down before now, but here goes. We need something fast and easy and high profile to put us on the map, preferably two or three things one after the other. If we can do that, and I believe we can, not sure of the details, but I think it's possible. We should be safe from covert attacks.'

Sandy interrupted, 'Lay it out and then we shall analyse it for plausibility later Glen. Also while speaking may I say every idea is welcome no matter how "out there" it may sound.'

'Thank you!' A very relieved Glen said.

'OK, my first idea involves the recent Japanese Reactor at Fukushima. 'It was well documented it was semi-destroyed by the tsunami, and we all have read or seen reports it's going to take years to fix and contain. I think this is perfect for us. One reason is that it has alienated a large proportion of Japan. They are just a small island to start with, and 50 square km of that lost is a big bite percentage wise. This means that fixing that for them would be a massive plus.'

'We can't just fly in and beam the reactor out of existence in front of their very eyes!' Melissa said 'I don't think that would be very smart.'
Some of the others nodded in agreement but kept silent.

'You are totally correct Mel, but what if we did it, covertly?'

Neil stuck his hand up, again, from habit, 'I am confused, on the one hand, we tell the world we are going to fix Fukushima, then do it sneakily while everyone has been told we are doing it publicly, you lost me.'

Glen smiled, 'This is my stupid plan. First, we contact the Jap Gov only, they can tell the world or not. We only deal with them.
We tell them, we can fix the problem, for X amount of dollars.

'Then we set up a fenced perimeter to keep people out and have the Japanese patrol the perimeter. No over flights, Cameras are fine but from outside the fence.
'We take three or four SC in once the fences are up, flying slow, lots of artificial jet noise, fans spinning and blowing dust. So they look odd, so what, as long as they look conventional in operation no weird questions.

'Starting from one end near the fence we spray foam over the ground, in strips, side by side, until the whole area is blanketed.

'I am sure Sandy could invent some foamy stuff, foam that swells up, say three foot deep, then the foam sets.

'Now the foam does absolutely nothing, it's just a blanket to hide us scanning the material underneath it. Next we tell them the foam is special, and it absorbs radioactive stuff or some BS like that, and we leave it to sit for two days, after all, no one can work miracles right!

'We also tell them not to touch the foam as it's acidic or whatever lie suits. This will explain why once we scan the foam away WITH the crap from underneath, why there is nothing left. With a few extra flights over the buildings, we can remove the building, dead reactor, and stuff. Then show that we filled the hole in with super hard concrete.

'Once finnished, we take the money, wave and fly away. That's my plan, lots of missing details I suppose but I am not the sharpest pencil in the packet.' Glen sat back and took a drink, 'so what do you think?

Paul was thinking behind steepled fingers, 'Crazy plan Glen, but IF it did work, it would give us credibility.
Glen looked relieved that someone was on his side.

Paul continued, 'Then when we were removing known stashes of dumped materials, not so many questions on where it went. This would give Oracle a definitive public profile. Meaning we would be safe from suddenly disappearing. Well safer than if no one ever heard of us anyway.'

Brad spoke up, 'You have been carrying all this around in your head? Well I have to say, it has taken me by surprise, in this case, I am going to defer to Kia for comment, she knows more than I do and I am the first to admit it.'

Kia shook her head, and Glen's face fell. 'I am as surprised as you are Brad, for years we kept everything under the table, been doing that for so long it's become second nature to hide everything. 'What Glen has suggested has a lot of merits actually. Technically it's very easy to do. Configuring the SC outwards appearance is nothing.

'That's why it already has fans in stubby wings. Manufacturing foam to spec is also a walk in the park. We can build a long cylindrical receiver and just transmit the mixture to that as it hangs under each SC. It probably would be best to fly off and return every few hours, to make it look like you could only carry so much foam blend. Next point, scanning under the foam. We can do that. Removing the debris and waste, we already can do that. Removing the reactor building contents and surrounding debris, also simple.

'To fill the hole, also easy, but we need to be SEEN to tip material back in. Not so simple but do-able. What other angles would need to be covered?'

'I think just scanning the foam away afterwards is the weak part of the plan' Neil said.

'When a magician spirits away the rabbit, everyone wants to know where it went. What we would need to do, is apply some overflights of laser scanning stuff, so they think we are burning the debris away. 'If people think they have a plausible answer to a question, then it's no longer a question to them.'

'Bringing an SC into public view may not be such a bad thing offered Miako, it would mean if one were ever seen, it would no longer be classed as a UFO or an alien invasion.'
She smiled at the grin on Neil's face, 'You laugh at me Neil, but just remember your first impression in the barn!'

Bree took the verbal floor, 'I have zero to contribute to planning, it's just not my area, but I will say though that there is a distinct difference between operating totally under the radar and operating secretly. Just because we are seen to do repair work definitely does not mean we have to tell anyone HOW exactly we are doing it.

This might satisfy both Kia's point to be secret and Glen's point to be visible. There has to be a middle point that balances that out.

No one picked up the conversation, they all sat deep in thought.
Sandy broke the silence, 'Glen your plan has merits, several of them. 'For one, in the future once we had removed important underwater targets. There would come a time where the next targets were no longer water based but land based. That was an issue that I had labelled for being dealt with when the time came.

'On the subject of shelving decisions, I suggest we do that with this one, at least temporarily, it is now just past midnight, and you all need to be on your "A" game at eight a.m. sharp.
'I will run scenarios based on Glen's suggestion, and when complete will inform Kia of the predicted success or failure.

'Well done Glen, I have something to do now, other than zap mozzies', and with a cheeky grin Sandy left.

Melissa laughed at the receding disc, 'I bet you can read thoughts as well Sandy! Well, folks, I for one am looking forwards to tomorrow, come on partner, you can escort this lady to her room.' Ray stood as did the rest, said their goodnights and headed for bed.

Chapter Ten

7.30am showed on Neil's watch as he sat on the low wall outside the main entrance, beside him were Miako and Glen.

'Anyone would think you lot were eager' came Bree's voice from behind them, as she and Brad descended the steps. 'Ray won't be long, he is marking time outside Melissa's door while she gets dressed.'

A low hum came from the right as the garage door rolled up, a SC slid out into the morning sunshine followed by another and yet another until there were five parked angle wise in front of the house.

The side door on the fifth one opened, and Kia stepped out. Dressed in her usual suit and soft boots. But this time they were blindingly white, more so in the sunshine. She waved to them as they heard more footsteps behind them. Everyone was now assembled, dressed in suits and eager to go.

Kia walked over and sat on the wall, 'Good morning, nice to see even Paul is on time!'

'Would not miss this for the world', he quipped back. 'You seem bright and cheery this morning, well, definitely bright!' He feigned having to shield his eyes from the glare of Kia's suit.

'Sorry', she said and reached up to the lapel stud and turned it, the suit went from white down to a dark grey.
'Hey! I didn't know you could do that!' exclaimed Miako!

For the next 30 seconds, everyone looked like chameleons as they changed colours.
Kia grinned hugely as Brad shifted to bright pink for a few seconds.

'Very nice dear, matches your bum' laughed Bree and hugged his arm as he got the colour back under control to a respectable grey.

'OK', Kia stood and turned to face them all, 'Sit on the steps for a quick briefing please', once they were all seated, she continued. Today will feel no different than your last few days in the sim, we are not going to be doing anything that you haven't done dozens of times before.

'The plan today is to head out WNW for about 200km and drop into the water. You have all played follow the leader for hours, so following is not a problem.

'Once we get to the target area, each of you will have coordinates on the screen designating your particular area to clear. If we get it done without issues I will see if Sandy can relay anything else for us to do. 'How does that sound?'

'Lead on fearless leader' Ray said.

Kia nodded, 'Grab your partners and lets go dance then. Brad takes SC-1, Neil SC-2, Ray SC-3, and Paul SC-4. I am in 5.'
Paul and Glen hi-fived each other, and everyone boarded their designated SC.

Kia moved to the edge of the standing area and the others fell in line behind. 'All good? She asked over the radio.'
Four affirmative replies came back. Grabbing the control yoke she shot forward smoothly and climbed to about 2000 feet. Each SC behind her mimicked the move with exact precision that belied the fact this was their first real mission.

Kia asked them to form a V formation, and it was done so smoothly she smiled.

'Go to auto and lets rock' she said.
To her left, a screen showed the formation and one by one the icons turned green indicating they were now locked on to her SC as if they were one. Smiling she took them to just over Mach 1 and did a few barrel rolls.

'Show off!' Neil's voice said.

Kia radioed, 'Set your G bias to about 80%, you will find the ride a bit better until you get used to seeing things move out the window but not under your feet.'

Less than 17 minutes later Kia throttled back to 450kmh and dropped into the water. Again, there was no feeling of transition from one medium to another. At 80ft lights flared on from each SC and shone off hitting nothing but a few fish.

At 940 feet the bottom came into view, Kia checked their speed, to just over 20knots, as they levelled 30ft above the seabed she issued a few check instructions and got confirmations back from all craft.

'Three and four go manual and follow your CoOrds. Let me know if you encounter any problems.' On the screen, #3 and #4 icons turned blue and peeled off.

They cruised on for another 4 minutes, passing over stacks of drums and other debris accumulated over the decades. Reaching a target point on her screen Kia, released #1 and #2 and watched as they peeled off.

'Happy hunting', she said and throttled up to 80knots heading for the last waypoint on her map screen.

Two hours later almost to the minute, Kia finished the last sweep of the quadrant that had been assigned to her. Apart from checks and a bit of chatter no one seemed to be having any issues. Swinging up and away from the bottom she punched in CoOrds and hit the autopilot.

Walking over to the right wall of the cabin, she flicked a switch. A three-foot wide screen lit up with a map of the area. Homing in on her quadrant she could see it was now coded green, whereas it was coded yellow when she had arrived. Sliding the map sideways she could see the progress the others were making, she guesstimated about another 30 minutes should clear this area.

Nodding her approval she then zoomed out a little looking for new targets. On the left of the screen was a separate window that scrolled known objects that were in the map area.

As she moved the map around the other window refreshed automatically. 'Sandy, is there anything close by worth taking the teams over to?'

Sandy's voice answered crystal clear from hidden speakers', A few things nothing really a priority. Have you anything particular in mind?'

'No, not really, just wanted to give them a bonus for all the excellent work they have done today, which by the way is a testament to your great instructional skills.'

'They were easy to teach, everyone took to the basics very well, Miako was a little hesitant and unsure, but once the confidence settled she caught up fast.
'Wait, there is something near', Sandy relayed the CoOrds straight into the memory of the SC, 'Waypoint plotted.'

'It looked like 45-50 shipping containers from the Sat Scans, Probably some cargo ship not lashing its load properly on a heavy sea.'

Kia answered 'Thanks, that will fit the bill nicely, can we send these into the yard as is? They can unwrap their own presents?

Sandy replied 'I can do that, I have an idea that will suit your request perfectly.'
She walked back to the pilot chair.
The SC was stationary exactly at the waypoint. She called Brad.

'Hi Kia, we have finished the sector and are approaching the waypoint.'
Brad slid silently to a halt not four feet to the left of Kia.

'Good job' she said 'just waiting for Neil.'

Miako's voice came in clear, 'Alongside now Kia, our sector is done. 'We had to re-run one leg I missed some on the first scan, sorry.'

'All good' Kia replied, 'OK lets go pick up 3 & 4. I have a small assignment for us, follow in order please.' Kia took off smoothly closely followed by Brad and Neil. They stayed outboard slightly for a better forward view.

All three slowed to a halt at the second waypoint. Ray and Paul were there already waiting.

'Greetings Earthling' Paul said. 'All present and accounted for. No issues other than Glen spilt my coffee.'

'Excellent' Kia replied 'Drop on the back and follow. I won't lock us this time. Keep reasonable separation and don't get lost. 'Actually, why don't you all swap with partners, not fair hogging the pilots chair.'

Bree's tinkly laughter came in', We just did that. Lead on.' Kia checked the new waypoint and cruised off at a respectable rate. She swung wide of a few seamounts and skipped over trenches and for 20 minutes or so everyone was treated to the world that very few people ever get to see, at least not in person.

A gentle chime interrupted an incoming story from Ray.

'Waypoint', Kia broadcast. 'BOL, shipping containers or similar.'

'BOL?' asked Melissa.

'Be on the lookout', explained Neil.

'Spread out in a line, my screen tells me about 310 meters 1.o'clock, you copy that?' asked Kia. All four confirmed screen contact. 'Lets just lift a few meters and slow to 10kmh. Give them a slow pass to check them out.'

Silently they glided slowly over the target area. 'These haven't been here that long.' remarked Paul, as he watched the containers slide underneath his SC.

'Not much silt build-up on them at all.'
Within a few moments, they had cleared the last one, slowing to a halt they turned and faced back the way they had just come.
'Paul, Ray, you guys pick 'em up, no need for all of us. We will follow you' instructed Kia.

'Brad, punch in home CoOrds, You can lead us home if you like.'

'Good as done' came Bree's reply.

As the others moved forwards scanning the containers, the other three SCs followed, slightly above the two leading craft for a better view.

It was strange to watch as each container flashed out of existence. Shortly it was all over.

'Good job people, Brad's got the point to lead us back, it's still early in the day so we might get another job in, that's if you are up for it' Kia said.

She smiled at the enthusiastic replies coming over the coms. 'OK, Brad, it's your show.'

'Roger!' Brad pulled forward, and everyone fell into formation behind.
The trip back in seemed shorter than the trip out.

As they approached the island Sandy's voice flooded in', Hi Scavengers! Welcome home. Please leave the SCs parked outside, and be aware there is a new building to the right as you land.'

Bree was already outside the SC as Kia was shutting down her craft. They all walked over and stood in front of the new building. It looked like an industrial shed. It was about 100 meters long by about 30 wide, the long side facing them had rolling doors equally spaced down the side. The closest door to them was open.

Ray was the first to speak, 'Well Sandy has some hidden talents! 'That was one quick construction job. It took the council back home nearly four months just to give me approval for a carport!'
Together they walked inside, footsteps echoing in the vast hollow space. Down the far end was a huge boxlike construction and a large conveyor belt about waist high and running along the back wall.

At the other end of the conveyor was a smaller box. The conveyor was obviously to take things from the large box and put them inside the smaller one. The building was lit by a mix of clear roofing segments and ultra bright lighting over the conveyor.

Melissa turned to Kia, 'Please don't tell me we are about to become factory workers!

'My mother worked in a place like this sorting potatoes when she was younger.'

Kia laughed 'No, not at all, but the principle is the same. All the data we scanned from the shipping containers is in the data tanks. We can reconstruct or "ReCon" anything we have stored as you know. So what we have here is a large receiver in the unit down the far end, and this end is a scanner. We get the receiver to put it all back together. As the stuff comes along the belt, anything of interest you can take off, and what is not wanted is disposed of in the scanner at the end.'

Neil nodded', Makes sense, that's why the receiver unit is bigger than the scanner. This is going to be very interesting!'

Glen looked surprised, 'You are excited about sifting through garbage? You are one weird hippy my friend!'

'No, you don't see the picture here. If we scanned and cleared an old Spanish Galleon off some reef, and sifted it here, there could be priceless relics, gold, jewellery, cannons, swords all kinds of stuff!' replied Neil enthusiastically.

Bree walked to the wall and grabbed a clear face shield from a hook. There was a dozen or so hanging up.

'Lets go treasure hunting, just like the old days hey' Brad?

Brad nodded, 'But without all the digging and finding rusty nails!'

Kia spoke up, 'We have rusty nails if you're feeling that way inclined.' Brad shook his head.

'Sandy fire it up please' Kia said and the conveyor started moving, at about half walking pace.

The first thing to appear on the conveyor was a stack of sturdy folding tables.

Kia motioned for them to follow her down to meet the tables as they slowly moved up. The conveyor stopped.

The boys flexed muscles in a few seconds a line of tables stood behind them.

They spread out about 4 feet apart as the belt started to move again.

'What is about to come next is stuff out of 3 of the containers we did this morning' informed Kia, she was standing behind them on the other side of the tables.
They were amazed at what came next, washing machines, furniture, industrial tools, and brand new motorbikes in crates. There was a small break in the flow then came pallets and pallets of paint tins, followed by boxes of assorted hardware and bundles of cloth.

Everyone had been picking stuff up and looking it over and tossing it back on the belt. Again another gap in the flow, then boxes of machinery parts, tractor parts, and huge wheel rims.

Kia pointed to three 4ft crates. 'Grab them please guys.' With a grunt they were dragged off the belt onto a table one by one. Next came a few boxes marked "TVs", some marked "Radios". Next, a stack of single mattresses, and lastly 12 boxes marked microwaves.

As the mattresses arrived where Kia stood, she hit a stop button and selected one from the stack and tossed it onto one of the tables.
'Unhappy with your bed?' Bree asked.

Kia grinned as she slid a wickedly thin knife from a thigh pocket in her suit. Slipping the tip of the knife just under the top edge seam, she slit the mattress from one end to the other. She cut both ends and flipped the top of the mattress back.

In the centre of each spring, a plastic bag had been taped. Cutting the tape on one bag and lifting it out, Kia handed it to Melissa.

'Here have 2kg of the purest heroin you can buy.' She then pointed to the wooden boxes the boys had grabbed before. 'Those have machetes in them, not in itself unusual, except that being marked machinery parts means they were going somewhere they shouldn't be.'

'How did you know?' asked Miako.

'I didn't, Sandy picked it up when a flag in the data store came up. I just thought it interesting enough, to show you first hand.

'Although we are clearing the waters, sometimes what we do also helps with problems on land. Not so much with this lot. It was too deep to be recovered easily by conventional means. 'What made me suspicious was that large container ships are very, very strict on lashing of containers. Yes, they lose some every year, but this many seemed a bit off.'

Brad hit the go button on the belt, they tossed the mattress and bag back on, followed by the crates.
In a few minutes, the belt was clear.

As they exited the building, Glen joked that he now knew where to get a motorbike if he wanted one.

It took less than 35 minutes before everyone had freshened up, grabbed a bite and a drink and was lounging around in the OpCen. Neil was off to one side talking with Sandy, and the others were at different terminals.

Sandy finished with Neil and moved over to the HUD. 'Listen up everybody. All eyes turned her way. Well done on your first run everyone! No one got lost, and you didn't beam each other out of existence.' She paused. 'I'm joking, there are safety protocols in place, it can't happen.

'I now have two new targets for you, I'm sending 1 & 3 to here, a section of the map blinked. The other pair 2 & 5 is going here, it's a bit further, but there is less at that location. I am sending you in pairs because you are still new at this.'

'Eventually, most of your missions will be solo unless the target is a large one. Paul & Glen will have a break, there are some things I would like to go over with them. Destinations and information are already uploaded in your respective SCs, have fun, and why are you still here?'
The crews sorted themselves out and bid farewell and left.

Chapter Eleven

Only Glen and Paul were left with Sandy.

'We in trouble?' asked Glen.

'Far from it' Sandy said and motioned for them to sit. 'I have been running scenarios non-stop since last night regarding your suggestion Glen. Kia and I have spent a few hours in discussion about the points you made. The reason I wanted you here was to ask you guys to work with me a little on this.

'As an AI, highly advanced as I may be, I know I have limitations when dealing with humans and human emotions. That's why it is critical to get your input. I may come up with something that logically will work, but emotionally "stinks". By emotionally, I mean suspicious or does not FEEL right. As unbelievable as it may sound, there are areas I am definitely lacking in.

'Paul has a background in high-end corporate circles, which to me is almost as good as diplomatic training. Glen, you are an expert on explaining tech stuff to un-savvy people. Both of those traits are required if we go with Glen's idea.'

'I think before we go ahead with the Japanese issue, it would be best to sort out the U-boat and the mercury issue off the coast of Norway. It will be awkward enough to approach the Japanese on a cold sell.

'If we do something on a smaller scale, it may make selling us to the Japs easier. Your thoughts?'

'Reputation is everything' Paul said, 'Especially in big business, if we get a good rep, we can just about go anywhere.

If we can get a rep of being a big, no-nonsense company, it will also help. Scrub that, big is not necessary. Powerful is good, and by powerful I mean financially. If a company looks like it has a lot of money, no one wants to take it on.'

Glen said 'When Microsoft was being dragged over the coals for supposed monopolising the market. Even the US attorneys office didn't want to take them on in the courts because the amount of money MS supposedly had.

'So I back Paul up here, Money equals Power. Secondary only to knowledge. Knowledge is the greatest power. You find the skeletons that companies hide. Especially the big ones, and they tend to walk quietly when you enter the room.'

Paul excused himself and left, he was back in a few moments with a can of soft drink in each hand. He tossed one to Glen.

'Sandy, please put up a list of the worlds top 10 richest companies.'

Sipping his drink he studied the list, 'OK, next a list of the supposed largest.' On the second list were eight of the names on the first list.

'Next, list any of those that have ties to government contracts.'
It took longer this time, but the list appeared next to the other two.
Paul pointed out several companies that were on all three lists.

'These are the heavyweights in the financial sector. No-one messes with these. We need to get these to either respect us or fear us, I don't care which. Then if we ever walk into a room, what we say gets listened to, that includes governments.'
Glen looked surprised.

'Yes, my friend', Paul continued 'because 99% of governments are backed by the money of big business, from funding election candidates to funding research and development. Please remember that this is the crème de la crème of the power brokers of the world. The ones we talked about before the other night.'

Sandy nodded her understanding, 'But we do not wish to become one of these do we?'

'Hell no.' Paul said. 'What we need to become is a separate class all of our own. These are bulls, big and powerful, they rely on their size and hard tactics. We need to be more like a Panther, quiet, sleek, just visible enough to keep them nervous.

'We want them to be wary of making any sudden moves because they don't want us to focus on them.'

'I am not sure I understand your animal analogy, but I get the main gist of it.' Sandy turned to the HUD, 'As for funds, that is not a problem. How much should we let the world know we have?'

Glen held up his hands, 'I am out of my comfort zone now, so I will sit back and let Paul do his thing.'

Paul dragged a stool over and sat. 'Firstly, how much is Oracle worth, as in the bank?'

'Well' Sandy looked at the HUD, and it cleared, several windows popped open and slid smoothly into a line. 'Currently, our assets are listed as 237 million, the island value, a few vehicles and minor stuff. We have opened several accounts due to the necessity of funding company registrations, permits and all that red tape.

'We have eight accounts with 15 million in each, to cover that. That's all that is currently on the books so to speak.'

'Hmm, approximately, 350 Mill' Paul said out loud. 'Not too shabby for a new company, but nothing that would scare any of the bulls.

Both Sandy and Ray remained quiet while Paul closed his eyes and put his razor sharp mind to work.

'We can't just increase the accounts drastically because that would be one of those things that smell "funny" to us humans.'

Ray nodded at that. 'Sudden riches always seem to allude to illegal conduct. Right or wrong, it's the first thought that comes to mind involving cash.'

Paul stood and paced back and forth furiously thinking, he stopped and snapped his fingers.

'Gold may be the answer' Paul said, 'If we contact an international bank and tell them, we wish to take some of our gold reserves and put it in their bank, that's a legitimate increase of wealth. Besides it's hard to procure gold illegally in any reasonable quantity.'

Sandy brought up a list of large banking institutions. 'Which one of these would you suggest suit our needs?'

Paul pointed to three on the list. 'Any of these would be good. They are close to the best, but not quite.'

'My turn for a question' Glen said, 'why not use the best ones?'

'It's all about the power and greed to be the biggest if we boost the holdings of one of these, that pushes them up the ladder.

 The others will then hunt down the reason they have been overtaken.'

'Although they are not supposed to talk, someone always does, and it will filter through the grapevine that Oracle has a lot of money. That's the result we are looking for.'

'Excellent' Sandy said, 'I electronically set up the other accounts, but we can't send the gold electronically.'

'No, we can't. This will have to be done in person. When Kia gets back, I will ask for some time off, and we can sort this out.'

Sandy said 'No need, I will sort that. Now, how much gold?'

Paul held his hands out and shrugged his shoulders. 'It would need to be a fair amount to cause the ripples we want to.

'How about a few kilograms and a promise of more if the bank performs well?

'Banks play the markets using the gold they hold as collateral, the better they play, the better the return.'

Sandy looked at the three banks Paul had highlighted, 'So we need to cause a stir, and rely on the people to be unable to keep their mouths shut, have I got this right?'

Paul nodded, 'You got it dead centre. The better the ripple, the better the result.'

'Great, I like learning!' Sandy smiled, 'I will arrange an appointment for you and Glen with these three banks. They will be told we are going to deposit exactly 5 tonnes of gold, with a further shipment, possibly larger, if they perform to our satisfaction.'

'Geezus!', Paul said 'That will send shockwaves, not ripples. I like it!!'

Glen cleared his throat, 'Um, this may be a rather stupid question, but do we have that much? Just asking.'

Sandy smiled, 'Glen dissolved in the oceans are thousands of tonnes of gold, no one has extracted it. Simply because with their current methods, the cost versus return is biased the wrong way.'

'Last estimates are 15,000 tonnes in suspended seawater.

'However, I know of several deposits on the floor that we can grab some from to fill our needs for this project. It will take me a few days to set this all up, but thank you both for helping with this problem!
Is there anything else we need to do to establish our credentials?'

'Not at this time' Paul said, 'We need to do this in a sequential manner. Without one of the steps done first, the next one cannot be taken.'

'Understood' replied Sandy.

Glen glanced at the time on one of the monitors, 'So if that is sorted, can we go play in the SC?'

'I would be up for that. I don't know when the others are due back, but it beats sitting around.'
Sandy cleared the HUD and brought up two maps. On each of the maps was a pair of green triangles with numbers in them.

'That's where they are, Brad's pair are on site and starting their second run, Kia and hers are still about 40 minutes from their target zone. There is nothing close that I could send you to, and I don't really like you going off on your own yet.'
Disappointment showed on both their faces.

'Hang on a sec. Kia, You there?'

'Yes Sandy, what's up?'

'The boys and I have finished our discussion, we have formulated a plan to start the ball rolling.

'However, now we are done the boys are hounding me to let them play in the SC.'

Laughter came over coms, 'Sure let them out otherwise they will just mope around and draw on the walls or something.

'Keep them close, and keep an eye on them, any problems let me know immediately. Set a flag on them and relay data to my SC, please.'

Paul and Glen hi-fived at the news. 'Mum is letting us out to play!' quipped Glen.

Turning to Sandy, he asked for a map of the surrounding area. It appeared on the HUD. Both of them stood studying the layout, zooming in on different features.

'This line here', Paul tapped the HUD, 'What's that?'

'It's the undersea fiber optic cable that we laid in.'

'OK and this dotted line here?'

'That's a trade route, main shipping channel.'

Looking north-west was a line of seamounts part of the Island chain they were on,

'We might go check out up here, doesn't look like much to get into trouble with.'

'If I send you to the last mount and turn due west there is another line of mounts running across there', Sandy said as the map centred on the areas she spoke of. 'You may find remnants of early wooden traders around that area, I haven't tasked any Sats to do detailed scans around there as yet. It will probably be another five years before we have mapped everywhere in hi-def. As you know, we are centred on problem areas first.

'So I will plot four waypoints for you, here and here, then west to here and south to this point. How's that sound?'

'Great', Paul said, 'Lets move land lubber' he said to Glen, who beat him to the door.

Sandy could hear them arguing who was going to drive all the way down the stairs.

She cleared the HUD except for a tracking screen showing the exact CoOrds of the pair that just left. Then she started looking for an armored truck hire company and started sorting hotels for bookings. Plus a hundred other details that needed to be done.

___Chapter Twelve___

Brad had his feet up on the corner of the console watching as his wife piloted the SC over their fourth run of the area. He watched data scroll up the scan HUD as they eliminated what looked like massive coils of wire and other debris below them. Bree was concentrating on the guidance, but not so focused that she couldn't watch the material through the front windows.

'I don't know what all this used to be', she waved a finger forwards, 'and it doesn't look like it's that dangerous compared the Nuke waste, but have you noticed the lack of fish and wildlife? 'Something amongst this it is tainting the water for sure.'

Brad nodded, 'Was thinking that before, but dangerous or not, all this is better gone.' He turned his head to the left and could see the other SC lights off in the distance. 'How are you guys doing, Ray?'

'All good' Melissa's voice came in clear 'We were just remarking on the lack of life over here as well. With luck after all this mess is cleaned up it will eventually return. There is a whale carcass to our left, was going to leave it, food for the rest, but if it's contaminated around here that may be as well, what do you think?'

'I would take it' Bree said, 'Better safe than sorry.'

About 850km to the NE Kia and Neil's SCs were at a total standstill, hovering about 30 meters off the sandy bottom. Neil and Miako were both leaning close to the front window.

'That's awesome!' Neil said, 'What exactly is it?'

'Check your scanner HUD, it will give you a better 3-d view.
'You tell me what you think it is, and I will let you know how
close you are.' Kia said.
Neil walked to the console, and zoomed back, what he was
looking at was a ship some 160 meters long according to the
info on the HUD. It was broken just behind the rear derricks
that hung limply over the side. Huge cracks ran from the keel
all the way to the handrail mounts.
    'Well from what I can see it is a merchant class ship, I can't
see a name or a home port on it. I will run a silhouette scan in a
sec. Total length looks to be about 163 meters long.'
    'Very good Neil, before you compare it to the database, back
up a little, it will give you a better view.'
Miako dropped into the pilot chair and reversed back. To
the right Kia's SC slowly sank onto the sand to give them
uninterrupted views both ways.

Neil ran a silhouette scan for known lost ships, as each outline
flashed behind his capture, he walked back to the window.
    'Amazing that no matter what we build or make, the wrath of
the sea is never to be underestimated.'
A chime sounded from the console, he walked back.
    'According to the results here, Kia, it's the Martin Brown, lost
1966. It was a crude oil carrier listed as 66,000 tonnes, home
port shows to be Aden. Umm, lost with all hands location
unknown. Suspected capsized in a large storm. There is a
captain listed and 43 crew.'
    'Well done, I got the same. Now, in this case, it's not
dangerous, but it's awkward to handle. We can't just scan it
out as normal, due to the fact crude oil is a liquid and the ship
probably still has 80% of it's cargo. If we cut it up, the oil will
escape into the sea. Which we can still handle, but it's a very
messy way to do this.
    'So, if it was just you two here by yourself, how would you
tackle this one?'

'So we can't just slice it up?' asked Miako.

'Well, we could Miako, with the 2 of us here one could slice, and the other takes the escaping oil. Kinda messy, but doable if there is not much current. We have a lot of time today, and once you are proficient you will be out doing this by yourselves, so not trying to be awkward, I'd like you to tackle this as if you were here alone.

'Just for the exercise if that's ok with you?'

'Sounds good to us, I love a good challenge! We are just going to look at it for a moment.'

Their SC peeled off and ran a few passes from bow to stern. As they returned next to Kia's SC, Neil reported.

'Well the scans show that out of eight compartments, six are still full of crude oil, the other two are on the broken line and obviously leaked out as it sank.

'Add to that there is also a fairly large, heavy oil tank, possibly their fuel tank, is showing a fair amount of oil. It's full, but Miako thinks the balance of liquid is sea water that leaked in. No other major contaminants we can scope.

'There is some asbestos used in the crew cabins as insulation, but that's it.'

'Good so far' Kia said, 'Now, in the Sims you were shown if the target is too big to take in one pass, We normally shave the target from the top down on parallel to centre passes.'

Neil added, 'So nothing can fall and trap the SC. I remember the lesson well! Shaving the top of this ship would expose all eight tanks and no way we could catch all the oil rising out of all holds.

'I'm just thinking out loud, sorry. Even shaving one hold at a time once we cut through the top, by the time we swung around it would be too late.'

Kia was smiling as she listened to Miako and Neil throw suggestions and ideas at each other just to end up discarding them for one reason or another.

'Alright, we give up, there must be an answer, but it escapes us at the moment, how is the best way to do this?'

'Stay where you are and watch. I will do the first one alone. You can do the others, and I will just cover you just in case' replied Kia.

'The first thing to remember, all rules have an exception, always. Secondly, think of the characteristics of oil and water. 'Have I given it away yet?'

'Nope, I'm still drawing a blank.'

'Fair enough.' Kia's SC ran the same parallel scans to get the data of the target as the others had done. Then she slid off the side of the ship and turned 90 degrees to face the hull. Moving sideways, she lined up with the stern and dropped almost on the sand.

Neil and Miako stood close to the front window watching every move intently. Two laser guides from the other SC marked from the stern to JUST inside the bulkhead of the aft hold.

'These two points encompass the entire hold widthwise, now watch.' Suddenly the section started to disappear from the keel upwards. Quite slowly as it was a rather wide section, as the hull was being scanned out, the SC rose at the same speed, keeping the cut perfectly level.

Neil slapped a hand on his knee making Miako jump, 'Of course! Oil floats! By shaving from the bottom up, the top of the tank stops the oil from rising! Therefore, no leakage!'

'Correct' Kia said. 'However, I have my finger on the scram button. If the hull shows any sign whatsoever of moving I am out of here. This is not the safest method to remove hulks. But in the case of oil tankers, it's normally the only way when alone. For the most part, if any of the teams come across a tanker, it's best to call for backup. Remember this. Never be afraid to call in help. There, all done.'

Kia looped back and parked next to Neil. In front of them was a hull with a perfectly flat stern. 'I must ask, did you notice anything else on your scan run?

'I have a purple flag up on my screen.'

Miako walk over to the scan HUD, 'We have a purple flag too, one moment I will bring it up.' Miako worked the keyboard a few moments. 'OH!, I see why. Further up the front, we have some human remains!'

'Correct, the ships been down since '66. We are at what, 1800m? Way below the thermocline, so colder water. There won't be much left, but obviously enough to set a flag. It's not military so won't be classed as a war grave.

'Just mind the flags next time, or set a tone for flags in your options, better to be safe than sorry. Don't beat yourself up over it, that's why I am here after all. Now your turn, take the next section off. Remember these points, slow ascent due to larger width, try to keep the cut as parallel as possible to avoid leakage, and most importantly, get ready to get the hell out of the way if she moves.'

Kia moved around the back and just above deck height facing down the middle of the ship to the bow. If anything went wrong she was in the perfect position to catch anything heading for the surface.

'Anytime you're ready.'
Miako elected to drive as Neil manned the scanner. The exact same process Kia used was applied to the second hold and in a few minutes the ship was another hold shorter, and nothing was spilt.

'Well done! Now we are on a roll, take the next section. This time be very aware of possible movement, it's where the hull has split.'
Kia kept the same height and bearing and just moved forward. Miako let the SC sink again and moved left in front of the next section, and repeated the process. Then again and again until one last hold and the bow was all that remained.

As they lined up for the last hold Kia said, 'On this last scan, the bow may fall forwards because of the rake of the leading edge, be very careful it does not topple towards you as well.

'Once you have removed the hold, I will take out the rest.'

Miako lined it all up, Neil gave the thumbs up, and they scanned the last hold. Just as they finished, the bow groaned and started to topple towards them, with the flick of her wrist Miako had them clear in milliseconds.
From a safe distance, they watched as the bow very slowly dropped sideways, billowing up clouds of silt.
Seconds later it was gone, and Kia's SC slid into view out of the billowing cloud.

'Nice job, that's several thousand gallons of crude oil that won't be a threat anymore. We can head for home, either airborne or cruise the bottom picking anything up along the way, your call.'
'We vote airborne for a change, be nice to see the sun instead of inky blackness.'

'Roger that', came the reply, 'You take the lead I will be wingman for the trip home. Watch for surface ships, don't want to bump your head.'

Neil asked Miako 'May I?' She smiled and gave him the pilot seat.

Neil swooped in and did a perfect landing next to the two SCs outside the house, touching down mere seconds before Kia.

'Someone is still out and by themselves.' Miako remarked as they stepped out into the sunlight.
They walked into the OpCen to find Brad and Bree going over the data from their last target.

'Problems?' Kia asked, perching on a stool.

'Oh Hi! No, not really' Bree answered, 'Just curious, our target was a lot of junk, a lot of wire, copper by the look of the corrosion. We didn't pay a whole lot of notice to the data when we scanned. It popped no flags. But it seemed strange there was very little if any, fish or wildlife around. Just wondering why.'

'Have you asked Sandy? She is the best data analyst we have you know.'

'Not yet, I was hoping to find it myself, but I will ask if I come up empty, How did you guys go?'

'Awesome!' Chipped in Neil, 'We took out this huge ship, a tanker!

'It had snapped in the middle and was sitting nearly upright on the bottom, you should have seen Kia! Awesome tactics, she asked us how we would do it. I totally bummed out trying to figure it out, when zappo she has gone and cut it sweet as, and not spilt a drop!'

'You're too kind, and you exaggerate too much Neil.' Kia replied 'Besides you pair did the rest very well.'

'Naw!', Neil went on, 'Just take a look at the mission tape!'

'Mission tape!' Bree exclaimed, 'Why didn't I think of that!' She leant over and gave Neil a kiss on the cheek.

He immediately turned bright red, Brad laughed. 'Relax she gets excited like that.'

Bree cleared space on the HUD and pulled up their mission tape. Spooling through it at 8x, she stopped in points and went back a few sections here and there. 'Damn it!, I know something is there, I just can't see it.'

Kia got off the chair and walked around the other side of the HUD. She pulled up a map of the area, and zoomed in close. Sliding the area back and forth and up and down, 'Hmm strange' she remarked.

'Told you so!' Bree said through the glass.
A disc hissed out of the wall, and Sandy walked over and stood next to Kia. She studied the map for a few moments, then lifted a finger and moved the map diagonally a few miles. Tapping her finger, she pointed at a section of the map without saying a word.

'Aha!' Kia said. 'Got ya.'

'Ah ha! What?' Bree said and walked around just in time for Kia to close the map. 'Nothing dear' Kia said and headed for the door.
'Oh no you don't' cried Bree 'We have no Ah-Ha's without giving reasons, that's so unfair!'

Kia stopped at the doorway and looked over her shoulder. 'Think currents my dear, currents! And left a spluttering Bree standing with her hands on her hips.

'SANDY!'

'Sorry Bree got to run' and vanished!

'Ooooh! Bree stamped her foot. 'WOMEN!' Brad laughed out loud until Bree turned her gaze on him.

'Err, I'm out, got to pee', and dived through the door just behind Neil and Miako. Standing alone in the room, she stood in front of the HUD again, staring, 'I know there is a reason for it, and I WILL find it!' she said to no one.

Chapter Thirteen

Glen was in the hot seat as the pair cruised five meters off the bottom, weaving in and out of small seamounts like a slalom skier. The scanner was set to auto and was vacuuming any man-made object from the floor as they cruised along. Using a live data link back to the OpCen, the system was set to raise an alarm or a flag as they were called if anything came up out of the ordinary.

Paul glanced at the scan HUD, 'Well my fine friend, just cruising around, we have rid mother earth of 18 tonnes of crap so far.'

Glen lifted his eyebrows, 'That's surprising, most of what I have seen is old drift and drag fishing nets, there must be miles of that crap everywhere. That and bottles, none with any messages in them so far, though.'

Paul grinned and settled back, 'I like this new life. Great people to work with, every day something different, you know, I haven't heard one of the crew ask about wages or holidays, none of the dreary day to day shit I used to have to put up with.'

Glen nodded, 'I wondered about wages once, not that any of us has spent a cent over the last week. Christ! It's only been a week! Since we have been here, anyway, I thought maybe the firm was new so money was tight. Then you and Sandy go throwing tonnes of gold around, just for kicks!!'

Paul grinned, 'That took me by surprise as well, and let me tell you something off the record. If they decide to go ahead with your idea, I can see you and me in a suit, in some of the best hotels in Europe.

'Walking past movie stars and celebrities as if they were paperboys on a sidewalk. OH and the Gold-diggers!! Hmm.'

Glen looked at Paul for a second. 'I am not sure I am the bloke for that kind of job Paul, I don't know the terminology, and I don't have the social etiquette skills, hell I don't even know what a Gold-digger is!'

Paul playfully punched him in the arm, 'Listen, if you are up for it, we could spend a few hours sorting that out. Most of the high rollers are eccentric, and people are used to them doing weird stuff all the time. A Gold-digger is a term for one of the women that buzz around rich people willing to do anything to get their hands on a guy with money. Never pick one up, they are hard to get rid of!'

Glen thought on it while steering through the uneven terrain, 'Aw hell why not, might be good for a laugh.'

A chime sounded, Paul looked at the screen, 'Time to turn south on the home leg.' Glen eased the SC round until the heading matched the flashing display.
For the next 35 minutes nothing of real interest passed by the window, they were not that deep, only about 40m or so. Enough sunlight lit the floor, although most of the colours were grey at that depth. Rounding the next mount they pulled up fast, the area between two mounts was just laced with long drift nets.

'Crap!' Paul said, 'I was enjoying the ride.'
It took nearly 15 minutes of scanning to remove all the debris. Glen circled the mounts a few times to make sure they got it all and lined back up on their previous course. Shortly they were back up to cruising speed, and Paul went back to make a cuppa.

A few minutes later he slid back into the seat holding two cups and handed one over to Glen.

Glen took it and sipped, 'You would make someone a good wife you know.'

Paul grinned, glancing out the window he stopped the cup halfway to his mouth, 'Something over to the left there', and pointed.

Glen swung a slow curve 90 degrees to the left, and brought the target up dead centre, more damn nets. Working like a well-oiled team, it didn't take long to remove the netting.

'Well, Well', Paul said after the nets were gone. 'Will you look at that.'

Glen put his cup down and slowly ran the SC along a shape that was half buried in the silt, 'Scan it in and lets see what we have got.'

Positioning at one end they scanned along the length of the dark shape, once clear at the other end, Paul punched up a silhouette comparison and waited. While he was waiting, he dragged a flashing flag open. 'Don't know what it is as yet, but it's got 61 flags set! 48 as human remains and 13 as UXB. The scan is complete, it's an unknown WWII Sub, that's all I got.'

'I think we leave this one alone, something for Sandy to play with.'

Glen agreed and glided off.

'You know, there must be a whole heap laying down here. Two-thirds of the planet is water.

Paul agreed but was looking out the window with more concentration than before.

90 minutes later they arrived back. They only made three more stops for nets and one for an old marker buoy.

When they walked into the house, Glen peeled of saying he was going to get rid of two gallons of coffee, and he would meet up in the OpCen.

Paul jogged up the stairs and walked into the main room.

'Hi Bree, how was your day?'

She turned and gave a small wave, 'Good, we cleared the zone fine, but something was off, and I am trying to figure out exactly what.'

'Ask Sandy' Paul replied.

She rolled her eyes, 'Not you too. I tried that, but she ducked and ran before I got a chance.'

'It sounds like they want you to figure this out by yourself then, but it can't be anything bad.'

'How do you figure that? It could be anything!'

Paul shook his head 'If it was something bad they would never have turned their backs. Simple 101 deduction.'

'You know, I hate your analytical mind, you are probably right, so that means it's a simple explanation, which makes it worse as I should be able to see it then.' Bree sighed.

'See what?' asked Glen as he entered.

'Never mind' Bree said, 'Long story.' She went back to her data read out and maps.'

'Sandy?' Glen called.

Sandy arrived, 'Yes boys, how was the trip?' She ignored the glare she got from Bree on the other side of the HUD.

'Not bad, we got rid of a lot of old netting, tonnes of the damn stuff actually, but around about here', he pointed at a map Paul pulled up. We found an old submarine wreck.

'You couldn't see it at first, it was swamped in old trawl nets.

'Paul ran a silhouette scan, and it came up blank, but, we ran a scan over it anyway, it triggered over 60 flags, 13 of them UXB and the rest human remains. We just left it alone and continued the circuit.'

Sandy was staring at the data from the scan as it scrolled past in a window. 'Now that is very interesting. I don't have anything in the database, but that isn't unusual. Most of my data comes from scanned archives and records. So if it wasn't in there, either there are some records I have yet to read, or this could have been a prototype or something like that.'

'I doubt it was a prototype' Paul said.

Even Bree waited to find out how he came to that conclusion.

'If it was a prototype, on a test run, I seriously doubt they would have put live ordinance onboard. I admit it IS possible but doubtful. Well, it's time to eat so I will leave you with this, I know you love learning Sandy.'

Glen and Paul left, Bree said 'Whoa there Sandy, you're not getting away this time!'

Sandy moved around to her side of the HUD, 'I think you have suffered enough dear. Look here is your zone you cleared. 'The ocean current is flowing from this angle here. If we backtrack about 700m, what do you see?'

Bree zoomed to the area Sandy pointed out, 'Thermal vents in the sea floor. I don't get the connection, though.'
Sandy opened a new window and in it was a chemical breakdown of the matter spewing from the vents.

'None of this vent is very toxic, but it probably makes the water smell like sulphur to the fish. Stinky water to them.

'So until it dilutes enough further away from the vent, fish will avoid the strong concentration area.'

'Damn! It's obvious when pointed out like that. Thank you, now I can go eat without this bugging me.'

Sandy said 'Well done girl, It was a credit to you that you went with a gut feeling and stuck it out. Excellent work!' And with that she vanished.
Bree cleared the HUD and went in the direction of the kitchen.

Chapter Fourteen

Down the dining room, there were people everywhere, some were still eating and the early ones had finished and were lounging about. Brad waited until everyone had finished eating and was settled, He then called for attention and got it.

'I have talked things over with Kia, and as you know I was selected as CEO of Oracle. I want to resign that post.'

A rumble of different comments rose from the others.

'The reason', he said loudly to be heard over the rumble, 'is quite simple. I really, and I mean really, enjoy being out in the SC. Also, you all know how long you have been with Bree and I, nearly two decades or more. To be truthful, I am over being a boss. I don't need the stress, and I don't need to be the one to make the hard decisions anymore. I, we, want to be one of the guys.'

He paused, collecting his thoughts. 'Let me explain without being overtly preachy. It's important to me that you understand my reasoning' He looked at everyone in turn.

'Paul takes the lead easily when it comes to areas of his expertise, Neil, Miako, every time any one of us has something to say, the rest of us listen. You don't NEED me to be boss man. 'Kia here is a much better choice. She knows things I am still trying to believe are true. I have watched her closely, the way she listens to what you and I have to say. I have watched her lead in times of confusion.'

'To me she has every ounce of the necessary STUFF, to lead the group. I for one am more than willing to follow her into any situation that we may find ourselves in.

'A bit more truth, I wholeheartedly believe, she chose me as CEO, because she knew, that if I had not agreed to come aboard, none of you would have either. Now, that's not a bad thing to have loyalty like that, and it makes me proud you have enough faith in me to follow, but in saying that, having me as CEO of a company that is as powerful and as advanced as this one, based on those selection criteria is foolish.

'I am way out of my depth and comfort zone as boss. Bree and I are more than happy to make our home here, and we are really looking forward to the future with Oracle.
'Well, that's just about all I had to say, I wanted to say it while we were all together.

'Tomorrow is the end of the week that we told Kia we would give her our decisions. I am hoping that tonight she will loan me the SC. So Bree and I can go back home, collect all our personal things. Then come back as permanent residents of this island.'

Bree stood up and held Brad's hand, 'This is something we both want to do. You are now all free agents. It's your turn to pick what you want to do, I am sure we can give you a lift home if you wish.'

Neil said something in Miako's ear and she nodded.
He stood and said, 'I want to stay, and Miako as well, there is no job, no employment, just simply nothing, that can compare to what I have done here. Nothing at all. I will go with you guys to collect some of my stuff, but I doubt I can get it all in one night.'

Bree laughed. 'I love you like a brother Neil, but sometimes you can be so stupid!'
 Neil was lost for words.

'Brad and I couldn't pack all our gear in one night either!

So we are just going to scan the house, leave the walls and take the rest. When we get back, Sandy will put it all back on the conveyor in the shed.'

Neil just shook his head, 'You are so right! Sometimes the obvious just bites me in the ass!'

Paul said 'I am in 100%, my life, my choice.'

Glen stood said 'Ditto' and sat down again.

Melissa leant over and kissed Ray on the cheek, 'We are in.' Ray just looked dumbfounded but managed to nod.

Sandy breezed in, stood by the doorway and silently clapped. 'Holos can't make noise, sorry' she said. Everyone roared with laughter. 'Not only have you all shown me an insight into the emotional side of mankind, tonight you just showed me that you are fully capable of some of the best flawless logic as well. 'As you just saw, I applaud you.'

She turned to Bree. 'Also, your idea of scanning the house for your personal belongings was pure genius that's twice today you have impressed.' Bree blushed. Sandy left.

All eyes swivelled to focus on Kia. 'Is this ok with you?' asked Brad. 'To be an effective leader you need to have a crystal clear picture of everything, I just don't have that.'

'You are truly a great man Brad, all of you are a fantastic team. Yes, that's fine by me if it's what you all want.'

'It is not only what we want, but it is also what we need. It will be tough for the company over the next few months to put ourselves where we need to be, and for that, we need the best-qualified person to lead us, if anyone here has that qualification it's you.'

'I second the motion' Ray said, 'Carried' said everyone in unison.

'I shall return shortly' Kia said and walked out of the room.

Neil was the first to speak, 'I think we did the right thing, and I think you are brilliant Brad.'

Brad shook Neil's hand firmly, 'All of us here have strengths that cover others weakness, and with Kia at the helm, I figure we are a rock solid unit.'

Kia walked back in. She gave them a card each.

'OK if I am the boss, and you are employees, there are some rules.'

'Rule #1, Always, I repeat always, speak up if you have an idea on any subject.

'Rule #2, You are all authorised to speak on behalf of the Oracle company. We will always back your play no matter what.

'Why? Because I have faith in each and every one of you.

'Rule #3, You will be paid nothing. There are no wages at all. The cards I just gave you each have two million dollars on them. If you empty the card, we will top it back up.

'Rule #4, Last rule, each and every mission, is on a voluntary basis, if you do not want to go, that's fine by me. Now, questions?'
Neil put his hand up.

'Yes, Neil?'

'I am going to put this card in my room, I will never need or use it, and there is nothing on the mainland that I want.'

'Same for me' Miako said. 'Maybe for a holiday now and then, but I know after a few days, I will be itching to come back.'

'Anyone else?' Kia asked. There were no further questions.

'OK, fine. Organise with Bree what you need to do to get your belongings sorted. Neil, Miako, when you have time can you talk to Sandy, please. Paul, you said you had tuition for Glen?'

'Bree might be best to take Ray and Melissa in a separate SC, less exposure time.' Bree nodded. 'I will be up in the OpCen if anyone needs me.'

Kia walked into the OpCen and sat down heavily. Sandy came over and asked her if she was OK.

'I think so, all the things I was worried about. How I was going to get all the people up to speed. How the company was going to pan out, and if Brad was going to be able to shoulder the load. All those things were resolved tonight.'

Sandy nodded, 'Yes, tonight's events have certainly strengthened us immensely. You asked Neil and Miako to talk to me, what is it that you want us to do?'

Kia flicked her hair back.

'I want them to design a new SC.' That made Sandy raise an eyebrow. An action she copied from watching Kia and Bree.

'I will explain it when they get here.'
Presently Miako and Neil arrived, Kia motioned them to sit. 'Sorted the stuff with Bree?'

'Yup, she's just about to take off with Mel and Ray, all good. So what's up?'

'Both of you are Sci-Fi fans correct?' They nodded. 'I want you both to design a new SC. We need a design that people are going to accept easier than the one we have. All the internals are obviously up to Sandy, but I don't think we need a SC large enough to carry 14 people.

'Something about half the size, if not smaller.'

'Oh wow really!' Neil beamed, 'I would love to do that!'

Miako said 'There are a lot of futuristic designs on the net, how about we do a search, then select, say, the top ten.
'Then we can tweak the best one to suit, it will save starting from scratch.'

'Sounds like a great plan Miako!'

Sandy cleared the HUD, 'Let's go hunting then', and so the search began.

Outside it was just getting dark as the two SC's lifted off and headed for mainland Australia. Bree radioed into the OpCen and said they would report back in when the task was completed.

Glen and Paul walked into the OpCen and sat at a terminal. Paul put his hand on Glen's shoulder. 'You are about to learn about some of the nastiest, most competitive traits of mankind. You think some governments are underhanded, wait till you see what the large corporations of the world are capable of!' He turned to the screen and pulled up some information. He then started to educate Glen on the basics of dirty corporation business, and within the first hour, he found that Glen was a damn fast learner.

While all this was going on Kia was going over the last few days data, when she had done that she started on some Sats info. Just filling in time as the crews did what they had to do. For the first time in years, she found herself at a loose end and decided it was a very strange feeling.

With all the data cleared and signed off, Kia turned and watched the people buzz back and forth, images flashing up on the HUD and either flicked into a holding pile or discarded.

The two boys in the corner, heads together, Paul speaking and gesturing, Glen is occasionally grinning or laughing.
She stood, stretched and said goodnight and headed for the sack. No one even noticed her leave, apart from Sandy.

Chapter Fifteen

Kia woke with a start, lying there listening for whatever it was that woke her. She got out of bed and looked at the digital display on the wall, it was already 10.33am! She couldn't ever remember being offline that long!

Walking over to the window, she looked through the blinds. Paul and Glen were standing by the open door of the shed talking to Neil. Miako came out of the door said something to Paul. Glen held out his hand and shook Neil's hand and then gave Miako a hug. They all looked pleased with themselves.

'What are you hooligans up to' murmured Kia as she walked over to the wardrobe.

Slipping on a suit, she powered it and turned to a light grey. Then slipping on boots and tidying her hair, she headed out to find what was going on.

She was met by Bree in the foyer, 'Hi boss, long night?'

Kia shook her head, 'No, I went to bed rather early for a change.'

Bree nodded, 'Sandy told us to leave you be, you had been under a lot of stress and needed time to charge back up fully. The trip out last night was a success, the most time was taken getting Neil's stuff, and for a single guy, he sure had a lot of stuff! And by the way he and Miako are acting he won't be single much longer. They have been getting closer as each day passes, but this morning they are almost inseparable.'

'I saw them with Paul and Glen out by the shed, they must be retrieving the gear you guys collected last night' replied Kia.

'I don't think so, we haven't started reclaiming any of that yet, for one there isn't enough space in our rooms for it. And also there isn't anything we need right now. But, I do know there is something in the shed you really must see, shall we?'

Side by side they walked outside and down the steps towards the shed. Neil saw them coming and met them a few meters from the door.

'Hi Ladies! Great morning!' He beamed a huge smile. Kia's eyes narrowed as Neil stood in front of her blocking the way to the shed.

'Neil, what are you up to?'

'Nothing! Just remarking what a great day it is, out here, outside the shed, with you, and Bree, together, us, here.'

Kia held up her hand, 'Stop it, Neil you are babbling, what have you done and what are you hiding in the shed? Tell me now or I will toss you over my shoulder and look for myself.'

'Well, actually it wasn't me, it was more Miako, I helped, a little, and so did Sandy!, but it was mostly Miako. Which I didn't mind, she was brilliant and...'
His words trailed off, as Kia grabbed him by the front of the suit and lifted him 2-3 inches off the ground.

'You are babbling again.' She put him down and smoothed out his suit. Now be a nice sweet lad, and tell aunty Kia what you, sorry, what the three of you have done. I haven't had my morning coffee yet, and I might be just a little on edge because of that, understand?'

Neil nodded quickly, 'Well, it's probably best you see for yourself.'
All this time Paul had been leaning on the door jamb, grinning as he watched. He stepped to one side and motioned her inside with a small bow.

'This I have got to see' Bree said and both girls stepped around a nervous looking Neil.
Kia stopped in the doorway, and her mouth opened slightly. A reaction mirrored by Bree.

Inside the shed, sitting on the conveyor belt was Brad, Melissa, and Ray.

Glen and Miako were also there standing next to them.

Kia looked at them and then back to the thing parked in the middle of the floor. Bree and Kia walked around the brand new S2 sitting in the middle of the shed. It looked sleek, it looked futuristic, but most of all, it looked...

'Perfect! What an absolutely amazing job Neil!'

Neil punched the air in delight, 'It wasn't me it was Miako, she found the base design and we just customised it. Based on what you told us it needed to look like. Sandy set the size based on the mechanics and electronics it needs to have. Sandy put it all in this awesome CAD program, and it just all flowed together, sweet as.'

Neil opened the door, 'Go inside and have a look!' Bree followed Kia in.

The interior was vastly different. There were two pilot seats side by side now. The scanning station was gone. There was a large wrap around HUD under the front screen.

The front screen was much taller and curved up over the seats, the sides wrapped around much further. Kia slid into one seat and Bree into the other. The view was panoramic. Neil flicked on the power, and the console lit up.

He showed the girls where everything was. Controls were now much easier to access. Scanning controls were now duplicated left and right. Anything that needed to be accessed by both crew was at the centre and on the console that flowed back between the seats.

'Wow' Bree said, 'Everything just where it needed to be!'

'You can thank Sandy for that' Neil said, 'she overlaid hours of our movements in the old SC and ergonomically worked out the position for everything we have ever used. She put the common stuff close and the other stuff outboard.'

Kia got out of the seat and looked around the rest of the interior.

There was enough room for four more people, and the ceiling was much lower and contoured. She walked back outside and did another circuit.

She took in the flowing contoured wings. Each of the jet fans were now twice the size from before and the wings highly maneuverable. On the rear was a shallow sweeping tail fin with the word 'Oracle' emblazoned on it. The centre of the 'O' was a graphic picture of planet earth taken from space.

'I am speechless' Kia said coming to a halt next to Neil and Miako. 'You have really excelled!!'
Miako elbowed Neil.

'Oh yes! I nearly forgot!' He reached into his suit thigh pocket and withdrew a wafer-thin card, pressing a button on the card. The S2 changed colour, pressing it again, it changed yet again.

'Wow' Bree said 'That's neat, who thought of that?'

'Kia did' replied Neil.

'I did?!'

Neil nodded, 'When you said, we would need to do something and then fly away to make it look like we didn't have endless resources. 'This way we duck out of sight, change colour and come back, looks like a totally different S2.'

'Brilliant thinking' Kia said.

'Actually no, just a different perspective, *THIS* was brilliant and Sandy thought of it after we suggested the chameleon paintwork.

May I?' asked Miako, as she took the control from Neil. She pressed a button, and the S2 disappeared!

'What the!' Brad said and slid off the conveyor, 'You didn't show us that before!'

'I saved this for Kia, if you look hard, you can see it is actually still there. Cameras on the other side reflect what they see on this side, giving the illusion of being able to see the other wall from here. It's not perfect and from some angles, the view is distorted a little, but at a glance, it works. If you fly over someone the underside will reflect the sky and clouds.

'If you knew exactly where to look, you might spot the deflection, but I would bet if you flew over a stadium full of people no one would see it.'

Neil smiled, 'I secretly think it's because I told Sandy how Klingons cloak their spaceships in the TV Show.

'We call it "Camo", short for camouflage.'   Brad was bobbing up and down, 'Well I tell you that is almost perfect!' He walked around the other side, 'And I can see all of you from here!'

Ray followed Brad around, 'Not bad, not bad at all! You definitely can see distortion when you're moving, but hey, nothings perfect.'

Brad looked at Ray, 'That was a bit negative don't you think?'

Ray shrugged, 'Just my opinion, if it distorts then anyone with a keen eye may pick it up.'

Miako asked if Ray thought he had keen eyes.

He nodded 'Pretty good, yes.'

'Then why haven't you picked up the other S2 at the end of the shed?'

Ray turned and looked. 'Where?'

Miako pointed the card at the seemingly empty end of the shed. Another S2 appeared!

'WOW! OK, I apologise, I will shut up now' he said with a grin.

For the next few minutes, they walked around the Camo effect totally enthralled.

Unbelievable, Kia was still shaking her head in disbelief. She took the control card off Miako and cycled some colours. Miako showed her that even though there were four colour buttons if you pressed a < > key you could lighten or darken the shade.

'Coffee!' Bree said, and a small cheer went up, together they all walked into the house.

Sandy was waiting for them in the dining room. She was literally beaming.

'You like?' She asked as they entered.

Accolades flowed forth from everyone. Sandy was fielding questions on the new layout of the craft and other points Kia was still deep in thought when Paul came over and sat next to her.

'Quite a job the kids did hey?'

She nodded, 'They excelled, I am so proud of them!

'Look at them now to what they were like ten days ago, and Neil has really come out of his shell.'

Paul nodded, 'Miako loves that fact, listen can we talk? Up in OpCen.'

Kia nodded, and they both threaded their way through to the stairs.

'What's on your mind?' Kia asked as they entered the OpCen.

'Last night as you know I took Glen through the basics of dealing with the big guys, banks, corporations and the like and he is a very fast learner. I think our chances of getting Oracle into a position of respectable influence is probably 300% better than when Glen first suggested we go semi-public.'

Kia nodded her agreement, 'With the S2 the kids came up with visual believability is also much better. However, I feel a "BUT" about to appear. What is the next hurdle you think we are going to hit?'

'You know you are almost scary with your mind reading capabilities', smiled Paul. 'Our next problem and I can see two that need addressing shortly, but one at a time, the next problem is this place.'

'I don't follow sorry', replied Kia.

'Once we become noticed, they are going to investigate us. That's not an issue. I always wear clean underwear. But they will look at the island, some of them will pay handsomely to get pictures of our HQ. Either by high altitude surveillance or the more influential will wrangle a Sat to take pictures.'

The others began filtering into the room, finding chairs, and listened quietly.

'It's what I would do if I were on the other side.' Continued Paul, 'Everything I can think of, everything that I would do, we have to expect at least that much, if not more.'

'Well even if they did, what would they see? A house and a long shed, and a garage, no big deal!' Chipped in Melissa. Paul just looked and smiled.

After a few moments of silence, 'OH! OH, I see! Yes of course!' Kia exclaimed.

'So once we have fixed that which may take a day or two, then we can do the Europe thing.' Paul leant back against the wall.

Melissa put her hand up, 'I got lost at the end, where is the harm in an overview of the house and shed?'
Brad spoke up', Mel, if you were to go and meet the CEO of a large company, and be invited to his house for a party, how would you react if your limo stopped at a wooden hut at the end of a dirt road?'

'I would think that either I was in the wrong place or had just been abducted.' She replied. 'OH! Now I get it! Powerful in their eyes goes hand in hand with big, large, or huge. A house and shed just doesn't cut that image does it!'

'So you have something in mind Paul?' asked Kia.

He nodded', I think I can set something up that will do two jobs. Firstly, radiate the impression we require, and secondly, be of benefit us as well. Oh and I can do it without destroying the charm of the Island.'

'So what do you need?'

'I only need three things, Sandy, Bree and the rest of you off the island for a while', replied Paul.

'Me?!' Piped up Bree, 'Why me?'

'Because you are better at colours and designing than I am, some changes are going to need a woman's touch. That is if it's OK with Brad' asked Paul.

Brad smiled, 'Sure I don't mind lending my wife for a good cause, but what are the rest of us going to do, we only have two S2s.'

'Actually', Neil said 'there is eight more in the garage. We bet on Kia liking it so we made ten. If we bombed out, we were just going to scan them out.'

'How about this for a suggestion. You and Bree get started on the design, and the rest of us will take the S2s out for the afternoon, Glen can pile in with Brad for the time being. That ok with everyone?' asked Kia.
She got nods of approval from the others.

'Great, see you outside in say half an hour then. I am off to freshen up.'

Brad walked over to Paul, 'If I come back, and you have a black eye, I will know you said no to one of Bree's ideas.' He hastily sidestepped to avoid a sharp finger in the ribs.

Paul laughed, and he turned to Bree. 'How about we start after we watch these clowns crash and bump and scratch the new S2s just taking them out of the garage?'

'That will be fun to watch' Bree said, taking Paul's arm and lifting her nose to Brad as they left the OpCen.

Chapter Sixteen

Almost to the second, four S2s took off for parts unknown, and Bree and Paul walked back into the OpCen.
Paul dragged a pair of stools over, and they both sat in front of the HUD, he rubbed his hands together and explained to Bree what they needed to achieve. She was quite surprised.

'You want to remodel most of the island tomorrow!'

He nodded, 'Yup that's the plan, so I will draw up a list of what I think is needed, then you, with your designer flair, can rearrange it all to make sense. If the kids can build a fleet of S2s overnight, this should be a breeze. Sandy, let us begin.'

Sandy appeared and stood behind them, 'This is so exciting!' She said with much enthusiasm, they both turned and looked at her.

'What!' She said, 'Hey! Normally I only get to crunch numbers!'

First Paul asked for a large detailed map of the island, and then he asked for a side view with dimensions. He noted that the height of the house above sea level was about 80 meters.

'Can you show me the island out to about 300 meters from shore, the maps changed slightly, so we have deeper water West and East, shallower North and South.'

'That matters?' asked Bree?

'Eventually, it will, we will have to design something to stop people coming here and taking our stuff, or at least trying to eventually.

So building right the first time will make that easier.'

'I hope it never comes to that' Bree said.

'Me too, but some of the jackals on this planet are pure heartless animals, besides I have a plan to stop them. Sandy, how did you build that shed so fast?'

'I have 6 ROVs in the back of the garage, and they have telescopic towers. Once in place they act like a mobile receiver. The shed took about 11 minutes start to finish. I can always make more ROVs if we need them.'

Paul nodded, 'Fine, for now, but once we have this layout done and built, I would like to install street lighting, but I want the poles also to be like the ROVs so if we need something in a hurry you can make it.'

'Something like what?' asked Bree,

'Oh I dunno, a couple of Sherman tanks for example.'

'Bree stared at him 'You jest right!?'

Paul smiled, 'Right now, yes, but I can tell you this in all earnest, no-one, not one of these creeps or governments are going to either hurt my friends or take this tech from us. Not if I can help it. If you think I am taking a tough line, just take a moment and think what a totally pissed off and angry Kia would do!'

Sandy said, 'I have only seen her mad once, it's really scary, and I never said this, but if Kia really got angry, not even I could stop her!

Please, lets not dwell on that. She let that sink in and in a lighter tone asked 'What's first?'

'Well lets select what buildings we need first, then we can worry about layout. We need eight nice cottages or more. Our rooms are just not up to it, plus Brad and Bree are noisy at night.'

She slapped his leg 'We are not!..... Are we?!'

Paul just laughed and put eight houses on the side of the HUD, 'Next we need...'

And so it went on for the rest of the afternoon.

As the sun started to settle in the west, the S2s arrived back home and were duly put away.

It sounded like a herd of children pounding up the stairs and into the room. Paul and Bree were sitting back studying their afternoon's handy work.

Brad came over and gave Bree a kiss on the cheek, 'Sorry you missed the first run in the S2s hon.'

She waved that off, 'I have had a great day, I didn't even have time to miss it, check it out' and she pointed to the HUD.

All but the designers clustered in front of the HUD. Each building was numbered, and there was a legend down the side of the screen explaining all the functions. Not only was everything in place, but it was done down to the finest detail of landscaping and pathways, change huts near the beach.

'Welcome to our new place Bree said. There might be a minor tweak here or there, but that is essentially it folks.' Neil pointed to the long runway that cut diagonally across the island.

'The S2 doesn't need a runway' he commented.

'No' Kia said, 'But any visiting dignitaries in the future may.' She turned the map from an overhead view to walk through mode, after a few minutes of walking around, she returned it to overhead.

'I need to find a better word to use than brilliant. Very well done, again, you guys excel at what you do.'

Paul said 'There is a reason for that Kia, it comes down to the interest and passion that people have for what they do. Most people succeed well, when what they are doing is also their passion.'

Ray took one last look at the HUD, 'I think we are well on the way, I can't wait to get to actually do something. I hate politics, politicians, and the utter crap that goes with it. Today was a great day, the S2 is a dream to work with, everything right at your fingertips, now this, he waved a hand at the HUD, and it is like the best dessert ever.

'As good as all this is. I am hooked on hunting with Mel in the S2.' With that Ray took a step back from the screen.

'I can't design like Neil and Miako, I can't build like Bree and Paul, so apart from hunting, which by the way, was my pastime and hobby back home. I don't have much to contribute at this time.'

He turned to leave.

Kia said 'Wait, please Ray. You are so wrong about how useful you are. Give me just one moment of your time. He stopped and waited.'

Kia looked at the others before continuing.

'Come over here, please.

He walked over to the HUD. 'Look at what they did today, then look at it again, but, this time, tell me, exactly, how many men and in what fashion you would take control of it. Show me its strengths and weaknesses.'

'I, I don't know what you mean' Ray stuttered.

'Yes, you do, I know you do. Whatever they put together tomorrow has not only got to shelter us from the sun, wind and weather. It's got to protect all of us, Melissa included, from the very assholes you hate.'

Ray looked at the floor. Kia turned to face him and lifted his face, she held her hands on both sides of his head and looked into his eyes, deep into them.

'Sergeant Major you are home, this is your family, and we will stand by you no matter what, today, tomorrow, and beyond.'

Melissa went to interrupt, but Brad grabbed her arm, he put a finger to his lips. Kia's tone changed. 'No lies, no bullshit, and most of all, NO ONE GETS FUCKING LEFT BEHIND ON MY WATCH! Do I make myself perfectly clear Ray?'

The pure venom in Kia's voice made Miako's skin crawl.

Ray nodded, 'Crystal clear lady.'

Kia dropped her hands to her sides, she said to the others, 'Mel, Paul, stay, the rest of you scoot.'

They got, in total silence, not sure what just happened.

Kia stepped back out of Ray's personal space, 'Now my friend, show me the best way to defend this place.'

Brad and the others were in the dining room. No one spoke for quite a while. Eventually, Glen cleared his throat and said, 'OK, what just happened up there?'

Brad moved uncomfortably, 'All I know is many years ago Ray was in the Special Forces. I also know that something happened, somewhere, and his team left him behind. I know that for two years he was gone, and finally re-appeared during some kind of prisoner exchange program.

'Ray and two others. Apart from that, that's all I know, and I only know that because 11 years ago we both got drunk as skunks at a bar. Hell, I don't even know if I remember it clearly, but we never talk about it, and I have never pried into it. Not my place.'

Miako stood up, 'I am going to use my terminal in my room, and I do not wish to make Ray feel uncomfortable when he comes down. Neil would you keep me company for a while, please.'

Neil walked with her to the door, she stopped and turned to the room. I feel very sad for Ray. I am also very frightened of what I saw in Kia's eyes. I once said I sensed the power in her. Well today, I actually felt both that power and the anger that she has. The worst thing is, I don't think what we just saw was Kia at her full capability.'

With that, she took Neil's hand and walked away.

Glen stood and wiped his hands down his pants, 'God help those who did that to Ray if Kia finds them. See you guys in the morning' and left.

Bree took Brad by the hand and headed for their room. After they showered and were lying in bed, Bree laid her head on Brad's chest.

'In the layout we did today, Paul has included a receiver near the new admin building.

'There is a circle of light poles that look innocent enough, but will double as a receiver. When I asked why, he said "just in case we need to make something fast, like tanks". Then he said he was "joking", after tonight I don't think he was.'

Brad stroked her hair for a while, 'I doubt anything bad is going to happen hon. But being prepared is not a bad thing. Worst case we jump in our S2 and get the hell out of dodge. She nodded at that and drifted off to sleep.'

Chapter Seventeen

They were woken early in the morning by an unholy racket out in the hallway, Brad pulled on his PJ pants and opened the door to check it out. Ray was walking up and down the hallway banging a serving tray with a spoon.

'Rise and Shine you lazy grunts! The sun is almost up and we have to vacate. Fish to scare and birds to terrify... He spied Brad standing in PJs, he broke into a huge grin. OH you're awake already, my bad! Come on, quick brekky and lets go!'

'Ray, one day I promise I am just gonna kill you. Go away for an hour.' With that, Brad shut the door.

Bree looked at her husband grinning his head off. 'What was that?'

Brad shook his head, 'I think we got the old Ray back and darted to beat Bree to the shower.'

45 minutes later everyone was standing outside on the steps. The sky was a perfect blue and not a cloud in sight. Miako was putting her hair up in a ponytail, and Neil was hopping in a circle trying to get his left boot on. Paul and Kia were standing off to one side, Paul was pointing out landmarks, with Kia nodding occasionally.

Melissa and Ray were standing talking to Glen. Beside them stood Brad and Bree, Bree was the only one not in a suit. Instead, she wore a light summer skirt and a tank top.

When Kia had stopped talking to Paul, she called them all together.

'Take a look around boys and girls, when we get back it's going to look different.

Now, as we have been kicked off the island for the day, I have decided we might as well do something worthwhile. We are looking at a 14 hour day approximately, all CoOrds are in the S2s, but here is the outline.

Rumour has it that there are three areas that were used as munitions dumps after the last war. There probably is a whole lot more, but just for today, we are going after three of them. 'Nothing especially hard about these, other than there is a lot of traffic in the areas. Be especially careful about bumping your head, or even running into something. I am not sure how good our insurance is.

If any of the ordinances does go off, which is very doubtful, the S2 can take it without any problems at all. But it will cause a stir with the powers that be. Each target area is quite large, so we will do each one as a whole group. Any questions? Good. Brad say goodbye to your wife, Glen say goodbye to yours. You two are teaming up again for today.'

'Bye, honey' Glen said to Paul, Paul curtsied in response.

'Mount up!' Kia said and led the pack away.

Bree stood next to Paul watching them lift, turn and leave. 'Yup', she said out loud, 'Definitely the best choice.'

'What, me as a wife?' asked Paul. 'No silly, Kia as leader.'

'Without a doubt' he said, 'Come on lady, we have a complex to build.' Side by side they headed for the OpCen.

When the sun rose that morning it shone on three tiny buildings. When the sun started to set that evening, it shone on a whole new gleaming complex. The job, though long and tedious, was done.

The new OpCen stood exactly where the old one had been, but instead of a three story building it was now an eight story high tower. With a circular balcony, wide enough for tables and chairs and a walkway. A super fast elevator took them from the ground floor to the top in seconds, although there was no sensation of movement. The windows went around the entire room and were all one way.

You could see out, but not see in. Sensors in the room kept the ambient lighting to a perfect level, automatically adjusting the transparency of the glass. Whether the sun was shining outside, or it was pitch black.

'A job well done' Paul said to Sandy.

'Indeed' she said, 'it was quite a lot of work, I had to lock in seven additional CPU banks at times!'
They looked around the new OpCen. Now there were four large HUDs from just below the ceiling, down to waist height. They were arranged in a square formation with room to walk through at each corner.

'Sandy, may I ask you now for a logical opinion? Are you happy with the new set up, and do you feel we forgot anything?'

Sandy pondered for a moment, 'I am more than pleased with the outcome, with the peripheral sensors and other equipment we fitted over the complex I feel I have everything covered, before I felt restricted to the house only.
 As for missing anything, we ticked all the mental boxes I had and then some. We did a formidable job today.'

Paul and Bree walked out onto the balcony facing south and leant on the railing.
 Even though the sun was just approaching the distant horizon, all the streetlights and path lights in the complex were on.
To the left were a dozen individual villas that were their new homes. Beyond that was a large complex of buildings, and offices. To the right, where the shed used to stand was now a garden complex and a park area for the many golf cart style vehicles. Beyond this were assorted building and laboratories.

Also a hostel/hotel type building with the capacity for 260 people.

Even further away was the Airport control tower, complete with runway lights and a flashing tower light. Even the OpCen had roof lights. Paul had joked that when the others returned they better not run into the new tower.

On the other side of the runway were assorted buildings, a machine shop and fuel storage. While the two on the balcony could never, ever have done everything down to the last little detail, Sandy both could and had.

'We need some more people' Bree said.

Paul glanced at her, 'How so?'

'Well, we need gardeners and groundsmen, mechanics and cooks, that kind of thing. We made this, but it's not ALIVE if you know what I mean. Any outsiders are going to think it strange no people are ever seen. They would never need to know what goes on up here, just like workers in any big company never know what's going on, on the top floor.'
'OK' Paul said, 'But won't they think it's strange that nothing seems to be going on here?'
'Not at all.' Came Sandy's voice from just inside the doorway.
'Not if we make something go on.' Paul walked back inside, Bree followed.

'What did you have in mind?' He asked.

'Well', Sandy said, 'What about we scan a few old wrecks and set up an area in one of the warehouses to store them. I already have thousands of relics and artefacts blueprints in the data tanks. Then invite a few crusty old archaeologists and the like to come and study them. The labs can have every conceivable scanner and tester known in them. They, in turn, can invite students to study under them. Hey presto, not only are we cleaning the place up, but we are furthering the education of the youth in matters of history. It won't be a front for what we do, it will more like a side venture.'

Bree laughed, 'Sandy you are becoming sneakier just like us.'

'I have said it before, and I will say it again, I really like learning!' smiled Sandy.

Paul walked over the HUD that showed the S2s locations, 'We have three green areas and four triangles about 15 minutes out.'

'They should be home about 45 minutes before the sun goes down, so they can have a bit of a look around' remarked Sandy.

'Although we worked all day, I feel surprisingly fresh. I still think we could add a few bits though' Bree said.

'Oh undoubtedly, I would like to see a shipping dock down the bottom end. That came to me when Sandy had her epiphany.

'If we collect relics, eventually they will need to be shipped back to their respective owners, and just by the way Sandy that will also boost our credibility by a large amount. Countries make a big thing about getting national treasures back. Even if they never knew, they had them in the first place. Also, not all visitors would come by plane so a working dock would be a bonus.'

Suddenly there was a flash overhead, followed closely by three more.

'The guys are back!' Bree said redundantly, and walked back out on the balcony to watch them circle the island slowly and drop one by one onto the allocated landing areas. 'They look so tiny from up here' she commented.

Brad was the first one out of the elevator but only by milliseconds, as the others rushed in gawking at everything. The only one walking at a reasonable pace was Kia and even she was checking everything out.

Paul and Bree stayed on the balcony and waited. They didn't have to wait for long, soon the rest came through the doors like a mob of paparazzi, rushing over to the railing they gawked and pointed and oohed and ahhed.

Glen walked over to Paul and said, 'I am home honey, love what you have done to the place! Something is different! Let me guess, you have had your hair done?' Much to everyone's amusement. He then shook Paul's and said seriously, 'Well bloody done, now show me what it all means.'

Both Bree and Paul took turns in pointing out features of the complex and answering a myriad of questions.

Kia came out onto the balcony with a tray of coffees. Everyone sat at a nearby table, turning their seats towards the complex. As the light slowly diminished the whole panorama took on a different feel. All the buildings were well lit, paths and walkways, the garden, the airstrip.
The balcony lights came on automatically, and one by one everyone told the stories of their day.

Kia summarised the days results with the occasional interjection of comments from the rest.
Paul brought up the comment Bree had made, and the idea that Sandy had, he also re-told the possible benefits to be had. Just that topic alone was discussed at length, and in the end, it was decided they would run with it, but a few months down the track. That seemed to fit well with all.
Paul was watching Ray during the evening and was happy to see he looked much more relaxed, not only in his demeanour but physically as well.
 Melissa stood and gave her glowing impression of what was achieved today, not only for the disposal of so much evil they had done but also the efforts of Sandy, Paul and Bree. The next thing she asked was that she would love a shower and to freshen up.
 'So where do I go?'
Bree laughed and took everyone over to the railing.
She pointed to the villas.
'The first one we reserved for Kia, it's closest to the S2s and the OpCen. It is positioned so she can see almost every building. The second one there', she pointed, 'I have reserved for myself and my man. The rest are up for grabs, each one is identical. However, every second one is a mirror reverse of the one next to it.
'All have two bedrooms with adjoining bathrooms, kitchens blah, blah, blah, It's up to you all if you want one each, there's enough for that, if you want to share, there are two bedrooms.

'If you want to pile in together, that also is an option. All of them have phones, net, and HUDs, every possible thing that we could think of.

'Depending on my flight status tomorrow, I will be going over to that building there, the one marked 'B', and will be reclaiming my knick-knacks and personal stuff, to make our villa more homely.

'Lastly pick your place from up here, because it's easier to see the layout.'

Paul added, 'One other thing, one floor down from here is a caféteria area, doubles as a dining room kitchen. So you can either eat at home or here. Restrooms are there as well. All that is in this tower now is all Sandy's stuff, a café and the OpCen.'

He turned to Glen, 'We sharing or going solo?'

Glen shrugged, 'I can go the room each route if you snore, I will move out.'

'OK, I opt for #5 the blue villa, that way we don't have to listen to all the rows at night.'

Paul agreed and asked Bree to give him a yell when she goes to collect the personal gear.

Paul and Glen took off down to inspect the villa. Bree hugged Brad, and they left as well.

Miako and Melissa looked at each other, and Melissa said 'Well this is a bit awkward.'

Miako smiled 'Not really, Neil is my S2 partner so he can be my house partner too, I am thinking.'

'Damn fine idea', Melissa agreed, 'You think you could cohabitate with your S2 partner Ray?'

'Hell, I will try anything once if it doesn't work, like Glen said there are enough villas to go round.'

Kia stood and laughed, 'You know Paul and Glen have got you four figured out dead centre.'

'How do you figure that' Neil asked blushing slightly.

'Real easy' replied Kia, 'They picked first, right?' Neil and Melissa nodded, in unison.

'Do the maths, not counting my place, three couples make the next available villa number 5?'

Kia smiled at the look on their faces and bid them all goodnight. She walked inside, spoke with Sandy for a few moments and disappeared into the elevator.

Those left on the balcony watched the tiny figure of Kia leave the building, check the S2s and head over to the first villa.

'OK then' Ray said, 'Lets check the villas out.'
All of them left bidding goodnight to Sandy, who was still working, checking the S2's day's data.

Chapter Eighteen

The early morning rays of the sun found Miako standing in a yoga pose under a sheltered sundeck in the garden area. She held the pose perfectly motionless for three minutes, then relaxed before moving into the next position of her routine. Fifteen minutes later she heard someone approaching and moving only her eyes, she greeted Melissa.

'Morning', she replied, 'I am off down the beach for a swim, care to come with?'

Miako nodded, 'Sure, I have about 15 minutes left of my routine then I will grab a towel.'

Melissa watched her go through some of the stances and positions of her routine, after awhile she remarked, 'You know if I could stretch and bend like that I probably would have a much better sex life!'

Miako lost her composure and rolled on the mat laughing, 'OK that is enough for me, I shall get my stuff, be back shortly.' She rolled up her yoga mat and jogged back to the villa.

She was back dressed in a floral bikini and sandals, 'I left a note for Neil when he wakes, lets go then.'
Side by side they took the path to the west beach.

Paul was sitting in a chair outside the villa. He had rocked the chair back against the wall and was drinking a large glass of fruit juice. Glen sat just off to his right finishing his breakfast. Both of them had seen the girls leave for the beach.

They talked about a whole range of issues, but were for the most part relaxed and at ease.

Glen pushed his plate back, and burped, 'Maybe I should take up yoga?'

Paul grinned, 'I can just see that now, you in a skimpy yoga outfit. Hell, even the seagulls wouldn't land near you!'
Glen balled up a hand towel and threw it at him.

'You know I never did thank you for taking the time to show me all that shit the other night. I grew up in a harsh environment, dodging fights and arguments, and that was just at home. School days were not much better, although I did well enough to get into a local Tech college. Midway through my last year, I caught a teacher and a female student making animal noises on a desk. I thought it was wrong, so opened my mouth about it, those two denied everything. I was branded a troublemaker and tossed out of the course.

'So I took up IT instead, graduated with a B-Class Cert. Bummed around for a while, chasing girls, occasionally catching one. Then I got wind of an IT job going so I tossed my resume on the table and got the job, thanks to Miako. The rest is history.'

Paul nodded, 'I didn't have it so bad.'
'Born to an upper-middle-class family, one brother, younger than me, a sister older. Was doing well in high School, happy home life, dad was into trading. Mum was a typical stay at home kind, all was sweet until one day I got off the school bus and found mum crying in the kitchen. Cops are standing there, Colin, my brother had wrapped himself around a lamp post in a car he didn't have a licence to drive.

'Home life went to shit after that, my sister moved out because of the atmosphere.
'Dad buried himself at work, and mum, well mum decided life looked better through the bottom of a bottle. A lot of bottles actually.'

Paul stopped speaking and waved, Glen looked up and waved as Kia and Ray walked down towards the new complex.

Paul continued 'I started hanging with dad more, mum mostly being incoherent most times. That's how I got into the trading market, it came really easy. I could pick up a trading sheet and look at it, and it was almost like the good ones were highlighted and the bad ones underlined.

'Dad called it a gift, I think it was more a gut feeling myself. I did really well, was making nice money.

'Then one day this guy comes into Dads office, asks for me, he heard I could 'Dowse the Market', a clicky term for predicting the market. He offered me an obscene amount of money to go work for him, and I did. Worst mistake of my life, well, no, maybe not a mistake per se. I found out that I had moved from helping Gran and Granddad invest their pensions and life savings, to a really dark culture that flowed under the surface. Paul paused for a moment...

'But hey, money was great and everything I got to do was just numbers and names on a sheet of paper, I saw companies and cabal climb and some fall, I saw nasty trading designed to lose money but kill another competitor in the process. It was all in the name of ladder climbing and dollars.

'What finally got my eyes open was I personally picked an up and coming competitor and told the boss I figured his company was going to give us a push. A push is used when we bid on a sub-contract job for say the military.

Even though we don't make what they want, we get others to make the parts for us, and we deal with the military at a grossly inflated cost.

'Anyway, a push is when another company bids for the same contract but DOES make the parts, that means they can offer a better cost per part deal, basically pushing us off the table. Anyway long story short, the guy was found about ten days later hanging in his garage. Been there a few days so the papers said, a suicide, a note stating his wife cheated on him, and he couldn't take it. Bollocks!!'

'I investigated that guy up, down and sideways before determining he may move to push us, Glen, he was as camp as a row of tents, his marriage was a front for appearances. She was gay as well, and it suited them both perfectly.

'From that newspaper article on, I started looking for other incidents and found way, way too many. I told them the pressure was getting to me, told them I wanted some time off, threw a couple of easy deals in the shitter to add weight to the story, and they figured I was burned out so let me go.

'They are nothing more than a bucket of snakes.'

Glen leant back, 'I guess sometimes it's hard to have faith in mankind.'

Paul said 'Isn't that the truth!' Both of them sat quietly, wrapped in their own thoughts.

Glen cocked his head, straining to hear something. 'You hear that?'

Paul rocked his chair forwards and listened, 'Popping noise?' Glen nodded.

Paul walked into the house and grabbed some runners. 'Lets go look, maybe one of my buildings is falling down already!'

Glen groaned. 'What?' asked Paul.

'You built the villas too right?'

Paul pushed Glen onto the path leading to the complex. As they walked between a few buildings, the noise was louder but sporadic. It would stop for a few minutes, then start up again. 'Definitely down this way', they rounded the corner of a warehouse. The path led to a smaller, long utility building. The sound was coming from inside.

Opening the swinging door, the noise went from a low popping to loud cracks. There was a connecting door between the front office and the warehouse area beyond, they opened the connecting door and stepped inside. BOOM, BOOM, BOOM, Glen held his ears.

Kia turned and smiled, she handed Glen and Paul a pair of electronic ear muffs each. The noise returned to low popping. In front of them were booths, Ray was standing, legs apart facing the far wall, Pop, Pop, Pop, he put down what he was holding, and took his ear muffs off. Turning, he spied the guys for the first time, 'Oh, Hiya fellas.'
He hit a button on the wall and something from the other end started travelling this way.
Paul turned and looked behind him. The end wall was covered in almost every kind of handgun imaginable.
The left wall held rifles and the right wall, shotguns.
'Kia figured that as I liked hunting, but wasn't allowed to hunt anything on the island, that she would do this as the next best thing. It's bloody great, have a go!'
Click, the target he had been shooting at stopped at the booth, Ray unclipped the paper and handed it to Paul. There was a fairly good grouping in the centre with a few stray's just outside the black.
Ray pointed to the strays, 'You can tell it's been a while hey.'
Glen turned to Kia 'We don't need to learn how to be commandos, do we?'

'No, not at all this is purely for sport and recreation', she replied. 'Or do you want to sit twiddling thumbs when there is nothing urgent to do? If you want to play tennis, we can set that up, or lawn bowls.'
Glen grinned at the bowls comment.
Ray said, 'I am more than willing to act as coach, he motioned to the walls, there is nothing here I can't strip and reassemble, so if you want to have a run just speak up.'
Glen said he would give it a go.
Paul shook his head, 'Maybe later.'
'Let me finish this set' Kia said, 'Then I will walk back with you and leave these two to plink away.' She turned and walked back into a booth. Picked up her handgun, called live fire, and fired a mag of 15 shots down range.

She dropped the mag out, cleared the gun and laid it back in its case with the magazine. Stepping around Ray, she hung her ear protection up with Paul, and they both left together.

Ray selected a box from the shelving and put it in front of Glen, he opened the box and inside was a brand new pistol. 'This is a Browning BuckMark .22lr, it's a nice little unit to learn on before you move up the calibre ladder....'
Kia and Paul walked in silence most of the way back to the villas.
Paul was the first to speak, 'I think you are a great leader Kia, not only do you focus on the tasks we need to do, but you take the time to listen and help the people around you, that is very rare today.'

'Why thank you, Paul, I have found it costs nothing to care but pays a lot in return.
Now lets find out where the rest of the lazy inhabitants are, shall we?'
'I saw Miako and Mel go down to the west beach, Glen and Ray are back there, only three to find.' Paul said.
All three were found in the OpCen. Neil was working on a HUD. Brad and Bree were drinking coffee on the balcony.
Paul dragged up a chair and sat next to Brad. 'Morning ladies' he said as he sat down. Bree grinned.
Brad asked 'Where you been? We buzzed the villa but got no answer.'
Paul pointed to the little warehouse, 'See that place there, Kia had it fitted up as an indoor shooting range for Ray to play in. We heard some strange noises and found them shooting away at some paper targets.'
Bree clapped, 'Oh goodie, wonder if Ray minds a girl as company!'
'You are a shooter Bree?' asked Paul with surprise.
'Hell yeah!!! Doesn't everyone! So does Brad but he normally shoots a different format than I do. My Dad taught me.

He used to shoot western action. Complete with gun belt and wide-brimmed hat' she laughed. 'It's fun, try it, you may just be surprised.'

Kia came and joined them, 'I see the girls are still on the beach.'

Brad turned his head and squinted at two tiny dots on the white sand, 'That's damn good eyesight you got there!'

'Not really, Paul told me he saw them going that way this morning.'

'So what's happening, we can't just sit around all the time. Not that I mind, I just get fidgety, ask Bree.'

'I just talked to Sandy, she has hired a small hangar just outside Paris. Tomorrow Paul, Glen and I have an appointment with the holding company at 1.pm. Sandy is still filling in the details and this evening we should have a full plan put together. Then the next day it's one in Italy, and the 3rd day one in London. Once all that is done, we let it stew for a while, I don't know how long it will take before things start to happen.'

Paul said 'I do, things will be simmering behind the scenes before you get to Italy and before you even get to London, it will be hot news. A lot of companies have gone the 50/50 deposit way hedging bets, but to my knowledge, no one has done a 3 way run on holding companies. On top of that, 250mil was the record back when I played the game. What we are going to drop on them will be huge.'

'Good' Kia said, 'We now look the part, and soon will be worth the part. This must be the first time anyone has had to build the company to explain its services, rather than get the company first then build the services. Sandy tells me that the London based holding company was started by a combination of a Singaporean and a Japanese Banking Cartel. So that might open the door to Japan a fraction.'

'I would say you have a fair to excellent chance the Japanese may open the door that fast it comes off at the hinges', replied Paul.

Bree got to her feet 'I am so over sitting on my bum all day, I am going to find Ray, you coming Brad?'

He stood and smiled, 'Only if you want to lose again sweet pea.'

After the pair had left Kia turned to Paul, 'So what can go wrong with tomorrows plan?'

He shook his head, 'Nothing really, not much can go wrong when you are spending money.
The only thing that could go wrong is if someone steals the gold from us.'

'I doubt that is going to happen. There won't be any gold to steal until the armoured car is parked at the loading dock', replied Kia.

'It looks like we are almost set then.'

****

Bree and Brad found the range building easy enough, inside Glen was pounding away at a target set at 10 meters with Ray standing close and instructing him. From the look of the paper target on the table, Glen wasn't doing too shabby either. They waited till Glen had shot his set before interrupting, Ray beamed to see them and got extra enthusiastic when he found out they were regular shooters!

When he asked them what they would like to shoot, Brad asked for a 45ACP and Bree wanted a Glock 19. Like a kid in a toy store Ray grabbed the necessary hardware, pointed to the ammo cabinet.

'Take booths 4 & 5. Just far enough away so that any ejected shells don't fall around Glen's feet and distract him.'
It only took fifteen minutes for them to get organised and step up to the line, Brad's target holder was at the booth, but Bree's was down range, stopped at the 50-meter marker. She hit the return button, and it came whizzing back to the booth. It still had a target hung in the frame.

Bree unclipped the used target, hung the new one and sent it downrange to the 15-meter mark. She took the used one to Ray and handed it to him.

'You left your target in the frame, nice 4 shot cloverleaf by the way.'

Ray frowned for a second, 'Ah, not mine Kia's, but she put a full 15 clip into it before.'

They both just looked at the target and said nothing. She took the target back to Brad and showed him. She said the same thing she had to Ray and Brad just stared when told it was a 15 clip target. Bree put the target on the table behind her and started filling her clip.

Miako and Melissa came back from the beach and showered. Changed, they walked up to the OpCen. Stopping at the café first, they grabbed a sandwich and juice each and continued up top. Kia was still on the balcony with Paul, and Neil was still at the HUD, Melissa walked out and sat next to Kia, and attacked her sandwich.

Meanwhile, Miako had given half her sandwich to Neil, and they both looked at a design he had been working on all morning.

'I see you have named it.' Neil grinned, 'Yes, I call it the ValKyrie, it will suit don't you think?'

Miako nodded, 'Perfectly!'

Melissa finished eating, leant back and relaxed. 'You took Ray away this morning, is he out on a run?'

Kia shook her head, 'No, he is down at the indoor shooting range, been there all day so far.'

Melissa sat up startled, 'Is that safe, you know, considering?'

'Relax, I was with him for awhile, then Paul and Glen came down, when I left with Paul, he was just like a little boy in a toy store and fussing over Glen like a mother hen. Brad and Bree went down not more than half an hour ago, besides, come with me a second.'

They walked inside, and Kia pulled up a screen of the indoor range, they could see clearly everything going on.

Melissa watched for a couple of minutes and smiled.
Ray was slapping Glen on the back, and smiling wildly.

'Thank you, Kia, I was worried about the old lug.'

'No need to worry yourself about him, he is as tough as old nails, he just needed a bit of refocusing. The fact that some of us are sports shooters like him, gives him a common ground he feels comfortable on, it will be good therapy.'

Paul came in off the balcony, 'Sandy I am going down to the err... OK, where would I be going if I wanted to get the personal stuff we scanned from my house?'

She smiled, 'I have already boxed it all up, and it's in your lounge in the villa.'

He stared, 'How did you manage that?'
Sandy continued, 'I heard what you said to Bree about defending this place. So, I now have a complete grid of receivers around the island. I can now put anything anywhere on the Island!'

'You are a true treasure', replied Paul and went to unpack.

Kia looked through the HUD at Miako and Neil, 'You two are quiet.'

'Just checking our online character scores and catching up with gossip.' replied Neil.

'Well, I'd like a meeting around 8 pm if that's OK', they nodded. Sandy let the others know about an 8 pm briefing in the café please.' Sandy saluted and carried on with her data sorting.

Seeing there was nothing left to do, Kia decided to have a look around the complex, she had already committed a detailed map to her memory. Instead of walking, she hopped onboard one of the many electric carts and hit the accelerator.

Chapter Nineteen

Just before 8.pm, Kia was sitting in the café looking through some notes on a tablet. Everyone was present and sat quietly talking amongst themselves.
Kia put the tablet down and looked up. They took that as a cue to drop the chatter.

She smiled. 'Before we start this briefing, I would like to recap what we have accomplished in the last nine days. The reason for this is because starting tomorrow it's going to get busy, very busy. Some of this is going to sound like it's out of a spy thriller novel. It is real.

'So are your accomplishments over the past week or so. You have literally progressed from a bunch of people who had everyday lives, with dreams of a better world. To a bunch of people about to make a better everyday world. You have also progressed within yourselves as well. Neil here is the best example, but I have seen it in all of you. You look at things we do, not with disbelief, but with a sense of accomplishment, and I hope more than a little pride. If you think I am overstating your progress, think back to last month.'
She paused, looking at each in turn.

'If someone was to ask you to build either a flying craft or 35 square kilometers of a complex. Maybe clean up 12,000lbs of live munitions, and you have less than 24 hours to do any of these, what would you have said back then?
'That is the extent of my patting you on the back. Right, now moving forward.

'We are now going to go, semi-public. Most of you know some or all of what I am about to say, but let me say it anyway. 'Semi-public means letting the world's powers that be know about us. There is no turning back from this once it's done. If anyone thinks we are not ready or thinks we should not do this, speak up now.'

Glen put his hand up.' Paul has tutored me on and off for a few days now, on the side of society I did not even know existed. It's been a real eye-opener. When I suggested going public, it was based on my 'then' view of the world, it seemed the best path to take. Now I have a lot more knowledge than before, I think what we are about to do is no longer the best path. It is now the only path!'

Kia nodded, 'I agree, to do what must or should I say needs to be done, secretly and covertly, which was my first plan, would so badly limit us from doing things effectively.

'The plan over the next few days is simple, we are going to go to a bank holding company in Marseilles France, deposit some money. Then on to another holding company in Italy and do the same there, then the third and last task, go to a London-based Holding company and deposit the last block of money with them, and then come home.'

Brad shifted in his seat, 'I take it, all of the above, is simple in a perfect world. However, we all know this isn't a perfect world. In fact, we all have made a living for years because it's not a perfect world. Otherwise, we would not have been working on anti-intrusion software. So who is going and who stays home?'

'We are all going.' Answered Kia.
That caused a stir and a ripple of chatter.

'I thought it was just the three of you, Yourself, Paul, Glen', Ray stated.

Kia shook her head, 'All of us Ray because I don't trust these people as far as I could throw them, but lets break the operation down into three parts.

'One for each deposit.'

'May I take the next bit?' Paul asked Kia.

'Be my guest', she replied.

'The ones that will be seen are us three. Kia will be the boss lady, Glen and myself, acting as advisors, assistants whatever. We can't carry the gold in, so we will need transport. Transport requires drivers and guards. We also can't arrive with an S2, so we need regular transport. Going in to make the deposit will be a breeze, they don't know jack shit why we have an appointment other than to make a deposit. What and how much they don't know. So getting in, doing drop number one, is a walk in the park.

'Now once we walk out of that bank, the word is going to leak. How fast I don't know, but leak it will. Hopefully, we will have got out of France before that happens. The French don't know we are going to Italy next. If we cover out getaway well, again the drop will go smoothly, but this time rumours of something in France may have reached the Italians ears. Now depending on what info was leaked, again no problems. In out and away. 'Two deposits that close together IS going to be noticed, and the name Oracle IS going to leak. That makes the UK deposit just that bit harder.'

'How so?' asked Miako.

Paul smiled at the question, 'They are nosy asses, they will want to interrogate us, they will want to see how much money we have, they will want to know why we deposited in France and Italy, what else you ask?

'God knows. It could be anything from stalling tactics while they recover and plan, to outright abduction. These guys might be good guys, or they might be the darker side, you can't tell from the outside.'

Nobody around the table was smiling now.

'Once we deposit in London, we are out of there.'

'Right, now you have told us, what we need to do, now tell us how we are going to do it', Neil said.

Kia took the lead, 'Originally I had planned on a three day Op. One deposit each day. In light of the urgency Paul has described, I have ditched that and hope we can knock it over the same day. This is what I propose, and it's coming out as I think, so join in anytime!'

For the next two hours, all the fine details were ironed out. Ideas were thrown in and out, cut, bent or moulded. Eventually, all conversation came to an end, simply because there was no more that anyone could think of to say. Everyone knew their part precisely.

Sandy had stood motionless for the entire meet, only answering questions when asked directly. However, she had not been idle.

As things were agreed on and put in place, phone calls and arrangements were being made in the background. Everything the group needed was being organised, and she hadn't even blinked!

Paul tossed a pen onto the table. Pages of mindless doodles in front of him, something he always did while thinking hard. 'Well, I think we nailed it, or as close as we can ever hope to be. I personally think it's going to go without a hitch, and even if it hiccups, we have allowed for that.

'They are at such a disadvantage and will be behind the eight ball all the way.'

A chorus of agreement came in reply to that.

Melissa spoke up next, 'I know we agreed to leave in the morning, but I am so hyped now, no way will I get to sleep.

'I put my hand up that we leave earlier. I know the holding companies won't open earlier for us, but I will probably feel less jittery once this is underway.'

'There is a name for that, it's called PMN in the military, not the ladies' PMS, Pre-Mission Nerves, it's what soldiers get if they have too much time to think about what they are about to do. Once they are on the plane or boat, it goes away', explained Ray.

'It's why, normally, those that plan do not tell those that go until the last minute.'

Kia looked at Sandy for an opinion. 'Everything we need, here, is ready to go, the things we need at the start point are organised, and they are in a different time zone to us here. France is all set to go, the Italians ditto, London is one hour behind them so I am still working on them.

'As you asked, I have set up all the stuff we need, but none of the appointments. Also, three hours ago I tasked three Sats, one for each location, they are now watching each area for any extracurricular activity that may arise after your arrival and departures. I will leave them there for an additional day or two. If you leave early, lets say 1.347 hours from now. Travelling west you will be able to follow an early morning twilight flight to France.'

Brad shook his head, 'Your organisational skills are impeccable Sandy.'

'Oh, you don't know the half of it yet, young man she smiled back. Now go on you lot, git!'

Ninety minutes later three S2s lifted quietly off, turned west and climbed to 50,000ft, in tight formation. Bree was running point and had Kia onboard with her. Off to her right was Miako with Neil, Paul and Glen. To the left were Melissa with Ray and Brad. They were cruising fairly slowly on a heading to take them over Japan. They were waiting for something.

Sandy was standing in the centre of all four HUDs which displayed a Sat view of all three destinations, and the fourth was a top down view of the S2s position and progress. Even she wasn't sure why she was doing this visually, it just seemed the way to do it.

Chapter Twenty

As they approached the Japanese border, the group slowed even more, until their HUDs showed a blip of an international flight that had just left Tokyo. The plane in front of them slowly climbed to 45,000 ft and headed in the same direction they were travelling. Bree closed the distance until they were almost directly overhead and about 1500ft higher. She then slaved the S2 to follow the shiny aircraft in front.

'Why we following this plane again?' asked Brad.
Melissa turned and looked at him. He was dressed in a Security guard uniform identical to the one Ray was wearing. Melissa walked over to him and helped him with a tie he was fighting with.

'At this height, we may leave contrails behind us, by following the plane any that we do leave will flow together with the plane, plus if we occlude any stars, it will be blamed on the plane. It's just one of the details Sandy sorted for us. If you ask me, I would rather be over cautious than careless.'

*****

In Miako's S2 Neil was standing in his boxers and a white shirt, he reached up and took a pair of immaculately pressed trousers off a hanger and drew them on, followed by a jacket with double row buttons. Miako watched him dress, when he was finished, he placed a chauffeurs cap on his head and asked,

'How does that look?'
She walked around him, picking off a piece of lint, and straightened a sleeve. 'My! She said you do scrub up well!'

'I have never worn a suit before, or in this case, a uniform. It feels... empowering!' He gave her a grin and a bow, 'OH shit!, shoes! He exclaimed, looking at his feet still in his runners.'

Miako giggled and gave him a kiss on the cheek. 'What was that for?'

'Just for being you and not the timid, shy guy you used to be.'

He coloured slightly, 'That's because I feel like I am part of something special for the first time.'

Sitting at the back Paul and Glen grinned at Neil, they were dressed identically. Ultra black suits, with knife-edge creases that were laser straight. Neither had bothered to tie their ties as yet and their jackets were undone, Paul was fiddling with a cufflink.

A watch on his wrist made the picture. It was an analogue one. Digital watches were for the crass crowd Paul had explained to Glen before.

Miako brought Neil a pair of mirror polished shoes, 'This will complete the picture, and I wish I had a camera.'
Neil stood up after slipping on the shoes and turned Miako around to face the back of the S2, he put his arm around her waist and said, 'Sandy take a picture, please.'

Sandy's voice filled the cabin, 'Done! And I agree you certainly look dashing! Forty-eight minutes till waypoint people.'

*****

Kia stood in front of Bree's critical inspection. 'Thank you, Sandy' she said in answer to the arrival update. She was dressed in a business jacket and a hugging skirt that was almost obscene in its short length. The skirt was crimson in colour and contrasted well with the brilliant white shirt. The shirt was a mixture of fine silk and lace with a plunging neckline. She had a multi-layered necklace on that was a mixture of yellow and rose gold, the links were woven and in regular spacing, jewels were woven in.

Everything just dragged your attention to her ample cleavage. She had matching earrings and multiple rings on most fingers.

She didn't wear a watch, but there was one included in a very ornate broach that she wore on the jacket. Black silk stockings and stilettos rounded out her outfit.

'So', Kia said, 'Your opinion, please?'

Bree just shook her head, 'You are an absolute killer vision! Just make sure you stay away from the guys!'

'What, why?' Kia asked raising one immaculately formed eyebrow.

'If you don't, dressed like that, you will have drool all over you!'

Kia laughed and gave Bree a hug.

'Careful!' Bree said, 'Even I am starting to drool.'

'Separation waypoint three minutes', Sandy informed them. Bree returned to the pilot seat, checked left and right, and down at the airliner they had been following faithfully. A chime sounded marking the break-off point and in perfect formation, they peeled off to the left and started a slow descent. The plane continued blissfully unaware it had been followed.

Kia kicked off her shoes and sat next to Bree in the other chair. She punched up a map and watched their progress towards a small private airfield called Villac Oublay according to the display. She checked the S2s were flying locked.

Bree was literally flying all of them. 'I know it's semi dark down there, but I am taking them in camo.'

The perimeter lights of the airfield were visible in the distance, Kia said nothing. Bree like everyone else knew their roles perfectly.

They were approaching the airport from the side, on a path that took them over very few houses and farms. Skimming the treetops Bree took them over the perimeter fence and slowed to a fast walking pace as they slid silently into an open hangar and put them down deep inside.

She switched off the camo, she didn't want anyone walking into the S2 in the semi-dark. Kia slipped her shoes back on, and everyone assembled just inside the hangar doors.

Neil was the first to receive both an eyeful and an elbow in the ribs at the sight Kia made walking over. '*Do not* make derogatory remarks about the boss', Kia warned before anyone said a word, 'It will reflect badly in your pay packet. We have a few minutes up our sleeve before we need to move out. Anything off the beam at the moment?'

'You could have warned us earlier that we would be fighting off people falling all over you. You know how the French are, and the Italians are going to need shooting!'

'Har Har', Kia said. 'Ray, bring the truck over please, Paul, Neil, the portable receiver suitcases out of the S2.'
Ray walked into the deep shadow of the hangar. A minute later an engine started and a security truck drove up near the door.

The sky was getting brighter fast. The boys returned carrying two suitcases each. They jumped into the back of the truck Ray had just opened. Out of the first case, Paul pulled out a box about 12 inches long and 4 inches square. He peeled an adhesive strip off the bottom and stuck the box to the base of the wall near the floor.
Pulling on a tag, a foil strip extended from the top of the box, which he stuck to the wall at the roof line. Opening the next case, he did the same near the back of the truck.

Neil was duplicating the same on the other side. Handing the empty cases to Melissa and Bree, they jumped down out of the truck.

'The receiver is set up and working.'

Kia turned to the three girls, 'OK ladies you are up, Sandy will feed you any data that you need, be careful.'
They nodded, and each climbed into their S2s. Miako lifted first, turned in place, then slid out into the dawning sky as she turned camo, she was followed out by Bree and lastly Melissa.

Neil walked off and grabbed the limo which was parked next to where the truck had been.

The limo pulled out of the airport and headed for the city, the truck was following about 100 meters back. Kia looked back just in time to see a twin jet plane land at the airport and taxi into the hangar they just vacated.

'That was lucky!' Paul said!

'Not really, on board are a woman and two guys who mysteriously won a three hour casino trip to Marseilles', smiled Kia. 'Shortly a black limo will pick them up, take them to two casinos', that just happen to be close to the holding house, then back to the airport and fly them back to Germany.'

'God, you women are damn sneaky!' Grinned Glen.

The run from the airport to the Holding house was about 90 minutes. They took their time and stretched that out by another 20.

'You are five minutes out' came Sandy's voice in everyone's ear.

'Thanks, mum, ' they heard Ray reply.

Kia looked at the clear sky, 'Nice day to spend some money she quipped.'

Miako's voice came in, 'Traffic accident about 2km up ahead. Might slow you up another 10 minutes or so.'

At the sight of the limo the traffic cop on duty let them through quickly, but the truck was stopped.

Neil eased back a little until he saw the truck 4-5 cars back slowly catching up.

Paul glanced at his watch, 'Holding house just opened the doors.'

Paul looked at Glen, 'Party time.'

Glen nodded, looking quite relaxed.

'Glen, when we get inside, ignore anything Paul, or I say. I want you to keep your eyes on the bankers face at all times. I need him to feel nervous, I am going to try and push him outside his comfort zone, this is his lair. But he doesn't need to be in charge.'

'Got it.' Glen nodded to Kia.

The limo did a right turn and slowed to a halt outside an impressive building with a wide set of marble steps out the front. At the top of the steps, stood two security guards in uniform. One each side of a revolving glass door.

Neil hopped out of the limo and walked around to the back door, he opened the door and stood rigidly straight as Paul climbed out and made a show of looking around. Next, Kia closely followed by Glen.

Kia looked around disinterestedly. She saw the truck pass the end of the street. It was going to the loading docks at the rear. Paul led the way up the steps, Kia a step behind him and Glen one back from her.

The security guards ignored both men and tried, unsuccessfully, not to gawk at Kia. She didn't even acknowledge their presence.Once through the revolving door, Paul stepped to one side, and Kia took point, the sound of her clicking heels making the guy at the reception counter look up.

'Monsieur DuPont.' Is all she said.

'Oui Madam, do you have an appointment?'
Kia, who had been absently looking around, turned a pair of Tawny-Gold flecked eyes onto the receptionist and said nothing.

__Chapter Twenty One__

'Err of course madam! This way, please!' He fumbled with the catch of the gate and shot through, leading them towards a large office down the rear of the hall. As he walked, he kept looking over his shoulder to make sure they were still following him.
Customers and staff alike stopped what they were doing and stared as Kia walked past. The receptionist knocked timidly on the door and opened it, he stepped back and bowed as the three entered the office. Quickly closing the door behind them.

DuPont was a short, tubby fellow dwarfed by the desk he sat behind. The walls of the office were sparse, a certificate hung behind where he was sitting. Two hard chairs stood in front of the desk, ergonomically designed to be uncomfortable. DuPont planned to be king in this realm. 'Yes?', he said in a gruff voice without looking up once since they entered, again power play.

'DuPont!' The sharp voice of Kia sliced through the air. 'Do you always act so ignorant when a lady enters the room?'
DuPont's head snapped up, and his jaw dropped!! 'My sincere apologies my lady!' He literally leapt out of his chair and almost ran around holding out his hand. Kia ignored the offered hand. DuPont stopped a pace away from Kia, she took half a step forwards. This made him have to look upwards to keep eye contact.
'I have come here to deposit some of our gold reserves. My assistant', she flicked a minute gesture towards Paul, 'Has recommended this', she paused, 'House.'

DuPont glanced at Paul and nodded.

Paul flicked a hand out, it held a business card. DuPont glanced at Glen as he took the offered card, and saw he was staring at him.

Despite the cool air, sweat started to bead on DuPont's brow.

'Please', DuPont gestured to the chairs, 'Won't you sit?'
Kia gave a slight shake of the head, her eyes never left his.

'I came here to deposit a very small portion of our company's assets. Depending on how your institution performs over the next financial quarter will determine if I recommend a further deposit or trade elsewhere. If you check your loading bay cameras, you will see I have arranged the delivery of five tonnes of gold immediately.'

DuPont stepped back behind his desk grateful to have a reason to move away from Kia's stare. He saw a truck backed against the loading dock and two security guards waiting. His hand shook slightly as he read the card Paul had given him.

'Oracle. I have not heard of this company.'

Kia leaned on the desk, 'I did not come here for a popularity contest. Do you or do you not, wish to accept this deposit?'

DuPont nodded, 'Five, five tonnes you said!'

'For now' Kia replied, she flicked a 10 ounce piece onto the table in front of DuPont. 'This is for your lab testing, it is disposable!' All the details you need are on the card, if you need to speak with us, contact our receptionist and make an appointment to talk to Paul Treman, my assistant. Now if you would be so kind as to unload my delivery. I will take the receipt now.'

DuPont had lost it, he nodded, opened a drawer and removed some paperwork. He picked up the phone and barked a few orders.

He quickly wrote on the certificate, stamped it twice, and handed the certificate over to Kia.

'Would you like some refreshments?'

'I have another appointment in Marseilles.' She glanced at the certificate and handed it to Paul. Paul read the certificate, nodded to Kia and put it into a jacket pocket.

Kia turned and strode to the door, halfway there she stopped and turned to face DuPont, 'I assume you will keep our transaction strictly confidential!'

DuPont smiled, 'Of course! All our transactions are treated in the strictest of confidence, and I can personally assure you of that!' He was starting to feel more in control as he started a spiel he had been using for years. 'All of our cust...'

Kia cut him off mid-sentence, 'I hope so, for your personal safety, I would hate to think you would mention this to your staff, or your wife.'

DuPont shook his head and was about to continue his spiel..

Kia took a step towards him, eyes never leaving his, 'That would include Marie and Corinda as well, of course.'

DuPont looked like he had been kicked in the family jewels. His mouth moved, but no sound came out.

'I can see that we now understand each other perfectly!' Kia turned, and they left DuPont staring at where she had stood, he suddenly didn't feel that well.

Back in the limo, they travelled in silence for a few minutes, Paul held the certificate out to Kia, she shook her head and smiled, 'File it away, we might need it later.'

Glen had not stopped grinning since they got back in the limo, 'Who are Marie and Corinda?'

Kia laughed, 'They are his mistresses. It's just Sandy paying attention to details.'

The truck caught up with them as they left the city and headed out into the countryside. Paul checked his watch, 18 minutes total, from in and out.

Neil turned into a little lane and pulled up next to a disused farmhouse.

'End of the line he announced', he got out laid his cap on the roof and ruffled his hair, 'Whoa that was awesome!'

Branches of the trees next to the limo swayed quickly, Neil turned in time to see Miako land next to them. 30 seconds later, Melissa landed in front of the limo. Ray climbed out of the truck, which had parked behind the limo and climbed in with Melissa.

Brad walked over and shook Paul's hand, 'Smooth job everyone.'
He patted Glen on the shoulder and jumped in with Melissa.

Kia took a few moments to look around, smiled and said, 'On to the next.'

Neil tossed the keys onto the roof, picked up his cap, and the three of them boarded Miako's S2.

They rose clear of the farm and watched Melissa scan out the limo and truck. Both went Camo and headed southeast. Bree caught up with them just before the border, she had been watching their back trail.

Italy went just as smoothly, except the manager there almost broke into tears. He insisted on walking them back out to the limo and holding the door for Kia. Glen said it was so he could see up Kia's skirt.

Chapter Twenty Two

Just before 1 pm, they arrived in London. Standing in a vacant warehouse, they had half an hour to kill. The manager at the London Holding house was known to go out for lunch at the local boys club until 1.30-2.00pm.

Brad and Bree were leaning on a windowsill overlooking the Thames River. Ray and Glen had just finished taping the mobile receiver into the back of the truck. Ray was explaining to Glen when Sandy sends in the gold it feels like the truck sinks into the ground by 2 feet.

Kia walked over to the pair at the window she had a jacket hung around her shoulders, and was sipping a hot cuppa. 'I miss my suit! It's damn cold here.'

Bree grinned, 'Well it's not like you are really wearing much.'

Brad smiled, 'In Italy, the loading dock is near the main entrance, you should have seen the stir Kia caused walking up the stairs!'

Paul walked over munching on a sandwich and carrying a cup in the other hand.

'After seeing the sleaze managers in the last two Holdings, I don't think anything has leaked as yet. Although' he sipped his coffee, 'Even if it did, I don't think it will affect us as much as I first thought.'

'This one might be different' Kia said, 'Sandy tells me the manager here swings the other way. That's why he goes to the boys club at lunch, emphasis on the word boys.'

Bree nodded her head towards the river, 'I wonder what's hidden in that, wouldn't it be great to clean it up, and I bet there is some history in there.'

Brad frowned, 'Explain history?'

'Well' Bree said, 'engagement rings thrown off the tower bridge by jilted or betrayed lovers, bicycles with flat tyres thrown in by a frustrated commuter. Bombs from WWII that hit the soft mud and never detonated. Bottles, from every generation. Lots of interesting things, maybe even the knife Jack the Ripper used!'

Brad grinned, 'Who knows, it's a mystery that may never be solved.'

'I bet Sandy would know', Paul said. 'Ask her when we get back.'

Bree nodded, 'I might just do that, good idea Paul.'
Kia handed Paul back his jacket, tossed the dregs out of the window.

'Time to play the final scene.'

Neil pulled the Rolls up outside the turn of the century building, he hopped out and opened the door. Just as before the trio walked into the building and to the inquiries desk.

The pretty receptionist smiled at their approach, 'May I help you?' she asked.

Kia smiled back and asked for Marcus Welby. 'One moment' she said, 'I will see if he is back from lunch.' A few moments later she returned, 'He has just returned, may I tell him who is calling?'
Paul handed the girl a card, 'Tell him it regards a deposit.'

She disappeared into the back again. On her return, she said, 'I am so sorry, Mr. Welby is busy, he asked if you would mind dealing with another associate?' Paul leant across and said something in her ear, her eyes widened, 'One moment sir!' and disappeared again.

Kia looked at Paul. Paul whispered 'We're being stalled. Welby is the only one authorised to take deposits like this.

This may get sticky be on your toes. I have met this guy before, but I don't know if he will remember me.'
Kia nodded her understanding.

The girl was back beaming a very weak smile, 'Follow me please.'
Paul stood back, and Kia followed first. They were shown into Welby's office, Welby was sitting perched on a corner of his desk. Another power play tactic thought Kia.

He had Paul's card in his hand. He stood as the door closed behind them, 'Paul!' he said and held out his hand, Paul Ignored the hand.

Instead, he turned to Kia, and said 'Marcus may I introduce Kia, she represents Oracle Industries, a new company.'

Marcus nodded politely, and 'What can I do for Oracle today?'

'Paul has recommended these Holdings as a place to deposit some of our assets.'

'Did he now? Well, I thank you, Paul', Marcus made is sound like an insult.

'May I ask the size of this proposed deposit?'

'Five tonnes', again Kia dropped an ingot on the desk.

Welby was rattled, but soon regained his composure, he picked up the ingot and turned it over in his hands, 'And this is for the purity test I assume?'
Kia nodded.

'Wonderful' Welby continued 'as Paul may or may not have told you, it may take quite some time to test the purity of your deposit, you see it's not unknown for new clients to bring us a deposit that is not as pure as the test piece they supply.
Now I am not saying that is the case here, but one cannot be too careful. We never know what kind of people we are dealing with sometimes.' Welby smiled a weak smile.
Paul could tell Kia was starting to heat up. He looked at Marcus 'Marcus, the gold is fine, there is a truck at the docks ready to unload as soon as you issue us a bond against it.'

Marcus, nodded, 'Sure, that won't be a problem, may I ask the origin of the gold?'

'You may ask' Kia said, 'Not that I am going to tell you.'

Welby nodded, 'Fair enough', he filled out the deposit bond and stamped it and gave it to Kia. She read it, and handed it to Paul. Paul held it up to the light.

Welby smiled 'it's a legitimate bond Paul.'
Paul read the bond folded it in half and went to put it into his pocket with the others, Marcus' eyes narrowed at the sight of the other bonds, his hand shot out to grab them. As fast as he was, Kia was much, much, faster, she grabbed his wrist and squeezed.
Welby dropped to his knees with a squeal.

Kia let him go, 'Do not touch my assistant!' she hissed.

Welby stood, rubbing his wrist, 'Touch me again and you will be sorry!'
Kia took two strides forwards and stood nose to nose with Welby.

'Are you threatening me?' she said through clenched teeth. 'I will let you into a little secret Marcus, just between us. There is nothing, absolutely nothing, I would like better than for you to threaten me. It would be nice to rip you limb from limb. I'd take one arm for Johnny Stillhouse, one for Stephen Baxter, I'd tear your throat out for Grant Stick.

'So am I slowly getting through to you by chance?'

With each name Welby went whiter, he stood trembling in front of Kia, 'Who the hell are you!' He nearly shouted.

Kia stepped back a pace, 'Me?, just another customer who's making a deposit, but I am also the last person you want to cross. Now have they finished unloading my truck? Good. Remember, I will be back, play nice with my money dear.'
With that, Kia strode out of the office.

Back in the Rolls, Paul breathed a sigh of relief, damn that was close.

Kia nodded, 'Very close.' Kia touched her earpiece, 'Girls, Ray sharpen the eyes, they were waiting for us, we got the job done, but we are not in the clear yet. Bree, watch the truck. Miako watch the Rolls, Melissa take a higher view and try and head us off if you see anything. Neil, lets get out of here, as fast as practical, but don't leave the truck.'

Chapter Twenty Three

They made the M1 and headed north. After 45km Melissa reported back that the Rolls had a tail. Kia swore.

'Neil, take the next exit and head for the open countryside. 'Ray stays on the motorway. Hopefully it's just us they want and will ignore the truck.'

Neil shot up the off ramp and headed east. After 20 minutes Melissa confirmed the truck was in the clear. Kia instructed them to dump and clear the truck ASAP.

Paul said 'We could just dump the tail and get out.'

Kia shook her head, 'I want to catch these minions and ask them who they are working for. It's always nice to know who is working against us, don't you think?'

Paul nodded, 'Fair comment.'

'Sandy, find me a deserted or empty place close please, and direct Neil to it.'

Kia looked relaxed as she watched the countryside outside the window. She looked at Glen. He was pretending to snooze in the corner. 'You OK?' she asked.'

He popped an eye open and smiled, 'Reminds me of when I stole my brothers bike, he chased me for ages. He was really pissed at me when I threw it back into a kid's yard that he had stolen it from a few days before.'

Paul Grinned.

Glen waved his fingers in the direction they had come, 'These guys have already lost they just don't know it, so yeah, I'm OK.'

Ray's voice came in over coms, 'The truck is cleared, and we are just behind your tail.'

'Thank you', Kia replied.

Neil spoke over his shoulder, 'Sandy says we are about four minutes from destination, then what?'

We stop, and we wait' Kia said.

A short time later Neil pulled into a circular drive and stopped in front of a cottage. A sign in the window declared the place available for lease, monthly or annually.

There was no breeze, the sky was clear and birds were chirping.

'Nice place she picked', Kia commented as she stepped onto the patio, and sat on an antique bench. 'You boys go on in and wait.' Everything was nice and peaceful. A flock of startled sparrows rose out of one of the trees and headed off over the fields.

Kia just smiled.

Fifteen minutes later a dark SUV pulled up behind the Rolls, two beefy men got out, one opened the rear door.

A very well dressed woman exited the SUV and looked around. She closed the door and walked towards Kia, flanked both sides by the men.

Just as she was about to step onto the patio Kia said 'The monkeys stay there.' Both men frowned at that.

The woman advanced alone and stood facing Kia. 'Nice place you have here, thinking of buying it?'

Kia shook her head and stood up, easily 2 inches shorter than the visitor. 'No, I prefer a view of the sea actually.

'A lot less vermin around that way.'

The woman frowned, 'My name is Veronica, not vermin!'

'Close' replied Kia, 'And what is it that brought you here Veronica?'

'I have a proposition for you.'

'Really?' Kia said, lifting an eyebrow in a taunting way, 'You don't even know who I am.'

'You work for a new company called Oracle, you're based somewhere offshore, your company is involved with scientific, environmental recovery. Your company is about four years old. How am I doing so far?'

Kia nodded, 'My! You are well informed, and who do you pimp for?'

'I am not at liberty to divulge who I work for, suffice to say it's a bigger organisation than the one you, how did you put it, pimp for.'

'Ah, mistake number one Veronica, I own Oracle, down to the last paper-clip. Whereas you are just a paid messenger. Now, dear, let me ask again. Slower if you like, what do you want and who do you work for? See simple questions, hell you remembered your name didn't you! So your turn, and if the next few words out of your Botox lined lips are not the correct ones, you are leaving.'

The guy to the left slid his hand inside his jacket and suddenly froze to the sound of a familiar metallic click. Looking to the left of the cottage he saw Ray standing, holding a semi-auto aimed at the centre of his forehead, he slowly removed his hand.

Kia smiled, 'Your monkeys are not well trained are they? Hopefully, you are, now I am a very busy person. It's a nice day, reach deep and come up with the right answers. I shall not ask again.'

Veronicas hands were balled into tight fists, and she ground her teeth slightly, 'I already told you, I can't divulge...'

Kia held her hand up. 'Now, you get your apes and your ass back in your car. You then drive back to John McFarlane and tell him, IF he would like to talk to me, make an appointment with my secretary Sandy. Sandy will get back to him in due course with a time and place of my choosing. Can you remember that? Here, take my card.' Veronica took the card in automatic response and immediately hated herself for it.

'Now toddle off while much more important people get back to work.'

Not waiting for a reply Kia spun on her heel, and walked inside the cottage.

Veronica stood speechless for a few moments and stormed back to the SUV. Not waiting for the door to be opened, she opened it herself and slammed it hard behind her.

Ray twitched the barrel of the pistol he was holding, the two guys slowly backed away and got in the car, never taking their eyes of Ray.

Moments later the SUV thundered out of the gate.

Ray de-cocked the gun and slid it back into its holster. When the SUV was out of sight, he followed Kia's footsteps.

Inside the cottage Kia stood with a wide grin, 'Now that was fun!'

Paul shook his head, 'What a cat fight!, as you were talking Bree was doing OOOOH and AHHHs, Miako too.'

Brad laughed, 'Even I was wincing!'

'You sure pushed a lot of buttons out there', Melissa said.

Kia nodded, 'Enough that she should have blurted info she really didn't want to. So, either she was highly trained, which I doubt. Or she actually knew next to nothing.'

'How did you know about John mcwhatsit?' asked Neil.

'Simple I stalled until Sandy could break the code on her cell phone, that was the guys name on her speed dial so I took an educated guess. Since we are in a cottage, I am going to get out of this outfit. Bree grab my cargo bag from the S2 please, while I have a shower, she looked at the guys, and you penguins might get changed as well.'

Half an hour later Kia was dressed back in her usual suit, with the makeup cleaned off and her wet hair in a ponytail she came down the stairs. She found everyone sitting on mismatched benches out the back of the cottage.

'So Paul, looks like we got away with it yes?'

He nodded, 'It has leaked, obvious from what we heard.

Not only has it leaked, but they have pulled the files on the company. We introduced you as the top lady in each holding, Veronica mentioned you worked FOR Oracle.'

Ray came out of the cottage and closed the door, 'The place is clean, can't tell that we have even been here, and the Rolls is gone.'

Kia nodded, 'Well done everyone, we came loaded for bear, ready for anything and didn't need it, to me that makes it a win!'

She wriggled her toes which were now back in boots, smiled and said',Lets go home.'

Kia rode with Paul and Glen, Glen piloting.

England is a narrow, but long country so they skipped out sideways over the sea and took an over the water route back.

Chapter Twenty Four

About three hours into the flight Glen informed Kia he was getting a lot of radar returns at about 2 o'clock in their current position. She stood up and walked up front. Leaning over Paul's shoulder, she saw what Glen had seen. The radar was tracking one or sometimes two aircraft that flew in a semi-circle onto the screen at 2 o'clock position and off the radar at 4 o'clock.

There were three other contacts on radar, but they were maintaining a steady flight path, indicating that they were probably airliners.

'Flick on the IDR and see if we can identify them.'
Little tags appeared next to each icon, the three straight lines were indeed commercial planes, the ones running on and off the screen were identified as military jets, FA18-E Hornets.

'It's just the boys playing with their toys, I don't think that the bankers have a fleet of FA18s up their sleeve.'
Glen flicked off the IDR, and the icons disappeared. Icons can sometimes hide a second aircraft if you just glance at the screen. Paul reached over and set a radio to scan mode, in a few seconds the voices of the F18-E pilots came in crisp and clear.

They were doing touch and go exercises off the flight deck, flying in lowering the landing gear, touching the deck then go- ing to full power and taking off again. That explained the loops they were showing on Glen's radar. Glen increased radar range, and there was the carrier they were based on, the USS Carl Vinson (CVN 70).

'Looks like they are having fun, wonder what would happen if we joined in?' Paul said.

Glen chuckled at the thought, 'I reckon the CAG would have a heart attack if we didn't get shot down in the process.'

'They can't see us', Kia chipped in. 'Besides we really don't want to rattle that cage at the moment.'

It was late afternoon when they finally they made it back, even though they were in the air several hours it was still daylight as they had been following the sun. It was a tired and hungry bunch that piled into their respective villas.

Showered and changed most made their way to the café. Brad and Bree opted to eat in, and Melissa dropped onto her bed and promptly fell asleep.

Miako and Neil were already eating when Paul and Glen walked in, they grabbed a plate each and helped themselves from the servery.

'Care to join us?' asked Neil and all four sat talking about the days events.
The elevator door opened, and Ray walked in beaming a radiant smile.

'You just come into some money?' Glen asked.

'Nope, today was a great day, well two days really, since we followed the sun back.'
Grabbing a plate full of food, he sat next to Glen.

'Today was like my old days, all the team striving for one goal, knowing they had each others back. That my friend, is what was missing my whole life, someone I could depend on.'

Miako put her hand on his arm, 'Ray, know now, everyone here has your back, each and every day.

'These are not just words, they are my promise.' 'Mine too' Paul said and shook his hand.

Glen waved a fork, 'Goes without saying.'

'So what do we do now?' Neil looked for an answer in their faces.

Paul cleared his plate, 'Well as far as the results from todays activities, it will take probably 48 hours to filter through to the lower levels. You can bet your ass that Oracle is a word being spoken in a whole range of places.'

'So now they will be watching for us to do something and hope that we fail right?' Said a voice behind them.

Kia stood behind them sipping fresh juice.

'Damn you walk softly!' Ray exclaimed.

'Easy soldier, I am not after your medals. Who was in the S2 at the cottage, the one near the cherry tree?'

'You saw me!' Neil said in surprise.

'No, but you startled a flock of sparrows, and THAT's what gave away your position. If we were playing paintball your S2 would be full of pink polka dots now. So, what shall we clean up, that is a high profile target, easy enough to do and won't get Neil covered in pink dots? After all, that IS really why we are here.'

All five of them looked at each other, 'Lets ask Sandy!' they said in unison.

'Good idea' Kia smiled, 'The last idea one of you came up with, had me walking around in a short skirt.' She put her empty glass on the table, 'And I don't wear underwear.' She said as she walked away.

Glen choked on the mouthful of coffee he had just taken. It ran from his nose, his eyes watered instantly. After a while he got the coughing under control.

This caused much amusement and ribbing from his fellow diners.

He turned, but the elevator doors were already closed.
'Bitch!' He sighed and wiped his eyes again.
This brought more peals of laughter.

'Hi, Sandy.'
'Hello, Kia, good to see everyone in good spirits.'
'Yes, moral is quite high at the moment, how did you go with that list?'

Sandy cleared some workspace on the HUD. 'There are a lot of big jobs available, but some of them quite complicated. Some are very sensitive in nature, and some I don't think we have the clout to pull off yet.'
The elevator doors opened, and the five from downstairs trooped in.

'Spill your coffee, Glen?' Kia asked sweetly.
Indicating damp marks on the front of his suit. Not waiting for his spluttering reply, she turned back to Sandy's display.

'So, OK leave out the ones you think we can't swing as yet, and crop the very difficult ones lets see what we have left.'

A list appeared on the HUD, 'The ones near the bottom are not environmental, but are currently high profile problems.'

'Hmm, we are after credibility rather than publicity, the man on the street isn't important as yet. That damn U-864 keeps coming back up. So be it, Sandy try and get us an appointment with someone that has some say in the matter, I don't want to deal with a desk jockey.'

The elevator opened and Bree, Brad and Melissa stepped out, 'See I told you they were planning something' Melissa said.

'Already finished you're too late' Ray said.

Melissa poked her tongue out at him, 'Why are you all wet Glen?'

'Never mind' he growled.
Bree walked over to Sandy and asked a question quietly, Sandy nodded, another disk slid out of the wall, and the other Sandy beckoned her over to a different HUD.
Brad went and joined them.

'Well, what shall we do? Got anything boss?' Kia shook her head, nothing as yet, not urgent anyway.'

'We could always clear the area around the island, we went for a run a few days ago around the seamounts. We found an old, unknown sub under a heap of trawl nets', offered Paul.

Miako looked at Kia, 'Is it ok if we go and play?'

'Sure', Kia said. 'Stay in touch, don't stray too far.'

Ten minutes later the first of 3 S2s lifted off. Kia flicked up a map of the island and a 1000km circle around it. Three green icons shone brightly on the map. Satisfied, she walked around behind Bree and watched what they were doing.

Bree had a map up of the main London area, there was a blinking red circle on the river and in a second window was data scrolling a list of possible items. Sandy was explaining that nothing small would show. There has not been a deep scan, just Sat overpasses. Meaning anything smaller than a vehicle or large fridge would not show up.
So far the list consisted mainly of old sunken boats of various types, a few shipping containers and various metal objects.
'Well, that's disappointing, so much for my romantic notions.' Bree wiped the HUD clear, and Sandy disappeared.
'Where did the others go?'
'They were bored so took off to explore the area around the island' replied Kia. 'There is a map on the other HUD if you want to catch up.'
Bree looked at Brad, he shrugged, 'Sure, why not and off they went.'
Sandy said, 'The kids have grown up and left home.'
Kia smiled 'Certainly seems that way, another milestone.'

Chapter Twenty Five

'Kia, I have Mr. Taren Johansen on a video link, Department of Environment, Norwegian Gov. Returning our inquiry. Putting him on HUD.'
A life-sized image appeared on Kia's HUD.
'Thank you so much for your prompt reply, Mr. Johansen.'
'Not at all.' Came the pleasant tenor voice. 'I thought it might be of benefit to meet with the one that has caused such a stir in certain circles just of late, please call me Taren.'
Kia nodded, 'Taren my name is Kia, and as you know I front a new company called Oracle. We currently are focused on solving environ problems that other companies or agencies simply cannot.'
Taren nodded. 'A noble quest. Most new companies normally only add to the environmental problem. It is refreshing to hear of one that works against the trend. So how can the people of Norway help?'
'Actually Taren, it is I that am offering our service to you. As you may appreciate, being new, we need to prove we can do what we claim to do. The reason that I wished to talk to you was about U-864.....'
'Ah yes! The bane of my office. Every time 864 is raised in conversation, lots of money is spent on lots of meetings, and nothing is ever done. I wish it would just disappear.'
Kia smiled warmly at Taren, 'Actually Taren, that is precisely what I was going to offer you. And at an exceptionally fine introductory cost of absolutely zero.'

Taren's eyebrows rose, 'Please fine lady this is no joking matter. This wreck is causing not only environmental damage but damage to our political office. The public cry out for us to do something, but the public funds are just not available to do so. Every year contractors contact my office and each year the costs are nearly double.'
Kia detected the genuine pain of Taren's situation in his voice.

'Well, we may be of service to each other if that suits you. Not only am I offering our service to remove U-864, but we will also remove all traces of mercury in a 1000m radius, which also includes any contaminated fish and shellfish.'

Taren's image smiled, 'Ah, but it is cruel to taunt an old man so, I have left less than 18 months in office before our next elections. Even if we were to agree on this, I would not have the time in office to be accredited as the man who got rid of the scourge.'

Kia laughed, 'You do yourself a disservice, and you are not old, just weathered by wisdom. Also, if you agreed and were able to officially authorise us to do this job, it would be done in 3 to 5 days.'

Taren sat upright, 'Please!, am I to understand that not only are you offering to remove this blight that is poisoning the sea life in an area that once was a prosperous fishing ground. In addition to that, but you are also offering to do this at no cost to the Norwegian government! Now you state to me that you can accomplish all this in a matter of days, not months or years!'

'That is totally correct in all aspects.' Kia replied soberly. 'Taren, we are like no other, it is both a blessing and a bane to us. I give you my word that we can do what is required, quickly, cleanly and with minimal fuss.

Our only concern would be that the site may be considered a war grave. We do not wish to have repercussions due to this.'

Taren's face was deadly serious. 'Issues pertaining to historical value and war grave issues were dealt with over three years ago when we first attempted to clean up this mess.'

'If you can incorporate those terms with your offer, I will have my secretary, Sandy, issue you the necessary documentation and email it to you within the hour.' Kia looked the image straight in the eyes.

'I know you have doubts, but let me reiterate, this is neither a scam nor an empty promise. This particular problem shall cease to be a burden to you within a week. I personally will attend your office and tell you face to face when the job has been completed.'

Taren beamed a typical huge Norwegian smile, Kia suspected the distance between them just saved her from a massive bear hug the Norwegians were famous for.

'I will need clearance for my crew to enter both your official waters and your airspace.'

He waved a massive hand enthusiastically, 'it shall be done!, I will go now, thank you so much for contacting me, and on behalf of each and every Norwegian, I thank you.'
Kia smiled and waved, the HUD went blank.

'Well, that went much better than I thought possible, excellent!'

She walked over to Sandy, 'This may be our big break we have been waiting for!'
Sandy had a map up in the corner of the HUD which showed four icons where each S2 was. She could see they were running grid lines about 450km away.

'Let the happy wanderers know they have a job on in the morning, it's been a long day so I am turning in. When the contract comes in from Taren would you be so kind as to put a hard copy on my table in the villa, please.'
Sandy nodded, 'Get some rest.'
One last look around the room, then Kia headed for the sheets.

Sunrise saw Miako on the garden deck for her morning yoga routine. Today she was not alone, Melissa had been her student for a few days now.

From her vantage point on the balcony on the tower, Kia watched her try to mirror the movements Miako made. Shifting her attention to the west beach she watched as four tiny dots moved on the beach. Each of the dots represented one of the boys, but from the balcony, it was impossible to identify them individually. The remaining pair of people was sitting opposite her at the table. She had left a message for them to meet her there. Brad was reading a document Kia had handed him a few moments before.

Bree had already read it, 'This is great news! It's the next step in the right direction for us. So this is our new job. I take it that the three-day timeline is to cover our asses. Still, we are going to give the Japs the same time frame, and it's a bigger job.'

Kia nodded. 'Actually, it's almost the same size job. Mercury has leached into the water and surrounding coral. That will have to be cleaned as well, and also removing contaminated fish and molluscs. It's a fair area to cover. I asked you two up here as I regard you both as our 2IC crew. It wasn't a choice made on ability, because you all perform well. The others are used to following directions from you and that just made it the obvious choice.'

'I can see the logic in that', Brad said as he handed the authorisation from the Norwegian Government back to Kia.

'It also means that you won't be leading our first official venture, which is a bit strange.'

'Oh, I would not miss this for the world, but I have another item I wish to take care of. About 280km NW from the U-864 is another sub. This one the Russians lost. It's a nuke, one of a kind, and intel on it suggests it has still got its armament, and reactor. They supposedly sealed it and declared it safe till 2025.

In my opinion, it is safe when it's gone. Designated the K-278 it sank after an accident, all the crew got out, so it isn't classified as a grave site. When the others are ready, we can pick teams. Three in yours, two in mine.'

Paul nodded, 'Sounds like a plan to me.'

Forty-five minutes later, everyone was standing in a semi-circle around the HUD. Sandy had brought up two maps, one showing the Norwegian Sea, the other the Barents Sea. Sandy was chairing the briefing.

'Todays mission ladies and gentlemen is twofold. 'Everyone goes to this point here.' An icon flashed on the map. 'Once you have said your tearful goodbyes, the first team of three S2s continues to this location.' An icon flashed at the coordinates just west of Fedje Island.

'There you will find the U-864. It's in 150m of water, scan it and remove. Then, using the U864 position, clear a circle of all man-made debris. You will also need to scan and remove, fish, molluscs, and anything else showing a high mercury contamination.

'This will speed up the recovery of the area by years. Norwegians are fishermen, they rely on the sea and losing a large chunk of the area has hurt them.

'The second team will continue to this point', again a flashing icon appeared, 'There you will find the K-278 Russian sub, a MIKE class. The one and only that they made. It has a hot reactor as well as live nuclear munitions on board. Supposedly only two units. I say supposedly because governments are famous for telling the truth, to the public and each other.' That brought a few comments.

'Again, according to official records, everyone managed to get off this boat. Although most froze to death in the cold water. The Russians sealed the boat and assured us simple folk it's safe till 2015 or 2025, depending who you want to believe. I suggest we remove it and a 1000m perimeter of all debris.

'The S2s scanners have been upgraded. Once you start your scan runs you will find you will be speed limited until the scan is complete. If you need to move in a hurry, no problems, but the scan will stop. This is to ensure we get a perfect, deep image when we scan stuff.

'Team two will probably finish first. It would be nice if they came back and helped team one out.

Brad is running the first team, Kia the second. Volunteers are being called for the makeup of the teams. I suggest mortal combat or just draw straws. Any questions?'

Neil put his hand up. 'What if we locate another wreck while clearing the perimeters, and it IS actually a war grave?'

'Good question Neil. Considering we are still on new ground, scan it and leave it alone.
However, I have noted that you think I may have missed something as important as that.'
Neil looked flustered at Sandy's reply.

The Holo smiled, 'Only playing with you Neil, relax. If you do find something I have missed. Again a slow scan will tell me, to the last item, what's on or in the target. If something triggers a flag, like a nasty no one has admitted to being there, I will make a determination on a per item basis if we leave it there or not. Also, Flags now auto chime so that you won't miss them. 'An example, if you find an item inside a scanned target that's dangerous, we may decide to remove just that item and leave the rest for now. Any other questions? Good.

One last thing, this is a multiple day operation, as Norway has a myriad of islands. I have chosen one as a base camp. It has a large cave above sea level. When you break off for the day, use that. It will save you from coming back here. Food and supplies are in the S2s. Pick your teams, and happy hunting.'

They scientifically selected the teams, by pulling names out of an empty coffee cup.

Glen whooped when he picked Kia's team, 'Well', he said in reply to their stares, 'she gets into more trouble than you guys do!' He ducked as Kia went to smack him.

'Grab breakfast if you haven't already, 30 min to departure', Kia then walked over to a vacant HUD, she dialed out and in a few moments, the smiling face of Taren was on screen.

'Hello Taren, just calling to let you know we are about to get underway. I hope nothing has arisen your end to interfere with the project?'

Taren shook his head, 'Not at all Kia, in fact, quite the opposite! Many of my colleagues are ringing us and portraying their personal thanks!'

Kia smiled, 'We shall not let them down. I do however have another favour to ask of you.'

Taren looked worried, 'It's not a complication I hope?'

'No, not at all, I have instructed my team to clear the U-864 and a surrounding area, they will remove all traces of Mercury from the water, as well as fish, molluscs, and others with a concentration of Mercury higher than recommended for human consumption. This should help your fishing industry recover much faster.'

'Oh, thank the Norse Gods!' Taren exclaimed 'You are indeed a blessing on us!'

Kia held up her hand, 'Please, it's what we do. Now the favour I have to ask you is this. Can you assemble a team of people, both archaeologists and historians, say a limit of 20 people all told? In about four or five days, I will issue an invitation to our island for them to attend.'

'That would be simple to arrange.' Taren said 'Though, may I ask why?'

'When we clear the perimeter, we are going to clear it of ALL man-made objects and items, and from the preliminary data, it looks like there may be quite a lot of old and or ancient relics. These we will make available to your team for appraisal and removal to Norway's museums and institutions.'
Taren's mouth just fell open!

'However Taren my friend, please vet your team very, very carefully. It will not be below certain criminal elements to try and insert spies or sleepers into your team. I cannot stress this enough!

'Our security here is airtight. However, anyone venturing into the wrong areas will have serious consequences, some of them may be fatal. So with this in mind, try not to broadcast what they will be doing', Kia smiled.

'I will deal with this personally. Three of my cousins are of the required personnel, and I can vouch for them', replied Taren elated.

'I shall see you soon' Kia said as she signed off.
'Visitors?' Sandy asked.
'Yes Sandy, sorry about the short notice and extra workload.'
'Bah!' Was Sandy's reply, 'I have yet to hit 3% CPU usage, and that's on my current bank! Although the complex construction gave me a bit of a tweak!'

Chapter Twenty Six

Kia slid comfortably into her pilot seat in her S2. Running a check over the console. She waited until last to leave. She caught up in less than a minute. Dropping into a V formation, Brad, who had point, locked them all together then she relaxed. Relieved of pilot duties, she pulled up an Intel screen on the K-278.

Displacement: 6,400-8,000 tons Submerged.
Length 117.5m
Beam 10.7m
Draft 9m
Speed 48-56kph Submerged
Test depth 1,000 safe 1,500 crush
Armament SS-N-15 Starfish missiles
 Torpedo tubes 6 x 533mm 53-65 carried.

'That's quite impressive', Glen said, after Paul finished reading out the specs, 'And it's all in one piece?'
They were checking the target out as well.
'Not quite. According to intel when it finally went down, five guys were still in it. But they climbed into the tower which was also an escape pod and fired it up to the surface. One got out before the pod, itself sank, or they all got out, and 4 froze in the water. Reports are a bit vague.'
'Guess we will find out when we scan it.' Glen nodded.
Paul got up and made a cup of coffee for each of them. Handing Glen his, he slid back into the seat. 'So what's your view on this 'war grave' issue?'

Glen took a sip and hung a leg over the armrest, 'Well I'm a bit conflicted. If it was my dad on the bottom, I am sure the family would want him back. I think it's all to do with the ones left behind really. Like all funerals are. Let's face it, dead is dead.'

Paul nodded, 'I think it's all about money.'

Glen grinned, 'With you, it's always about money, but pray tell, how you get to that conclusion?'

'Simple, analogy coming up. In a war, say 150 people die when their sub sinks, and it sinks 8,000m. It becomes a supposed war grave, right? Now another sub sinks, 150 people die, but they sink in 40m of water. All the bodies get recovered, and go to their respective funerals, and the dead sub is salvaged.

'The last one, 150 people die in a plane crash, again the bodies are collected and attend their respective funerals, and the plane wreckage is removed. Now for the analysis.

Over the three examples, the only time the bodies are not recovered is when it becomes too expensive to do so. Various departments and organisations have the tech, to get to the wreck. But because you can't just dive or walk to the corpses, they deem it too hard and slap a war grave or just grave tag on it.

'Money my friend, the assholes in power love to hoard it. When the American sub 'Thresher' went down, in peacetime. They located it, eventually, took pictures with an ROV. Saw it was broken, said stuff it, no one survived, lets keep the money and leave them.

'You ever see a coach wreck on a highway and just leave it there, or a train wreck?'

'That's quite a compelling argument', Glen admitted, 'Still seems morally wrong though.'

Paul laughed, 'They don't have morals unless someone is looking. If something goes wrong and no one sees, they cover it up if possible.
Even they have double standards on "war graves".'

Glen looked surprised, 'Explain double standards.'

'OK', Paul continued, 'They dig up an ancient site and find human remains, they wave the bones around like trophies! 'Look what I found Ma! Stick it in an old bucket and drag it out of the hole. Don't you watch Discovery Channel? Time, that's what they wait for. Once there had been enough time go past, so all the relatives and families die off, then they go and mess around with their supposed 'war graves.' In 1000 years, if mankind hasn't killed itself off. Stuff left from WWII will be collectors items, just like they do with the Egyptians now. Personally, I believe, everyone deserves to go home, sooner or later.'

Glen nodded, 'I can roll with that.'

Just over 85 minutes later the waypoint came up, Paul had been watching England and Scotland roll past to the left.

'It looks like we are getting wet' as they started to descend. Glen stowed the empty cups and checked the HUD.
Brad's voice came in over the speaker, 'Eyes on radar folks, this is a very busy area, surface ships and fishermen. Please do not get caught in a net! Also, military underwater craft from various countries like to slink around and play war games.'
They entered the water like an arrowhead. Levelling out at 150m gave them enough depth to miss surface traffic, but not nets. 45 minutes later they came to the separation point.

Kia and Glen dropped off the back of the other three as they veered right towards the Norwegian coast.

Glen pulled close to Kia's S2 and said 'Lead the way boss lady.'

 Kia responded by dropping down to 30m off the seabed, flicking on her lights and selected TFRS.
Glen followed suit, also engaging the Terrain Following Radar/Sonar. They were 90 minutes from the zone icon, soaring over the bottom.

Paul and Glen were watching in total amazement at the volume of debris lying on the bottom. It almost seemed like every 150m something loomed large on the sea floor!

'Geezus', exclaimed Glen, 'This is like a junkyard, look at it all!' He banked left slightly to miss a huge floating net that had been snagged on a wreck. 'This is bad.'
It did not get any better the further north they travelled.

Kia throttled back 50%, and informed them they were approaching the outer limit of the zone. Glen swung 50m to the left of Kia. Both of them slowed to a crawl, the slower speed just brought more debris into focus.

'Got it' Glen said.
Coming to a complete stop and hovering, the lights illuminated a huge cylinder shape laying on the floor, 'Hello K-278.' Glen kicked to the left and travelled the length of the sub to the bow. There he found the torpedo tubes and a huge hole at the front. 'It looks like one might have cooked off' remarked Paul. 'Either that or someone cut that hole trying to get to the munitions.'

Kia appeared from round the front, 'At least it's in one piece, almost. I will start the scan, can you run a second scan behind me, about 20m separation, please.'

Glen confirmed. Kia's S2 rose over the bow. Twin lasers slashed through the water and straddled the bow, slowly the S2 travelled down the length of the sub.
Glen turned his S2 and rose, exactly mimicking Kia's manoeuvre. Again lasers cut through the water each side of the bow.

Paul hit the scan button and the S2 automatically started forward.
Kia turned off after finishing her scan and watched as Glen finished his.

Both of them hung motionless in the water while the data was uploaded to Sandy. Less than 90 seconds later Sandy's transmission came in, 'Received scans, both good, give me a few' moments to assemble.'

Glen saw several flags pop on the HUD, each one accompanied by a warning tone. 'I like these new scanners, look at it go!'

On the HUD in front of them a 3D representation was appearing, from bow to stern, same direction as the scan was taken. Each flag had a line from the flag to a place on the model.

Kia's voice came in, 'These scanners are a hell of a lot faster than the old ones and are more discriminating. Just to confirm I have flags for the reactor pile and three spare rods, also 16 torpedoes and three missiles.'

'Copy that', Paul said, 'We get the same.'

'Good', Kia returned, 'You may do the honours if you like.' Glen travelled back down the sub and turned around, lining up again. This time, he punched a different sequence and as he travelled the length of the sub it was disappearing along the laser line. Eventually, it was completed. K-278 was no longer a threat.

'Well done' Kia said, 'Now to clear the area and call it good.' Starting from the centre of where the wreck used to be, they separated 15m apart and set a spiral course and set the scanners to both scan and remove. Again on auto, the S2s slid silently through the water about 10m off the bottom. Occasionally flags would pop, this kept all three of them busy, checking and identifying the flags.

In one section flags popped every few meters Checking the flags it was found to be an old minefield. Most of the mines had filled with water and sunk to the bottom. The mines, the chains holding them and the concrete tethering blocks were all removed. It still made them nervous, especially the few mines that were still floating.

The array of debris was amazing, shoes, bottles, tin cans. Anything that could and would float and eventually sink, either lost overboard or from the mainland. Dingy, yachts, barrels, shipping containers. The list seemed endless!

Occasionally they came on other large wrecks. These were scanned in detail. If no flags popped for human remains they were removed.

Several human remains were located and scanned, these were located with no wrecks found. Several WWII aircraft were scanned. Considering this was just a 1000m circle, it took close to five hours before they were done.

They doubled back over the area. It was a stark contrast from how it looked before they started.

Kia put a call out to Brad to check how they were doing.

Chapter Twenty Seven

'Slow', Paul said U-864 was gone, they had recovered human remains and munitions. They had also managed to recover 45 tonnes of Mercury still in phials.
Brad went on to say that they were still cleaning the site and the immediate surrounding area. 'It's like a junk yard down here! They had at least another two hours just in the immediate area.'

Kia informed Brad they had finished their area and were heading their way.
   'Great' came the reply 'We need all the help we can get.'
Kia took off, Glen followed, back in the wingman's position. It took Kia and Glen almost two hours to catch up with the others.
On arrival, they found a long indent in the coral where the keel had lain for so long. For a distance of 800 meters, the sand was clean and pristine. A testament to the hard work Brad and the others had been doing. Everyone except Brad was running the slow circular courses that Kia had been doing not so long ago. Brad was running a parallel pattern close to shore, working his way outwards. Kia asked him, 'Where he would like Glen and her to start?' His reply was 'There is stuff everywhere you look, help yourself.'
Kia said they would run out to the 1500m perimeter and work their way in.
   'Sounds like a good plan to me', came the reply from Brad.
Kia kicked her S2 away from the shallow water and headed out 1500m from zone centre.

A quick test on the water showed Mercury concentration was still a bit higher than allowable. They ran further to 2500m and tested again. This time, the sample came back under the limit.

She let Brad know. Telling Glen to start here and circle clockwise, she would run anti-clockwise, 'Be careful', she said, 'There is an island around here somewhere.'
Glen grinned, set all the parameters into the Nav system and started his cleanup runs.

If they thought there was a lot of debris near the shoreline, further out from the coast, the area looked like a municipal tip! Running round till he got to the coast, Glen spun 180 degrees and shifted 15 meters to the right. The floor was clear here, obviously Brad had run up the coast the extra 1000m.
Running back and forth, Glen and Kia passed each other once each sweep. Occasionally one or the other would see Brad at the end of their Sweep. The concentration level was high, flags seemed to be chiming every few minutes. On the HUD the cleaned area was slowly getting larger, the track from every S2 clearly marked.
Three hours later Kia, reached a turning point and let the S2 settle to the bottom. Miako noticed Kia's icon standing still.

'Kia, Miako, You OK over there?'

'Yes Miako. Just having a breather.'
Everyone understood, while they were in pairs and had been able to share the load, Kia was alone in her S2.

Brad called for everyone to end their current sweep at the next turn point and head for the cave. He asked Kia to go straight there.

Within the hour all five S2s were parked in a neat line.

It was bitterly cold in the cave. The air was still and clean. They sat in a circle around a small fire that Neil had made from the abundant driftwood. None of them were cold, their suits saw to that, except for fingers, and they were easily kept warm holding steaming cups. It was dark outside, but not pitch black due to the moon and stars.

In the cave one of the S2's had its lights on so the area was well lit.

Exhaustion showed on their faces. The job was easy. It was dealing with all the flags that took the concentration.

Bree was telling how she and Brad had found a sunken wooden tender, 'Millions of flags popped on this little boat, the reason turned out to be cases and cases of hand grenades. The wooden crates had disintegrated, and the grenades had rolled all over an area the size of a football field, washed there by tidal action.'

Many stories were told some quite hilarious, Melissa had found a standing statue that had scared the hell out of her for a moment.

Neil had scanned a large old drum, which released, according to him, a huge monster octopus that had been hiding in the drum.

Fishing nets seemed to be the most abundant item. They all agreed it must be wrapped over and around almost everything.

'Where did all the stuff come from' Paul asked?

Kia pointed out that this area was and still is, one of the most prolific trade routes used since man climbed into his first boat. The Vikings, the Romans, modern man all used and still use these waters.

Not to mention smaller inter-island traffic. Thankfully not all the oceans would be this contaminated. Only the areas close to shore. Although they were well rested, Brad called it quits for the day. He told everyone to get some sleep, and they would go again in the morning.

His reasoning was due to the rather shallow shoals, ambient light is better during the day. No one complained at that, one by one returning to their S2s. Closing the doors and flipping down the comfortable bunks, most were asleep within minutes.

They started late in the morning. The first S2 hitting the water at 9 am. A 20min transport leg saw them all resume scanning by 9.30.

Brad was correct, it was much less draining with ambient light. It gave a much better field view. It still took nearly ten hours to clear the 5000m diameter zone.

Glen ran the last sweep as they were on the outside. The HUD in all S2s showed a perfectly clear light green area.

'On me', Kia said and headed for the shoreline. Picking a deserted beach she dropped her S2 onto the short grass. The rest landed in a row. Kia put a call through to Sandy. Sandy confirmed the success of the mission and all data had been received and checked. She opened the door and walked out into the brisk air. The sun was still shining but not raising the air temperature by much.

Brad and the rest stood waiting for what was going to happen next. 'I am going to put a call into Taren and let him know the job is done. The next bit is a bit worrisome, I am going to fly the S2 into the local airport, and meet with him as promised.'

'Not alone you're not' Ray said!

'You go we all go. So far this has all gone without a hitch, that's because we are in our element out here, no-one can reach or touch us. In there, it's a whole new ball game.'

'So what do you suggest?'

'Give me a moment to think' replied Ray. 'OK, my suggestion, boss, is you take Bree, and Melissa with you. You three land at the airport, meet the locals, make sure the meeting takes place at the airport, I am sure they have a VIP lounge or something. Neil and I will prowl. Neil can fly the pants off anyone here, and I have no problems with shooting anyone, if necessary. 'Alternatively, you can send us back and go in alone.'

Kia smiled', And let me guess, that won't happen.'

'You can bet your ass on that' Bree said.

'OK well, lets see what Taren has to say first.'
Kia returned to the S2 and asked Sandy to connect her.

'Taren's face appeared on the screen. Good evening Taren, I am pleased to announce that project is almost complete.'

Taren clapped his hands and almost burst into tears. He must have said thank you at least ten times if he said it once. Kia could not help grinning at the outward display of emotions on his face.

Once he began to settle, Kia continued. 'Also, as I promised, I shall attend your office in person, and thank you for your faith in our company and abilities.'

Taren nodded. 'Umm, there is a slight problem with that.'

Kia tilted her head in an inquiring gesture.

'I have been called to Oslo by my superiors. They, in turn, were summoned to speak with Haakon Magnus. He is my superior's superior.'

'Haakon himself, spoke with me at length and is now fully aware of what you and your company have done for Norway.
'He has requested to meet you at his residence in Oslo. I take it you will be arriving by air.
'I have the coordinates here for you. I will also be in attendance if that is not an inconvenience?'

'That is not a problem, Please give me the CoOrds and I shall be there in a little over one hour.'
Taren read the numbers out for Kia, and they bid each other goodbye.
She punched the numbers into the Nav system and walked out of the S2.

'Right, I have told Taren, I would meet him in just over an hour. His boss called him in to explain what we were doing and apparently would like to thank us as well. So Ray, what did you come up with?'

'Kia/Miako in one, Brad/Bree and Melissa/Paul, you three make up the delegation, Neil and I will run a perimeter.'

Glen stood up, 'And I am just going to fish off the beach?'

Ray grinned, 'You wish, you can go with Neil or with me, your call.'

'I'll go with you, Neil makes too many funny noises when he's flying.'

Neil spluttered a denial, 'I do not!............... Do I?'

Everyone left him there waiting for an answer as they got ready.

'Just remember to turn on the fans and noise makers', Ray said over his shoulder.

Standing outside the S2, Kia selected a deep burgundy and set the other two midnight black. Miako came over, 'Reporting for duty Capt'n', and threw a mock salute. Kia grinned and waved her inside.

55 minutes later, five S2's crossed the Oslo boundary, one red, two black, two in camo.

Sandy's voice announced, 'Destination in seven minutes.

'Thank you, Sandy' replied Kia.

Sandy continued, 'You ARE all aware that those CoOrds will drop you fair and square in front of the Royal Palace?'

'WHAT!'

' Are you sure?'

'Indeed, and just to bring you up to speed, Haakon Magnus is not only Taren's boss, but he is also HRH Haakon V, The Crown Prince of Norway. He is currently acting as regent for his father who is recovering from surgery. Don't forget to curtsey!' And with a chuckle Sandy disconnected.

Chapter Twenty Eight

No one had a chance to gather their wits!
A chime announced the destination was in sight. Kia hit the controls that retracted the covers from the fans in the stubby wings, and they burst into life with a muted roar. Heaters supplied superheated air into the outflow, giving a very credible impression of mini jet motors.
Neil and Ray peeled off in opposite directions and started scanning for possible threats. They were the only ones not making any noise.

For the last few minutes of the ride, everyone had checked their hair and suits, damn Sandy for not saying anything earlier!

Kia's S2 did a smooth twist turn and pulled up about 3ft from the car park surface, slowly settling onto the surface in a cloud of leaves, dust and small stones. She was closely followed by Bree and lastly Melissa.

As the turbines wound down to a stop, Kia and Miako closed down all the internal systems. Leaving the outer video feeds hot, for Ray and Neil to access. Standing outside the closed door, they waited for the rest to arrive. At last everyone was together. They looked nervous. 'Relax guys. Lock your S2, wouldn't want to have someone steal it', advised Kia.

Standing on the top of the steps, Taren, called out and waved them up. He shook Kia's hand vigorously, then everyone else's hand as he was introduced.

'Come, come inside where it is warmer, follow me. Oh, this is simply a wonderful day!'

'Excitable isn't he!' whispered Melissa to Paul.

Taren led them through a magnificently decorated hall to a side door. The room beyond the door was decorated as opulently as the hall. Two other people were in the room, both stood to welcome the new arrivals.

'Kia may I introduce to you Klaus Hartman from the German Embassy here in Oslo. Klaus has been very instrumental in getting clearance to remove U-864.' Kia shook hands with Klaus and introduced him in turn to her party.

The last man in the room was wearing a suit but had taken his jacket off and laid it on the arm of the chair he had been sitting in.

Taren Smiled broadly and said 'Kia, it is my greatest pleasure to introduce to you our regent, HRH Haakon Magnus V.'

Kia shook his hand and bowed. 'It is a great honour to meet you, your grace. I am humbled to be invited into your home.'

Haakon smiled, showing a perfect set of white teeth. 'Rubbish my dear lady! We are indebted to you for what you have done, not just for this country, but for the hope you have given others facing their own environmental crisis.'

Kia, then led Haakon down the line introducing everyone one by one. Haakon had a few words of praise for each one. Refreshments were brought in, and they all sat for just over an hour fielding questions from the Regent and Klaus.

A messenger poked his head around the corner of the door, he spied Haakon speaking with Miako and gestured he was wanted on the phone.

Haakon apologised and excused himself from the room, following the messenger out the door.

Kia led Klaus off to one side while there was a bit of a lull in the conversation. 'I would like to thank you kindly for allowing the project to go ahead.

Klaus waved off her thanks, 'It's the least we could do, after all, what was the alternative? We were concerned about losing the remains, but compared to all the things being contaminated.......'

Kia raised an eyebrow, 'I don't understand. Did Taren not explain to you that all remains and their personal items would be fully recovered and presented to the German Gov?'

Klaus did a perfect imitation of a rabbit caught in a spotlight look.

'All the human remains are being cross-referenced with DNA databases. We have positively identified all bar one of the remains, and even that one we have narrowed to living cousins so far.'

Klaus just stared at Kia for a few moments, 'Wunderbar!!!' He exclaimed. 'We were under the impression that once the sub had been removed all was virtually lost!'

'Originally with early scans that was the case, however, we have been improving our technology, and our techniques. Like with every new venture, there is a learning curve. Now we need to sort some reliability issues and code separation issues, and we will be a lot happier. All of the contents of the U-864 were preserved as best as possible. After all, our main aim is to resolve these problems, with the minimum of fuss and risk to all concerned.

'We have invited a few archaeologists to attend our main storage facility. We would be more than happy to have a German representative group as well. As we asked Taren, select your people carefully.'

Haakon had returned and was deep into an animated story with Paul. For the next two hours, everyone got to know each other much better, and the start of long term friendships started in that room, on that very day.

'No, it's fine! WE understand, while we were protecting your combined asses in that leaky old building, it is perfectly understandable that you would be drinking champagne and slicing the most delicate triple smoked ham from the bone. And you forgot to tell us everything was fine....'

Neil and Ray were really throwing a beautiful artificial tantrum, trying to make the others feel bad. It wasn't going to work. No one was paying them any attention!

They were already over half way back to the island, Kia opting to stage a take-off in the dark, just to make things a bit more awkward for the photographers to get a clean shot of the hardware during lift off.

'Well, I believe all in all that went very well for us, do you not agree?' Miako started a round of applause going, 'Well done one and all.'

'May the next step be as successful as the first', Paul raised a glass of cola and clinked Glen's coffee cup with it.

Brad dropped his duffle bag onto the lounge back at the villa. 'Hell, we were only gone for two days but it seemed like a month's adventure', he said to the back of Bree as she headed for the showers.

Chapter Twenty Nine

Early next morning Kia had just finished her run and was leaning against a pole talking to Miako and watching while she went through her rigid yoga regimen. Normally Melissa would be working out with Miako, but there was no sign of her so far this morning.

'Melissa sleep in?'

'Not sure, haven't seen her so far this morning. I haven't seen anyone but you so far.'

Kia shrugged, no matter. 'I'm going up top if you need me for anything.'

Miako just kept skipping to her inner beat and waved.

Stepping out of the elevator doors into the OpCen, Kia was not surprised to find a woman sitting patiently in a chair on the balcony. She walked outside and pulled up a chair next to the woman.

'Lovely morning.' She received a nod in reply. The woman lifted a fairly thick file out of her lap and handed it to Kia. Kia placed it on the table in front of her and walked back inside, crossed to the elevator and went down to the café.

She was back in the chair on the balcony in less than three minutes. Placing one of the two mugs of tea in front of the woman, she picked up the file in one hand and her mug in the other.

Glancing at the woman she smiled, 'Don't worry, I nearly never kill anyone until after my first cup of the day'. With that she started reading, and, drinking.

Exactly 38 minutes later Kia stood, drained the cold dregs of tea out of the mug. Closing the file she tossed it on the table.

'The first lie in the file says your name is Jennifer Wall. Care to correct that typo?'

'Katelyn Hedges.'

Kia nodded, 'Follow me, Kate'. Kia walked into the OpCen and stood in front of a blank HUD. 'Put both of your hands on the screen palms first, fingers spread and smile.' Once her hands and eyes had been scanned Kia called Sandy.
Sandy appeared, and Kate merely lifted her eyes to the disc and back to Sandy's face.

'Run with that for me will you please Sandy. Kate has interrupted my morning routine, so I shall take her with me until I decide what I am going to do with her if anything at all.'

Sandy smiled and nodded, 'I shall give you a yell later.' Kia headed for the elevator, and Kate followed.

Ray was already at the range and had just finished cleaning an S&W 686 series revolver that he had been training
with previously. Open on the bench beside him was a case containing a Beretta 90-two type F which he was going to use over the next hour.
Kia walked into the range just as Ray snapped the case closed on the S&W and slid it back in its place on the shelf.

'Good morning Ray, mind some company?'

'OH Hi Kia, you are always welcome', Ray's smile never wavered as he noticed Kate but it had left his eyes immediately. 'I will play up this end and stay out of your way.' Kia just nodded.

Ray lifted two mags out of the Beretta case and shook a handful of Remington 147gr HPJ onto the table and started feeding the magazines. Kia walked along the range until she came to the gap in the booths. A space of around 5 meters allowed people to stand with nothing between them and the far wall.

Turning to Kate, 'you can either sit over there or find something that suits you to play with, or if you want to do your nails, there is a bench just outside the entrance we came through.' She turned away and opened the double doors of a tall cabinet.

Reaching in she grabbed a fully customised western style gun belt from a circular hanging holder. She strapped the belt around her waist and tied the holster pigging strap around her thigh.

She glanced at Kate who was slowly walking along the back wall, checking out all the many and various items available.

Opening a drawer Kia removed a pistol case and closed the drawer. Inside the case was a pristine Army Colt 45 revolver, one of the newer models from the Colt factory.

It had a better safety system that allowed it to be carried with all six chambers full, unlike the earlier model. Deftly flicking open the loading gate Kia thumbed six shiny new rounds into the chambers, spun the cylinder gently and dropped the gun into the holster on her thigh. Sliding ear muffs over her ears, she turned and faced the target line. She adjustied her feet spacing until she felt comfortable and then relaxed.

The move was oh so fast! No straining for additional speed, just a smooth flowing grasp of the grips, thumb cocking the gun as the barrel cleared the holster, and the finger pull as the gun lined dead centre of the target.

It seemed like the recoil put the revolver back in the holster, it was that smooth.

Ray grinned and shook both fists, he was a true gun fanatic, but he just loved watching Kia when she went all western on him. He missed the next one as he blinked. She moved again, this time firing twice, back in the bag. Again, two shots and back in the holster.

Kia hit the retrieve button, and the target came rushing back to the firing-line.

A nice 5 and 1 group showed in the centre of the target.

Glen looked over her shoulder, 'hmmm one good one and five bad ones.' Kia grinned and poked her tongue out at him.

'So who's the visitor?' Kia looked over where Kate was still looking over the impressive array of hardware.

'That Ray, is why I came down here. Let me put the Colt away and I will intro you to her. I am after your opinion.'

Ray nodded and took the colt off Kia and started clearing the empties from the cylinder. 'Leave the box out, I will clean this with Glen next time he's in. He has a knack with the mechanical and likes that side of things.'

Kia dropped the gun belt back onto its special shaped holder and hung it back up in the cabinet. 'You can put the Beretta away you won't be needing it' Kia whispered in his ear.

'OK Kate, Your turn. Sandy, all to the café, please.'
The three of them left the gun range together, Kia in front, Kate in the middle and Ray bringing up the rear.
That was the same order they left the elevator, at the café.

Everyone was there, talking amongst themselves until they spotted the new face, then everyone fell silent.
Kia kicked a chair over to the wall and indicated Kate to sit in it. She then turned her back on her and bid everyone good morning. 'Paul, what's the news on our Holdings front?'
Paul was sitting on his chair backwards and using the backrest to support his arms.

'Well, from what I have read on the grapevine, Oracle is now a well-known entity, in fact, those that as of today have not heard of us, are probably the good guys. All the bad ones know. Incidentally, Veronica met with some unfortunate accident, apparently.'

Sandy started her report next. 'The newspapers in Norway are full of the removal of the U-864. Even the other sub got into a few footnotes. General public reception has been on the positive side. Especially with a few scientists showing pie charts and graphs on TV talk shows about the amount of area that was cleared and blah blah blah... So all in all two giant steps, both successful, both in the right direction.'

'Excellent news' Kia said, 'Congrats to all, any other business you guys have? Or questions? None? I will sit down with Sandy shortly and start the next job rolling. Right, next item on the agenda.'

We received an email from Haakon last night, asking for a small favour. Sandy a HUD along that wall, please.'

A picture of Kate appeared on the HUD, 'According to the file this is Jennifer Wall. Real name Katelyn Hedges, 32, Single, good education, recruited out of college to join MI6 in Sheffield England.

'Originally was attached to the foreign affairs office in Paris.

She did data and information vetting, looking for nasty people planning to do nasty things, that kinda thing. Did that for five years, and rather well from performance reports. About a year ago while following a trail of dirty money and people smuggling, she and three colleagues were killed. Turns out Kate and her friends, found that the money was not coming from bad guys in the UK to bad guys in Europe. It was actually coming from good guys in the UK to bad guys in Europe. 'So, long story, shorter version, she and the three others started running.

'A newspaper report said all four had died in an unfortunate minibus accident. Sandy backtracked the emails from the reporter who wrote the article, seems it was a cover story to cover the disappearance of the four. Both the good and the bad guys still wanted to kill them, again.

'Now, apparently Haakon, through one of his charities, got wind of a people smuggling ring and when he sent someone to check it out, they found Kate and eleven others gagged and bound in a shipping container. Along with stuff that goes boom.

'So he took them home. Gave them a safe place to stay. Most of the others were able to be relocated with family. With Kate, it soon became obvious that not one country would take her and guarantee her safety. So, people that is the short story.'

Brad stood up and walked to the sink, poured out the cold coffee and refilled his cup. 'So what are you either asking or suggesting?' He asked as he perched on the corner of a table.

'ME? Personally nothing. I don't trust her as far as I could throw her. She's Ex-Gov, and she's Ex-MI6. That's two strikes against her in my book. The only thing in her favour so far is that she gave me her real name at the first request. If anyone thinks I am going to let her wander around the island, they need to half the dosage. I have programmed Sandy to kill her if she steps one foot out of bounds.'

Bree walked over to Kate and dragged a chair with her.

'Hi Kate, my names Bree, that's my hubby Brad. He will tell you that I have a knack of sounding people out. So tell me your story and lets see what my gut comes up with. Lets start with what you want from us?'

Kate gave a weak smile. 'Bree, I want nothing more than to be able to sleep longer than 15 minutes at a time and not wake bathed in sweat.

Kia stood up and stretched, 'Time for the OpCen for me, I will leave you guys to do whatever you want.'

Miako said 'I will stay with Bree, why don't you others do something useful?'

'It sounds like a plan' Paul said as he headed for the elevator with the rest, leaving only Bree and Miako talking to Kate. Sandy was busy at the HUDs as normal, when they all exited the lift.

'So dear Sandy, any dirty laundry on these four as yet?'

'Not that I can find. Do you want my opinion?'

'Sure', Kia said, 'Always willing to listen.'

'As far as I can sort out, all of these people were doing a great job, just for the wrong people. None of them have bad backgrounds. Obviously MI6 have checked them out, but that means nothing.

'What I mean is *I* have checked them out, and they came through with a pass mark.'

'That's a plus in their favour then. How did she get onto the island?'

Sandy pointed towards the complex. 'She arrived in Haakon's private Lear Jet. The only reason she got to land on the island.'

'OK well, lets shelve that for now, we have work to do.'

'Brad, Sandy has five target areas to clear, you got everyone less Glen and Paul, I need them for something else.'

Neil was smiling, 'Love it, time to work!'

For the next hour, Sandy ran through all the target areas with the boys.

Kia walked off during the briefing and put a call through to Haakon's office and talked at length with Haakon himself. After she had closed the video call, Paul and Ray walked over.

'Sandy says you have something for us?'

'Paul, time to contact the Japanese and see if they are receptive to having that reactor sorted out. Glen, lets go back down and see how the girls got on with Kate.'

Glen headed for the elevator with Kia.

Walking into the café it was apparent that the three women were no longer on hostile ground, but whether they were on friendly ground was not apparent either.

Miako looked up at their approach and smiled. 'We have formed an opinion that Kate is not an imminent threat to Oracle.'

Kia nodded, 'So I do not need to dispose of her remains this afternoon? Excellent, I had other things to do.'

Miako blanched white, she was still more than a little uneasy when Kia was hard to read.

'Talking about other things to do, Brad needs you upstairs. He has a fistful of targets and zones for today. Miako and Bree said "bye" to Kate and headed up to the OpCen.'

Kate looked from Glen to Kia and back. 'So what happens now?'

'Now we find you something to do. I have just the job for you in mind. Again, follow me', just as Kate stood Kia turned back to her. 'Have you eaten?'

Kate nodded 'Yes, Bree got me something before.'

'OK.'

They left the OpCen and walked over to the bank of carts parked to the right near the gardens and jumped in, Glen in the back, Kate in the front with Kia.

No one spoke for a while as Kia took the cart down into the complex and pulled up outside the hostel. They walked into the hostel and over to the managers office, opening the door, she stepped aside and waved them both in.

'Right Kate, of all the meetings, briefings, memos or any other form of communication you have ever had in your life, these next few facts are the most important. I am going to ramble on for a few minutes, and when I am finished, you are going to make a decision.'

Kate nodded nervously.

'What we do here and how we do it are two different things, we do not care that people know WHAT we do here. We do however care that they never, ever find out HOW we do it.

'Spies and snoopers will invariably meet with fatal consequences, and none of us has a problem with that, at all'. She let that sink in.

'I am offering you a job here. I do not care what name you choose to go by. Your job will be to run this entire complex. In three weeks or less, there is going to be a delegation from Norway coming over to the island to sift through material recovered from the seas off their shores, and probably a couple of German guys as well.

'So I am going to give you and your ex-partners, if they surface, the opportunity to form the management to run this complex.

'Sandy is, as you have gathered the AI for our main computer system and will assist in all your training and anything else you need.'

'In exchange, we will protect you from any and all threats.

'You have my personal word on that. You may leave at anytime you wish. You will meet and deal with many, government people, Also deal with a lot of large companies.' Kia paused to let Kate absorb the info.

'If you recognise anyone from your past who may wish to harm you, firstly, tell Sandy, because Sandy is always here. Secondly, you tell me. If this is a scam on your behalf, I strongly suggest you let me know, here and now, simply because from this moment on, the result will be fatal for you, and all your co-workers and chain of command. This is the one and only time I am going to ask.'

Kate shook her head and looked directly into Kia's eyes, 'I am not a spy, nor working for someone. 'I am grateful for your offer of a fresh start and a safe place to live. I will try to be both an asset to Oracle and hopefully a friend in the future, because right now, I don't have any.'

'OK, I have the assurances I required. I suggest you hang around the OpCen and get up to speed on what's going on around here. We basically are fixers. We fix problems others can't or won't.'
Glen here will show you around, then take you to the next available villa so you can get changed and showered and up to OpCen.

Chapter Thirty

Kia stood next to Sandy watching four S2s at work.

'They seem to be able to clear that quite well.'

Sandy nodded, 'This is the third zone for today, and they are about 22 minutes ahead of projected schedule.'

Kia tapped a coms icon on the screen, 'Hello boys and girls.' Various styles of greeting were returned.

'You guys are looking good, third zone and 22 minutes up on the schedule. Well done.'

Brad's voice came back in reply, 'We seem to be getting the hang of these sacks and pointy sticks.'

A rude comment was received from Melissa much to the chuckling of others.

'OK be good, if you do find a bit of time in a zone, always try and run another pass or two. If you have time on the home leg, run a scan/collect course. The more we clear, the better it all gets.

'Oh, and by the way, Neil, you missed some! Ciao!'

Kia signed off and grinned as one of the green icons spun 180 degrees and backtracked its last scan lane.

'Neil, you are so gullible sometimes!'

Paul came and stood next to her.

'We have had a bit of to and fro from the Jap Gov so far this morning. Yes, they know who we are, they also know what we did off the coast of Norway. They do want the mess cleaned up.'

'There's a but coming, isn't there?'

Paul nodded, 'Yes, a really big one.

'They are more than happy to have the problem removed, as long as we sell them the tech and the equipment to do the job. 'I ever so politely told them that was never going to happen. 'The Jap Gov is like a large onion, lots of layers. Unfortunately, I haven't got down to a layer with enough clout as yet. But the day is still young, it's not even noon yet. How did you go with Kate?'

'She seems genuine, has all the right body language, ticked the right boxes. Besides Haakon asked if we would look after her, as a personal favour to him. He had faith in Oracle and gave us a chance, so I am just paying back the trust, so I offered her a job.'

'Really? Doing what?' asked Paul.

'Managing the complex. Looking after the people when they get here next week. Sandy will work with her, she should be fine. She has good organisational skills, and good pre-emotive feelings. Sure, it's applied in a different job, but overall the skill set isn't that different, besides it's a way she can earn her keep. She is aware of the consequences of trying to cross me.

'If you or Glen are looking at her as a possible companion, let me make it clear up front. If she turns out bad, I will fix it, permanently.'

'Speak of the devil', Paul said, as Glen and Kate walked into the room.

'You missed me already?' Glen said.

'I didn't notice you had left my dear friend.'

Sandy flicked on the overhead speakers, there was some frantic chatter going on.

'What is this?' Kia asked Sandy.

'There is a carrier 250km off the west coast of the USA, around about level with Bakersfield. They have been doing exercises off the carrier for the last few days, the weather has been excellent and virtually no swell to speak of. However from what I gather they have had a mid-air event.

'One plane is in the water. The pilot ejected safely. It is the other plane is the problem.

'It looks like the pilot is either dead or non-responsive, the plane is locked on autopilot. It is running TFR at about 800m and is running wide open. Just to add the cherry, it's headed this way.'

Kia thought for a few moments, then shrugged her shoulders.

'It won't get here, in fact, it won't even be flying in the next hour. It will be out of fuel and auger into the sea. It's not carrying nukes, is it?'

Sandy checked her data, 'No it's just a training flight.'

'All good then. Note wherever it goes in, and we may pick the wreck up later.'

Kia flicked her hair clear of her shoulders and walked outside onto the balcony. Paul and Glen exchanged puzzled glances but said nothing. Two minutes later Kate walked out onto the balcony and approached Kia.

'May I ask a question, Kia?'

'Sure go ahead, ask away.' She looked over Kate's shoulder as Paul and Glen stepped up and leant on the door frame listening.

'That plane, the one heading this way out of control', Kate said.

'Don't panic about it Kate, it hasn't got a hope in hell of reaching this far, so you are safe.'

'I understand that, but what of the pilot flying it?'

Kia's brows dipped together, 'What about him? If he is dead, he's dead, and if he is unconscious, then he may revive in time to take control of the plane, slow it down and eject. Either way, it's not our problem.'

'So there isn't anything that can be done to save this guy at all?' Kate asked.

'No, not really. According to Sandy the fighter, I take it it's a fighter, is heading outbound wide open, that means at best they may be able to fly alongside it, and even then only so far. The others have to make it back to the carrier.

'The damaged fighter doesn't. So they, the Yanks, haven't really got a hope in hell, well nothing I would bet on.' Kia looked at the clock on the wall. 'It's probably going to be all over in 20 minutes, 25 max.'

Kate wrung her hands together, 'Could you do anything about him? The guy, the pilot of the fighter, could you help him somehow?'

Kia looked into Kate's eyes, 'Possibly, but why would I want to do that?'

Kate stared back with all her strength 'Because it's the right thing to do! I have lived my life by the old saying, "For Evil to triumph all it takes is for Good men to do nothing". Please, please can you do something!'

'Kia held Kate stare easily. For near on a minute, eventually Kate broke the eye contact.

Kia looked past Kate at the boys, 'Paul takes Kate, Glen, you're with me.' Kia walked past Sandy on the way to the lift, 'CoOrds in Sandy?

'Yes dear locked and hot, see you when you get back.'

'Stick close Paul, it's going to be a fast run.' Kia virtually peeled concrete up as the S2 took off that fast.
Pulling up the intercept CoOrds, Kia opened the throttle almost wide.

Glen looked up from the HUD, 'It's still running like an arrow, there are five aircraft further back, but I think they are just scanning for the impact point.'

'USS Nimitz, this is S2-1 from Oracle do you copy, over?'

'Oracle S2-1 this is the USS Nimitz, please clear this frequency immediately. This is a reserved military frequency, over.'

'USS NumbNutz, I normally would comply, but you see there is a F18-E pilot in a bit of trouble, and I thought since I was out this way, I might bring him back home. Now I am going to be busy for a few minutes, so how about you clear the deck off and find someone with brains and more important for me to talk to?'

18 minutes into the flight Glen started throttling back, keeping one eye on the HUD radar and one on the Nav screen he was trying to juggle two craft, both travelling faster than bullets but heading towards each other.

Glen pointed down to sea level, 'We are about to pass him going the other way.' Kia nodded and rolled the S2 upside down and headed for the surface, she levelled out at 800m, 500m behind the single F18-E. The S2s flashed up to the tail of the fighter.

'Paul, this is going to be a real bitch for timing, I want you to scan the F18-E.'

'We can't take the pilot out! We will kill him!' replied Paul.

'I know, what I plan to do is span over the top and put three anchors through the airframe. However, I don't have time to scan where the fuel lines are and other stuff, so just before I spear it, I want you to take all the fuel out of the thing. Get me?'

Paul grinned, 'Got yah smart cookie. Lets do this..'
Kia slowly slid her S2 over the top of the high speed F18-E. Paul approached from behind and below and scanned the fighter.

'Ready when you are.'

'Glen, target the nose cone and inside the leading wing edge by about 800mm. When I say go, you fire the grapples, Paul you remove the fuel, ready 3, 2, 1, GO!'

'You got him!!' Paul yelled into the coms.

'OK, indeed we did' replied Kia. 'Lets take him home.'
Kia turned a nice casual 180 degrees and headed back the way the fighter had come.

'Sandy, can you locate where the other F18-E was ditched? We can be nice and give them what's left of that one back as well.'

'USS Nimitz, this is S2-1 from Oracle Industries do you copy over?'

'Oracle S2-1 this is the USS Nimitz, we copy you 5x5 Captain Bergholt Speaking.'

'Good afternoon Captain Bergholt, my name is Kia. We have successfully captured your runaway F18-E. I have had to put three small holes in it, but besides that its only other problem is it is out of fuel. The pilot seems to be breathing, but not conscious. I highly suggest a medical team on deck in about eight minutes.

'Also, as the landing gear is up I suggest something soft to put it on, or I can just hold it above the deck while you put the gear down. Over.'

'Thank you for the update, Kia, I shall clear the deck so you can land. Over.'

'Not necessary, we are capable of vertical landing. I have S2-2 with me, they are diverting to recover the other F18-E that dropped in the water. That will also be placed on your deck. Over.'

As Kia broke off contact, they passed the other five jets going the other way. The carrier became a bump on the horizon and in a few minutes Kia was hovering just off the deck. The emergency crew scrambled to the F18-E, the hot air jets and screaming high noise from the S2 just didn't seem to bother them.

It had taken seconds before the medivac team had the pilot out and on a gurney and running for the doors. Kia backed the S2 over the lift and waited for the techs to manually lock down the landing gear.

Once she got the thumbs up, she neatly popped it on its wheels and dropped the three lift cables. Sliding sideways Kia put the S2 over a vacant park bay and dropped it onto the deck.

'Come on Glen', Kia said, 'meet the locals.' She stepped out of the S2, flicked the remote to lock it and slid it into her pocket. She leant back against the nose of S2-1 as Paul arrived with a dripping wet, badly twisted jet suspended under his S2.

Three deck hands showed him where they wanted it put and nice as pie, Paul placed it on the dot. He parked next to Kia's and climbed out and locked his S2 as well.

All four of them walked over to the open double doors where the medics had disappeared. They were met there by Captain Bergholt. He introduced himself and shook everyone's hand as Kia introduced them.

'Please follow me, our C/O would like to thank you in person.'

'Lead the way.' They followed Bergholt up a few levels and through a maze of passageways, to a briefing room door. Bergholt knocked and entered at a command.

Captain Bergholt came to attention and snapped off a smart salute.

'C/O. Ron Baker may I present Kia and her crew from Oracle.' Bergholt then stepped back.

Baker stepped forward and shook Kia's hand. Just over 6ft with a stocky build he had the typical close shaved hairstyle and an easy smile. 'Come in', he said 'have a seat, can I get you any refreshments?'

'No that's fine Mr. Baker, we only stopped to see how the pilot was. I have some things on the go this afternoon I need to get back to shortly. So how is he doing?' Kia asked.

'The doc suspects he has a severe concussion and a suspected broken nose. They will know more after X-Ray's. Which is minor compared to hitting the surface at high speed. Thanks to you and your help we expect him to make a full recovery.'

Kia smiled and stood, 'Well that's great news, now before you ask, and I know you are dying to. I can't tell you anything about them. That is classified, which is a term that you are more than familiar with. I can tell you it was our pleasure to be able to help with your F18-E issue, and I think the evening meal tonight, will taste much better with todays outcome.

'Are you familiar with what we at Oracle do?' Both the C/O and Captain Bergholt replied that they had no idea. Kia sat back down and for a few minutes, gave a fairly in-depth explanation about Oracle, making it clear on the political stance of the company.

Standing, Kia continued, 'If it is OK with you I would like to drop back in tomorrow, and I will bring you something that really should have been returned to you many years ago.'

Ron stood, and shook Kia's hand, 'May I ask what it is that we have lost?'

Kia picked up a pen off the desk and wrote something on the back of an Oracle card, she placed the card in his hand and the pen on the desk.

She turned to Captain Bergholt, 'With the C/Os permission, we would like to go back to the flight deck now, please.'

Bergholt looked at Baker for direction, he was still staring at the card. 'What? Oh yes, yes of course!'

Back in the S2 Kia, watched the officer of the deck check no one was near the jet blast area. He finally gave her the thumbs up. Kia hit the start up and after 30 secs of noise, lifted smoothly off the deck turned and disappeared in a beeline for home, closely followed by Paul and Kate.

When they arrived back at the OpCen there was a line of S2s parked in the sunshine. Kia and Paul parked next to these and made their way to the tower.
They found everyone seated in the café. Greetings were exchanged as they walked in, Brad asking where they had been?

'I had a small errand to run for Kate.' Kia said, looking at Kate as she said it, Paul just grinned in tandem with Glen, and they made their way to the servery.

'I am just going up for a few moments, Glen get me a coffee, will you? And I'll be back shortly.'

Kia walked into OpCen and stood next to Sandy.

'Hi, fearless leader', Sandy said, 'Well done today! Although you did lead Kate on a dance there for a while!'

'Well, yes, I wanted to see her morals and price she would put on life. I think she did ok don't you?'

Sandy nodded, 'So what can I do for you?'

'I need to locate the A-4e exactly and make preparations to give Mr. Webster back. I'd like to do this around 1.38pm tomorrow. Time is significant as you can see.'

Sandy nodded, 'OK, now do you want to give the Skyhawk back as is or restored?'

' I don't know Sandy, ask Brad and Paul what they think and lets go with those results.' With that, she headed back down to the café.

As the elevator doors opened the volume of cheering and shouting was huge. Paul stood on one leg on his chair imitating some kind of stork in mid-flight. He grinned sheepishly being caught in such a pose.

Kia held up both hands, 'Hey, I ask no questions and see nothing!' She sat between Bree and Glen and picked up her cuppa.

Bree leant over and said 'Congrats on your fishing trip, I hear you caught a fair sized one today.'

Kia laughed, 'Yes, but I had to give it back. So what's with Paul's impression of Swan Lake?'

'Ah', Bree smiled, 'He was mimicking your swoop and capture move I do believe.'

'So how was your day' Kia asked, Bree nodded, 'It went well the zones were fairly easy to clear up.

'We finished a bit early, so Brad got us to do a line sweep, but he had us running 45 degrees back and forth. 'During this sweep we came up to a beautiful old tall masted sailboat, was fairly deep about 9-9.5k. You should see it Kia, absolutely stunning, OH!!!' Bree's eyes shot wide open!! 'I have an idea! Can we recon it and put it on a hard stand area somewhere!? It would make a brilliant display!'

Kia laughed, 'Bree you can do anything you want, start a collection if you want.' Bree lunged at Kia and gave her a massive hug, 'What a fantastic Idea!'

Paul came over and put his hand on Kia's shoulder, 'I am going to see if there is any progress on the Jap issue.' Kia just nodded as Paul walked out.

She was watching the antics and gestures of everyone as they retold stories with an exaggeration factor that was impossible to measure. Even Kate seemed to be a bit more relaxed, answering a question occasionally.

One by one people started to disappear upstairs. The OpCen was always a popular place to hang out in the evening, simply due to the lovely balcony views, easy access to the internet and other vast databases of info.

Miako was talking to Kia and Melissa near the HUD.

'I think Kate has caught on that you would have gone after that pilot anyway.

Kia nodded, she is an analyst and a thinker, I would expect her to. Like I told Sandy, I wanted to find her level of morals and humanity. I still know very little about her, and I don't give trust very easily, and we all know respect must be earned. Mel, tell me, how Ray is doing now?'

Mel nodded her head, 'He is great, he still is the annoying little argumentative shit he always was. But the boy underneath now seems calm and content. The Range was a great idea, although I was concerned for a while. He is the kind of person always needs something to do.'

Kia smiled 'We all are. Only Miako here can put her brain into neutral and idle, the rest of us need that constant pressure level. Kind of like water, while under pressure we don't boil and are happy.

Bree had a new idea tonight. Apparently, you guys came across a tall ship today?'

The girls nodded, 'Yes, it was magnificent, even in its condition you could almost see pirates running around on deck and up and down the rigging.'

Miako agreed, 'Definitely something out of the ordinary.'

'Well', Kia continued, 'When she was telling me about it before, she came up with the idea to restore it on a hard stand somewhere, if it was OK with me. Hell it's fine with me, I told her she could start a collection if she wanted to!'

'Now that's a damn fine thought. Not everything has to be lost forever does it.' Melissa said.

Paul wandered over, 'Ladies, may I steal Kia for a moment?' They nodded and moved out of earshot.

'There has been no response from the Japs on our offer to clean that mess up.

However, I do believe they are watching us with a high level of interest. Our run in with the USN today was rather fortunate and gives them something to babble over with their sushi tonight.'

Sandy came over. Kia asked her if there was any update on the other three missing analysts from Kate's team.

Nothing as yet, should she bump it up the priority list?

Kia shook her head, 'Nice as it would be it's not a necessity as yet. Although, look at them all just standing around, lets see what Kate's management skills are like shall we?'

'God, you're a schemer!' Paul said.

'Listen up people, gather round my little lost puppies. We are still waiting for the Jap Gov to make its mind up whether it can trust us to save its ass or not. So that little excursion is on hold for now. 'Tomorrow I'd like a team to volunteer for a run out to the Ryukyu Islands just off the coast of Japan. It's international waters so that's a blessing.

'Any volunteers? Neil and Paul, great thanks. This needs to be a quick run, no time for cleaning strips there or back.

'At those CoOrds, you should find what's left of an A-4E Skyhawk fighter. On board is a Lt. JG Douglas Webster and a 1 Megaton Nuke.

'This came up in conversation when you first got here if you remember. Anyway, as a token of how nice and sweet we are I offered to give Mr. Webster a lift home where he deserves to be. Apart from it's the right and moral thing to do, which the USA Gov does not care about, I have other reasons for doing this.

'Firstly, there is a nuke lying on the floor in an area known for seismic activity, it's pure stupidity to leave it there. And piss weak for the USA not to have addressed this issue, but hey just my view.

'Secondly, as we just gave the navy two fighters back, it's seemed a good idea to make it three.
It's NOT a war grave per se as they were not at war when the accident happened, and it also is not the result of enemy action. BUT it pushes the buttons close to the debate on war graves. My plan tomorrow is to take the A-4E back, a coffin with Mr. Webster's remains, and a crate with the Nuke, less fissionable materials of course. There is a twofold reason for being a bit showy. A, because we can, and B, the Japs will hear about this, hopefully in a positive light. I gave the carrier a days notice. They are prowling up and down the USA west coast, less than three hours from L.A and Berkley.

'Sandy informs me that before us dumping the F18-E's on the deck, flights in/out to the Nimitz from land based points, total three in nine days. Since we dropped in, eleven, in the last few hours. So with that info Ms Kate, what would you surmise from that?'
Kate had physically jumped at the mention of her name, caught out by the question.
'May I have a sec to collect my thoughts, please?' Kate asked.
'Sure, take your time', Kia replied.
Kate took a deep breath, 'I don't think it's the A-4 or Webster that they are getting excited about.

'The possibility that you are doing to drop a nuke on their main flight deck that has been submerged since 1965 is probably the most worrying thing to them.

'The next thing will be how come you could find it and they couldn't. Again I suspect they actually stopped looking for many years, but may have restarted searches due to the 'Terror' threats we all now seem to face.

'Why would the terror stuff make any difference now?' Melissa asked.

'Oh hell, an easy one to answer', replied Kate, 'When this warhead went overboard, most of the worlds population was thinking fantastic! great! Wish they would all fall into the sea.

'No one actually WANTED a nuke back then, but now, every minority group would give up their testicles to get their hands on a 1MT warhead.

'So while no one wanted them, no one looked, now groups are actively seeking them, the governments of the world will begrudgingly start looking again.'

'As a side note, if Kia plays the right cards, it's possible someone may sneak around her window one night and drop a list on the floor that has a lot of missing stuff and issues never known before. Figuratively speaking, of course. Think tanks all around the globe are going to be watching what happens tomorrow very closely. This will have far, far reaching effects. Much further than a good old, found this here have it back issue.'

'Nice analysis Kate', Kia said, and Kate almost blushed. 'So anyone else has thoughts on this? Next question, what are the chances they will try and hold us captive tomorrow. I think it will be fine, but I know some like Glen don't like governments in any shape or form. Another question, do we go in with just one S2 or do we make a more impressive appearance?'

Kate hesitantly raised a finger.

Neil smirked, 'See, I am not the only one with manners.'

'I don't think there is going to be a problem with them trying to abduct you, but you can lay bets that there is going to be more scanning, sampling, filming equipment being fitted to monitor that flight deck than ever before.

'I would not be surprised if the stripes you see tomorrow to mark where you park are temperature and air sniffer strips, they may even have a false panel so they can see how much an S2 weighs.'

'Sneaky sons of bitches!' Exclaimed Glen.
Kate and Kia smiled at Glen.
'OK, thanks, Kate, then tomorrow we will take six S2s, four will land, the other two will go into a holding pattern. These will squawk an FF signal just so everyone else knows they are there and that we are security conscious. Volunteers to be the outriders?'
Glen and Ray put up their hands a full second before anyone else. 'That was a given. OK, lets move on to the next item. Everyone upstairs please'

Chapter Thirty One

'Kate here as you know was placed in our care by Haakon, nice fellow, his heart is too big. Anyway, Kate was part of a team that went missing. Three of that team are still missing, be nice to find them. As you all know, I do not like loose ends.

So all those with nothing better to do stand here in the middle of the four HUDs screens. Sandy clear all screens.

Right, Kate will sit on her ass here. Kia put a chair near the wall.

'Kate close your eyes, do not open them again unless you need to visually check something OK?' Kate nodded and shut her eyes.

'Now ladies and gentlemen, a game. Kate is going to tell you the three names you will be looking for, you may ask her as many questions as you like. She will keep her eyes closed and rely more on memory. YOU ask questions, one of them may nudge some small item free in her mind.

'Keep at it until you find them or are too tired to continue. 'Sandy will work the outside of the HUD and send all of you any little iota of information that may help. OK, are we ready?' Nods and thumbs were shown all around. 'Kate, the three names and anything else you can remember to describe them, ANYTHING.' Kate nodded.

'Layla Brooks, Jess Brown, Gina Aubrey.' Kate said, Ten pairs of hands went to work, Sandy was included in the count. The questions came one after the other. For hours - questions/ answers more questions. Miako stepped back from her HUD and walked over to where Kate sat with her head in her hands.

'Kate?', Miako slid a picture onto the HUD in front of her, 'Is this one of your team?'

Kate lifted her head and opened her eyes, 'YES! Oh my God, yes, that's Gina!'

Kia walked outside of the HUDs square. She pulled a copy of all the info to her HUD.

'OK people take a break, anyone who was chasing Gina, flick what info you have over here', asked Kia.

Kate was just staring at the picture. 'That was amazing to find Gina in a few hours!'

'Not really, what we just did is what I call a varied view search, everyone in the room has a different perspective that means many other paths are searched. OK, one down two to go.' And so it started again, this time with just two names.

76 minutes later, Ray and Mel got a hit on a pair of hitchhikers in Sweden matching the pair's description. Sandy found a room they stayed in and programmed a Sat to do a VERY slow scan looking for more information.

'Well done everyone!' Brad announced, 'Sandy has it all now, let her run with confirmation and we should know by morning. So go on everyone scoot.' He then walked outside to where Kia was sitting on a chair semi-dozing.

'You alright?', he asked, Kia smiled 'Yes, just tired, and a bit annoyed I suppose as well.'

'Annoyed? How so?' Brad sat.

'When we designed Oracle to do what it is now starting to do, one of the mainstays was for it to be non-political.'

'Today, we are playing politics with the Japanese Gov, also now the USA Gov, Kate was a problem given to us by the Norwegian Gov. Arrgh it's just so frustrating!'

'We ARE non-political Kia, but what we are even more so is adaptable. I have seen both you and Paul step up and deal with, lets call them Outsiders. It has not made a bit of difference where, or what these Outsiders have been.

Oracle has been able to adapt to get our mission accomplished. That is always the most important thing, striving to get the mission done. By simple definition, everything we do is political to a certain extent, and as long as we keep that extent to the minimum required to get the mission done, we have succeeded.
Now boss, get some sleep, tomorrow you get to meet the second most powerful force on the planet.'

Kia rolled out of bed just on sunrise, she threw herself into the shower and let it alternate hot/cold until she was fully awake. Towelling off, she walked into the wardrobe and grabbed a suit and got dressed. With a glass of pineapple juice in one hand, she walked outside and sat on the bench in the garden alcove. She watched Miako going through her relentless Yoga regime every morning. When Miako was finished, she came over and sat opposite Kia. Throwing her towel at her Miako demanded to know why Kia never seemed to work out but still had a tight butt.
Kia laughed, 'I worry too much to get fat.'
Miako nodded, 'I am beginning to believe that is true.'
An S2 went flashing overhead followed by a deep rumble of its sound wave. 'Neil, huh?' Miako nodded.
'He volunteered to go and scan the A-4 last night, and he had to draw straws to beat Paul in who was going to be pilot, but got lucky this time.'
'So how are you and Neil getting on? And stop blushing! Miako for gods sake we are not stupid. For what it's worth Neil seems to be 500% better now than the day I met him in Brad and Bree's house.'
Miako smiled, 'He has much more confidence in himself and his outlook is much, much better. He is sleeping a lot quieter too, he used to toss and turn frequently, and be up and down every 40-50 minutes.
'Now that he sleeps better, his biorhythms seem to have improved a lot.'

Kia nodded, 'This is excellent news, and how are you doing yourself? Do you feel this line of work suits you?'

'Kia, to be honest, I was not sure that I would like this kind of work, but after seeing some of the wonders and doing some of the things we have done, I cannot see myself doing anything else.'

Kia nodded 'I am sorry to ask so many questions, I just worry sometimes.'

Miako smiled 'You worry for no reason, and if you doubt my words just wait for the next five seconds.'

Neil came walking over, 'Good morning Neil' Miako said, 'how was the trip?'

Neil grinned from ear to ear, 'AWESOME! So lucky we don't have radar guns over the water hey.'

'Kia and I were just talking, we might need you to help out in the complex', and Neil nodded 'That's all good.'

'Well, it might mean you won't be flying the S2 for a few months.'

Neil's face fell, 'Naw, you can't do that!, please don't do that!'

Kia put a reassuring hand on his shoulder.

'Neil, we would never do that to you. I was just saying to Miako that I was just worried about you liking your new job.'

'It's the best job on the planet! No one has a better job than me! I must go, time for breakfast! Bye for now.'

'See I told you so' Miako said as Neil disappeared from view.

Brad called Kia over coms to come down to the B warehouse. Miako tagged along. Inside the warehouse, there stood a derelict fighter plane, the A-4 Skyhawk. It looked quite bad.

Sandy was there under her disk.' I think we can clean it up a little. It doesn't need to look this bad. '

Kia nodded, 'Lets clean it up to a 'Surprisingly good condition for its length there' kind of look, without attracting too many questions.'

Sandy said 'OK, how about this then?'
It was strange to see a fighter slowly restore itself. It was like watching a time-lapse film running backwards.

Suddenly Kia held up her hand, 'About there I think. What do you think Brad? Miako?'

'Hmm, not sure, lets invite Ray down, he is the military man.' Ray walked in a few minutes later, 'Oh WOW, you can tell it's been there awhile hey.'

'We gave it a bit more Resto, so it didn't look too shabby. So you think that is acceptable?' asked Kia.

Ray nodded, 'How about its payload?'

Sandy put the Nuke on a trolley. 'That looks OK as well.'

'Now, what about part three?' Kia said.

'That's all done, the remains are quite good considering they were locked inside the A-4, so no scavengers to spread the bones around.' Sandy reported

'Well, it's only 8.00am, delivery is at 1.38pm, 2.5 hours to cruise there, still got a few hours to waste for today then.' Everyone started making their way back up to the OpCen, ignoring Sandy's taunt that she would race them back.
Ray walked into the OpCen first. Kia and the rest having stopped at the café next floor down.

'Hi Sandy, you only just beat me back', that brought a grin from the Holo.

'Any news on the three missing?'
Sandy said 'Actually yes, it looks like the two in Sweden are doing the holiday work and move on routine. Probably safest at this point. The other one, Gina, the last place I can positively place her is in Belgium, close to the Dutch border, but that was months ago. She is a little more elusive to find. Also, there are several people looking for the pair, but strangely no-one is looking for Gina!

'Every time a record gets accessed the file directory is updated, now, me being an AI, know all of this and have been following it from the other side. Anyway, I have facial recognition software running in all major railways and bus terminals, so have two other agencies, unfortunately, although their software seems to be working fine, it isn't. Can't understand why!'

'Well, I suppose a feed, then time to do the returned soldier bit.' Ray stepped into the lift and dropped into the café. He grabbed a mug of hot coffee and went and sat next to Melissa and Paul.

The others started filtering in, and it didn't take long before everyone was there and just killing time till departure. Sandy materialised and called for their attention.

 'Ten minutes to lift off, people, as per usual, it's a purely voluntary trip.

  Kia is hooking up the A-4E to her S2, so I will be doing the briefing.

'Shortly we will visit the Americans on one of their most powerful war platforms. There we shall meet and greet the hungriest, most selfish war mongers we have ever met. They may try to capture us, imprison us, hurt us, with beatings and steal your S2 from you. Apart from that, lets try and have a nice time. Oh, Kate, Kia has told me that if you wish, you may accompany her. The choice is yours.'

 'After your description you just gave, I wouldn't miss it for the world.' Kate headed after everyone else. Six S2s were flying in a diamond formation of 4 and two outriders, towards the west coast of California. Kia and Kate were in the lead. Everyone was transmitting an FF coded signal. Just so the carrier knew they were coming. The S2 Kia was in, had a clear shield protecting the A-4E that was nice and snug underneath. They picked 8000m as the best height for contrails, and they were running just a fraction under Mach 4.

  All designed to put them over the carrier by 1.38pm as promised. The exact time the A-4E fell in the water in 1965. Glen and Ray were in the two outside S2s both more than happy not to have to deal with the carrier crew.

  Brad was carrying the coffin in a sealed container, and Paul was carrying the deactivated nuke. Neil was happy sitting in the back of the formation. No one was saying much, not even inside the S2s.

<u>Chapter Thirty Two</u>

5km from the carrier, the radio burst into life. 'Approaching aircraft, this is the USS Nimitz, please identify. Over.'

'USS Nimitz this is S2-1 from Oracle, accompanied by S2-2 through S2-6. Permission to enter the 5km air perimeter?'

'S2-1, USS Nimitz permission granted.'
Kia pulled back on the throttle, and all S2s slowed as one unit. The USS Nimitz was dead straight ahead.

'USS Nimitz this is S2-1, requesting permission to land on your flight deck. S2-2 through S2-4 to follow suit. S2-5 and S2-6 will maintain the safe perimeter.'
This time, there was a slight delay in getting the reply.

'S2-1 through 4, permission granted.'
Kia had held them motionless at 4km from the carrier. Everyone activated their fans and hot air systems. She nudged them to 100kph, slowly closing the gap. Each knew their part so unless the carrier or crew did something stupid, it was all going to be fine.

Kia pulled to a halt 20 feet from the side of the carrier. They had approached at right angles to the centre line. She nudged forward and very gently started lowering the A-4e to the deck. As the airless tyres hit the deck, two deck handlers appeared and fitted chocks and disappeared back into their gopher hole.

Kia released the Skyhawk and slid sideways towards the bow. Over an empty parking bay, she lowered the S2 and shut it down.

Brad had moved forward and lowered the sealed capsule with the Nuke to the deck.

He then slid next to Kia's S2 and parked his S2.

Paul moved forwards and lowered the container to the deck in front of the Skyhawk. He hit the releases and behind him, Neil scanned out the container, leaving a coffin exposed, draped in the appropriate flag.

Paul slid next to Brad and parked and then Neil parked next. It went that smoothly, they looked like they did this every day. All the S2 crews stood in a line as six marines in full dress uniforms, marched slowly out of the carrier main doors, collected the coffin and returned inside the carrier.

Captain Bergholt came out of the main doors and approached Kia. She smiled as he drew to a smart halt and saluted her.

'C/O Baker requests your attendance in the forward officers mess. If you would be so kind as to follow me.'
With that, he spun neatly about and marched off in the direction he had come from.

The Officers Mess was the size of a large hall. As the Oracle crew were ushered in it was plain to see there were a whole lot of personnel that normally would not be found dead on a carrier.
Kia looked for and found Ron Baker, she walked up to him and shook his hand, 'Nice to see you again.'
Kia reached into a suit pocket and withdrew an envelope.
'These are the DNA results for Mr. Webster and also the certification that the B43 was disarmed and is safe.'

Baker smiled, 'There were a few who were worried you may just toss the B43 on the deck and say, "Not sure if it's still working!"'

Kia matched Bakers smile, 'Actually Ron, if I may call you Ron, the thought had occurred to us, just to add spice. However, it is harmless. Only fit for a museum piece, maybe with the Skyhawk. How is your other pilot by the way?'

Ron nodded 'He is doing well, he is awake and eating, no signs of permanent damage.'

'That is great news, I am pleased to hear that' replied Kia.

Ron motioned to the large table in the centre of the room, 'Please sit, we have some landlubbers who want to waffle on, and that might be more tolerable sitting.'

Ron took the head of the table. Oracle sat down the left side, and the assorted dignitaries took the right-hand side. Once everyone was seated, a young cadet was ushered into the room.

He gave a speech and a certificate of recognition to the members of Oracle from the Webster family. The cadet was the great grandson of Douglas Webster.

Paul accepted the award. There were a few speech givers, thanking them for the F18s some for the A-4E, hardly anyone mentioned Douglas Webster, and that ticked Kia and the others off a bit.

All was going fine, many asked questions on the S2, some were answered, and some were politely bypassed.

Then a Dudley Fairbanks arrived, he introduced himself as the secretary to the Department of Defence, Development Section, DODDS. Ron swore under his breath when Fairbanks was brought into the room. Kia touched him on the forearm, 'Is he your boss?'

Ron replied 'Hell no!'

'OK, can he affect your career?'

Ron shook his head, 'No, he is just a major pain in the ass and embarrassing to boot.'

Kia smiled sweetly, 'Please leave him to me.'

Ron looked into a pair of Tawny-Gold flecked eyes and suddenly felt sorry for Fairbanks.

For the next 45 minutes, all was cordial, and the conversation was a two-way street, the crew was explaining what Oracle does, and the carrier crew filled in details about life onboard a floating city. That was about the time Fairbanks had his fourth scotch.

Fairbanks wrangled himself a chair directly opposite Kia and Paul, he stared at them for a while, probably thinking he was intimidating them in some subliminal way.

'So Paul, tell me about this S2 craft of yours?'

Paul looked at Fairbanks and smiled, 'and what is it you would like to know?'

'How fast are they and how much to buy one or maybe two?' said Fairbanks.

'Well, Mr. Fairbanks, They are not mine. They are the property of Oracle, Kia runs Oracle and therefore has the authority to answer your questions that I do not have.'

Fairbanks switched his attention to Kia, 'Well?'

'Well, what Mr. Fairbanks? I missed your question I'm sorry.'

'I asked how much for one or two of your S2s parked out the front?'

Kia Smiled, 'I am so sorry, Mr. Fairbanks, you wouldn't have enough money to buy one, never mind two of the S2s.'

Ron put his hand over his mouth to hide a huge grin, as Fairbanks spluttered. 'Do you know who I work for!?'

Kia nodded 'if I recollect you said you work for the DODDS is that not correct?'

'Indeed it is' Fairbanks half roared, 'And you say that we could not afford to buy an S2!! Preposterous!'

'Actually, it isn't at all, you do not have enough money to buy one, and secondly they are not for sale. Now before you get upset and stamp your feet, let me tell you it is not just you.

'They are not for sale to anyone. We do not sell them, hire them out, loan them, or give them away to anyone. So you see there is no reason to get upset, we are not singling you out at all. It's the same for everyone.'

'We could always just take one off you! They are after all parked on USA property.' Ron moved to say something Kia held his arm.

'Mr. Fairbanks, you look like an intellectually smart person. Someone who knows what he wants, and will stop at nothing to get it.' Fairbanks grinned and nodded.

'Unfortunately, in your case your looks are deceiving, you are neither very intelligent nor are you smart. You do not have the means even to touch one of the S2s parked on deck. You could try to abduct one of us, or hold us hostage and demand that we give you an S2, but I seriously doubt even you would be that stupid. I have no idea who sent you here, I sincerely hope it was your idea, and you were not sent because that would mean there is more than one fuckwit in the DODDS. The best thing you can do is finish your drink, and leave.'

Fairbanks stood and stared daggers at Kia.
'You will live to regret those words, I promise you that!'
He turned and pushed his way through to the door and slammed it after himself.
Ron threw back his head and roared with laughter. 'It was about time someone put him in his place.'
Kia smiled, 'My pleasure', she held up one finger, 'Ray, Glen, keep an eye on the S2s. A dick by the name of Fairbanks might try something stupid. Try NOT to kill him.'

Ron heard all of this and leant over to one of his aides.
'Make sure Fairbanks is in his cabin and stays there, for his own safety.'

'Ron, I have no problem telling people what we do, and why we do it, I just cannot tell people how we do it. Some technology is just too dangerous. The reason we picked up the B43, can you imagine it in wrong hands? There are 92, sorry 91 known nukes out there. Please don't tell me you are naive enough to believe that USA, USSR China UK and others have told the TRUTH, and that's all there is?'
Ron shook his head, 'I see your point.'

Peace and normality returned. After a few hours the meeting broke up, and everyone went back onto the flight deck. The A-4E was gone as well as the B43. Ron shook hands with everyone and so did Bergholt.

'Thank you for Mr. Webster back, I didn't care much about the rest, but it's nice to get a serviceman home.'

'Our pleasure', Kia said. 'If you get in a fix that we can help with, give any of us a yell.'

'Actually, there is.'
The lift at the far end of the flight deck lifted to the top, laying on the lift was the remains of the F18-E that crashed.

'There is nothing useful left of that. Can you get rid of it for us?

'Normally we would just push it over the side, but now, I think you might get upset if we do that.'

Kia grinned and shook her head. 'So the powers that be want a demonstration hey? Sneaky way of asking!

Glen, remove the wreck for the nice men, please.'
From out of nowhere Glen's S2 appeared, scanned the wreckage and took it in one pass, less than two seconds start to finish.
Glen then turned and faced back up the centre line of the flight deck, just hovering.

Kia turned to Ron, 'There! Neat and tidy.'

Kia lifted off first, and soon all were back in formation, Ray and Glen took outboard positions, and they hit the throttle for home.

Chapter Thirty Three

6.30pm that evening everyone was in the café watching the news segment telecast from the deck of the Nimitz that showed the handing over of the lost fighter and pilot, and few candid shots taken in the Officers Mess, and the departure of the S2s.
The removal of the F18-E was not included in the telecast. Paul turned back from the HUD, 'Well that turned out better than I had hoped, apart from Fairbanks, I did not detect any overt or covert hostility. Anyone else?'

Neil put his hand up, 'The only strange question I was asked was if the S2s were armed. I shook my head and told him none of the S2 craft carries any arms or ordinance of any kind.'
Bree was the last one to report on her side of the day. 'Most of the questions I was asked was about what we did with all the stuff we collected, they used the words collected a lot, I think they had this impression we are physically picking this stuff up somehow, or at least physically rounding it up.
'Since we removed the fighter wreck, that may have changed now. A few asked who we worked for, or if we were attached or annexed to any country.'

Kate had listened to everything Bang and finally said, 'It seems that they don't know what to make of you. Large beasts take a long time to react. Fairbanks was probably their easiest to find asset. To them, you are still just a fancy new salvage company. May I say something? Based on past experience and analysis?' Kia indicated for her to go ahead. Kate drew a deep breath.

'OK. Lecture coming up, I get how you guys are trying to get recognition, but in all honesty, you're at the wrong end of the stick.

'Doing the Norway thing, the fighter capture and now the USA returned soldier, it's all good, but none of it will really ever connect.

'Let me explain if I may, this is right down my alley.
'Governments are full of people, who have eyes, but they are, for the most part, blind. They mainly run on what they are told by various think tanks.

'What you did in Norway, will hit the outside filter of a think tank, and be deemed not of political or military interest to them and tossed in the back of the information drawer.

'What you did today will receive better treatment by a Russian think tank or a Chinese one, but a USA tank will file it away. That's how it works, the only ones noticing and linking together the things you have been doing is the general public.

'Mr. Public will know about a football riot, but the British diplomat won't as a general rule. Anything that is not directly linked to his job is not reported to him.

'I am still not sure why you are even bothering to gain public recognition? From what little I have seen, you guys are top of the pile in what you do. You are the best there is. So just go and do what you need to do!

'Stuff the world, always be polite, always treat others with respect and do your job well. That's what I was taught growing up.
'What you really need is a damn good PR department, and trust me, you have the best in the world in Sandy.

'Start an Oracle website with news, blog, add articles and full-colour pictures about artefacts found. Give Bree her Tall Sail ship, put pictures up, within days, you will reach millions of people.

'Ask Neil how successful websites are, how many people visit UFO sites, and stuff like that.

'Start a lost and found museum, stuff that full of artefacts that history lost, and that Oracle found. Take one of the warehouses in the complex, and fill it full of history. Remember the old "build it and they will come" quote. Well, it's true, and it can get huge.

'Thousands of people will come, will learn, will leave and take with them the message to clean their shit up.

'Last but not least, put together a resume of what we do, email it to secretaries around the world, both corporate and governmental. The world runs on secretaries. Let them know if the shit hits the fan, you are the guys to contact.
Screw the rest of the world! You all just go right ahead and make this a better place.
'Now, after all that I need a drink.' She walked off to grab one.'

Kia was sitting deep in thought, rolling a pen through her fingers over the back of her knuckles and back again, totally unaware she was doing it. Bree was sitting one side of her and Melissa the other, none of them speaking.
Kate had found herself a drink and sat opposite Kia.

Eventually, Kia's eyes refocused, and she saw that she had been staring at Kate, for who knows how long.

Kate waved and said 'Welcome back!'

Kia smiled, 'I have decided not to kill you, as annoying as you are.'

Kate sipped from her cup and nodded her thanks.

Kia continued, 'These other friends of yours, are they worth the trouble? Would you lay it on the line for them?'

It was Kate's turn to stare at the floor. After a while she looked at Kia, 'Gina I have known since high school, been everywhere, done everything with. The other two I have known for 11 years in the tank. Also BTDT friends. In all honesty, Gina scores 7/10 for the trustworthy score, the other two probably a 9.5/10. Not sure why my gut tells me that, but it does.'

Kia nodded, 'Good enough for me. You tired?'

Kate shook her head 'Not particularly, why?'

'We might go and find them. I think we need our own think tank.'

Bree nodded, 'I think you're right, Sandy is 101% accurate to logical and logistics, and we have been providing the human viewpoint, which she loves to get. It's just too much Intel overload, for us. If we can get a high-class act like Kate and her crew interfaced with Sandy and her abilities, it's got to make life easier.'

Melissa added, 'I can do on the spot decision making and general planning, but to do a week or more in advance taxes my imagination and gives me a headache.'

Kia turned to Bree, 'Would you and Mel and Miako please start setting up interviews for staff for the complex? I was going to get Kate to manage it, but that would be a waste of talent on such a menial job.

'We need the lot, grab some of these useless males and put them to work.'

Neil grinned as he heard that. 'You! Kia said, grabbing his ear... Get to work on the best kick ass website there has ever been.. And if I see the word PWNED on it once, I shall staple you to the wall outside the balcony, do I make myself clear?' Neil nodded, but his grin never got smaller.

'Make it professional. Lets go, Kate.'

S2-1 tore off into the early night, heading for Norway airspace. Kia was running that high they actually skirted the edge of space. They ran like that for just over two hours. Dropping on a slow curve designed to put them somewhere over Norway.

Kia hit the HUD, She punched a few numbers and waited. A chime sounded, and Haakon's face appeared on the HUD, 'Kia! Nice to hear from you!'

'You too Haakon, I have a favour to ask. May I have permission to use Norwegian airspace? Please, it's in regards to the package you sent me.'

'Indeed, you may! In fact, you may do so permanently at any time you please until I rescind the authorisation in person.'

'Thank you kindly, I may need to cross into Sweden and search for two fair ladies before an untimely event befalls them.'

'I will make a call or two on your behalf. It will be fine.'
Kia thanked him closed the link. Next, Kia pulled up the Sat lock that Sandy had affixed to the area the two girls were last seen. It was still active, slaving the Sat info into the Nav unit made finding the approximate location much easier.
'So Kate asked, where are we going to start?'

'Sandy last had them in a little bed and breakfast here in a place called Bydalen, Sweden.'
The HUD showed an overhead of the small town. 'The main highway is the E4, and from all pointers, they seem to be moving southwards.
'So what I am going to do is drop us into a lake about a half days travel from the bed and breakfast. Then you are going to find them for me.'
Kate lifted one eyebrow, but said nothing.

Just after midnight the S2-1 was sitting happily 12mtrs under the surface of one of the many lakes that cover Sweden. Both Kia and Kate had a satellite feed up on their HUDs. Kia had opted for a 100km radius search area and was checking all low budget hotels/motel B&B, pretending to be a relative looking for the girls on a working holiday.

The water was crystal clear at this depth and Kia was watching some fish swimming slowly past as she waited for the umpteenth B&B to answer the phone.
She had taken her boots off and was wriggling her toes on the carpet. The phone line rang out.... 'Shit!'

Kate leant back in the chair and arched her aching back. 'We just don't have enough Intel. This is a huge leap of faith here, and it's only going to be luck that helps us find them.

'They might not even be in a B&B for all we know they could be camping in an old hut or under cardboard in a ditch.'

'Would they have mobile phones or any kind of electrical equipment with them?' asked Kia. 'Is there somewhere they would check in? Like in the movies, a website or phone number.

'Scratch that, they know the home guys are after them as well, so even if there was they wouldn't trust it anyway.'

Kia pulled her boots back on and slumped in the chair, thinking hard. She sat up, 'Sandy?

'Yes?'

'Pull up a 150km area around where we are on the HUD. Now filter with infra-red. Ignore all houses, looking for barns, huts, lean to's or similar.'

'OK, give me a few moments, please... That leaves 47 possible sites, 31 to the north of you and sixteen to the south. All still in the 150km diameter. There are plenty more, but I have filtered out ones showing only animal or more than two heat signatures', replied Sandy.

Kia and Kate stared at the 47 red icons on the HUD.

'Stuff it!' exclaimed Kia, 'Watch that HUD and guide me to the first southern icon.' The S2 burst out of the lake turning Camo as it shot off to the south.

Kate gave Kia the CoOrds and in less than 30 minutes they had scanned the first Icon. Kia asked for the next location, again, they drew a blank. It was slowly starting to get lighter outside as Kia hovered over a little shack. Wrong again. It was a father and son hunting trip. Kate punched in the next icon vectors, and Kia took off.

The fourth icon was also a bust. Kate read out the vectors for the fifth icon as the sun slashed its first rays of the day over the land below.

Just short of 1000m to the next mark Kia got a chime and a flag, 'What the hell?' Kate touched the flag and a dialogue box opened.

'It's a helicopter approaching this way.' Kate said.

Kia pushed the S2 into a sweeping curve to clear the area. 'I don't want him to fly into me while we're in Camo mode.

'We can only check this one with IR now, with the sun coming up the IR is next to useless.'
They settled on a hilltop about 500m away and waited for the chopper to clear the area.
The helicopter came into view, but slowed and circled a barn structure near the bottom of the valley.
Kate said 'I have a bad feeling about this. That's the same point we were heading to.' They watched it land to the left of the barn, and the two occupants dropped out and ran hunched for the barn.
Kia gunned the throttle and slid to a halt next to the helicopter.
Opening a drawer, she grabbed its contents and opened the door. As she ran, she slapped an adhesive holster onto her thigh.
Getting to the side of the barn she could hear shouting inside, and screaming. Creeping round to the front door, she looked in where the gap for the hinges in the door was. There were two women being handcuffed on the floor by one man while another stood over them with a semi-auto pistol. The guy doing the handcuffs stood up and viciously kicked one of the women in the ribs.
She quietly stepped into the barn. The guy with the gun was laughing and kicked the other woman.

'Now that's not a very nice way to treat a lady', She purred.
Both guys spun around to face Kia. 'This has nothing to do with you bitch so just back out of the barn and bugger off.' Said the guy with the gun, 'Or you might just get some of what they are going to get.'
Kia smiled, 'Please do not point that gun at me.'
The guy just grinned, 'And why the fuck not?

Kia's right hand flickered, and a hole appeared in the guys front teeth where the projectile went in before severing the brain stem from the spine on the exit. Not much blood, but an immediate effect. The gun toting guy dropped to the floor in a boneless heap.

'Now, please release my friends.'
The second thug fumbled for the keys and released one of the women. He dragged the other to her feet and stepped behind as if to unlock the cuffs.
Suddenly he was holding a knife to the woman's throat. 'Drop the gun! No one move!!'
Kia shot him twice in the forehead before he even noticed she had moved. 'What an idiot. You two stay!'
Holstering her pistol Kia walked to the barn door and motioned Kate to come in, then walked back to the two women, 'Your names are?'
'Layla and Jess!' came Kate's voice as she ran forwards and hugged them both.

Ten minutes later they had calmed down enough to be coherent and talk to Kate. Meanwhile, Kia had searched both guys and their helicopter.
'Be back in two minutes' Kia told Kate. Kia climbed into the S2 and scanned both the barn and the helicopter. Reading the data on the barn and helicopter she parked the S2 in the doorway.

Kate had them both settled by the time Kia was back in the barn. 'I have told them you are one of the really good guys.' Kia nodded her thanks.
'Kate has told me about you a little. You are both think tank analysts, so, therefore, you should be used to thinking on your feet, am I correct?' They both nodded.
'Good, firstly, strip off, and I mean everything, ring, necklace, earrings, nipple piercing, everything off. Kate grab two suits, please.'

The women were undressing slowly, Kia nudged one of the corpses on the floor with her foot. 'These guys knew exactly where you were, so, one or both of you is wearing a tracker. The longer you wear it, the easier it is for more of these guys to find you. Please, take your time.'
They moved much faster, virtually flinging clothes off.

Kate walked in with two suits, she gave one to each of them.
 'Put these on before you freeze. Kia ran her hand scanner up and down both of them before they dressed. Then over the discarded clothing. She stopped and picked up a belt. Looking at the buckle, she tossed it to Kate. Kate looked and swore. 'This is a standard uniform issue, they must track everyone.' She tossed the belt on the floor.

Kia walked up to Jess, she reached up and hit the stud on the suit and did the same to Layla's suit. 'Right girls, listen close to me. Your choices start now.
I am willing to walk away and leave you here. Now you don't have the belt on, you will probably get free from this group. Or you can come work for me, actually work for Kate, who works for me.
 'You will live on an island 6000km away from anywhere, you will not get paid, you will, however, get everything you need. You may quit and leave at any time. Oh, and if you are a spy or turn rogue on me, I will kill you.'
Kia looked at Kate. Kate nodded, 'That about covers it, so yes what do you say, Layla? Jess? In or out?'
Layla looked at Kia 'If I join, do I get to keep the suit?'
Kia nodded. 'Indeed you do.'
 'Even though it's a yucky colour, it's so damn comfortable!' Jess said.
Kia reached over and dialled Jess's suit to a dark grey. 'That better?'
Jess's jaw dropped open. Layla said, 'Good enough for me. Lead on boss!'

Kia took the remote out of her pocket and turned the S2 back to its normal burgundy colour. 'OK girls, get in.' Kia backed out of the door of the barn and scanned the mess in the barn out.
She then rolled the S2 towards home.

Kate said, 'Not going camo?'

Kia smiled, shook her head. 'Someone recently made a damn good statement and said "Screw the World..'
An hour later they were in Norwegian Airspace. Kia flicked on an FF beacon, S2-1 Oracle Ind., It proudly broadcast, and Kia liked that idea.

Chapter Thirty Four

Kate sat in the back of the S2, answering a heap of questions and making sure the girls had food and drink. Kia started climbing well before the East USA coast, giving the American Airspace plenty of room.

Sitting with her feet on the dash, she was reading a printout from Sandy. Kate came and sat in the seat next to her.

'Thank you for this Kia, they may only be words, but they are all I have to show how much I appreciate what you have done. '

'That's OK Kate I shall no doubt work your ass off in return', she looked behind her, both Layla and Jess were sound asleep in the fold down cots.

'One thing I would do if I was you, keep an eye on them, until your gut tells you you're wasting your time. Like mine did about you yesterday in the café.'

Kia tossed the printout on the floor as a flag popped up on the HUD. It was an inbound message: "Hello from Bergholt. Baker in bad trouble. Got a few minutes?"

Kia frowned, pulling up the map on the HUD she could see she was not more than 45 minutes away from the Nimitz. She typed on the screen, perm to land? Threat level?

A few minutes passed, and she got her reply, "Granted. High."

'Sandy?'

' Yes Kia?'

'Anyone over this way?

'Nope, they all in the nest right now. Problem?'

'Possibly, ask a couple to meet me at the Nimitz. Urgent.'

Kia, looked at Kate, 'Lets see what the fuss is about.'
Kia ramped the throttle up and went into a long dive, the
Nimitz was 703km away, but it wasn't going to take long.

Bergholt was standing in the main control room watching Kia
approach. The duty officers eyes were glued to the radar return
figures. 'There is something wrong with the radar sir! It says
that bogey is coming in over Mach 5!'
Bergholt grinned, 'She obviously is not in a hurry today.'
Klaxons blared as the S2 screamed down the centre of the deck
to stop perfectly aligned with the first empty park bay between
two F18-E's.
'Stay here, you are safe as houses in here, don't let them out.
Just sit tight and wait for backup if we need it.' Kate nodded.
Kia locked the door behind her. She walked over to the officer
of the deck and asked for a way to Bergholt, he pointed to a set
of stairs.
'Three flights up, door marked 3001.'
 Kia thanked him and started climbing the stairs. On the third
level, she found the door marked 3001 and knocked. It swung
open instantly, and Bergholt stepped out.
'Follow me quickly!' He led Kia up to the bridge.
Commanding Officer Ron Baker was sitting in the chair
overlooking all flight deck operations. A duty officer was setting
up what looked like schedules.
Kia walked over to Ron. 'Afternoon Sir she said. I come at
your invite, how may I help?'
'You have been lured here under false pretences, not by
Bergholt or me, but by a delegation of DOD stiff necks. They
will be here shortly. My guys are bringing them the long way so
I can warn you. They want your bird and are willing to be nasty
to get it.'
Kia nodded and Smiled, 'Thank you for the heads up.'
Kia pushed a button on her remote, and the S2 disappeared,
a massive boom of the sound barrier being broken rattled the
windows.

Kia then selected a seat and sat crossing her arms, 'So how have you been?'

Ron smiled at her calmness, 'Very good, and much happier that I got to talk to you first. Oh, here we go, heads up!'

The door burst open, and five guys marched into the room. One of them was Fairbanks.

'YOU!! Are under arrest for trespassing on US property! And we are impounding your aircraft!' Fairbanks was that excited he drooled slightly.

Kia stood and faced Fairbanks. 'Firstly, I was invited here and have transcript, proof of that, and secondly I do not have a craft on this US property, and thirdly you are still a fuckwit.'

An older person stepped forwards. 'My name is Don Phillips, Fairbanks works for me. I am the minister for the DODDS, I am sorry we will have to take you into custody. You will be required to answer some questions, and it might take some time.'

Ron stood to say something, Phillips turned on him, 'Don't make this harder than it has to be Ron, I can cut your career short faster than you can blink.'

Kia looked Ron in the face, 'This is not your problem, Don here is taking all the blame for everything that happens from this point forwards. You see Donny my little fellow, you and your title don't frighten me, you and your muscles on these marines don't frighten me, you are an insignificant little bureaucrat, who needs to be put back into his place.'

Don laughed, 'and you think a 2-bit company like yours is the one to do that? Cuff the bitch. We are leaving in 30 minutes.'

Two large marines stepped forward towards Kia. She kicked one in the crotch and chopped the other across the throat, smashing his larynx. The one who was kicked started to get off his knees. Kia reached around his head and with a swift jerk snapped his neck.

In less than three seconds, there were two dead marines on the deck. The third marine went for his service pistol.

Kia somersaulted over the chart desk, picking up a steel pointer as she did so. She drove the pointer through the guys wrist and into his pelvis, stopping him from drawing the weapon.

Kia then extracted the gun and kicked him in the side of the knee breaking his leg. Kia held the gun loosely at her side.

'Mr. Bergholt, please take a seat by the window and dismiss the officer here', as the duty officer turned to leave Kia asked him to close the door behind him, and make sure she wasn't disturbed.

'Fairbanks yelled that she was in deep shit now, and nothing would save Kia from Guantanamo.'
Kia casually shot him through his right kneecap. She leant over him while he screamed and writhed on the floor, 'You open your fucking mouth one more time, and you will NEVER make another sound again, do you understand me? Not one sound!'
Fairbanks nodded, biting his lip.

'Now, Mr. Phillips, over to you.   Look what your little pissing contest has achieved. We have two dead career military, one over there hurt. Fairbanks doesn't count, he is the epitome of wasted oxygen, and I may still blow his lights out just to do the USN a favour. No, Mr. Phillips, you don't scare me. The fact people like you are actually in a position of power, now THAT scares me.

'I was so hoping we could get along. We probably still can, but let's set some ground rules, shall we, and we will keep them simple.'
Kia dropped the mag out of the pistol and racked the slide to eject the loaded round. She dropped both the gun and the mag in a trash can.

'First of all, the island on which Oracle lives is out of bounds. The 50km limit surrounding the island is out of bounds. US personnel are allowed on the island by either request from us or approval of a request from you. Any other personnel found within the 50km area will be executed. Any attack on Oracle staff or equipment by the US will be deemed as an act of war.

Our response will be both immediate and severe.'
    Fairbanks passed out, and his head hit the side of the desk, three people smiled at that, Don wasn't one of them.
'Now I think that's enough rules for a working relationship, don't you? Now if you think I am bluffing, or you think that I am making empty threats take a look out of the window.'
Don walked sideways to the window not wanting to take his eyes off Kia for a moment.

    'There are 10 F18-E's parked out there, they cost 30-60mill each, so playing fair, lets say 400.000 million dollars for all 10.'
    Kia waved a hand, and all 10 F18-E's disappeared. 'You just lost your government 400 million dollars. Now if I was really pissed off, which lucky for you I am just annoyed, it would take me and four of the six S2s circling the deck, less than seven minutes to kill everyone on the Nimitz, and destroy the Nimitz itself.
    'So Donny boy, take your dead, and your wounded off the carrier, sack that fuckwit, Fairbanks, file your report stating it was your entire fault, and then resign.'
Kia walked right up to him almost nose to nose, 'That is, unless you think you are man enough to do something about it your-self?' Phillips paled visibly beneath his tan. He tried to outstare Kia but failed miserably.
    'I thought not, you gutless prick.'

Kia walked over to Ron and shook his hand, 'If this pig lies about you and I find out..... Thank you for your hospitality.'
She leant over and whispered, 'Sorry about your toys. I will give them back later.'
    Ron smiled, 'They don't deserve that, but thank you, that would be nice.'
Kia walked to the door waving to Bergholt on the way, she stepped over the corpse and opened the door.
Standing on the flight deck, she pulled out her remote and got the S2 back.

Inside, Jess and Layla were amazingly still asleep, while Kate was wide-eyed and wide awake. 'Are you OK?' She asked.

Kia nodded, 'Yup, time for home and a damn good shower.' She took off on the final leg home, noticing six green icons on the HUD behind her. And two slowly circling the Nimitz.

Kia touched down and shut everything down. 'Kate, take sleeping beauties to your villa. Sandy will set them up with whatever you need. I am going to head for a shower, and some shut eye for a while.'
Kia walked into her villa and quietly closed the door.
Kate dropped Layla and Jess off at the villa and told them she would be back in a few hours. If they needed anything pick up the phone and the receptionist, Sandy, would answer.

Kate walked into the café and sat heavily in a chair. Brad and Bree walked over, Bree handed her a cup of hot sweet tea. 'So what happened out there? All we know was Sandy scrambled everyone to assist with a possible situation Kia was in.'
'Speaking of Kia, where is she?' asked Paul as he and Glen arrived. Three minutes later everyone had arrived at the café, including Sandy.

Kate looked at Sandy, 'Sorry, the receptionist was the first thing I thought of.'
Sandy smiled, 'It's fine.'
Kate looked at the puzzled look on the others faces, 'Never mind.'
'OK, short debrief. We found Layla and Jess, eventually. We arrived to pick them up same time a chopper with two undesirables arrived. 'The two guys went into the barn to get the girls. Kia walked in to stop them. 'One had a gun and tried to shoot Kia, the other threatened her with a knife. End result, bad men 0 Kia 2.
'We found out that the girls were wearing a short range tracker. I got them into suits, and we headed back here. Just as we reached the West US coast, an incoming message pops up.

'It's from the Nimitz. 'Ron Baker in trouble, high threat risk, but please help if can.''
She sipped some tea.

'And...?' Ray said.

'Kia left me on the flight deck with orders not to leave the S2 no matter what. So I sat there for maybe ten minutes? Next thing I know I am moving at a very high rate away from the boat. Sandy tells me everything is sweet and just to relax. 30 minutes later the S2 returns to Nimitz. Sandy is telling me it's all over, and you guys are there. Kia walks out gets in, and we come home.

'That's all I know. She said she was heading for a shower and sleep, and would see us all in the café in a few hours.'
Glen turned to Sandy, 'What happened on the Nimitz? I know you shadow Kia like a hawk.'

'I am sure she will tell you when she's refreshed. I will, however, tell you she put part of the US Gov back in its place, and she served Fairbanks his just desserts. Now I suggest we get back to work. We have had over 2311 application results for the jobs listed, and Neil the website is live, but has framing issues, that I have had to fix several times already.'
'Kate, your guests just rang me looking for you.'
Several groans could be heard from the group as they moved towards the elevator.

'Anyone NOT busy is welcome to help sort through the Sat data.' There was a concentrated rush to the elevator doors before they shut.

Kia walked into the café looking like she had had a full nights sleep rather than three hours. She was the only one there. She grabbed a sandwich and a large bottle of juice and headed up top. There were people scattered all around the OpCen, all stopped to say hi as Kia walked in. Spying Kate, Miako and the two newbies on the balcony Kia continued out and pulled up a chair at their table. Unwrapping her sandwich she ate while the others chatted. The new girls were asking questions and Kate and Miako were supplying answers.

She was also watching Bree and Melissa through the doorway, they were busy scrolling through pages of applications. Bringing her focus back to the table Miako had just asked Jess what she thought of the island so far. Jess thought for a while and said, 'It's the perfect haven, for the first time in months I feel safe. Obviously, it has nice views and fresh air, but all islands do. On this island, I feel safe.'

Layla nodded her agreement. 'Lots of places we have been lately look nice, or touristy, but nothing beats this feeling of security.'

Kia washed the last of the food down with a mouthful of juice. She looked from one of the newcomers to the other.

'Well, I hope you like it here because this is now your office.

'You three will be one of our layers of protection, Sandy has a dozen or more Sats collecting data. Add to that the scanning data we do, plus radio and web crawlers, she is capable of collating all this logically, and will tell you herself she likes interacting with humans and learning things.

'I know you currently think of Sandy as a big computer, trust me that won't last a day once you start working with her. So that will be your primary job.

'Your secondary job will be to keep an eye on what is happening in the complex once the staff has been selected. 'There may be several institutions that will try and infiltrate us, I'd like you to be aware of that. Now I will give you the same promise I gave Kate.

'You will be safe here, we will all see to that, especially me. Just like in the barn, there is a price for pissing me off.' Both Layla and Jess nodded, remembering what price Kia asked from the guys that were out to hurt them.

'You may pretty well come and go as you please, if you need anything just ask. If you're not sure who to ask, ask Sandy, and last but not least, like I also told Kate, if you turn on us I will fix that permanently.'

Layla and Jess both said they understood.

They were saved from brooding on Kia's last remark as the OpCen guys poured out onto the balcony creating pandemonium, as usual. Kia smiled at the mob, 'So, great saviours of the world, what did you accomplish today?'

'Ray said, 'I managed to accomplish all my tasks that I set for myself today, and I must say it was all done to an exemplary level of perfection!'

'God, you're full of it today, Ray', Melissa said, 'I doubt you could make coffee without spilling it!'

Brad squatted next to Kia, 'We have sorted a staff roster for the complex, now do you want to vet the selected people?'

'Hell No!' Kia said, 'You think I am sadistic and like hurting myself?

'Draw it all up on a HUD, layout a staff ladder and flow chart, like the positions to the applicants, then turn the lot over to the three witches here and get them to sort it.

'Sandy can book a charter to fly them in. The Coven, nice name for these three, they can sort the placements out working with Sandy. Miako, how you feel about designing a staff uniform for the island staff?'

Miako smiled', I would love to have a go at that.'

'Thanks, dear, something simple. Also need ID tags for all staff and a way of tracking them that only Sandy can access. 'No need for us to know, Sandy can tell if there's something suspicious.

'Well, that's the end of my thinking day Kia said stretching. I think Glen and the boys should fire up the new BBQ over there and treat us Ladies to a nice meal and a glass or six of wine.'

Glen turned at the mention of his name and spied the new eight burner BBQ, 'Oh YES!!, now that's a sight to warm a man's heart!'

When told about the fresh meat tray in the café fridge and everything they needed the boys stampeded to the elevator. 15 minutes later they were back with two trolleys loaded with everything they could find.

Chapter Thirty Five

Paul and Glen were sitting on the front deck of their villa having breakfast. Paul was reading the latest newspapers that Sandy put on the kitchen table every morning.
While he read, Glen was watching a line of female bodies doing yoga under the garden rotunda. 'I think Kia likes me.'

Paul looked at him over the top of the paper, 'What the hell makes you think that?'

'Well, look at all the new scenery that she has provided for me.' Glen smirked.

Paul followed Glen's gaze and laughed. 'Well the scenery is better, but I am at a loss how you figure it's for you. Don't answer that' Paul held up his hand. 'Your poor logic will ruin a perfectly satisfying breakfast.'

Glen cleared the plates and refilled the mugs. 'Well, I hope we do something exciting today, it's been a bit quiet of late. It's 6.28am, and I am already getting bored.'

'You could always wash the S2s' Kia said from behind him.

Both of them jumped, 'Damn you walk quiet' Glen accused her as he wiped spilt coffee off the table.

Kia sat next to Glen, Paul folded the paper and tucked it out of the way. 'So young lady what's on your mind?'

'Nothing really, I am sort of in the same funk that Glen's in.'

'So', Paul said standing up', Lets see what kinda trouble we can find today.'

'Hell yes!' Glen agreed. 'Must have been at least 16 hours since we were in trouble.'

Up in the OpCen Sandy was her usual cheery self', Hi guys, how are we all this morning.'

'Honestly? Sandy, bored out of my skull', Glen said.

'I am not surprised' Sandy said. 'You guys are the hunters and for the last 5-6 days have done no hunting. Housework is good for the occasional change, but you need to get out there.'

'Well, give me something to do' Glen said.

Sandy nodded 'You as well Paul?'

'Yes, please.'

Sandy pulled a map up, '466km WSW from here are three shipwrecks, no data, look approx 1944 vintage, go clean them up. This time take an S2 each, there are now 18 in the fleet. Also, here and here are abnormal readings, check them out for me, please. Once done, call in and if anything else has cropped up I will relay it to you.

'Take another crew with you if you like that means you can clear wider strips.'

'Whatever it is we will take it' Melissa said as she arrived with Ray. 'I am going nuts sitting around. What did we get?'

'A few shipwrecks and 2-3 unknowns. Taking an S2 per person, you good with that?' said Glen.

Melissa said, 'Fine by me, was wanting to try a solo run.'

'Love it', Ray said, 'I get to choose the radio station for once!'

Sandy continued 'OK, I am prepping S2-10 through 14 be out the front in ten.'

'I hope they didn't get all the best jobs!' Bree said stepping out of the elevator.

'Oh yeah, Sandy just gave us a line on 2 USO's on the bottom, so there!!'

'No!!' wailed Neil. 'That's so unfair.'

'Relax Neil', Sandy said, 'They are unknown objects. Besides, I have stuff for you as well.' She looked at the other four, 'Go on scoot, you're holding up the parking spaces.'

As Paul opened the elevator doors the newly formed and named Coven walked out. Kate waved and stood to one side with the others.

Sandy turned to the others', OK any of you have a problem taking an S2 each today?' Brad looked at Bree, she smiled, 'All good with me.'

Miako agreed, 'The peace will be a pleasant change.'

'Righto', Sandy said', you guys are heading NNE, up there you will find two old wrecks, clear them, and also there is about 8 Sq km of plastics and debris, it's almost thick enough to walk on, please remove as much as you can. As a lovely bonus, there is a semi-sunken ship there with 4-5 guys living on it. Please do NOT scan the Flip-Ship.'

'The what?' Brad said.

'Awesome! Neil's favourite word echoed around the room. 'A flip-ship is a boat they tow to where they want to take scientific studies, and they sink the stern upright. Kinda like a single legged oil rig, it stands upright until they want to move it again. 'It's really neat.'

Sandy broke the conversation up, 'Your S2s are out on the pads, they are clean, bring them back that way. As I told the others, collect everything in sight.

'Ladies!' Sandy called the Coven over, 'Would it be of benefit to us either now or in the future to stop by a high tech, well known environmental company, and introduce ourselves?' 'Especially as they will be able to bear witness that we are removing 300+ tonnes of floating plastic.'

Layla finally spoke, 'Word of mouth advertising or praise, out values anything you could buy, it's almost priceless in the right ears.'

Sandy nodded. 'As you heard, if you do stop and say hi to the Flip-Ship, it wouldn't be a bad thing. Now Vamoose!' They went out in high spirits, obviously glad to be doing something as well.

'Right, Ladies, see those three screens I fitted over those windows, it's your workspace. You know I am a Hologram. If you need help, call.' Another Sandy stood next to the first, 'There is a lot of me to go round' both Sandy's said in tandem. One disappeared, and the disc slid back into the wall.

Kate took the others over to the new area and picked the centre HUD, firing it up and sitting on a stool each all three started setting up their terminals to suit.

Satisfied that was running smoothly Sandy turned to Kia, 'Now boss, just you and me. What do you want to do today?' Kia thought for a moment, 'I asked Ron Baker to bring his boat further down the west coast. His planes can't reach this far in fuel.

So probably around 4 pm, he should be close enough to take half his F18s back. So really, if you have something close to do, let me know, if not I might just potter about close to base.'

'C/O Baker informs me he has midair re-fuelling available, so any time is fine by him.'

'Oh! OK, then I might do that. The F18s ready to go?'

'Yes, fuelled, charged and washed.'

Kia walked over to a HUD and put a call through to the USS Nimitz.

Acting Commander Anderson took her call, He explained that C/O Baker was rostered off for two days. Kia smiled at the young Officer, 'We all need time off. I called because I promised I would give you guys back ten little birdies.'

A/C Anderson smiled, 'That would be most kind of you.'

'Well, if you would like to prep five pilots, I shall pick them up within the hour, and they can bring the first batch home. Just yell when you are ready.'

'Yes, Ma'am', came the reply.

Kia broke the connection. She then pulled up a map showing all the S2s locations. Sandy said 'They are fine Kia.'

'I know, it's just habit I guess. I see they are all proudly using FF beacons now.'

Sandy nodded, 'Yes they wear them proudly, and they also have done this. Eight screens popped up next to each other.

Each one listed materials recovered and quantity. They have started score sheets on themselves, and make believe badges and awards. Like a stats scoreboard.'

Kia laughed, 'That's why they didn't mind taking an S2 each this morning! No need to share scores now. Nothing like a bit of friendly competition.'

'The best thing is', added Sandy', That there can be no cheating. Scanned data does not lie.'

'Well, I shall take my time and cruise to the meeting point. Keep those three busy and get them into shape. Any news on the last one of the group?'

'Yes, I have located her, she is back in the UK, but there is something strange going on. It looks like she is back with MI6. I need to analyse this further.

Kia frowned at that, 'OK keep me in the loop. Get the Coven to start hammering out the staff levels. The Norwegian and German teams are going to be here in a few days.' With a last look around she headed to the elevator.
Four minutes later she was in the air, another three minutes later she was skimming along the sea bottom.

****

Melissa was voted as leader for the day so she took point. She took them above water half way and then descended to skimming mode, four abreast just off the bottom. With the craft to craft coms set open they could hear and talk to each other as if they were in the same room.

Occasionally one of them would get a flag that needed personal attention, but for the most part, the trip out to the zone was uneventful.

Paul spied the first wreck, it stood upright on the sand, like someone had put it down and forgot about it.
They circled the hull, no signs of why it would have sunk, no name on the back or port of registry. Ray started a scan from the bow rearwards, closely followed by Glen.

At the end of both scans, Sandy confirmed good data transfer and Paul beamed it out, as they had started to call it.

Melissa did a few small circles around the site looking for any debris around the wreck and cleaned anything she found.

Arriving back, she came across the guys waiting for her. 'That was strange that one, ok boys line up on mama, and we go to the next waypoint.' Smoothly and silently they moved off. Behind them was a large depression on the bottom that the sand was already slowly filling in. Soon there would be no trace a ship had ever been there.

****

Brad was leading the other team's effort for the day. They chose to skim the water all the way to the first waypoint. 1000m from waypoint they dropped into the water and did a slow spiral to the bottom. It was very hilly in this region.

'The terrain is going to be a PIA!' Bree said, 'Lucky most of the stuff we are looking for is floating.'

Everyone lined up, the new S2s allowing them to see each other from the wrap around screen. At Brad's signal, they started their search. They found their first wreck after 20 minutes. It was a midsized fishing trawler, and it looked like it had caught something large in its dragnet as the back of the trawler had been ripped out.

They probably snagged one of these seamounts', Bree said. Over the next three hours they located and removed 13 wrecks, this definitely was an area of convergence of ocean currents.
Most of the wrecks were fishing vessels. Four of which raised flags for human remains. What they mostly found was tonnes and tonnes of debris that would have floated at one time, but over many years became waterlogged and sank. This convergence zone was almost like a natural occurring rubbish collection area.

The biggest plague was, once again old fishing nets.

Miako found a huge ball of nets in a hollow sand basin. The current had obviously been rolling the netting around and around as it slowly formed into a ball. Picking up more pieces over the years.

Neil found two old WWII mines from flags. Surprisingly, they found the centre area of the zone fairly clear of debris.

Neil and Miako started a two craft spiral clearance run to the surface, checking just how much suspended plastic there was in the water. After the third run to the surface, it was found that the contamination level was not as bad as they feared it might have been.

Halfway through the day, they ascended to the surface. Even the winds in this area seemed confused which way to blow. The air was still apart from a few breezes, and the water was like a lake. Neil spotted the movement on the Sonar HUD first. It was 400 metres below the surface and approaching from the east. He tapped the icon on the screen with a finger, and a dialogue bubble opened up.

USS Olympia (SSN 717) 110.3m x 10m x 9.8.

Current Command CDR MJ Boone.

'Oh hey guys, look we have a big fish approaching.'

Brad's voice came in. 'We will stay on the surface, that way we don't bump into them.

'Sandy', Brad called, 'Is there any way to get in touch with the Flip-Ship? It's not here that we can see.'

'Hang on a moment', came her reply. 15 minutes went by.

'Prof. Mark Brandon is in control of the Flip-Ship, and he is, now, aware of your presence. I explained what you are doing in the area and asked him if he would be so kind as to share any data with you.

He is most enthused to meet you. You have the waypoint in the Nav.'

'Thanks, Sandy, We are on our way.' They stayed stationary until the Olympia had passed out of range of the Sonar, then turned and followed the Nav data Sandy had sent.

As they approached Brad gave them a call.
 Prof Brandon answered the call after a few minutes of chat Brad told the professor they had them in sight and would see them shortly.

The Flip Ship was a very strange sight, for those that didn't know what it was. It looked like a ship had started to sink bow first. Stood on its nose and stuck the bow into the sand and stayed there. Stern clear of the water. That is literally what it was. A ship that they could deliberately sink upright, to turn it from a ship into a tower with a research facility on top.

This time, the ship was not touching the bottom, but floating free and had ground anchors out to hold it in place. There were some steel booms out sideways from the ship that looked like they housed an array of antennae and one long boom out the front for loading supplies off tenders.

The S2s came to a halt at the base of the ship. One behind the other.

Neil was last in line and moved down the line picking up first Miako, Bree, and then Brad. Once all were on board, he lifted up level with the lower platform on the Flip-Ship and nice as pie magnetically locked the S2 in place. All four disembarked into the clutches of Prof. Brandon and the astounded scientists.

Deck chairs appeared and a large folding table. After a round of introductions from both sides, everyone took a seat.
Brad took the lead and explained what Oracle was about, and its current work charter. He also made it clear he couldn't divulge how they did what they did, but gave a simplified explanation.

Mark and the other guys, were more than happy to share info they knew about environmental issues not only of this location but of many others that they had charted.
Hot chocolate was brought out by the jug full, and many stories flew across the table over the next hour or so. Mark was very surprised to hear that the most common pollutant was fishing nets.

Bree shook her head, 'That stuff is everywhere.' Bree handed the conversation over to Miako to explain about the large ball she had removed earlier. Mark and the others were absorbed, listeners.

'Do you have a laptop handy?' Neil asked.
One of the hands ducked into a doorway and was back with a laptop. He held it out to Neil. Neil put it on the table facing the Flip-Ship crew.

'It has Wi-Fi yes?' Mark nodded. Neil put an ear piece in, 'Sandy?'

'Yes, Neil?'

'Can you sync with this laptop on the Flip-Ship?'

'Give me a few moments to relay from your S2. OK, got it.'

'Please play the video cap we took on Miako's S2 of the ball of netting.'

A few seconds later the laptop screen burst into life with a high resolution video of what Miako had found. Mark and the others were totally stunned at the content!

At the conclusion of the video, the conversation turned to plastics. Bree explained they had run tests from 2000m to the surface and were surprised that there wasn't a higher concentrate of plastics.

Mark explained 'That's because this convergence area was a deep one. Meaning mostly from 500m down had a convergence effect.' He grabbed a map and marked three areas.

'These are shallow zones, so from the 500m level and up to the surface. These areas are the places that the floating debris was more prolific.'

Conversation travelled across many and varied subjects, but all in all, the guys from the Flip-Ship were pleased that someone was doing something about the state of the water.

'We are willing to clean a mess up once, but we are not going to do it again and again. Mankind has to learn from its mistakes and modify its habits.' Brad said.

The scientists agreed fully with that comment.

Bree stood and shook hands with Mark, 'You have our radio and contact details. If something happens you think we can help with, just give us a yell. Time for us to get back to work.'
There followed a round of handshakes and pats on the shoulder, and the guys jumped back into Neil's S2. He dropped them off at their craft and joined the outside formation as they dived for the bottom.

*****

The next waypoint on Melissa's Nav was one of the unknowns. They were all in scan/beam mode as they cruised onwards. 18 minutes later Melissa pulled everyone up.
There in front of them was the unknown object. Paul laughed.
'Now that is something you don't see every day!'
Glen circled right around the target. In front of them on a flat lava outcrop, was a complete steam locomotive and coal tender.

'That had to have fallen off a transport ship, probably in rough seas' Ray suggested.

'No!' Mel said 'I thought it made it this far and ran out of coal! Of course, it fell off something, or it was dumped off if some transporter was trying to shed weight. Ray, you may do the honours, Glen can do the second scan.'

They all took one last look, and it was gone. Melissa punched up the next waypoint, and they headed off, again in scan/beam mode.

The next wreck they came to was a huge ore carrier. It was in at least six pieces. It looked like it had failed at every third bulkhead. After scanning it Sandy asked them just to remove the ship. The thousands of tonnes of iron ore could stay where it was. It was no harm to the area. The defragmented nature of the wreck kept all four of them busy for a while. Finally, it was done.

'All right, one unknown left, then back to base.

Paul can take point.'
Paul punched the waypoint into the Nav, and they formed up on him as he left. It took them quite a while to arrive at the next waypoint, not so much because of the distance involved, more due to the amount of debris and fishing nets they encountered on the way.

Finally, Paul swung around the last seamount and came face to face with the unknown.
'Well, don't we just have a day full of surprises', Melissa said. Paul scanned the object and punched up a silhouette search. All of them slowly circled the object.
'So', Glen said, 'What is it? I mean I know what it IS, but not exactly what it is.'
Ray got the results from the search.
'That my dear friends, is a DC-3-362 cargo plane.'
Melissa read out the barely legible tail number, HS-000.
Sandy, joined in the conversation.
'HS-000 was a DC-3-362 cargo plane belonging to the Thai Government. It was logged as lost on July 25th, 1966, with the loss of all crew. It had a crew of three according to the info I have.'
'Thanks, Sandy. The scan shows three flags, the crew I take it', Paul said.
'Beam it out' Sandy said, 'we can sort the Thai Gov out later..'
Everything about the plane looked like it was intact, it even semi-stood on its landing gear. The cockpit glass was intact but covered with silt. The entire plane looked like it had landed there on purpose. Tendrils of algae hung off the wings and body like it was trying to hide from the world.
'Funny that they would put the gear down even while making a crash landing. I know it was a crash landing because none of the props is bent', explained Ray. 'That means the props were not turning when it hit the water. There is no obvious damage to the plane. Might pull this one up one day, just to see what's inside.'

Melissa and Glen ran a scan from wing tip to wing tip, and Paul beamed it out.

'All good, last waypoint is home so Sandy has plotted a scan and burn run for us as an option if we don't want to fly straight back.'

'Sounds good to me', Ray said, 'Load us up in autopilot and watch the scenery.'

Melissa took point and selected the route Sandy programmed.

They all did the same and off they went. Now, just passengers to the Nav system and the TFSR.

*****

Bree was running point by the time they were at their next waypoint. The Flip-ship was 55km behind them as they slowed at the waypoint.

'Nothing here that I can see', commented Neil.

'Me neither' chimed in Brad. 'Lets do a 300m circle around the waypoint, just in case it's not accurate.'

At the end of that sweep nothing major was located, so it was decided to take it out another 300m.

On the second sweep they started to get a return in the sonar HUD, Miako was on the outer end of the line and saw the target first. Laying on its side was a container ship, one of the smaller versions.

It was on a gravel slope, uphill from the wreck were track marks. They showed the wreck was slowly sliding down the slope and had moved 500m easily in the last few weeks.

'Ah-Ha!' Miako said 'the mysterious case of the moving waypoint! There obviously is enough air trapped in the wreck and containers to make it almost neutrally buoyant and the bottom current is pushing it down hill.'

Neil and Brad did the scan of the wreck and Bree beamed it out. Miako followed Bree back up the track the wreck had left and picked up a few containers on the way.

Miako put a call into Sandy. 'We are at the last waypoint before home. It had moved, but we found it.'

'Excellent news' Sandy said.

'Now the route back you gave us, wanders off line a fair bit. Is that correct?'

'Yes, that route back closely follows one of the trade routes. Statistically, trade routes have the most debris field along them. The route you were sent has been taken from old, very old maps.

It is different than the modern route taken by modern ships. The route you have is designed to use trade winds not diesel to travel along it.'

'Righto, now it makes sense. See you when we get back.' Brad took the left outer end and Neil the right outer end as they lined up. Set in Scan/Beam mode, they set off. Following the Nav and TFSR.

Chapter Thirty Six

Kia was enjoying the ride. It wasn't often that she was free of stress. She had two screens locked on where and what the others were doing, another screen was locked in TFSR mode. She had headed east towards the US coastline and turned north just before the US water boundary. Safely 100m inside international waters, Kia set in Scan/Beam mode and followed the coastline. Two hours into the run up the coast and Kia got a call from the Nimitz informing her that the pilots were assembling as requested. Kia thanked the radio operator and told them she would be there in 20 minutes.

She kicked off the scan/beam mode as it reduced maximum speed, and replotted a direct route to the Nimitz.
8km from the Nimitz, Kia was still skimming the bottom when all hell broke loose. The Nav broke off the set course and took evasive action. Collision warnings sounded, but the S2 was too nimble. Kia pulled up to the right and stopped, not more than six feet away was a submarine slowly heading away from the direction of the Nimitz.
Kia turned the scanner on and ran along the sub from props to tip.

Looking at the return data, she said 'Well, well, well, what are you doing here, Hmmm?'
She took some pictures and spun around and headed for the surface.

'USS Nimitz this is Oracle S2-1 requesting permission to land.'
'Oracle S2-1 permission granted, be aware, several craft on deck.'

Kia surfaced about 100m behind the Nimitz and nice and neatly set the S2 down close to the doorway in a vacant area indicated by the deck controller. She was met just outside by Ron Baker dressed in jeans and a T-shirt.

'Must be nice to get a weekend off.'

Ron grinned, 'It's not often enough, but the worst part is, even when I am off duty, there is nowhere to go.'

Kia laughed, 'Can you take me up to see your man in charge at the moment?'

'Sure', Ron said, 'is there a problem?'

'Not sure, I don't think so.'

Ron walked onto the bridge first and introduced Kia to the acting commander. Kia then told him about the Sub she saw slinking from the area about ten minutes ago and handed a handful of pictures over to A/C Anderson.

The sail number identified it as a Chinese Ming Class Sub.

Kia said 'It was in international waters, JUST, but I thought you would like to know.'

Ron looked through the pictures and handed them back to Anderson.

'I am officially off duty for another 48 hours, so you can worry about these instead of me.'

Kia said, 'OK, where are these pilots of yours?'

Anderson said, 'They should be on the flight deck by the time you get there. Can't you take Ron as well, he is a pain in the ass when he's off duty.'

Kia, thought for a moment, 'Actually, that's not a bad idea, I'll bring him back tomorrow afternoon.'

Ron's eyes opened, 'Really!!, that would be exceptional.'

'Love my carrier, but a day away is nice too. What do I need to bring?'

'Nothing', Kia said, 'lets go.'

Back on the flight deck, there were five pilots standing out in the sun.

'Follow me, guys and girls.' Kia opened the S2 up and showed them to the four seats at the back.

'Someone is going to have to sit on the floor, sorry.'

The tallest guy smiled and said 'No problem Ma'am, as long as I have something to hold on to.'

Ron stood in the doorway, 'Sit here Ron', and pointed to the second pilot chair.

She shut the door and leant against the seat.

'Before we go, there are two ways we can do this, the comfortable way or the painful way. The only difference between the two is you guys. My craft has G-force dampers, now if you don't mention that, I can use them, and we have a pleasant trip. If you remember that I said that, I couldn't use them, and it becomes a rough ride. So it's your call.'

One of the female pilots spoke up, 'Scuse me ma'am, but can you speak up? I haven't been able to hear a thing you have been saying.'

Kia smiled and dropped into the seat. She lifted off and turned on the spot. The deck officer checked she was clear to go and Kia accelerated down the centre of the carrier runway, and promptly dropped straight into the water!

That made the pilots cringe. Ron laughed, 'That was the only time you guys are allowed to do that!' He said over his shoulder to the pilots.

Kia punched in some CoOrds and called Sandy.

'Sandy, on the way back with my passengers. On the way in, I passed a sub lurking about. You got a track on that?'

Sandy said she didn't but would go looking.

Kia said 'Never mind, I have it on sonar now thanks.'

Kia closed at an alarming rate until she was just over the screws of the sub. She pulled to the left and slowly travelled the length of the sub. 'There you are Ron, that was your visitor.'

All the pilots and Ron were mesmerised by the sight of a sub so close it looked like they could touch it.

'Well, like you said it's international waters, but it's still unnerving to know they are prowling so close.'

Kia agreed and took off heading up to the surface.

About 1500 meters in front of the sub she broke the surface and headed for the Island.

One of the pilots pointed to a number on the Nav HUD and asked if that was the height over the water because it seemed a bit lower than that out the window. Kia glanced at the 2800.78 figure, No she said, that's our speed in KPH.

'Holy Hell!' Ron said, '2.8 that's not bad for a sub!'

Kia smiled, 'Neil, one of the young guys you have met, has wound his out to 9.7 before running out of room. Me, I actually like to see things.'

The rest of the trip was made up of a question and answer session. Kia was used to that by now and was pleased that people cared enough to ask questions. On arrival at the island, Kia took the S2 down the airstrip and dropped it onto the concrete before one of the large hangars.

As everyone climbed out, the massive doors started opening.

Inside, lined up nice and neat were 10 F18-E's Kia stood and watched as the pilots went through their well-trained routine prepping the fighters for flight. Walking to the hangar wall, she took down a clipboard and tore the top sheet off. She walked back to where Ron was standing and handed him the sheet.

He looked at it and then raised a questioning glance to Kia. 'This looks like a fault sheet.'

'That was all the faults Sandy found with the fighters and repaired them.'

Ron folded the sheet and put it in his pocket. 'I know a master sergeant that's going to be happy to see that list.'

One by one the fighters spooled up and made their way outside and lined up, down the runway. With a last test of the control surfaces, each one thundered down the runway and up into the afternoon sky with a powerful roar.

She led Ron back to the S2 and made the short jump up to the normal landing pad.

Together they walked into the café, where Kia showed Ron the restrooms and coffee machine and food bar.

Kia handed Ron a beer from the fridge which he took with a smile. 'Now how did you know my favourite beer?'

Kia sipped her hot chocolate, 'Because a good host always knows what her guest likes. You have shown me yours now let me show you mine' Kia said leading him to the elevator. Up one floor, they walked into the OpCen.

Kate came over, and Kia introduced her to Ron.

All three walked over to the Coven's work area, and introduced Ron to Jess and Layla.

Kia asked Kate if they were busy on anything at the moment.

'Nothing that couldn't wait a while, what's up?'

Kia smiled and held up one finger in the "wait a min" posture.

'Ron, I would like to introduce you to Sandy. Sandy this is Ron Baker. As you know, he is commanding officer of the USS Nimitz.'

Sandy's voice came out of thin air. 'Welcome, Commander Baker to the Oracle Operations Centre.'

Ron smiled, 'Sandy is your computer! Wow, Hello, Sandy!'

Kia smiled, 'Oh she is much, much more to us than a computer. Sandy come out and say hello properly.'

A disc hissed out of the receptacle high in the wall and hovered silently over in front of Ron and the girls. Ron took a step back as the Hologram burst into life.

'Sorry Ron, I am a bit shy with newcomers.'

Ron laughed, 'This is amazing!'

Sandy turned to Kia, 'You were about to ask Kate something?'

Kia turned Ron to face the closest HUD, please bring up the sub that we saw hanging around the Nimitz. Instantly there was a picture of the sub. 'What can you tell me about it?'

'Well, going by the sail number. It is the new SSK QING class submarine. There is no solid data on how many of these China has. Suffice to say that they have at least one that is operational. From the scan you took Kia, it has 12 top hatches and six forward and four rearward torpedo tubes. It is 122.6 meters long and 12x10 meters wide.'

'Crew size 65-73 worked out on the dimensions of the hull and averaging out the crew to the volume of 17 other types of sub.
I have transmitted this information to A/C Anderson.'
'Thank you', Ron said.
Sandy cleared the HUD and displayed an overhead map of where the Nimitz was, also the five F18s and the air tanker.
'The sub has left the area, and the planes are on course for the tanker that is orbiting here. With each statement the HUD showed icons.'
Kia turned to Kate.' Would you be so kind to see if there is any info on why the sub was in the area? If you find anything, relay it to the Nimitz.' Kate nodded and got to work.
'Brad has just landed. Melissa's about 32 minutes out. Brad's crews total for today is just shy of 176,000 tonnes.'
Ron cleared his throat, 'Tonnes of what, may I ask?'
Sandy opened another window, 'Mostly scrap steel, plastics, fishing nets, shipping containers, basically garbage that mankind has been tossing in the oceans and seas since he first found the shore.'
Kia took Ron by the arm and led him out onto the balcony. She asked Layla to grab another beer for Ron and a refill for her.
Ron was looking over the complex and watching the crew approaching the tower. So Kia, tell me honestly, what was your real reason for bringing me here? I know it wasn't because you felt sorry that I was bored.'
'It was a little, and also because I wanted at least one guy in the US military to know for sure what we did, and the fact that we do not present any threat to them at all. Let me be brutally honest here. If the US Gov decides they want our technology and try to take it from us. It's going to get very ugly, very fast, as you saw on the Nimitz. I know they can't do it. You are informed enough to be unsure. It's a situation I want to avoid like the plague. This tech is not for the war machines of this world.

'Each and every one of us is willing to die to make sure this never ends up in the wrong hands.'

Ron nodded somberly.' I do hope that common sense prevails. I believe it will. Just hopefully sooner than later.'

'I have a favour to ask, Ron. It's not mission crucial, but it would be nice if you could find someone to talk to regarding getting the crew and remains of both the Thresher and the Scorpion back. I would be much happier if they were no longer on Eternal Patrol and two reactors and several nukes were no longer rolling around the bottom of our oceans.'

Ron nodded, 'I don't know who is in charge of that, but I do know of several people who may know. A kind of, friend of a friend situation.'

'Fair enough', Kia said, 'I can't ask for more than that.'

At that moment the elevator exploded with highly enthusiastic and charged up people.

'As you can see half of the unruly mob have returned, and here comes the other half.' Ron swivelled in the seat to watch four S2s circle the tower and slide one after the other into the landing pads no more than 3-4 feet apart.

'OK', Ron laughed, 'So these things are actually silent?'

Kia grinned, 'We do have some secrets!'

'You guys are amazing! I just wish I was younger.'

'We have no age limit. If you ever do retire from the Navy, come look us up. You never know.'

Brad and the crew spilled out onto the balcony. Spotting Ron, Brad grinned and shook his hand warmly.

'So nice to meet you again! Hope we are not in some kind of trouble?'

'Not at all Ron smiled, Kia gave me back five of my fighters and invited me for a look-see.'

'Great, then you will be staying for our new found pastime, breaking in the BBQ!'

Three extra tables were dragged over and chairs for everyone.

The second crew piled into the OpCen and talked to Sandy for a while, then they too joined everyone on the balcony. Sitting in a huge square made by the three tables together Ron was entertained by stories of things that the crew had seen. Sometimes the story was embellished somewhat and subject to good-natured ridicule. As the sun slowly started to set, the BBQ was dragged out with great enthusiasm, and for the rest of the evening, a great time was had by all.

Early next morning Kia was up in the OpCen. She was discussing the staff applications that the team had processed over the last few days.

'So they all filled?' asked Kia.

'Most of them are on paper, we need to get the majority over here from the mainland and get things moving. Some will stay, some will leave. It will take about six months to settle into something fairly stable.' Kate replied.

'Just get it all happening please. I don't want any additional headaches.'

Kate replied, 'Understood.'
Brad and Bree had arrived with Ron Baker, who had stayed as a guest in their villa after the BBQ last night.

'I am sorry Ron, would it be OK if I get Brad and Bree to run you home and return with your Pilots for the remaining F18s?'

'That will be more than fine, and I have to thank you not only for the help but your hospitality from you and everyone here.'

Kia gave Ron a quick hug and shook his hand. 'Remember, we are just a call away if you get stuck.'
Ron waved goodbye to all and left accompanied by Brad and Bree. Just a few short minutes later an S2 zoomed past the windows and headed towards the Californian coastline.

'Right, what's next? Who's next?'

Sandy said ',The other six are in one of the hangars near the airport, and that's all I am going to say.'

Kia looked at Sandy, 'They are worse than kids sometimes!'
That had Kate and Jess laughing.

Chapter Thirty Seven

Kia found them in the next hangar over from the F18s. 'What are you overgrown hooligans up to?' Kia said as she entered the hangar. Standing in the middle of the hangar was a DC-3 with a tail number of HS-000. She walked around the plane, 'Well, that's different, you guys found this on your last trip out?'

Melissa nodded, 'It was one of Sandy's unknowns.'

'Have you a story on it?'

Ray supplied the background info. 'Apparently, it belonged to the Thai Gov, went missing in 1966, and was used as a cargo plane. The only reason we wanted a look at it was because it was standing with its landing gear down, props as you can see not bent. So it was a bit of a mystery why it was where it was.'

'I think it's good that you want to learn and discover the reasons behind some of the stuff we will come across. You won't be able to ReCon anything dangerous or nasty as Sandy won't let you. There are fail-safes in place just for that reason. If you want to investigate it more, ask Sandy to analyse it.'

'Well, we wanted to look kinda for ourselves, rather than read a list on a HUD.'

'Fair enough', Kia said, 'But she can still make it easier to investigate.'

'How so?' asked Paul.

'Easy' Kia said, 'Would you like a demo just this once?'

'Hell yes', Paul and Neil said together.

'Sandy get rid of the DC3 please', and it was beamed out. 'OK, put it back, on the floor, cut up the centre nose to tail.

'Three feet apart, please. Chock wing tips.'

The DC-3 reappeared, but this time as per request was cut from nose to tail perfectly and was laid on the floor with plastic wing-tip chocks to stabilise the two halves.

Kia walked down the centre of the plane easily seeing what it contained. 'Sandy, any theories why?'

'No good ones, however, the CoPilot and Nav guy both have bullet holes in the back of their skulls, and the pilot has one from the roof of her mouth through the top of her head. Yes, the pilot was female. The gun is laying in her lap. This suggests she shot herself after the impact with the water. If she shot herself before, the gun would probably be on the floor from the G-Force of impact. The cargo seems just various innocent cargo, nothing of great value.'

'So it's not like it was a heist to get 400kg of raw diamonds to a certain spot in the ocean, or gold bars. That is as far as I got with this.'

'I suggest you get the Coven to look into all the cargo and paperwork, and then loading manifests from where ever it departed from if you need to find out more.'

'Thank you, Sandy' Melissa said.

Paul stood looking at the skeletal remains strapped in the pilot seat. Corroded gun in its lap. 'What a mystery you are, look at all the questions you left behind. One day, not this day, but one day I will revisit you, and look for more answers.'

With that Paul and Kia walked out of the hangar, leaving the others to look around the cargo.

Kia was leaning on the railing when an S2, came sliding into view and dropped neatly near the airstrip. She couldn't see it on the ground, but knew what it was doing. A short time later there came the sound of jet engines spooling up to speed.

Then came the thundering roar as two, four, five F18-E fighters took to the air. They circled the island once formed up in a diamond formation and did a flyby past the tower.

She waved as they went past.

The S2 skipped over the buildings and landed on its pad. From where she was standing she could see seven people get out. Checking the clock on the wall, it was 8.37am. Damn these early mornings she muttered to herself and headed inside.

'Sandy, get me the Russian Environmental on the phone, please. Preferably a Sergei Donsky.'

Sandy stared for a moment and then nodded.

Six minutes later, Sandy called Kia over to a HUD, 'Sergei is online, no video.'

'Hello Mr. Donsky, how are you this morning?'

'Fine! Came a deep baritone voice, and what can I do for Oracle this morning?'

'Mr. Donsky, are you aware of who Oracle are and what we do?'

'We are aware of who Oracle are, and we are also aware that you like giving the USN a bloody nose.'

She smiled, 'Mr. Donsky, Sergei, if I may call you that, my name is Kia, and I think we need to meet.'

'I would like that', Sergei said, 'Where and when?'

'That is totally up to you, I need a days notice, and can be anywhere you ask. As long as I get clearance for Oracle to use Russian airspace for the day. I really would prefer not to give out any more blood noses.'

Sergei's hearty laugh came as no surprise.

'If you have an office somewhere with a lawn big enough for a helicopter or a helipad close that would be just fine. There will be just the three of us, myself and two others.'

'Of course, you will have security close by no-doubt?' Sergei asked.

'Do I really need to, Sergei?'

'No, Not at all, how does 1 pm tomorrow sound?'

'That's fine, I should be finished with the Royal Family from Norway by then. Goodbye till then.' Sandy cut the connection.

Kate walked over 'Did I just hear right? Are you walking into the lions den in the heart of Russia?' Kia nodded, 'Yes, and what's more I am taking some of you with me.'

'What are you up to? You are worse than the kids for being sneaky!' Asked Sandy.

'Nothing much, I am just going to sort out Russia.' With that, she walked into the elevator and closed the door before either of them could get their mind around what she had just said.

Down in the café Kia was sitting with her feet up on another chair when Ray and Melissa walked in. They waved, and she waved back. A few moments later, armed with bacon and eggs, toast and hot coffee, they sat down at the table next to her. She asked them if they found anything else strange about the DC-3 after she left.

Mel shook her head, 'We opened a few of the cargo crates but found nothing of value.

Miako came up with a theory that maybe they dropped what-ever it was off by parachute to a boat before flying off else-where to ditch the plane. Who knows, it could have been a love triangle between the three of them that went bad. It's just frustrating not knowing', Melissa grinned.

Kia nodded, 'I think the frustration comes with any job.'

The sound of the elevator chime signaled the arrival of more people. Half an hour later all the breakfasts were mostly over and done with, and all the plates cleared away. Neil turned to Kia and asked her what she had planned for them today.

'The next few days are going to be a bit hectic. We are get-ting plane loads of staff in today to start bringing the complex to life, Sandy is busting her CPUs doing a gazillion things that need doing. The Coven will be down here shortly. So relax while you can, from what I understand from the lists Kate has, rest is going to be in short supply for awhile.' She stood, 'I will be upstairs in the OpCen if you need me.'

Kia was looking at weather patterns over northern Europe.

Sandy came over, 'You aren't joining in the welcoming committee, Kia?'

Kia grinned, 'For the worlds smartest AI you ask some silly questions sometimes. That's going to be all kinds of hell down there, no thank you. I am much happier taking on the Russians.'

'Oh Yes, you're going to take over Russia, I remember that bombshell', Sandy said.

'Well, not take over exactly, more like, assist in their environmental issues.'

Sandy just stared at her.

'Come on Sandy, you know it makes perfect sense. That country is just about on its knees, from being one of the worlds superpowers to being the most screwed up country. I know it, you know it and you can bet your ass they know it. They do not have the time, the money, or the ability to fix it. We have.

Sandy still said nothing.

'They have no other option, do they? Take 60 seconds of CPU time, and then tell me I am wrong.'

Sandy looked at Kia, 'I don't need 60 seconds, and I am going back to work, here comes the first arrivals.'

Kia smiled at Sandy and walked out onto the balcony to watch the approaching airliner land.

After touchdown, Kia walked over to the elevator, 'I might have a look after all.'

Chapter Thirty Eight

Kia stood off to one side in the arrivals lounge watching all shapes and sizes of people milling around. Some already had made friends, some still unsure.
It made her smile. Life really is one big adventure.

There was an orderly chaos to everything. Neil was having a ball, racing back and forth with the buggy. Ray was smiling, hell everyone seemed to be on the plus side of happy.
Bree stopped next to Kia.' Hey boss, came to see the circus?'
Kia laughed, 'So how is it going?'
'Fairly smoothly, we only had one case of the ego monster, and she ran into Miako. Instant fix, we don't exactly know what Miako whispered in her ear while she was shouting, but she now is a model guest.
'Now the complex has life, now it feels to me like a real entity, I know this may sound stupid, I don't like crowds, but I don't like being alone either. Big island and eight of us was a bit lonely.'
Kia nodded, 'I get that totally. In fact, I think I may come down here occasionally, just to feel the ambience of people moving about, different voices, and different laughter.'
'Perfectly put', agreed Bree.
Melissa whizzed past with eight people on a trolley headed for the accommodation sector, she smiled and waved on the way past.
 Bree continued, 'You do know that by giving these people a good place to work and a good job. Oracle is adding more good Karma to the planet.

'These happy people will make our guests we invite happy. They, in turn, will make the people they interact with happy. It's a pay it forward situation.'

'So you don't think this is a bad idea then?' Kia asked.

'Hell no. Look at us, you came to us with an idea to clean up the planet. That's it. Scan the shit, beam it out, move on. Now while that will work all by itself, we have tweaked it a bit, instead of just beaming it out, we now use some of it to educate. Sometimes about human history, sometimes about the human future.

'That is a huge bonus, it is almost as important as your original idea. If we could click our fingers and the planet is clean in one day. What do you think will happen in 30 years? Some of the errors made in the past will just be repeated, make that most of the errors. Education is paramount to avoid future errors.'

While they were talking Glen had loaded the last of the new arrivals onto his trolley and zoomed off with them.
Bree and Kia walked over to where Kate, Jess, and Layla were sitting at their counter.

'How did it go ladies?'

Kate looked up from her tablet, 'Actually, quite painless.'

A few hours later they stood on the balcony of the OpCen, looking at the complex with lights in windows that had stood dark for so long, and listening to the distant sounds of people moving around.
Even up on the tower balcony, they could hear the music and laughter. The whole place had taken on a feeling of home, instead of just a head office.
Miako said what most of them were thinking, 'This is much better!'

Kate explained that while nothing was happening in the complex tomorrow, the day after, the research crews were arriving from Norway and Germany.

Kia sat everyone down and said she had a few things to do tomorrow, and would like Melissa, Ray, Glen and Paul with her for one or two days. The others can help Kate with the settling in process. However, if she needed them for any reason, be prepared to haul ass. 'Tomorrow they are going to pay the Russians a visit, and it should be quite interesting.'

As pre-arranged, at 6 am the next morning, four S2s lifted off and turned towards the Bering Strait. Just after midday they were approaching the White Sea, having made most of the trip over water. As they crossed the coast, Ray and Glen turned off their FF beacons. They all knew the Russians had been tracking them for hours, but now they could only see 2 S2s.

Kia and Paul were in the lead S2, and Melissa was in the second with Neil. Neil had asked to join at the last minute. At 12.58pm Kia landed at the CoOrds she had received from Sergei. Neil dropped in next to her. Only Kia and Paul left the S2, Mel and Neil making sure no one touched Kia's craft. Perched not more than 600m away on the top of a flat-roofed church, were two other S2s in Camo mode. Just sitting very still, like vultures.
Sergei Donsky and two guards met Kia and Paul at the entrance to the office building they had landed in front off. After introductions, they were escorted inside and up to the top floor where Sergei's office was.
The guards stayed outside the building entrance.
Sergei sat in an old overstuffed chair after waiting for his guests to be seated.
'I am very pleased to meet you' he said 'And at the same time very interested in why you would want to talk to us.'
Kia smiled, 'Sergei, you are a smart man. I know you probably have a file on both myself and Oracle. However, we both know it's a very thin file. I also know that normally you record all the conversations held in this room. But, not at this moment.'

'This conversation is off the record at this point, and after I have finished telling you why we are here, I think you will understand.'

Sergei smiled, 'I told them that this would happen, but you know old habits die hard with Russians.'

Kia nodded, 'it's quite prophetic that you chose those words, they are exactly the reason why I wanted to talk to you face to face.'

Sergei pushed a button, within seconds an orderly appeared, 'Coffee please', he asked and the orderly bowed and left again. 'We don't all drink vodka every day he said with a smile.'

Paul had a chuckle at that, 'Probably not, but I have a feeling we will all want one or three before we are done here today.' The orderly was back with a tray, he placed it on Sergei's desk and left.

Sergei did the honours and poured everyone a cup. Sitting down he took a sip, 'Let us begin, I am a very good listener.'

Kia began, 'Firstly, I would like to make it clear, I do not lie. Anything I say to you that I or we can do is the truth. Secondly, we are not politically motivated. You probably already know that, but it doesn't hurt to make it clear from the beginning. From the time you sat back down in the chair, this conversation is now being recorded.

 Not only by your people, but by mine as well. You are aware we have two additional units close for my protection, and I am aware you have three squads standing by close at hand. None of these will be necessary, but as you say, old Russian habits die hard. I came here today to start a dialogue between our two parties.

'Russia, as you know, is just about stuffed. Your economy is almost dead in the water like most of the European countries, your food supply is dwindling. 70% of your ground water is poisonous and undrinkable. Public dissatisfaction is high.

'Most of the world looks at Russia as a has-been superpower who is slowly falling to pieces, and actually, they are correct.

Russia, as it stands today, is just about screwed. We are here to help you fix that.

I would like you to get me an audience with your President. Once I have spoken to him and got his views on what we have to offer. Then a decision can be made whether Russia is going to self-destruct, or if you are willing to let us help fix it.

Sergei, was quiet for a moment, looking directly at Kia over the rim of his cup. 'You paint a very bleak picture of the future of Russia.'

She nodded, 'It's not your fault, and many things were done over many decades by your previous governments and leaders. 'There is a large cost to be paid to be such a powerful nation. All the previous rulers, ignored that cost or bypassed what needed to be done.'

'Now the people of Russia are paying for those bad decisions. Again I say, not this government's fault. It's a situation that todays Russians have inherited. Some of your current government knows what needs to be done to fix things, others are still in denial and believe it will be just fine, even so, Russia does not have the finances, the ability, or the means to fix what needs to be fixed at this time.

'We do, and we can. We can help kick start the recovery that you and your country need so desperately. It will cost you, the Russian people, for us to do this. It will cost you not so much in money, or favours or goods. It will cost you both in faith and also in the commitment to accept changes that will drive Russia back out of the ugly future it is heading for.

'I have explained all of this because I know the President is listening to this conversation. He is the first Russian that needs to have faith. Every great journey begins with the first step. We know precisely what is needed to start the recovery of Russia. We also know there are many that are going to sweat blood if this happens.

'We know who is robbing Russia blind, we know who is lying, and we know who is feathering their own nests.

'IF the Russians who can really think and the ones who do care about the motherland, wish to go down this path, it will need to start with a meeting of the President and the leaders of the opposition factions in one room at the same time.'

Kia took a sip of her drink. The silence in the room was deafening.

'That is my offer. The reason I offer this to the people of Mother Russia is simple. At the moment you have the most to lose, and you are the ones in the worst condition. The rest of this planet is willing and happy to sit by while you all die off or self-destruct. It is time for Russia to think about Russia. It is time for the rest of the world to be put back in its place. Some hard decisions will need to be made, but only hard for the crooked and tainted. I will leave my card with Comrade Donsky. You have 48 hours. Then Oracle will move on.'

Kia stood and shook Sergei's hand. 'Thank you kindly for your time. Hopefully, my message will get to the right ears.'
Sergei nodded solemnly. 'I hope so as well, because, to be honest. Nothing you have said today is a lie, and it's hard to swallow, that the supposed great leaders of the past, set us up for this.'

Kia and Paul again shook hands with Sergei on the steps. They walked over to the S2 and opened the door, Paul entered.
She stopped and turned and stared straight into the eyes of a sniper on a rooftop, two streets over. He squirmed under her gaze, 'How the hell does she know I am here!' He thought.

Kia closed the door behind her, 'OK ladies and gents, we have an area in the Barents we can clear before heading home. Waypoint on the HUD, follow me.'
With that, Paul took off and followed the Nav towards their destination.

Paul was quiet for a while. 'Penny for your thoughts', Kia said.

Paul smiled, 'I thought you were nuts back there telling the Russians they are screwed, but the more I think about it, the more I think you are right, It's just too horrific to contemplate.'

'Well, we don't need to, heads up people, getting wet. We have a mustard shell dump to clear out.'
Using direct data feeds from Sandy and the Sats, it didn't take too long to find the dumping area.

Mustard gas is relatively safe dumped at sea, any that leak, the salt water kills, but that was beside the point. Many fishermen had been badly hurt dredging one or more shells up in their fishing nets.

Spread four wide it still took three hours of running in an expanding spiral to clear the dumping grounds. The ordinance looked like piles and piles of cylinders, all different calibers, and styles.

Unlike other foreign material that had found its way underwater, no barnacles or growths had attached itself to the shells. Almost like nature knew these things did not belong there. Eventually, they did a last spiral circle and found no more shells. Completing two more circuits to be sure they got them all, they headed for home.

Behind them, the environment was 235 tonnes of mustard munitions cleaner, and that was always a good thing. It didn't seem that long before they were dropping onto the pads at home.

The OpCen was buzzing with activity over by the Covens screens.
Kate waved Kia over as soon as she walked in the door. 'What's up?' Kia asked as she walked over to Kate's HUD.

'You really dropped the cat amongst the pigeons.' Kate smiled, 'I haven't seen this much Russian inter-office traffic since the Kursk incident. Not only that, but there is a fair bit of traffic in the USA and UK offices as well. That tells me there are a few tainted officials feeding info out of Russia. Jess and Layla have identified at least 11 crooked people.'

'That's fantastic' Kia said', I need proof positive of as much corruption as possible. If they go with my idea, I am going to cut the lifeline to as many of these hidden sleepers as possible. 'There has to be a public culling and a public showing of accountability. I am no politician as everyone knows, and I don't need to be, but I do know that justice needs to be seen to be done.

'We need to foster a mindset change from despair to hope, then and only then will life start to improve in Russia. At the moment everyone else is rubbing their hands with glee that Russia is failing. Like vultures they are waiting to see what they can strip from the remains.

'Be it land grabs by the militias that will spring up, the cells after weapons, other companies offering a pittance for resources, like coal, gas, and minerals.

'Now I don't particularly favour the Russians, nor do I have anything against them, they have polluted the last 200 years badly, but there aren't many others who haven't either. I have been working on this for weeks. Is there anyone here with an opinion or angle on this?'

Bree was the next to speak, 'What will happen if we help them out and once back on their feet, they start to become the way they were before the end of the cold war? I don't know if I would want to help push this planet back into that kind of uncertain balance of power.'

'That is a fair comment', Kate said, 'But it will never be the way it was. It was trying to maintain that level of power, that level of threat capability that broke the Russians in the first place. I only found out last night what Kia had on her mind, and my first thoughts were that she had flipped, and was certifiable crazy.'

'I thought if she does this then, several scenarios will play out, but, you know when you start running each possible scenario out, instead of ending in doom and gloom, the results were actually showing positive signs of growth! Trust me, no one was more surprised than I was!'

'Let me give you an example, there are thousands homeless in Ukraine, just over the border, how would we fix that? Anyone?'

Neil put his hand up, 'Build more houses. Lots of houses.' Kate smiled, 'So you would think, but no. We clean the reactor mess out of Chernobyl, and Ukraine instantly gets one of its largest cities back.

Also, then Russia gets to shed some of the stigma it received from that event.

'Yes, the city needs fixing, but fixing is better and cheaper than building, and fixing means workers and jobs. With jobs come wages, and that money starts the economy moving again. '

'So what sounds like the worlds most ridiculous idea could, in fact, turn out to be the most brilliant idea of the decade?' Ray said.

'Indeed', chipped in Layla. 'No one thought of this because no one can do what you guys can do. I personally think this is huge!'

'I am going to play devils advocate here, don't get me wrong, I am all for this, but just for the sake of argument, I am going to ask negative stuff.' Kia nodded at Brad.

'OK, Brad give it your best shot.'

He continued, 'I am going to give you everything you want, and once things are in motion I am going to take it all off you.'

Kia smiled, 'The Yanks tried that, twice. It cost them millions in equipment. Yes, we gave the stuff back, but we didn't have to!'

Kate stood, 'May I explain something here Brad?'

'Be my guest, the floor is yours.'

'Today a lot of things happened that may or may not have been obvious to you guys.

'No disrespect intended. Kia and Paul did not simply HAVE a meeting!'

Brad said, 'OK then, please enlighten this poor boy, because that's all that I thought that happened.'

'The Russians knew all this, not only did they know , they actually mentioned about knowing it. They also knew we had two extra S2s in the area.
Kia made sure they did, and on top of that, she gave them hours of free time to hunt them down. They failed miserably. She also told them about the hidden men they had stationed around the area. Supposedly well hidden.

Next, We turned off all their surveillance and communications, then turned them back on again, at will. Furthermore we told them we had done it. We also traced the feeds all the way back to the President, and again told them we knew he was there. That means we also knew where all their 'secret' communications stations and relay stations are. Not only did we know that, we nicely traced through all of them seamlessly and with ease.

'Lots of small items that by themselves mean nothing, but when the Russian think tank adds them all up, the message will be clear.
'They got owned on their own soil, in their own back yard.'

Brad, thought on the points Kate had pointed out, 'When you put it in that context, I see what you mean.'

Kia continued, 'I have no doubt they will try, and am expecting that they will. When they do, I will put them down hard. There is no room for error in this. The way Oracle acts now will set the precedent for any other like situations.'

Ray said 'You're wrong Kia, it's not when YOU put them down hard, it's when WE put them down hard. I am in this boots and all. Yes, it may get dirty and may get difficult, but nothing worthwhile is ever easy.'

'Lets not get ahead of ourselves just yet', came Miako's calming voice. We do not know if they are going to accept the second visit as yet, and even then, they need to agree to the terms Kia will present them with.'
With that, the meeting broke up.

Ray looked at Kia as she sat on the balcony looking over the complex. 'You don't look that happy, lady.'

'I understand the complex here, Paul explains we have to look the part. Plus Bree's idea of using what we find to educate and inform the current generation. That I also get, no use cleaning up if others are just going to mess with it again.
But now we have taken this extra step, and I know it was my idea, but I am not sure it was a good one.'

Paul came out with a tray of hot drinks, 'Just how DID you arrive at this idea? Don't get me wrong, I think it's a good one, and whether now or later, eventually it's a step that would have been necessary.'
'It started while I was searching our database for Kate's girls. I was hunting for abandoned houses and such they might be using to hide in. It seemed like every second search referred to abandoned buildings in Russia, old missile silos, contaminated ground water, contaminated farmland, rusting, sinking Nuclear Subs, all Russian.

Kia took the coffee Paul held out to her.

'Of course, once my attention was drawn to Russia, then the real scope of the tragedy that the population lives there under became apparent. Even today, with the technology they have, they continue to do things either the hard way or the worst way.
'The top businesses are still just sucking the life out of the population with no conscience at all. Life isn't going to get better there without help. I think that's what angered me the most.
Both Ray and Paul nodded in understanding.
Paul said, 'You know it is our ability to adapt to situations as they arise, that is our main strength, and without that ability, we would be no better than others that have gone before.

I have said that before, and it's still true.'

Ray finished his cuppa and stood up. 'I suggest we all get some sleep. The Norwegian, and German fossils arrive tomorrow, the Russians still have nearly two days to answer, if they do at all. Nite.'

All three left for some needed sleep.

Chapter Thirty Nine

As Kia was getting dressed there was a knock on the villa door, looking around the doorway, she saw Miako at the front. 'Come in, I won't be long.' Miako walked in as Kia was brushing her hair, still barefoot, she smiled, 'You're up early this morning.'

'Actually, it's you that's running late, and I have already finished my yoga for the day.'

'Really! Damn must have needed that sleep more that I thought', replied Kia. 'So what brings you here?'

'Sandy informed me this morning she had finished laying out stuff from the Norway scan in warehouse 3 and 4, and the German Sub contents in warehouse 5, so I decided to have a peek.

'Oh, my god! You should see it all! Sandy has laid it all out like a museum, complete with a timeline based on a similar system like carbon dating. I was amazed and wanted to see your reaction to it all. We are all waiting for you out front.'

Kia grabbed her boots and slipped them on, flicked a hair tie around her hair and took Miako by the arm, 'Well then, lets explore, shall we?

Standing outside warehouse 3 was an impatient group of people. Neil was grinning like he always seemed to be, 'Miako has peeked inside but got us all to promise to wait for you.' Brad laughed, 'I tried to peek, but the girls stopped me.'

Kia put her hand on the door 'Well, lets see what has Miako all excited then shall we?'

She opened the door with a flourish and waved them all in first. The overhead lights in the warehouse were on.

Everyone stopped and stared at the sight before them!

Under the bright arc lights, there were rows upon rows upon rows of display cases as far as the eye could see, laser straight and equally spaced with a precision only Sandy could produce.

On the front counter were several stacks of catalogues, each one listing the contents of each row. Everyone was speechless!

'It will take days if not weeks to see everything here!' Melissa said.

'If the other warehouse is as full as this one, it will' agreed Glen.

Sandy appeared, 'Hi guys, so what do you think?'

'This is amazing', Kia said. 'All this was from clearing around the U-864?'

Sandy nodded 'and also from the other reef you cleared around the K-278. If I were to add in other FFs that you have recovered to date, we would need a bigger island! Most of the stuff is organised into a timeline the best I could determine, give or take a year or so.

'There is a section in the centre of the warehouse you should all see, I collected most of the valuables in a specific area, for safe keeping. Jump in a cart and have a look.'

Parked along the end wall was a whole line of golf cart type transports. Jumping in one Kia waited till it was full and shot off down the centre lane. In the centre was a roped off area, she stopped, and they all got out.

The roped off area contained rows of display cases, all sealed and bolted to the floor. Each case had either, gems or jewels, gold coins or similar items laid out on contrasting material.

One case Kia stopped at held only one item. It was a beautifully designed gold necklace, and it was huge! There were at least 30 interwoven gold chains and discs, mounted jewels and other intricate carvings. Sandy appeared and stood next to Kia.

'From my dating info it's about 1500 years old, probably worth 13-14 million in today's market for the gold alone, as it is, it would be priceless.'

Kia moved over to the next display and then the next.' This is stunning', she said in a whisper.

Sandy nodded, 'Most all these were located in two of the wooden ships that were removed, where they came from and where they may have been going, well that's up to the guys flying in to decide.

'All artefacts are sealed in these displays, only someone from our team can open them. They are bullet proof, fire proof, and I have an eye on them all. As you can imagine, theft is not possible.

'Each one has an embedded molecule specific to us at Oracle. I could trace any item anywhere on the planet, even if they melted it down. 'Also, I can faithfully reproduce anything here. The plane isn't due in for another 92 minutes, so you all have plenty of time to look around.'

'Also, in WH5, is all the material recovered for the German team, all the Sailors remains are in coffins, any personal items relating to each sailor is in a locked container with each coffin. There are dental images where possible and DNA sheets with each one. So that should please them as well.'
Kia nodded, 'Again, you have excelled Sandy.'

'Bah! This is easy, it's just data sorting. You are the guys that found all of this. This is the result of what you scan.
Without that scan data, none of this would be possible.'

Kia wandered around for about an hour, totally mesmerised with the antiques and artefacts that had lain in the silt and sand for hundreds of years. The pottery, the workmanship, it was all just amazing to see.

Sandy called Kate and Kia to the front of the warehouse, 'Time to get things ready for the visiting teams, they needed to check the staff was up to speed.'
 Kate said she had been checking on them every few minutes since they arrived and all was in the green.

Kia waved her hand at the warehouse, 'All this is searchable on a terminal database yes?' Sandy nodded, 'OK, keep tabs of who searches for what, just for the hell of it.'

'Consider it done' Sandy said. 'Let's welcome the guests.'

In the reception lounge, there were several staff members, neatly dressed in a uniform that Miako had designed. It was quite novel and pleasing to see the complex start to work in reality. Kate and Layla were sitting with Kia when the Lufthansa airliner swooped out of the clear blue morning air and landed in a roar of reverse thrusters. Once docked at the terminal gate, people began flowing out into the reception lounge.

'Kia!' a huge voice roared, she turned to see Taren walking towards her with a huge grin and arms wide open, warning of the huge Norwegian Hug coming her way. Once released from the bear hug, Kia introduced Kate and Layla, explaining that they would be assisting them in settling in.

'I am surprised to see you here' Kia said to Taren. He grinned. 'I have many holidays available, and as my cousins are here as part of the selected team, it was a perfect holiday opportunity!' Two huge bear like people stopped behind Taren. They were obviously related by the similar faces and mischievous smiles like Taren sported at the moment.

'Ah!' Taren said as he spotted the new arrivals, 'Kia, please meet my cousins Henrik and Ivar.' They bowed as they were introduced, 'They both are linked to the historical museum in Oslo and other facilities' Taren went on to explain.

Layla took control of the three huge Norwegians, 'Please gentlemen if you will follow me. We shall get you settled in and in a few hours will take you to the areas you shall be working in.'

Kia waved as they moved off to the exits followed by a dozen or more who had been waiting for the two professors.

The next group that had disembarked was the German party, and it didn't take Kia long to locate the familiar face of Klaus Hartman in the party.

She made her way through the crowd of people to where Klaus was standing talking to a tall, well-built woman.

Klaus spotted her approach and smiled and held out his hand, 'Kia so nice to catch up with you again. Let me introduce the leader of our party, Ms Trudy Gartner', Kia shook Trudy's hand. As she had expected, it was a very solid and firm handshake, which Kia had returned in kind, bringing a smile to Trudy's face.

'So very pleased to meet you', Kia said, 'If you and your group will follow me, I will find your attendant. She will set you all up and get you settled, and then I will return and take you to the warehouse.' Trudy smiled and said 'Thank you' in almost accent-free English.

Kia turned to Klaus, 'How was your flight?'

'It was good, but as always the food was terrible.'

Kia laughed, 'Well, you have the choice of a large caféteria, two restaurants and several cafés here. Hopefully one of them will suit your palette.' Klaus nodded with enthusiasm.

Kia spied Jess approaching the group, 'Jess, this is Klaus Hartman, German attaché to Norway, and this is Trudy Gartner, she is the German team leader.' Jess shook hands and asked them if they were ready to be lodged.
Handing an ID tag to both Klaus and Trudy, Jess led them off in the direction of the transports.

It reminded Kia of school kids on an outing. She walked to the entrance behind the last of the German group, inwardly grinning at all the excitement that showed plainly on the faces of the people.
Outside they were all loaded on a train of trolleys and whisked off down the pathway. A quick glance at the clock on the airport tower told her it was just after 9.00am. With a loud beep, Brad and Bree stopped their cart in front of her.

'Fancy a lift to the OpCen?' Bree asked, Kia nodded and hopped in the back as the cart took off towards the top of the island.

'That display in the warehouse is amazing', Bree said.

'It truly is! Agreed Kia, 'All it needs now is identifying, Sandy sorted age, but now the team needs to sort origin.'

'I personally think it's priceless doing this for humanity, there are some not interested in history, but most are to a varying degree. I didn't get to look in the German warehouse, but Brad took a peek, he said they are in for one hell of a surprise but won't elaborate.

Says I have to see for myself!' Bree punched him on the shoulder.

Brad pulled up at the base of the OpCen tower and held the door open for the ladies.

Up in the centre, they found Paul and Glen surfing on terminals. Neil and Miako were sitting outside on the balcony.

Kia ruffled Neil's hair up as she sat down with them. 'Well, boys and girls, another idea you had has now become a reality. As of today, present day homosapiens get to learn a bit more about their ancestry and history. I also admit, it was short-sighted of me to be willing to convert everything found into an inert sand compound.'

From where they sat they could see people walking back and forth on their new daily routines.

Paul came outside and sat next to Kia, 'It looks like our Holding Houses are doing quite well, and one of them is now into the top five slots. I think it's safe to say your plan to establish Oracle has worked out quite well, Kia.'

Neil smiled', it is quite amazing what we have achieved as a group.'

Glen sauntered out chewing on a sandwich. 'Ray and Melissa are almost on site, I suppose we could find something to do, although helping those nice German ladies out seems a fun idea.'

Miako laughed, 'Typical Glen, always willing to lend a hand to the ladies', she held a finger up to Paul as he opened his mouth to say something, 'Don't say it, hand, will do nicely thank you.'

Kia was also smiling at that comment. 'Where did Ray go?

'Sandy located a rumor of a mustard gas dump site just off Fraser Island, Australia. So they volunteered to go check it out since it's not that far away', Glen replied.

Kia said 'Well, I am committed to taking the Germans out to WH5 at midday, so I won't be going out today.'

Paul said 'I am hanging around to back Kia up if something comes up.' Glen held a finger up indicating he was with Paul but had a mouthful of sandwich. Neil indicated he was in and Miako as well.

'Well, that means we have a few hours to kill, too short to go anywhere, too long to do nothing.' Kia stood, 'I might have a shower and get cleaned up. That will waste some time.'

At 11.50 Kia walked into the hotel and asked the girls behind reception to let Klaus know she would be waiting in the main bar. Kia ordered a Lemon/Lime/Bitters and sat on a bar stool to wait.

A few minutes past midday Klaus and Trudy came into the bar dressed in casual khaki jeans and jackets. They spotted Kia and walked over, 'Hello again, here we are.'

Kia took the last sip of her drink, 'All right then, lets get started, where are the rest of your team?'

Klaus indicated over his shoulder with his thumb. 'They are all standing outside, very excited, and eager to get started.'

'Well lets not keep them waiting, we can walk to WH5 from here, it's only a few minutes and will burn a bit of the energy of your people.'

Kia stood and led them out the door. She kept talking to Trudy and Klaus as they led the procession of people down the pathways towards warehouse 5.

'Now I have not been in there myself, I have just been way too busy, but my people tell me that all the remains that were found have been respectfully enclosed in their own caskets.

Attached to the caskets are both dental information and also DNA results. We hope this will allow satisfactory identification when you arrive home.'

Klaus nodded, 'This is a good thing you have done for us.'

Kia stopped at a large pair of glass doors, 'Here we are, and she opened the doors and led them into the front office area. OK, before we go in, I just want to say, everything that is in there belongs to Germany. You are more than welcome to take any and everything you wish. Anything you do not wish to take back, we will dispose off on your behalf. Any questions?'

No one had anything to ask so Kia walked over to the main warehouse entrance doors and punched in a security code into the panel near the door. With a loud audible clunk heavy bolts withdrew from the doors. She pushed both doors wide open and waved the group inside.

<u>Chapter Forty</u>

They walked inside by about 15 feet, then came to a dead halt. Not one person spoke, and everyone was dumbfounded by what was in front of them. Even Kia took a moment to get over her shock. Even though she had been expecting the rows upon rows of display cabinets like in the other warehouse, she definitely was not expecting the sight of the U-boat in person!
Sitting in a cradle the U-boat took up a whole side of the warehouse. It had been cut down the centre lengthwise and walkways constructed to allow people to walk from end to end and view the entire interior of the sub.

Kia recovered from her initial shock, 'OK people' she said, grabbing their attention, 'Down this side of the warehouse is everything that we could recover from the interior of the sub and surrounding area.
'As you can see on this side of the warehouse is the submarine itself. The sub has been cut straight down the middle and the halves separated so you may all see where each artefact was recovered from. All the munitions have been removed, and although the torpedos are actually still in place, they have all been disarmed.
'Last but not least that doorway into that enclosed area over is temperature controlled and is where the caskets are stored. I highly suggest you ask Trudy if you wish to open any of the display cases. She has the codes and they are monitored.'
Kia pointed to another room off to the right, 'There is a lab in there that has the equipment you may use to examine the artefacts.

'Toilets are here, and there is a drink/coffee station in that corner. That about covers it I think, enjoy!'

As Kia turned to leave both Trudy and Klaus stopped her, 'This!' Trudy waved her hand at the contents of the warehouse, she was visibly shaken to the core, 'This is unbelievable! How was this even possible?'

Kia smiled, 'Please, don't ask and I will not have to lie to you.'

Trudy's smile increased in size. 'I understand that logic 100%.'

'I must attend to the others for a while, I shall drop in from time to time to see how you are going, if that is ok with you?' Kia said.

'Indeed, it's fine with us', declared Klaus. I am still astounded, and may be more coherent when you come back later.'
Kia smiled and waved as she left them to do whatever professors and understudies do.

She walked over to WH3 and entered, although there were 22 people in the Norwegian group they still looked just a few inside the warehouse. Kia found Taren and his cousins in the centre section like she thought she would.

Kate was there as well. Henrik saw Kia coming and shouted a 'Hello' that echoed down and back the full length of the warehouse.

'My god this is amazing, he said with his enthusiasm controls turned up to ten plus. What magnificent pieces of art and artefacts! All this history and all this workmanship' Henrik said, 'It will take us weeks, to study it all.'

Kia smiled, Henrik was just as enthusiastic as his cousin, 'Henrik, you may take as long as you like.
'Just remember though, if you find anything originating from another country, they will have to be informed of its recovery.

Now as I just informed Klaus in the other warehouse, anything that belongs to your country or that you have claim over you are welcome to take back with you. Anything that you do not require, like 2000 clay pots all identical for example, we will arrange disposal for you. This warehouse and the others are open 24/7. You may come and go as you please.

All artefacts are tagged, not that any will go missing, but it's my company's policy to do so. 'Kate told you about the lab and other things?'

Kate nodded, 'Yup, just finished when you arrived.'

'Fine then, I shall let you start your wonderful journey of discovery. Kate and I shall leave you for now and drop by from time to time.'

'Thank you so much!' came the chorus from the guys.

Outside, Kate turned to Kia, 'Thank you for getting me out of there. I endured 3 bear hugs and think I have broken ribs.'

Kia laughed, 'Come on, I will treat you to lunch.' Instead of heading up to the OpCen café area, Kia opted for one of the newly opened and staffed café in the plaza between the staff hotel and the guest hotel. Kia ordered a muggaccino, and some toasted fingers. Kate went with a pot of tea and a ham and cheese croissant.
The waiter asked for a signature as payment.

Kia smiled, 'I hadn't even given payment a thought! Damn, I am out of touch!'

Kate looked at Kia, 'Can I ask you a question?'

Kia nodded 'Sure, go ahead.'

'Did you guys really find all those artefacts near a Norway beach?'

'Yes, we did indeed, actually it was recovered from a semi-circular area about 5km in diameter from where the U-864 was lying.

You see that area is one of the high traffic lanes that seafaring travellers have used for years. It would not be unreasonable to suggest that there are thousands of tonnes of artefacts lying on the sea floor from man's first trading voyage to this very day.

'Hell, shipping companies lose approximately 100,000 shipping containers overboard every year. Some float and are recovered, but mostly lay on the bottom as modern day pollution.

'The real reason we cleared all that stuff you see in the warehouse, was simply due to the tonnes of mercury leaking into the water and the ecosystem around the sub.

'If it had not have been for that, we probably would not even have looked twice at the situation. Our priority has been and still is toxic and/or dangerous debris. The rest, like that in there is just happenstance. One day we hope that cleaning general pollution is the main priority, which means all the bad stuff has been dealt with.

'It was Bree I think that mentioned the benefit of using what we collect to educate people. It seems to be a win-win situation so far.'

Kate slowly shook her head, 'It makes the mind boggle just exactly what is out there, both good and bad. The girls and I are so lucky you found us when you did, and for what it's worth, we are 100% committed to helping any way we can.'

A shadow dropped over the table, they looked up and it was Bree and Melissa. 'Hi there, take a seat' Kate indicated a pair of vacant seats. 'What brings you girls down here?'

'Shopping' Bree said, 'They have actually got a mini supermarket, with a great ladies section!

I know Sandy could make anything, but it's the hunt that makes it fun!'

Kia asked Melissa how she went with the hunt off Fraser Island.

'Quite good, actually it turned out there were two dump sites, neither one particularly large, and we had a 100% clean up success', was Melissa's reply.

'All good then' replied Kia, 'I can't speak for you ladies, but I really am getting, fidgety and restless. It's annoying.'

Bree laughed, 'That's one of the reasons we came down here, I personally can't understand people that love to laze around all day, I think it's your fault Kia, you showed us how interesting life can be. So days like this seem to drag on forever.'

'Why am I always the one to blame?' Kia laughed.

'Actually, I might brave the Norwegian guys and go for a wander through the warehouse. That should help pass the time for a while.'

Kate stood, 'I will give that a miss thanks. Three massive bear hugs from them was enough, besides, I want to see what the rest of my girls are up to.'
They said bye to each other and went their separate ways. Bree and Melissa staying, and ordered coffee.

Back in WH3, Kia started in the first row on the left and spent nearly two hours, walking down one side and back up the other of each row, totally absorbed in the vast and varied artefacts that were on display. Eventually she bumped into Ivar, who was studying a fairly large breastplate. 'Hello! It is the fair lady who brings this fabulous wealth of history to us.'

'How is it going Ivar?, and what is that you have there?'

'This', Ivar said, 'has all the markings of being a Viking breastplate from a ship's captain of some wealth.
Vikings were actually pirates did you know? It was a name given to warlike pirates in the area.

'There were no land-based Vikings. No Viking villages or peoples, at least not in the beginning. Anyway, this plate has a pictorial engraving that tells the story of the owner being the master of three long boats.'

'That is amazing', Kia remarked, 'and what about a time period?' Ivar shrugged his massive shoulders 'That is hard to say. My colleague who would have more on this, unfortunately did not make the 20 person limit. As it was, we went over by one person, not counting Taren of course.'

Kia looked around at the massive area, remembering that there was WH4 next door that even she had not yet visited, 'Ivar, you get on the phone to your colleagues. There obviously is much more here than we anticipated, please invite whoever you require. Let's lift the cap to say 100. If that becomes a problem we shall revisit this when the time is necessary.

'Also NO hugging!! You Norwegian guys are just way too strong for us frail women!'

Ivar roared with laughter, 'Yes, yes we can be a little boisterous sometimes. Thank you so much, I shall go make arrangements right away. I also have 2 Swedish colleagues, I would like to invite, is that fine?'

Kia nodded, 'Just remember, the green fence on the north edge of the complex is the limit. There is dangerous and potentially fatal, equipment north of that fence line. We do not wish to have any accidents. It is a boundary that cannot be ignored.

'We have technology that others may wish to take from us. We cannot allow that to happen.
The same methods we use to collect and preserve all this, can be misused in the wrong hands.'

Ivar nodded solemnly, 'I understand completely, as a scientist, I fully appreciate how equipment developed for good, has been bastardised for evil purposes in the past. I will personally choke anyone from my team that violates the boundary with my bare hands!'

Kia laughed, 'Ivar that, hopefully will not be necessary.'

He bowed, 'I take my leave and go to call my friends, they will be most pleased!' Ivar gently placed the breastplate back in its display case and closed the lid, again bowing to Kia, he rushed off in search of a telephone.
Kia smiled at the back of Ivar as he rushed away. Such dedication to both his job and his hobby. She checked the clock on the wall near the entrance doors, 5.18pm. Time did move faster when busy, she thought, and made her way to WH5.

Inside WH5 She found Klaus sitting on a chair at a desk reading some of the catalogue listings, and pulling certain items up on the HUD attached to the desk. Kia pulled a chair over and sat next to him.

As she sat down he became aware of her presence, 'Kia! This is amazing!'

Kia smiled, 'Not really Klaus I have sat in a chair before.'
It took a second or two for the penny to drop. He grinned widely when it did. 'Some of the contents of the sub were sealed in containers that almost remained waterproof. 'We have some of the original drawings of the V1 Rocket and other items that were supposed to be taken to the Japanese during the later part of WWII.

'Incidentally, one of the remains is a Japanese scientist sent to accompany the sub safely through Japanese waters.
I have informed the appropriate people that we have one of their scientists remains. They are very keen to get him back. It is part of their custom.'

'That's fine' Kia said', if you arrange it with their people we can make a personal delivery to them for burial, or you guys can do that. Either way it's not a problem. So, how is it going?'

Trudy walked over as Kia asked Klaus, she answered for him, 'Kia this has been a fantastic insight into our history. What we expected to find when we arrived here is less than 1% of what you have managed to supply us with. This is almost as good as being there on the very day. We really owe you a huge debt of gratitude!'
Klaus nodded his agreement with that statement.

At that moment a Claxton Siren sounded and Sandy's voice came from overhead speakers.
'6.00pm, all personnel in warehouses report to the caféteria for dinner. Lights out in 15 minutes, lights back on in one hour. Thank You.'

Klaus laughed, 'That lady knows how to treat researchers! Come Kia, please have dinner with Trudy and myself.'
With that, the three joined the stream of people walking out the main exit.

Chapter Forty One

Seated in the corner of the caféteria, Kia, Trudy and Klaus were discussing the days events. Klaus was saying, 'The idea of recovering all lost U-Boats probably never has been contemplated.'

Trudy said, 'It certainly would never have crossed my mind! It would be a massive undertaking.'

'Not to mention expensive!' said Klaus.

'Well, eventually they will all need clearing out. I just thought you might give some thought to it in the future.' Kia said. You have met Paul who works for Oracle?

'Paul was a marketing specialist many years ago, and to Paul everything boils down to money in the end, and in this case he is correct.

'If every lost U-Boat was lying dry on the sands of a beach. 'We would not be having this conversation, but because most are deep underwater, governments do not either have the funds to remove the mess they made during the war, or are highly reluctant to spend what is necessary to do it.

'It is an out of sight, out of mind situation. They hide behind the words 'War Grave.'

Trudy looked slightly indignant at that, 'But they ARE war graves, of some of the finest young men of our country!' she said in defence.

Kia held her hand up, 'You will get no argument from me on that Trudy, but let me use the example Paul uses to explain my last comment.'

Trudy still looked defensive as Kia continued....' Please answer me one question. If the same 66 sailors had been unlucky and died in either a train or a bus crash, would their remains still be left lying next to the road or the tracks?, and if not, what is the difference?'

Trudy looked conflicted, all her professional career, she had accepted the war grave excuse and mentality, and never felt the need to question it. Kia continued, 'For the most part nearly every civilised country tries to appear to do the right thing when it comes to disasters and accidents, but in the background are the bean counters, and when they say enough is enough and that the cost outweighs the return everything stops.

'I personally think that just declaring a site a war grave is a very poor excuse not to bring sons, daughters, husbands and wives home. Maybe they couldn't do it back then, but as you have seen we can surely do it now.'

Kia stood and said to the both of them, 'It's only an idea, and the U-864 may have been the key to bringing a lot of your people back home. Some may still have living relatives, brothers and sisters. Thank you so much for dinner, there are some things I need to take care of plus I need to make sure my people are not just lazing around.' She shook hands with Trudy and Klaus and headed out towards the OpCen.

'Hey Sandy', Kia said as she entered the OpCen, 'How is everything going?'

Sandy smiled; 'Actually, everything is going perfectly so far. How are the visitors going?'

'They are extremely happy and most of them send you their thanks and regards', smiled Kia. 'So how are things going off the island?'

Sandy gave Kia a detailed report of Sat scan results, things the Coven brought up and basic news from around the world.

'So we are not headline news?' laughed Kia.

'No' Sandy said 'but you guys are starting to creep onto the middle pages more and more. The Norway situation, the USS Nimitz, there was even a mention in a blog from the Flip-Ship about a new weapon being developed to help fight the environmental war. Everything so far has been positive. That is the most important thing, although personally I don't really care what they think. What needs to be done, needs to be done, simple.'

'Got to love your pure logic Sandy', smiled Kia. 'So moving on, where is everyone?'

'Most of them are in the warehouses or caféteria, except for Ray and Glen. They are in the shooting range. Miako is down in the café, she just arrived back from the warehouse. Speak of the devil here she is.'

Miako exited the elevator as Sandy was speaking; 'I thought my ears were burning a little she said. What's happening? hopefully you have a full day of work for us tomorrow, and I am going stir crazy. I have been bitten by the treasure bug after walking around the warehouses today. I can't get Neil out of the damn submarine! He thinks he is Captain Nemo or something.'

Kia grinned at that. 'Well I think we shall have to find something to do, I am the same as you, extremely restless.' Sandy stopped what she was doing.

'Oh! Here is something interesting, incoming video call from a Ms Sika Hiratsuka, for you Kia, background check show she works for the Japanese War Veterans Society, NWVS.'

'OK bring her up on the HUD. Stay Miako, you may be of help.'

A picture appeared of a young lady, it was hard to judge her age, anywhere from 24 to 35 Kia thought to herself.

'Good evening, Ms Hiratsuka, my name is Kia, how may we help you?'

The image bowed, slightly and politely, 'Please call me Sika. Our office has been contacted by an Herr Klaus Hartman, I do believe he is an acquaintance of yours.

'Herr Hartman informs us, that you have successfully recovered one of our lost sailors. He also informed us that you have offered to return his remains to us?'

Kia glanced at Miako, 'Yes indeed. Your lost sailor was recovered when the U-864 was recovered off the coast of Norway. We informed Klaus earlier today, that either the German delegation could return the remains, or if he wished we would do it on their behalf.'

Sika smiled, 'That would be most appreciated if you could do so. I am in the position to arrange anything you need to make this happen, and arrange any payment as necessary.'

Kia shook her head, 'There is no payment necessary, and we are pleased to do this for the people of Japan. All we need is a time and place of where you would like the transfer to take place. Time wise, we can do this anytime from sunrise tomorrow, unless that is too soon for you?'

Sika bobbed her head, 'Tomorrow is wonderful, and we try to settle these matters promptly.'

Kia smiled, 'Just tell us where. We will need the same room as a helicopter would normally use.'

Sika again bobbed her head, 'That makes life much easier. 'Please excuse me one moment', she lifted a phone on her desk and spoke quietly into it for a few seconds. She nodded a few times at whatever she was hearing and then hung up. 'I am sorry for the interruption. I have arranged for you to receive the necessary clearances and authorised your attendance at the department of defence warehouse on the outskirts of Tokyo. All documentation and approvals will be sent to you within the next few minutes.'

Kia nodded 'Thank you, we shall see you around 10.00am tomorrow.'
Sika smiled and bowed, then cut the connection.

Kia turned to Miako, 'So you sense anything out of place with that?'

Miako shook her head, 'No she seemed legitimate to me. On the phone, she was asking for flight clearance and best location for delivery, so nothing sinister there.'

'All good then, we shall do that errand in the morning. After that, we might take a run up to a known convergence point, NE of Japan. The Sat data is showing a large concentration of debris in that area.'

'There are quite a few wrecks on the way back around the Midway islands, also some that haven't been listed as found according to records as well.' Sandy chipped in. 'Also, Neil should be pleased, information on the artefacts found and sub pictures are generating a lot of website traffic. So a few pictures of missing ships will increase public interest, obviously there will be no location data included.'

'OK well you can upgrade the Web page to reflect that the missing Japanese sailor, is returning home. Just don't say when, also I suspect that he wasn't actually a sailor. More like a technician or scientist considering the sub was full of rocket plans and sample parts', added Kia.
Brad and Bree arrived. Waving "hi" they walked out onto the balcony.

'Well', Kia said 'it's pushing 7.30pm, so there won't be much more happening tonight I hope. Once everyone turns up, I will ask who wants to go hunting after our delivery in the morning.'

'Talking about hunting' Sandy said, 'I went through some Sat data after you guys cleaned out the U-864 and K-278 subs. You did a nice job on the semi circle clearance zone too, I might just add, but, 2.3km from the U-864, I have located what I believe to be the U-486, lost with all 48 hands. Tracking through a paper trail and websites, it looks like the U-486 was torpedoed. As it's a non-nuclear boat, it doesn't matter. Just thought you would like to know.'

'I shall mention it to Klaus next time I see him' Kia said.

Miako grinned and said 'Ok, 846 and 486 we know about, what about the 648? Just to have all the numbers.'

'Ha! , I knew you would ask that! U-648 was lost in the North Atlantic, somewhere off Portugal. According to records it never sank or did damage to any ships. It did however, manage to shoot down 4 aircraft during its time at sea.'

'You are just too smart for me Sandy!' Miako laughed.

'We are very lucky that she IS actually that smart, our asses depend on Sandy quite a lot', Kia remarked, 'and I for one would never try to play chess against her!'

Chapter Forty Two

'Against who?' asked Neil as he and Ray followed Melissa out of the elevator. Kia pointed to Sandy. 'Hell no!' That would be tantamount to suicide! So, any news on some work for tomorrow?'

Kia nodded, 'Possibly, just awaiting the rest of the crew.

Melissa said, 'Paul and Glen are getting drinks in the café and I saw the Coven walking this way as we entered the door downstairs.'

Kia said, 'Good, we can work out who is doing what tomorrow.'

Less than 15 minutes later Kia had everyone in the OpCen sitting in a circle next to a HUD.

'OK, tomorrow, we have an appointment to take our Japanese casket to the Japanese at 10.00am. I would like to take 2 S2s to do the job. Any others that tag along can stand off until delivery is finished. After that job is complete, I was thinking of heading out along the islands of Midway. See if we can locate any lost items of interest, then swing north. North of the Midway island chain is a convergence zone, noted for its collection of debris.

'So was going to skim through that area as well. Sandy will scan the banks for data on that area and let us know in the morning if she finds anything. Everything in the complex is working fine, and I have been going stir crazy. So who is volunteering to come with, and you can either take an S2 each or double up, your call. So show of hands please.'

Everyone, including Sandy put their hands up.

Kate stepped forwards, 'I know we are not operational staff, but would it be possible for us to accompany someone, for the experience, please? There is currently nothing of importance for us to do, and if something does surface Sandy assures me there is a HUD in the S2s we can use.'

Kia thought for a moment, 'Well Kate, I will leave that up to these guys. If they are happy for you to tag along, it's fine by me.'

Kate nodded her thanks.

'Alright final call, who is going solo, hands up?' All hands went up.

'OK, looks like we don't love each other anymore hey?'

Miako smiled, 'It's not that, we stand a better chance of increasing our stats when flying solo, besides we are all coms linked anyway.'

'Fine', Kia smiled, 'Kate and Layla and Jess, are asking for a ride. If you want to offer a seat, let them know. I have taken Kate before, she rides well.' Kate poked her tongue out a Kia.

'So I will take her tomorrow.

It will be an early start, 7.00am departure. Don't get lost on the way to the pad.'

Standing in the morning sun at 7.03am, Kia watched the last of the people arrive. On the back of Kia's S2 was a specially made container that carried the casket and whatever else was going to Japan.

So nine S2s left one after the other, watched by quite a lot of the complex staff, who had heard of the S2 craft but not seen one as yet.

Kia peeled over the complex and let them all get a good look as they formed up on her S2 and let the whole formation rip through the sound barrier in less than 500 meters. Just far enough away not to break any windows.

All nine craft were running FF beacons, which anyone could track.

It was the way they travelled mostly now. On Kia's HUD there were eight orange icons, showing all S2s were on the same open Com channel.

'Thank you for flying Oracle Airway's, Kia said, 'we have about 1¾ hours till destination.'

Layla and Jess's excited chatter was easy to pick over the other guys. They had a million questions, but plenty of patience as well.

Neil said, 'Gee, was I ever that excited? That brought roars of laughter from every S2!'

Glen said, 'Neil my friend, you are one of the most excitable characters I have ever seen.'

'I wouldn't be too sure of that', Kate said, 'those Norwegian cousins are dangerous to stand near when they get excited.'

Kia kept a close eye on the Nav HUD, but all was fine for the trip.

The general banter between the craft showed how happy the crew was to be out and about again, and not stuck on the ground.

As they started to approach the Japanese international water boundary, Kia asked the other S2s to drop off the back and stay on the open side of the boundary. They split up and the other three kept travelling forwards, three turned left and headed south and three turned right and headed north.

'They know you're coming Kia', Sandy's voice echoed in all nine craft, they have spooled up four SU Jets to accompany you in.' Kia acknowledged the info and pulled up a radar window on the HUD opposite the Nav HUD.

She could see nine icons of the S2s and four red icons approaching from eleven o'clock, but were still eight minutes away.

Kate asked if they were in any danger from the fighters.

Neil's voice came back over the coms, 'Hell no, they are just like mosquitoes, Firstly the S2 is at least twelve times faster, and although we are not armed, as such, we could scan each jet and take it apart rivet by rivet.'

Kia smiled at the thought, 'OK heads up, our escorts are here. In we go, won't be long guys.'

The leader of the SU flight contacted Kia and asked her to please follow him, and he would guide them through the busy flight paths of Tokyo's busiest airports.

Kia acknowledged and fell in behind the leader with the other three jets following them in. 'Bet the cameras are rolling pretty hard on those jets behind you' Paul said. Bree suggested that the pilots probably have six or seven SLR cameras around their necks. That caused a lot more than a chuckle.

The Nav HUD chimed and showed the LZ and a track line from where they were to where they had to land.

As they got close to the LZ, the jets peeled off and headed away from the city. Kia and her escort slowed to a walking pace and very gently landed on the exact CoOrds they had been given. Just before Kia touched down, she turned 180 degrees then landed. 'Come meet the locals, Kate.'

Kate looked surprised, 'Are you sure? Don't you want someone watching the S2?'

Kia pointed out the window, 'That's what they are here for.' Kia and Kate stepped outside, the air was heavy with pollutants. They walked around to the back of the S2. Kia opened the cargo container. Inside was a casket, covered in a Japanese flag and two briefcases. Kia handed the cases to Kate.

Hearing footsteps coming their way, Kia saw a petite little lady walking towards them followed by six large soldiers in dress uniform.
Kia bowed and smiled at Sika. Sika smiled back and bowed as well.

'Welcome Kia, I am so pleased to meet you. I have been researching your company, Oracle, and it seems that you have a reputation for surprising people.'

'That is nice to hear', Kia replied, 'I like to keep people guessing, but first let me release your countryman into your care.'

Kia pulled the casket forwards slightly and a pair of drop legs with wheels folded from under the casket. She pulled the casket further and another pair folded from the far end. Kia rolled the casket to the nearest four guards of honour and Kate gave the briefcases to the other two.

As the guards marched off with their charges, Sika asked Kia and Kate to follow her. Kia said they would, however, their available time was, unfortunately, short, which would make their stay shorter than they would like. Sika bowed in acknowledgement.

Kia looked around the compound they had landed in, three high walls and an official looking building completed the four sides.

There was a large gate in one of the walls. It was chained and locked shut. Satisfied the S2 was safe, Kia and Kate followed Sika towards the stairs of the building.

Inside a very simple but clean office, Sika offered chairs for both Kate and Kia. She opened a drawer in the desk and withdrew a box about 12 inches square. Inside was a picture frame containing a certificate of recognition from the people of Japan to Oracle, for their assistance to the returned soldiers league. Sika presented the gift to Kia with thanks and a short speech.

After a few pleasantries, Kia and Kate stood and bid their farewells and Sika escorted them back to where the S2s were parked.

Kate shook hands with Sika, and Kia held out her hand and did the same.

Sika said 'if there was anything that she or Japan could do for her, to let them know as they owed Oracle a favour.'

Kia just smiled and said. 'Actually, you could find out one thing for me.'

Sika looked a little surprised to get a request, but nodded 'if it were something I could help with, I would be more than happy to do so.'

Kia smiled, 'I would like you to find out if the offer, we sent to help the Japanese government remove the damaged reactor from Fukushima and clear the surrounding area ever made it past the first receptionist.'

Sika's eyes widened slightly as she listened. It was obvious she had not heard of anything on the matter.

Chapter Forty Three

The S2 lifted slightly and turned back to face the right way,
'You boys awake?' Kia asked
Both of them gave her cheeky replies.
   'We got a fancy certificate to hang on the wall in the OpCen.'
   'Oh how nice, a second one!' Sandy said.
Kia's party rendezvoused with the others just outside Japan's
border.
   'So what do we do from here?' Bree said.
   'Well, I figured we would drop down to the bottom of the
Japanese shelf, and follow that north till just before the Bearing
Sea, then turn east and head for this convergence point. Just to
see what's there, and according to Sandy's report this morning
that may be quite a lot.
We can clear small stuff as we run, and anything else can be
decided on as we come across it. As it is a fair area, I suggest
we close ranks to about fifteen meters apart, so we don't run
too slowly.'
   Receiving confirmations Kia dropped into the water and
headed for the bottom. Setting themselves at the fifteen meter
spacings, Kia set her TFSR at eight meters off the bottom, and
in a line, they took off a few degrees right of true north.
   It didn't take very long before the signs of mankind's
footprint on the planet became obvious even deep under the
water. The debris was scattered far and wide, occasionally
a concentrated patch was found associated with wreckage.
Small fishing vessels were the most common item, shipping
containers a close second.

A lot of the debris was rubbish that had just been thrown overboard.

They had been travelling and clearing for just over two hours when Brad called for a stop. He was on the far right end of the line.

'Just hang on a min', he said, 'There is something off to the right I would like to check out.'

While the others held formation, Brad peeled off to the right and headed for a mark on his sonar HUD.

A few minutes later Brad called in, 'it's a few shipping containers.'

Neil chipped in', that's a large scan return for a few shipping containers.'

'Well' continued Brad, 'that's probably because they are still chained to the ship.'

'That might explain it', Melissa said.

The others broke formation and converged on Brad's location.

'It's been here awhile by the looks', remarked Miako, 'look at the amount of build-up on everything.'

'About four years I would estimate' Kia said, 'Brad, take Glen and Ray and run a scan from the end. The girls can follow you if it's clean and remove it.

'Meanwhile, I shall do a perimeter run, Just in case something fell off on the way down.'

As Kia took off on her run around the wreck, the boys lined up side by side and started a deep scan starting at the stern.
They cleared the bow, all the data was sent via satellite to Sandy.

Five flags appeared during the scan, three were human remains. The other two were generated by a container that was lashed to the deck behind the main steering house.

It took a few seconds for Sandy to analyze the scan data. She informed the crews that the suspect container actually had two sealed cylinders that contained radioactive rods.

They matched the dimensions of rods used in power generating plants. 'So let's remove those first.'

Melissa glided silently over the offending container and within seconds it was gone and no longer an environmental issue.

Bree and Miako ran in tandem along the ship, shaving off an easy 30 feet of height, they were followed by Melissa and Brad taking another slice. As they cleared the midway point Ray and Glen started their run.

By the time Kia had finished her perimeter run, Neil was lining up for a run along the rapidly disappearing wreck. She stopped and held off to one side and watched as again and again the crew sliced off another layer and swept back to the stern and lined up for another run.

'Well Sandy, looks like I am becoming redundant!'

'I think they are more focused on their tonnage stats than trying to replace you.' That made Kia grin.

Once the ship was taken care of, everyone slid back into formation, and they continued back on the original heading.

On reaching their waypoint just before the Bearing Sea, the whole formation smoothly swung east and headed for the marked conversion point on the HUD.

After a large amount of debris and several hours later Kia called a halt as they approached the waypoint flashing on the HUD.

'OK ladies and gentlemen, this is where you start work. Just over the next sand ridge is the junction of three main ocean currents.

A large percentage of material in those currents has been deposited over a 4500 square meter area according to basic Sat-scans. Sandy has some advice for us. Take it away Sandy.'

'According to a basic scan and data that I have at the moment, there is a large mound of assorted debris in the convergence zone. I do not have a good data read on what's there, so before you all go charging in I would like you to do a grid scan and feed me the info so I know what we are dealing with.

'Then, if there are no issues or hiccups, you can decide the best way to deal with the situation as you are there and have a visual.

'Sounds fair to me', Melissa replied, 'So how do we proceed?'

'On your HUD are waypoints that I have plotted for each of you. Follow the tracks and let the S2 do its thing. You will only have something to do if any flags pop up. Any other questions?

'OK off you go and when done Kia will decide on the next step.'

Glen slid into the pilot seat of his S2 after making coffee. He punched the necessary commands, and the S2 took over the rest, following the preset courses laid in by Sandy. 'Adios Amigos', he said as he started tracking.'
Within seconds there was nothing left at the meet point as everyone took the lead from Glen.

'Hell', Bree said over the coms, 'I have never seen so much stuff in one area! What a mess!'

Brad grunted his agreement, 'Be that as it may, but I am getting a LOT of flags and haven't had the chance to look out the window.'

Rumbles of agreement came in from everyone else, and for the next five hours, there was very little chatter from the speakers. Finally, Neil slid his S2 softly onto the sandy bottom, completing the circle of craft at the meeting point.

'Well, I had nearly 560 flags during my scan, some the programming took care of but a lot I had to recheck myself. That was hectic, to say the least.'

Sandy chimed in, 'It will take me at least 20 minutes more to correlate the data, so feel free to go for a walk and stretch your legs while I make some sense of this data.'
Most of the guys were reviewing data and checking the list of flags and notices that they had all been swamped with.

Bree sighed and put her feet up on the dash and stretched to relieve stiffness in her back.

'That has got to be the biggest pile of junk I have ever seen. According to my data it was over 79 meters deep in places! That equates to a huge amount of trash!'

'Oh, I doubt it is all trash', Paul said, 'In fact, I would not be surprised if that lot was valued in the trillions of dollars.'

Glen laughed, 'Trust you to think of the monetary value. What I would like to know is where all the nasty stuff came from. I found quite a lot of munitions and other not so friendly stuff. Kia, your thoughts?'
Kia was slow to answer, 'Sorry, just checking something.

'One of the three main current streams comes from down south of here, and if you remember where we are, it's north of where the Battle of Midway was fought during the Second World War.

'That means it's entirely possible that most of the nasty stuff has been collected by that particular stream and brought here.

'Most of my flags on ordinance I scanned show it to be mostly from that era, although I did find six newer torps from the last 15 years, they could just be training rounds that did not detonate.'

Everyone had their own story to tell on flagged items they had scanned but the most potent comment that made everyone pause and think came from one of the Coven.
Layla said 'I was shocked at the amount of human remains! I saw Miako deal with at least 130 HR flags before I lost count, which just seems awful to me.'

Sandy returned at that point, 'Yes, Layla, together, you all scanned a total of 976 HR flags, most of them seem to be from WWII era but not all. I obviously have not dated them, but a quick cross section poll shows most in that time frame.'

Kia asked Sandy for a generalisation of the data if possible.

'I have several CPU banks working on it now, but a broad-ish outline shows 7823 flags will need the attention of one of you in person.

'These flags comprise of mainly live munitions, chemical waste in barrels, Three HR for Kia's attention, and a few oddball ones that I would suggest someone deals with.

'Apart from that, unless I find something else in the scan data, and there is a high probability that I will, I estimate you have around eight, maybe nine weeks of work if you decide to clear the convergence.'

'Wow', exclaimed Neil, 'I knew there was a lot of material here, but didn't think it was that much!'

'Oh yes', Sandy replied, 'You have over 800 years of deposits here.

In amongst all that clutter is at least one if not two complete triple masted clipper ships.'

That caused a wave of comments.

'OK people listen up, we have been out and about all day, so I suggest we head home and start this first thing in the morning. The amount of flags Sandy has kept for us is more than I can organise, so Sandy, can you set up itineraries for each of us by morning and feed it live to the S2s?'

'Sure can, it probably would be more efficient that way anyway.'

'Good' Kia said 'saves me a lot of unnecessary thinking.

'Right, I am off for the surface, eight+ hours down here is enough for one day.'

With that, Kia lifted off the bottom and headed for home. One by one the others fell into a tight formation behind her and chatted amongst each other about the finds of the day.

It was after sundown by the time they reached home. The island was ablaze with lights as they touched down. Although tired they were still amazed at the night time sight of the hustle and bustle going on in the complex.

Freshly showered and fed, Neil was the first one into the OpCen.

'Hi Sandy, back again.'

'Hi Neil, you back to work on the project?'

'Yes, I think it's all done, just checking some code and then ready to boot I think.'

Sandy nodded, 'Well, you have been slinking in all hours after everyone has gone to bed for the last few weeks.' Neil jumped as the elevator doors opened, Miako walked in.

'There you are, thought I would find you here' she smiled at Sandy and sat next to Neil at the HUD. She looked over the work that Neil had been doing. 'So it's finished?'

Neil nodded slowly. 'Yes, I am just about to recheck the code and then it's over to Sandy to boot it up.'

'You sure you want to do this without telling Kia first?' asked Sandy. You know how she likes to be "kept in the loop" so to speak.

Neil looked nervous for a while, he finally shook his head, 'No... No I don't think so. If all goes well, this will never be used or even needed, then no harm. If things go sideways, we will need something like this to back her up. Besides, it's easier to ask for forgiveness rather than permission.

'Kia has always had our backs and looked after us all, but who looks after her, no slight on you Sandy!'

'None taken', Sandy said. 'OK then, lets be naughty together shall we when you are done with your checks let me know, and I will initiate the project.'

Miako finished proofing all the code Neil had up on the screen, 'It looks fine to me Neil, I feel it is a bit open ended, but in a situation where we would need this, that may not be a bad thing.'

Neil saved and encrypted the files and told Sandy it' was as good as he could make it.

Sandy nodded, and the code vanished from the screen, 'OK initiation sequences are running. We will know by morning if we have made any mistakes. If so, the initiation will auto shutdown. If all goes as it should, we have another asset at our disposal.'

'Well, that is a load off my mind, but this I hope will be just what we need in times of trouble. So where is everyone?'

'Paul and Glen are in the café downstairs. Brad and Bree are still in their villa. Mel and Ray are in the complex talking with some of the Norwegians at the bar. Kia is having dinner with Klaus and Trudy, and lastly The Coven is walking this way.'

Chapter Forty Four

Sitting in a corner booth of one of the new restaurants Kia was listening intently to the descriptions Trudy was giving of the finds they had been investigating that day. She was describing how they had a visit from a group of the Norwegians, who brought over some artefacts that were of Germanic origin. In fact throughout the day they had brought over no less than thirtysix items, in display cases.

Kia smiled at that, 'Those guys were told that if anything turns up that belongs to other countries that, they need to be returned. Obviously, they took advantage that you are just in the next warehouse to do just that.'

'We had a three week deadline to sort out the U-Boat and associated items. If they keep bringing things to us, we will run over that schedule', Klaus explained.

'I fail to see the problem', Kia said. 'You are more than welcome to stay as long as it takes to get the job done.' Trudy and Klaus nodded at that, 'But you see', said Klaus, he looked at Trudy before continuing, 'Trudy is actually standing in for her sister-in-law. Trudy is retired and was asked to join us because Kirsten, who normally would have come has just had a baby girl, and was not able to make the departure time.

'Kirsten is employed by our department, and Trudy is being paid out of our very limited budget. I have been informed that Kirsten will be sent to rejoin us by the end of the week. This means Trudy will have to leave. As I said our budget is limited.'

Kia absorbed all the information, 'I have a clearer picture now. So what will you do when you get back Trudy?'

Trudy smiled, 'I suppose I will sink back into retirement, tending my garden and cooking, which is a hobby of mine. It's nice and peaceful out in the country, although I would trade it all to be back at work in a heartbeat!'

Kia nodded and rose to her feet, 'Talking about being back to work, I supposed I had better do some work myself.' Kia hesitated as she turned to go, 'Trudy, I will give your predicament some thought, see if something comes up that may help you.'

Trudy shook Kia's hand, 'That would be nice, but please don't worry too much about it, I will be fine.'
With a wave to Klaus, Kia threaded her way past the people and headed for the OpCen.

As she walked into the café under the OpCen Kia found the three girls that made up the Coven sitting around a table enjoying after dinner cuppas.

'Hungry?' asked Kate.

Kia shook her head, 'No thanks I just had a meal with Klaus and Trudy, and I don't think I need to eat anything for a week after that! Oh! Talking about Trudy, she tells me she is being replaced by the end of the week. It turns out she was sent here to fill in for another antique guru.

'Do me a favour when you girls are surfing. Keep an eye out for a position vacancy that would suit Trudy. It seems a shame to retire someone as sharp as she is.'

Kate smiled, 'Will do.'

Kia grabbed a juice out of the fridge, and all of them headed up to the OpCen.
Kia found Miako and Neil sitting on the balcony overlooking the twinkling lights of the complex below.

'What are you two up to?' Kia smiled at the way Neil jumped at her voice.

'Nothing at all', Miako said as Neil tried to gather his thoughts. 'We just finished checking over todays data and chatting to friends on the net.'

Sandy walked out onto the balcony and stopped in front of Kia. 'I got a reply from the Russian ministry. They would love to sit down and have a chat with you, but they have a crisis looming on the border with Ukraine and need a few weeks to sort that out. They explained they hope the reply within the time limit you gave them will be sufficient for the time being.'

Kia nodded, 'Fair enough. Although I would like to have had the meeting as soon as possible, a positive reply is sufficient at the moment. Anything else happen that I need to know about?'

Neil shifted uncomfortably in his chair.

'Nothing at the moment', replied Sandy, 'Anything you need me to do?'

Kia shook her head, 'No, everything seems to be running well, I just get a little spooked when everything is quiet.'

Sandy smiled, 'Well, enjoy it, who knows when something will pop up. By the way, I hired some more workers. They are going to finish the work on the harbour, we spoke of a few weeks back. I have built most of it slowly, but now need actual people to be seen working in the area. It would be strange for the harbor to materialise all by itself.'

'Besides, we are going to need to staff it for loading and unloading the boats. Some of the artefacts are either too big or bulky or too heavy to air freight out all the time.'

'Well done, and on that note, I shall hit the showers and get some shut eye. There is still a lot of stuff at the convergent point to clear so I want to get an early start.' Kia stood and stretched, 'Good night all', and waved to the Coven as she walked past to the elevator.

*****

Early the next morning while everyone on the island was still in bed asleep, Sandy was flitting about in the OpCen. Why she used a Holo when no one was around she had not given any thought to. At exactly 02:12:337 she froze.

For an instant the Holo flickered and the night lights in the complex flickered for a millisecond.

Sandy stood perfectly still as she analysed what had just happened. Finding absolutely nothing wrong, she tasked several banks of CPUs to run micro-diagnostics to test everything from the ground up.

'Strange', she murmured to herself, 'something just happened, but I am not sure what.'

Everything ran as smooth as silk for the rest of the night, test after test was coming back all in the green. Instead of making her feel happier, Sandy grew more determined to find the cause of the glitch and restarted the whole battery of tests again. At 05:03 she found what had caused the glitch.

'Well, Well, I certainly did not expect that!' She returned to sorting data and information again, satisfied she had solved the issue.

Sunrise the next morning and everyone were seated in the café. Breakfast was just about over, and there was a drone of conversation as everyone relaxed before heading out for the day.

Kia tipped the dregs of her tea into the sink and stood the cup on the side. 'Well folks, time to give Mother Nature a helping hand.'

Paul stood and took his plate and grabbed Glen's as he stood. Glen quickly snatched a piece of bacon on the plate as Paul walked off.

Bree laughed at the sight of Glen, coffee mug in one hand and bacon in the other. 'Thankfully Brad has better table manners!'

'A man has to eat!' Glen said winking, as he followed Bree to the elevator.

Outside in the weak morning sun, everyone stood around the line of S2s. Kia was the last to join them. She had just finished being briefed by Sandy. 'OK boys and girls, today and for the next few weeks we have a huge man-made mountain of debris to remove.

'Thankfully Mother Nature collected it all in one place for us. So, when you are ready, climb aboard your trusty ships and follow me.'

Four minutes later the last of the nine S2s flashed over the top of the OpCen and quickly disappeared from view.
Kate watched them disappear from the balcony. Walking back inside she stopped next to Sandy at the main HUD.

'Sandy, can I run an idea past you for your logical opinion?'

'Sure, go ahead.' For the next few minutes, Kate outlined an idea she had and between them they tweaked and twisted the basic idea into something that looked like it would be worthwhile.

'Thanks', Kate said, as she walked back to her console, 'I will bring it up with Kia when she has a few minutes to spare. 'However it would be nice if I had a day, maybe two to set everything up.'

Sandy smiled, 'I think I may be able to help with that, I will get back to you.'

As the S2s arrived at the destination, everyone moved into their designated positions without having to be told. Not just because the points were in the HUD, but also in part because they were now equally as good at their work as each other.

Kia pushed the "go" button, and everyone swung into action. There was a reasonable amount of inter-craft chatter at the beginning, but within the first hour that dropped to just a few comments from time to time as everyone dealt with flags as they popped up and items that Sandy had deemed necessary to have a personal intervention.
'Attention ladies and gents, finish your current tasks and head to the assembly point. Well done guys.' Sandy said.

Brad looked at the HUD clock, it was hard to believe, but they had been hard at it for 11 hours straight! 'Damn, where did the time go! It only feels like we were here one, maybe two hours!'

Glen replied 'I stopped for a bite and drink about an hour ago thinking it was near lunch. It's been busy in this quadrant today.'

Mel said, 'I am not tired, but I do need a shower, I thought Paul had left his socks in here, but it's actually me!'

'Miako, you can take us home, I am going to lay flat on the floor and straighten my back if I can' Kia said.

Once everyone was back at the assembly point, Kia slaved her S2 to Miako's and wriggled out of her boots and indeed laid flat on the floor.

Chapter Forty Five

Freshly showered and in clean clothes, most of the crew filtered down into the complex centre to eat. Not because the café in the OpCen was closed, but it seemed good to be around the hustle and bustle of people after spending the entire day in almost silence.

Kia spotted Trudy sitting alone at one of the outside tables in the centre square of the complex. She was just sitting watching the antics of the students and professors as they walked past in various-sized groups or pairs.

'Mind if I sit down?' asked Kia.

Trudy jumped slightly, 'OH! You startled me, sure please do, always a pleasure to chat with the boss', she added with a smile.

'Oh, I am only the boss because I couldn't give the job away! Believe me, I tried!'

Trudy laughed at that, 'Well dear, you are a damn fine boss, and you will have to put up with me for an extra few days. It seems there has been some kerfuffle with paperwork, and my sister-in-law has been delayed a few days.'
They both sat in silence for a while, only interrupted when a waitress came and took Kia's order.

'This reminds me of my university days', Trudy said, 'scholars and students bustling about. Some smiling some deep in thought about some hard to fathom issue. Of course, the weather was not as nice as here on this beautiful island.'

'Klaus not joining you tonight?'

Trudy shook her head, 'No, he is deep into the catalogue manifests, there was and still is so much work to do!

'I took a tour in the Norwegian warehouse when they brought some stuff over to us this morning. I thought we had a lot of work to do. Let me rephrase that, we do have a lot of work to do but nothing compared to what they have!

'It must have taken weeks, no months to collect all that and clean it all!'

Trudy looked at Kia. It was plain to see Kia was thinking hard by the look in her eyes.

She was going over in her mind a plan that Kate had cornered her with just before she left to come down to the complex. All credit to Trudy, she saw what Kia was doing and waited patiently for her to finish the internal processing.

'Trudy', Kia finally returned to the outside world, 'How would you like to come and work here full time, as a consultant, a resident artefact guru?'

Trudy was stunned and just stared. Her mouth moved, but she uttered no sound at all. Kia picked up her tea and took a sip. It was her turn to sit and wait while the inner workings of Trudy's mind tried to comprehend what she had just heard.

'What would I do? I mean I know what I would do, but every-thing here is being sorted and catalogued!'

Kia threw her head back and laughed, 'My dear Trudy, if you knew how much stuff we have collected, you would suffer a heart attack but, first things first. I would like to take you to meet the core of the Oracle crew... and explain to you what we do here in more detail. I know you will not tell anyone what I am about to show you, but I have to ask you not to anyway.'

Trudy just nodded, still trying to settle her racing mind.

'OK then, drink up and I will give you a tour of the real system.'

Trudy stood, 'What! Right now?'

'No time like the present', Kia said and finished the rest of her tea as she stood.

Side by side, they walked north through the complex. Kia unlocked one of the gates that led up to the top of the island where the OpCen was. As they walked Kia was giving Trudy a very basic rundown on the aims and agenda of Oracle, and the main mission statement that all the guys worked under.

Occasionally they came to a halt while Trudy tried to absorb some of the most incredulous information she was hearing. Eventually they got to the entrance to the OpCen. In all honesty, Trudy could not have told anyone a thing about the walk from the café. She didn't even remember the villas as she walked past them.

They entered the elevator and headed up to the top. In the OpCen was the Coven and Miako, Neil and Mel. Out on the balcony Kia could see Bree and Brad. Sandy was nowhere to be seen, but she had expected that.

Miako walked over, and Kia introduced Trudy, then, in turn, she pointed out to everyone present and Trudy got a smile and/or a wave from everyone as they were introduced.

Kate was the last one to be introduced and walked over to shake Trudy's hand, wincing slightly at her grip.

'I remember that grip from when you arrived', Kate said with a smile.

'You can thank Kate here for your job offer, I had asked her to look out for a position that may suit you.

'Little did I know she was scheming to give you a job here, which I must admit, is now a brilliant idea, but one that had not crossed my mind.'

Bree and Brad came in off the balcony and introduced themselves properly. Trudy had actually seen them all at one point or another, but this was the first time that full introduction was made. It was physically obvious that Trudy was now much more at ease and had gathered her wits back together.

'It is so nice to meet you all finally! You are the ones that made everything in the warehouses possible.'

Brad smiled, 'There are three others that helped', 'four', broke in Bree, 'There are four others that make the crew.' Paul, Glen and Ray chose that moment to walk out of the elevator.

'AH', Bree said, 'These three are the office boys, Trudy, they don't contribute much, but they are handy for lifting heavy things and taking out the rubbish.'

'Am I in trouble again?' asked Glen, 'Because I am sure it was Paul that did it, whatever it is.'
Each, in turn, was introduced to Trudy and shook her hand. 'That only leaves Sandy for you to meet, Trudy.'

She nodded, 'I have spoken to Sandy many times on the phone. She is extremely helpful and has a surprising grasp of history and artefacts. I look forward to meeting her!'

Kia smiled and took Trudy's hand in hers, 'Well lets do that right now, shall we? Sandy say hello to Trudy.'

'Hi Trudy, I finally get to meet you! came Sandy's voice. It seemed to float out of the very air in the OpCen.'

It took a few seconds to register with Trudy, but she caught on very quickly, oh! OH! Sandy! You are a computer?!

Sandy laughed, 'No, dear, not just a computer, I am the most advanced AI on this planet, even if I have to say so myself, and it is with great pleasure that I hope you decide to join with us.'

Trudy looked around at everyone and saw them all smiling and grinning, 'Well ladies and gentlemen, I must say, I doubt anything else, could surprise me after these few weeks and now meeting you all!'

'I would not bet on that yet' Kia said, 'Sandy, stop being a snob and come meet Trudy properly.'
A disc hissed out of the wall and stopped a few feet from the wall, Sandy slowly appeared and when fully formed, walked over to Trudy and smiled. 'My apologies. Hello Trudy, nice to finally come face to face.'

Trudy giggled like a school girl, 'Well I never! A Hologram! You never cease to amaze me, Sandy!'

Kia said', Kate, Sandy, take Trudy over to the seats, and enlighten her to the specifics of the position we are offering and answer any questions that she may have. I need to catch up on a few things and will slip over later if needed.'

Most of the others went out onto the balcony except Neil, who went back to the HUD he was working on earlier. Sandy appeared beside him, 'Hey young man, good news, she said in a low voice, your program booted fine and is running. However, there is a small problem.'

Neil looked at Kia who was busy on the other side of the room.

'A problem?'

Sandy nodded. 'Just a small one, the program is running, but I can't find it!, I can feel it running, but its location is masked. I am sure it's nothing, but just wanted to let you know.'

Neil looked nervous, 'I don't know what to say. I hope nothing bad happens!'

'Relax, Neil, I feel no threat from the program, quite the opposite. It seems to be reading a lot of stored information, all information, like it's learning and studying.'

Neil was sweating and feeling quite nauseous. Miako came in off the balcony and walked over to Neil, 'Are you OK? You are white as a ghost!'

Neil shook his head, 'I really need to go lay down.' Miako took him to the elevator, keeping herself between Neil and Kia. As the elevator doors closed behind the pair the second Sandy faded out. Kia's eyes flicked around the room, 'I wonder what those three are up to?', she thought to herself. She finished reading the daily logs that basically gave an overview of all systems and issues both of what was happening around the complex and any items of interest either the Coven or Sandy had found.

Kia glanced at Sandy and Kate deep in conversation with Trudy and walked out onto the balcony where the rest of the crew were lazing around in the warm night air.

'Howdy boss lady!' Paul said, as Kia dragged a chair over and sat down. 'So what's the deal with Trudy?'

Kia threw a glance over her shoulder into the OpCen, 'I asked Kate to keep an eye out for a vacancy that might suit Trudy as she is leaving this weekend and being replaced.
Turns out Kate and Sandy have decided that she would be a great asset here with us.'

'How so?' asked Mel.

'Well, after the Germans and the Norwegians have done their thing and left, who is going to sort out all the stuff we have scanned that's historically important or useful? We can't keep asking nations to turn up here to pick things up, plus I am not keen on the idea of having an open house.

'Kate worked that out, so she suggested that we build a small team of our own that can bag/tag stuff and when we have a certain amount assembled, ship them off to where ever they belong.
'As Sandy pointed out, that would keep the visitor count to a minimum, and personally, I like that idea.'

'That makes a lot of sense', Bree said, 'Sandy can auto-sort most of the stuff so I understand, and the stuff she has an issue with Trudy and Co could handle.'

'Does that mean the complex will be redundant?' asked Glen?

'No, not at all, from what I am led to believe it will be a small team, but they would need assistants and packers and movers stuff like that. Plus anything that is sorted will need to be viewed by the respective countries and people concerned. Also, Kate said something about historical student classes. I really have left it up to them to sort out.'

'I am calling it a night.' Mel said, standing and stretching. 'We have to go back to that underwater mountain tomorrow, and I need some sleep, night all.' That signalled an exodus from all the crew towards the villas.'

Kia checked in on Kate and Trudy, but she doubted they heard her say goodnight. Sandy was flashing pictures of things they had scanned, and Trudy was totally engrossed in the display.

Early next morning the crew arrived at the parking lot where the S2s were parked, but they looked different! Under the belly of each craft was a large non-reflective disc. Kia was nowhere to be seen so the crew headed up to the OpCen.

Kate and the girls were all on their respective consoles, and Kia was talking to Sandy over near the main HUD.
After exchanging greetings, Brad sat on one of the stools and waited expectantly with the rest.

Kia looked at them in turn and said, 'Is there a problem?' That caught everyone off guard for a few moments.

Brad spoke first, 'Well depends on your definition of problem. It seems that the S2s are a little.. Umm pregnant?'

Kia turned to Sandy, 'See I told you they would notice!'

Sandy just grinned, 'Just a lucky guess Kia... OK, people gather round. Yes I modded the crafts, yes they are slightly different. No I am not going to explain, not here, when you get to the underwater mountain as Melissa called it, then I will show you what the disc is for. So off you go and have a great day.'

Kia pulled up first, almost central to the mass of debris that had collected in the convergence zone. The huge amount had collected over centuries and although the team had already removed an unimaginable amount, it hardly looked like the collection had diminished at all. Sandy appeared in eight of the nine S2s

'Ladies and Gents, it is time for a demo and explanation of the disk. Kia will now demonstrate what it's for, and I will answer any questions you may have. So Kia when you are ready off you go, and I will explain what you are doing.'

Kia's S2 slid sideways over the rocky outcrop close to the debris. she scanned a rock and cut a slice off the top leaving a perfectly level smooth area on the rock.
Carefully moving back over the smooth flat surface Kia hovered for a moment before the disc dropped loose from the craft and landed on three stubby legs on the fresh flat rock.

She then moved clear so everyone could see what happened next.

For a few seconds nothing happened, suddenly there were three puffs of dirt, one for each leg base.

Sandy spoke. 'The disc has now attached itself to the rock. So everyone find a suitable rock, and scan a flat surface on it the size of the disc.'

Once everyone had done that and was hovering over the fresh surface, Sandy continued the instruction. Here on the HUD you now see a new command Deploy. Once over the prepared surface tap the Deploy command. Next, once the disc has dropped free, move over to one side.'
Eight discs dropped almost simultaneously and attached themselves to the surfaces.

 'Well done, Sandy said, 'Now next to the deploy button is a counter display, dial in 10 for now.' This was done, 'Next we normally set a boundary to the area we are going to work in. I have already set the boundary for a 2km circle.

'You will pick this up easily as you get used to the disc. Right now, lets recap, clear an area for the disc, place the disc, select an area size you want to work in, and dial 10 in the box, any questions so far?'
Neil immediately cut in, 'I think I know what this is and if it is all I can say is WOW!'

'That, technically, was not a question.' Ray said.

'OK', Sandy cut back in, 'Now, you will notice the deploy button is now flashing after you entered the number 10.
Kia will now hit her deploy button so you all can see what happens.'

The disc Kia had placed showed a white light around the outer rim. The light got brighter as the disc separated at the rim and the top rose about two feet from the bottom half, in a second, a slightly smaller disc shot out from the inside, then another and another until there were ten discs hovering in an arc from Kia's S2.

'Ladies and gentlemen' Sandy said, 'Say hello to ten little scan drones. The large disc we dropped onto the rocks is called a Hive Disc, and these are the drones it manufactures.'

'YES! 'Neil said, 'I thought so!'

Sandy continued, 'These drones do what you were all doing yesterday, they scan and remove the debris in the perimeter we assign. Now on your drone HUD, you will see the drones as they work.' Sandy paused to let the new info sink in.

'If one locates a flag, it will hover over the area for 60 seconds waiting for an instruction from you. If it does not receive an instruction, it will continue on its merry way, but will avoid the flagged area until one of you clears the flag.

'Now on the HUD are several options, one of which is Local/All, this toggles from seeing everyone's drones to just seeing your own.'
'I suggest for beginners, we leave it set to Local so as not to be confused. Now, it is best to learn by doing, so everyone hit your deploy commands.'

In less than 60 seconds, there were 90 drones hovering in the water.

'It looks like an alien invasion!' Bree said.

'Right, the zone has been set, hit the GO button and lets earn our keep, shall we?'
Nine fingers stabbed the release command symbol, and 90 drones shot off in seemingly random but carefully preset routes.

'Won't they bump into each other?' asked Mel as she watched the scene in front of her with awe.

'Not at all, ' replied Sandy, 'Each one is talking to the hive disc, and each hive disc is networked to the others. If one area gets cleared out, the hives will re-assign the drones to other areas until every little piece of debris is gone.'

'Then what happens?' asked Paul.

'Then the drones return to the Hive Disc, and it scans each drone out and closes down and waits for further instructions, Ray one of your drones has thrown a flag.'

Ray shot off to the offending area and sorted the problem out. Within a few moments, more flags started popping, and everyone went to work.

Although working, Sandy kept up the instructions, 'If a drone is damaged or gets stuck, or fails, the hive will kick out another drone.

This replacement drone will locate the failed one, scan it out and take its place seamlessly. You may not even notice it was done.'

Sandy carried on the instruction and answered questions over the next two hours.

Everyone picked up the new system quite quickly and was astonished how much was being cleared while they dealt with flags and issues as they arose.

By early afternoon the flags were dropping off significantly as they removed the most modern debris and got deeper into the older material.

Just after 1 pm Kia got a call from Kate and told the crew, she was needed back in the OpCen. Everyone but the drones stopped for a rest and a drink.

'Go ahead' Brad said, 'We got this under control, almost.' Sandy re-tasked Kia's drones amongst the rest of the crew and instructed Kia's hive disc to go back to the island. With a cheery wave through the window, Kia peeled off the bottom and headed for home.

'So', Glen said 'we now have 11 drones each?'

'Nope' Sandy said, 'I was waiting for the boss to leave, tap the square where you entered the number 10 and when it flashes enter 50 and hit deploy.'

Three minutes later there were 410 drones flashing through the water devouring debris like it was candy.

'By my calculations, we should have this mess cleared by 6.43pm today' Sandy said.
It turned out Sandy was out by 1.8seconds.

After all the drones slid into the hive discs one by one, and the hives closed and reattached themselves to the S2 hulls, the crew made a wide sweep of the area and saw nothing but a clean, and pristine area.
'Mother Nature will be very happy with this', Miako said as they followed Bree in the direction of home.

Showered, fed and clean, the crew slowly gravitated to the OpCen. They found Kia relaxing on the balcony talking to Trudy and Kate.
Brad and Bree went out to the balcony to join them. ' Boss, we are back, and the convergence point is no longer a historical rubbish dump', declared Bree as she plopped down next to Trudy. 'So, all in all, I think it has been an exceptional day all round.'
Trudy looked at the smile on Bree's face and laughed, 'You really do enjoy what you do here!' Bree nodded in reply.
Paul and Ray walked out onto the balcony, they handed a cold beer to Brad and asked the ladies if they needed drinks. All declined.
'Now that area is clear where to tomorrow, boss?' asked Brad.

'Nowhere', Kia said, 'as of now all the crew are on notice to leave the island and not come back for a week, I don't care where you go or what you do, but this place is off limits to you for the full seven days.'
The rest of the crew had heard what Kia said and came out to stand around the seated group.
Miako said 'You mean we have to leave!'
Kia nodded as she stole a cold beer from in front of Paul, 'Yes Miako, you ALL have to leave. Kate and the girls too.

'Trudy's replacement will come in on a flight tomorrow, and I am going to take Trudy home after the handover is done. Kate called me back as you know, She and Trudy have put together a list of retired or semi-retired historians who would make an awesome team sorting out the stuff we have in storage.'

'None of us has had a day off really and even on quiet days none have taken a break from this place. All of you are millionaires in your own right, and not one cent have you spent.

'The trip with Trudy will take almost a week, so you mob may as well have a break as well.'

No one spoke for a while, then Melissa said, 'I don't need a holiday, but it would be nice to visit some friends and do some shopping.'

'Good' Kia said. 'In pairs, by yourself or as a group find something else to do. Take an S2 with you, Sandy has made passports for all of you. Once you have arrived at your destination, she will bring the S2s home, for two reasons. Firstly, you then can't sneak back, and secondly you can't lose it.

'Use the OpCen and find some mountain to climb or beaches to lay on. Now go on get!'

They got. Some were soon scanning for holiday destinations, others already knew what they would like to do or go. Trudy shook her head after they had disappeared inside, this place still never ceases to amaze me. Your people are the best suited for this job, how did you find them all?

'It's a short story, Trudy, they found each other. They were already a smoothly functioning and successful group when I found them, and as for suitability for the job, well, no one has done this before.

'They have adapted very quickly and also extremely well. As you have yourself Trudy.'

'Me! How do you figure that!?'

'Well, if someone told you a few weeks ago, you would be assembling a team to examine any and all artefacts raised from the planet's oceans, and would be chatting with a Hologram as if it was a real person. What would you have said? Hmm?'

'OK, I stand corrected. Well, I shall go back down and get my stuff organised for tomorrow. 'Klaus is very worried and needs to be calmed before he explodes.' With that Trudy stood with Kia and gave her a hug, 'I feel like a student again, the day before an expedition.' As Trudy walked through the OpCen, she waved to everyone and left in the elevator.

Kia finished the beer and sat on a stool against one of the blank walls in the OpCen, just watching the bustle of activity. Bree came over and sat on another stool next to Kia,

'Thank you for the time off, although I don't think we need it physically, it will be nice to mentally let go for a while. Brad and I are going back to the house. There are a lot of friends and families we would like to catch up with.

'Mel and Ray are looking at going to Mexico, she has always wanted to go there, and I think Ray would follow her just about anywhere on the planet.'

Kia laughed at that, 'I agree with that analysis.'

Kate joined them on the balcony. 'It looks like Miako and Neil are at a stalemate with what to do.'

Bree nodded, 'Miako wants to do the Orient side of things and Neil wants to see the northern lights in person. They will eventually work out that they can do both with their money and resources.

'Finally, Paul and Glen have decided on a road trip style week, travelling all around the UK where they both grew up. Plus it allows them access to all kinds of female company.'

'And what about you and the girls?' asked Kia.

Kate thought for a while, 'We are kind of different, we came here as fugitives so we are a bit hesitant about going anywhere. But I have convinced them to come with me to see my aunt.

She lives in a very small quiet Yorkshire town just outside of Sheffield in England. There is not much there, a pub, some shops and some really beautiful cottages. Paul and Glen have agreed to drop us off there and start their road trip adventure from there. Which is handy as none of us feels confident taking an S2 anywhere, even with Sandy's help.'

Kia smiled, 'Sounds like a plan. I am looking forward to meeting these people you and Trudy picked out, I have a knack of reading body language well, and would like a meet and greet away from here. Sandy has all this and the complex locked up and running, plus that mass that came in today will give her something to chew on.

'Talking about today, did you give Sandy the idea about drones or was it one of the others, like maybe Neil? He has been sneaking around the OpCen late at night for a while.'

'Nope', Kate said, 'I don't think even Neil knew, She told me about them late last night while I was running a few trackers for her.

'I think she came up with the idea herself, not really surprising the amount of net data she has absorbed. Drones have been used in many things over the years. She may have just realised they could be handy for us as well.'

Kia stood, 'I am about to head off to bed, anyone got any problems?' She received a chorus of no's in return. 'Right then, have fun. Be back here ready to get back into it next Saturday morning. So when I leave, you will all be gone when I get up in the morning.

'Sandy will give you a phone number to call, and you all know the email, only to be used if there is an emergency.' With a wave, Kia entered the elevator and headed for her villa.

Chapter Forty Six

The fresh morning sun found Kia sitting at a table outside one of the cafés in the complex talking to Trudy and Klaus, the empty plate with crumbs showed she had already finished breakfast. The current topic was the impending arrival of Trudy's replacement by her sister-in-law.

'I must say, you are taking the handover of the project rather well', said Klaus, I thought you would be a little more, subdued, for want of a better word. I know how much you like working, and now to become unemployed again must be a vast disappointment.'

Trudy smiled and shook her head, 'No Klaus, this is not the end for me, but a whole new beginning!'

Klaus raised one eyebrow, 'A new beginning? I don't understand. I thought the historical society was complaining of lack of funds and possibly reducing its members even further!'

'That is true' Trudy said, 'but it has nothing to do with it, Kia has offered me a job here! On the island! Can you believe that? Oh, I am so excited!'

Klaus grabbed both of Trudy's hands, and Kia thought he was going to kiss her for a moment! 'Well, that is magnificent news!'

He looked over at Kia, 'Thank you so very much for this, his English faltering slightly under the emotion. This will mean a lot, not only to Trudy but to me. We have been friends for so long it saddened me to see such an impressive mind so easily discarded for a few pennies!'

Both Kia and Trudy filled Klaus in on the new position Trudy was going to have and for the next few hours there was a lot of smiling and laughter at the table. Sandy's voice whispered in Kia's earpiece.

'Sorry to intrude Kia, but we have an inbound aircraft shortly due to arrive. I suggest Trudy makes her way to the reception lounge. Touchdown in 18 minutes.'

Kia relayed Sandy's message to Trudy and Klaus. Finishing her drink, Trudy said she would quickly freshen up and meet them both in the lounge.

The chirps of tyres and the thunderous roar of reverse thrust was muted somewhat by the thick glass of the reception lounge windows as the A320 plane slowed and turned onto the taxiway, making its way to the front of the building. Stairs quickly appeared and soon about seventy people streamed into the reception lounge.

Just for a fleeting moment, Kia panicked as she thought of the Coven not being here, but a detail from the hostel arrived and Taren and brothers arrived and everything was back under control.
Trudy broke through the crowd closely followed by a tall woman. They stopped in front of her and Klaus as Trudy breathlessly made introductions.

'Kia, may I please introduce my sister-in-law Kirsten! Kirsten this is Kia, she is the wonderful woman who made all this possible. She is the boss of the whole complex.'

Kirsten smiled the typical wide smiles like only the Teuter descendants can, and shook Kia's hand warmly. 'It is so very nice to meet you at last!'

Much to her surprise, Kia felt a tinge of colour in her cheeks! 'Welcome to Oracle, and I hope your stay is a pleasant one.' With that Kia let Trudy take over with Klaus and they led Kirsten away in the direction of the hostel.

Back up in the OpCen, she found Sandy glaring at the HUD.

'Problems?' she asked.

Sandy turned to face Kia, 'Oh hello, no, not really, I put some code to one side, and I can't seem to locate where I stored it. Strange, I know, but I was busy over the last week.'

'Talking of locating things, I have been meaning to ask, where are you storing all the scanned stuff?'

Sandy pointed to the floor, 'Apart from the itty bits we have reassembled, most of the inert stuff is under our feet. Actually, that's not quite true.

'This chain of islands is a result of volcanic activity, and most are hollow with massive side caverns deep under the seabed. So I picked a deep cavern, sent a receiver right to the very end of the deepest point and have been backfilling from there.

'This does two things, gives us massive storage space and secondly stabilises the whole chain of islands and the surrounding area.'

Kia nodded, 'Makes sense, I just never really gave it much thought until the other day. Now I have all afternoon to waste. Trudy, and I are leaving in the morning.'

'Well, you could assist in the data sorting from today's clearing.'

Kia lifted one eyebrow, 'Today's clearing? I thought I told the crew to be gone before I got up.'

'You did, and they did.

'In fact, they are all where they said they would be, with the exception of Miako and Neil. Those two argued over where to go and compromised. So they are in Switzerland.'

'Switzerland is a compromise?' Kia said.

'Well, yes, sometimes you can see a few of the northern lights there and it has mountains that Miako likes.'

'OK then, if they are all where they should be, who scanned debris and stuff today?'

'I did!' Sandy said proudly', I sent nine hive discs out and placed them in three rows of three. I then put out 300 drones per line and started them moving directly south.

'When the back line of drones caught up with the hive discs in front, I set them to leapfrog over that array and start a new line in front. Was exciting mathematics!'

'Sandy, maths is necessary, but I would hardly call them exciting! But hey, each to their own. So you had fun today' replied Kia.

'Still am. They are still out there working, anything they cannot handle is marked on my revisit map, and they move on. I am going to run this experiment for the week and see how it turns out, so far so good.

'I am hoping that eventually, the Hives will do all the work, and the crews only need to attend the Flag Revisit List or FRL.'

'That would be excellent. I think they will appreciate the promotion too. The hives and drones are safe? No one can steal them?

Sandy smiled, 'Nope, they are all linked and at the first sign of trouble will return to the hives. Besides, I am watching their every move.'

'OK fine. Trudy has a list of candidates she would like to interview this week. Most of them are older and either retired or work for themselves.'
'I might grab a cuppa and research the names, see if everything is as it seems with them.'
Kia went down to the café and grabbed a mug of tea and a sandwich and headed back up to the HUD. Dragging up a stool she sat down and went to work.

Early next morning Kia had just finished her shower and opened the front door to come face to face with Trudy who was about to knock. 'Good morning' they said in tandem and smiled at each other.
'You all ready to go?'
Trudy nodded, 'Indeed, am I too early?'
'Nope, you are exactly on time.. It will be dark when we get you home so that will work out perfectly.'

Side by side, they headed for the S2 parked in front of the OpCen.'

Once they were airborne and on their way, Kia reached into a pocket on the side of the command chair and removed a large wad of files. 'Well, dear Trudy, here is all the information that Sandy could find on the names that you picked. I know that you are familiar with each of these people, but I would like us to go over each one, one at a time, and maybe you can fill me in on details that are not here?'

'Certainly, and I can understand how important it is for Oracle to make sure we have the right kind of people on the island. Hand me the first persons file and let's see what we have.'

Totally oblivious to the clouds rushing past, far below them, both ladies got to work.

Chapter Forty Seven

At the exact time Trudy flipped open the first file, several thousands of kilometers north west Miako and Neil were walking arm in arm down a crowded street in Switzerland. The whole street was a mass of party goers and bands. There were food and drink vendors parked on nearly every street corner. Neil was holding Miako's hand and in the other had a huge oversized hot chocolate drink with an outrageously spiral and twisted straw.

'Are you happy we came here?' Asked Miako. 'I know this isn't what you asked for when we picked a place to go.'

Neil shook his head, I think this is amazing! It's nothing like I thought it would be, you know, snow and mountains don't sound that exciting. But this, the rave parties, the music, all this great food and stuff! 'The people are fantastic, so yes, I am happy and really glad we came here. Look at the snow, it covers everything, and I have never been in snow before, not like this.'

Miako laughed, Neil looked so damn cute all rugged up and with the woollen balaclava he bought yesterday with the silly flaps over his ears. She stood on tiptoe and kissed him on the cheek.

They spent several hours joining in the merriment and watching all kinds of street performers doing their many and varied acts.

The sunlight faded very fast down in the valley. Thousands of lights sprang into life. Not just street lights, but the houses were blanketed with lights and moving scenes.

Even the hills were floodlit by powerful beams, the snow reflecting the colours everywhere.

Miako was amazed by the colours and patterns that seemed to climb almost to the top of the nearby mountains.

Neil squeezed her hand, 'lets find a seat in a café somewhere and have something to eat.'

Together they threaded their way through the mass of people partying and throwing snowballs at the other people on the opposite side of the street. It was not much quieter in the café they picked, but they were lucky and got a table close to the street window with a good view of the celebrations going on outside. Neil picked up the menu and mused over the selection.

After they had both eaten, they headed out into the mayhem that seemed to encompass the whole town.

For four full days the festivities continued almost 24 hours a day. Miako and Neil saw lots of street performers, magic acts, and plays. Each night they fell into bed exhausted but having had the time of their lives.

Late in the evening of the fourth day they both booked a ride to the top of the highest ski lift, not to ski down the mountain, but as part of a tour group for star gazing. High in the air the stars seemed massively bright and Neil was treated to a glimpse of the northern lights on the horizon.

On the way back down Miako squeezed Neil's hand, 'Sorry the Aurora Borealis was not as bright for you as I thought it would be.'

Neil smiled, ' I got to see it, even just a little, and that's good enough for me, besides, it has been one hell of a party so far and we still have two days to go!'

Midday the next day found them both back in the mayhem of the main street. There seemed to be no end to the entertainment. All through the week they could not remember seeing the same act twice!. By early afternoon the fast pace caught up with them.

Neil dragged Miako into a street side café and they managed to get a table by the window. Even inside it was packed with party goers.

'We must be getting old' Neil grinned. Miako laughed 'It is hard to keep up, so many sights, so many shows!'

Neil grinned, 'Lets have something to eat and go back to the hotel, I need the rest!'

Miako left her menu on the table, and it took him a minute to realise she was staring at him. 'What? Something I forgot?' She smiled, 'No, not at all, but we have been eating at cafés and snacking on the food stands, so I thought it was time we went to a real restaurant and had a proper meal. We are, after all, millionaires like Kia said.'

Neil thought for a moment, 'I know, but it seems strange to me. I am not used to having money, not like this, money anyway.' Miako stood up, 'Come on Neil, lets spend a little. We are on holiday after all!'

Leaving the café, they jumped onto one of the many sleighs-taxis trolling up and down the main street and jumped out at their hotel.

Just under an hour later they returned to the kerbside and hailed another Taxi, 'Please take us to the best, most expensive restaurant in town' Miako told the cabbie.

The driver nodded with a huge smile and shot away from the hotel and headed back into the bedlam of the main street.

Dodging through the throngs of people, he finally swept into a large circular driveway and stopped in front of a massive stone building.

'Now this is impressive!' Neil said looked up at the three story building.

Miako giggled, 'It looks like a palace! OK, lets see how the rich people eat!' Arm in arm they mounted the stone steps to the front door, which was opened by two impeccably dressed doormen and ushered inside.

Chapter Forty Eight

Kia swung the S2 nice and neatly onto the grassy field just behind Trudy's cottage. The trip had been totally uneventful and seemed very short as they went over the possible members of Trudy's team one by one. Standing outside the S2 Trudy looked around at the landscape and the cottage. The Twilight made the view look like a huge artist picture.

Standing next to her, Kia was absorbing the view as well.

'This is really, really something Trudy. What a lovely place to call home!'

Trudy laughed, 'It is a wonderful place, but until a few weeks ago, it was also my prison. I love to work, to see the many wonderful things that our ancestors left for us. This place is nice, and I miss it sometimes, but this place is also a death sentence to an active mind.'

Kia raised one eyebrow, 'That's a different way of looking at it I suppose.'

'Come, lets not dwell on these thoughts, my future now looks much brighter, and this cottage is once again a nice retreat for holidays and not a place to wither away.'

Kia turned to the S2 and grabbed a pack from the doorway, closed the door and turned on the camo. She followed Trudy through an old turnstile in the low brick wall that separated the cottage garden from the field.

Producing a huge old key Trudy opened the back door, and ushered Kia inside. She took Kia to the spare bedroom in the back of the cottage, the shower is through there, 'I will start the fire to get hot water, and find something for us to eat.'

Kia dropped the bag onto the huge doona on the bed and sat down next to it. She breathed deeply and closed her eyes, the cottage air was slightly stale from being closed for so long, but still it had the smell of a hundred years or more of habitation.

The ceiling had huge hand cut beams that had been ornately carved by some long dead craftsman, but his work was legendary, witnessed by all the detail and intricate carvings that looked almost as fresh as the day he laid chisel to the wood.

Kia stood and unpacked the bag. Grabbing a few things she headed for the shower. Thirty minutes later dressed and a loose shirt and jeans with her hair up in a towel she followed her nose to the kitchen.

'What IS that wonderful smell?'

Trudy turned from the old stove, 'OH! You showered, the water can't have been very warm!'

Kia shrugged, 'Cold water never hurt anyone. What is that I can smell?'

'That, my dear, is some fresh bread in the oven. It will take a while before it's ready. I was thinking I might grab my old bike out of the shed and nip into the village and make a few phone calls while it is baking.'

Kia laughed, she walked back to the bedroom and returned with two laptops, 'Here Trudy, a present for you', and handed one to her.

'That's nice, but there is no internet here. In fact, we only had proper power supplied a few years ago.

Small villages are not high - priority, and the winters here play havoc with the exposed lines.'

Kia sat at the solid kitchen table and opened the laptop, there may not be internet here, but these are slaved to the S2 outside, and it has a satellite connection everywhere on the globe.

'Really!' Trudy quickly washed her hands and removed the apron she had been wearing and sat across from Kia.

Opening the laptop, she was greeted by Sandy's smiling face. 'Hi Trudy, I hope your flight was comfortable?'

Trudy grinned, 'Yes indeed, it seemed short, being busy and all.'

'Excellent, ok Trudy, what would you like to do first?'

Trudy thought for a moment and opened one of the files, 'I thought I would call or email the people I have on the list and put out some feelers on their interest. Then maybe set up a meeting with those that show interest over the next few days.'

Kia looked up from her screen 'That sounds like a plan, let's go with that. See if you can set up the meetings around two per day if possible. Obviously, travel distance is not going to be an issue.'

Several hours later Kia was standing in the rear doorway, a hot mug of tea in her hand and a huge chunk of freshly baked bread spread with delicious farm produced butter in the other. Trudy was just putting away some stuff when her laptop chimed, incoming email.

Several of the people she had contacted had answered the phone directly or were starting to send reply emails. Sitting down in front of the laptop she brought up the incoming message and after reading gave a little squeal of joy and clapped her hands. Kia turned and looked at her questioningly.

Trudy looked up, 'Sorry', she smiled, 'Karl and Misha just replied that they are definitely interested in talking to me about the project. 'They are married and have eidetic memories. Both are a powerhouse of knowledge, I was really hoping that they would be interested.'

'Oh good!' Kia said, 'Just what we needed, another few know-it-all people like Sandy!'
Trudy looked up and saw that Kia was teasing.

'You know that when we get back, I am going to blackmail you into baking this bread at least once a week.

'Even under threat of firing you if I have to. I have never tasted anything so delicious!'

Trudy laughed, 'OK, deal, I shall set a meet up for tomorrow, then head for bed I think.'

'Another good plan', Kia said, she drained the last of the tea and closed the door.

Chapter Forty Nine

Kia was not the only one full and happy, Neil and Miako were slowly walking arm in arm up the street towards their hotel. They had opted to walk to try and burn off some of the huge meal that they had just finished.

Miako squeezed Neil's arm, 'I do not think I shall eat for the next few days!' Neil chuckled, 'I feel the same, but it was definitely fun.'

Even though it was late the streets seemed just as full of revellers as before. Slowly threading their way through the people, Miako and Neil eventually made it back to their room at the hotel. A hot shared shower, and they both headed for bed.

Early next morning Neil swung his legs out of bed and rubbed the sleep out of his eyes. Miako was already finished with her morning yoga routine and was back in the shower.

'Hey, sleepy' she called, 'what are our plans for today?' Neil shrugged, even though Miako could not see him. 'I don't really know. I saw some brochures on the front desk, there might be something in there of interest.'

The sound of running water stopped, and Miako came out dressed in a huge bathrobe, towelling her hair. 'I don't want to sound ungrateful, and I know we still have tomorrow here, but really I am starting to get itchy about getting back to the island.'

Neil nodded, 'I am getting a bit that way myself. He stood and headed for the shower. 'Lets see what we can do today first. If we get too homesick, we can always ask Sandy to pick us up early.

'But YOU explain to Kia why we are home a day early.'

Showered and dressed, they took the elevator down to the foyer. Off to the left, was the dining hall and some wonderful smells were wafting out.

'Feel like breakfast?' asked Neil.

Miako shook her head. 'Not after last nights banquet! I could go a nice hot mug of coffee, though.' So off they went in search of the barista.

Neil grabbed a handful of brochures on the way in. Armed with cups of hot coffee, they sat at a table in the corner and together they went through the local tourist attractions. Eventually, they settled on three possible options. Just as they were about to leave a shadow fell over the table.

'Excuse me for interrupting.'

They both looked up at the person who had spoken. He was fairly short but dressed in an excellently tailored chauffeurs uniform. 'Are you by any chance Miako and Neil from Oracle?' All the colour left Neil's face as he felt his heart rate climb, Miako looked the man straight in the eyes and relied on her senses for her answer. 'Yes, we are, and who might you be?'

The man reached into his jacket pocket and withdrew a gilt-edged envelope, 'I have been asked to deliver this invite to you both, and if you wish to accept, please let the manager at the front desk know, and someone will come and collect you.' With that, he turned smartly on his heels and strode out of the room.

Neil stared at the envelope like it might bite him. Miako grinned at the look on his face. 'Relax, it's only paper!' She opened the envelope and withdrew a card.

She read the card, then slid it across the table to Neil. Neil picked it up and read, 'You are cordially invited to attend the Mountain View Chalet at 11.00am today.'

The card was not signed. 'Hang on, I just read about that place!' he shuffled a few of the discarded brochures on the table, 'Here this one.' He handed it to Miako. She quickly read through the pamphlet.

It was a history of the buildings that made up the centre of the township.

"The Mountain View Chalet is one of the oldest and most historic buildings and has the panoramic views of the entire town and surrounding mountains. Accessible only by a private lift, the chalet is not open to the general public, but is used mainly for visiting dignitaries." Miako read out aloud. 'Well, that's interesting! I wonder who it is that would invite us up to the most exclusive place in town?'

Neil shook his head, 'I have no idea, but I am not sure this is a good idea. We might be kidnapped and held for ransom! Remember Kia told us to be careful!'

Miako giggled', you really are a sweetheart, and do you think that if someone wanted to kidnap us, they would ask so politely?'

'I felt no bad karma from the man's aura. He seemed at ease and not a bit nervous. I say we go and find out! It will be fun.'

'OK, if you say so, we have nearly an hour before we have to be there, so what shall we do?'

Miako pushed back her chair, 'Well if the brochure says it's for dignitaries, I suggest we get dressed slightly better than we did for a snow outing.' They headed back to their rooms, both quiet and thinking.

Back in the foyer in just under half an hour, Miako walked over the manager at the desk, he looked up and smiled, 'May I help you?'

'Yes, I would like a ride to the Mountain View Chalet, please.'

The smile on the managers face disappeared, 'I am very sorry, but only special guests and people are allowed to the chalet. May I suggest other good places of interest?'

Neil looked at the manager, 'No thanks, we want to go to the chalet, we have an invite.'

The manager gave Neil a look of disbelief. 'That is not possible sir! May I see this supposed invitation?'

Miako slid the gilt-edged card across the table directly under the manager's nose. 'Read for yourself.'

The change in the manager was both, immediate, and drastic!. His face paled as he recognised the specific design of the card, he picked it up and read the invite. He handed the card back to her, and the change in his attitude was highly noticeable. 'My deepest apologies to you both! Please take a seat and I will attend to the matter personally.'
Without waiting for an answer, he almost broke into a run to his office.

As they sat in the huge lounge, Neil remarked 'Well, didn't that just light a fire in his pants! I thought he was going to just brush us off there for a second.'

'He recognised the design of the card. I doubt he has seen many of them, not the genuine article anyway.'

The manager materialised beside them, 'Please Sir, Madam, if you would follow me, your limousine is parked out the front waiting for you.'

At the curb outside the hotel was a black car with the driver holding the door open for them. He was not the same one that had delivered the letter that morning.

'Hello, my name is Jurgen, I will be taking you to the chalet. There is no road access, so we will drive to the base of the mountain and take the private cable-car the rest of the way.'

Sitting in the back Neil was grinning to himself. Miako looked at him, 'What are you grinning at young man?'

'I feel like a Rockstar or someone important in here.' She kissed him on the cheek, 'To me you are important.'
The drive was less than fifteen minutes to a car park in the shadow of the mountain. In the park zone, there were two other limos and a large wooden building.

Jurgen stopped the limo close to the door of the building and leapt out and opened the door for Miako and Neil. He ushered them inside the front door of the building and closed the door behind them.

Inside, there were two security guards and the man who had given them the invite. Beaming a smile, he asked them to follow him. They walked down a wide hallway to a large glass door. On the other side of the glass, recessed into the back of the building was a cable-car. Opening the glass door, they all entered the car.

Miako turned to the man. 'Can you shed light on who sent us the invite? We are on holiday here and do not know anyone from around here.'

The man smiled. 'Do not worry, I have been asked not to tell you. However, you will meet him in a few minutes.'

The cable-car jerked slightly and then smoothly began the ascent to the chalet. Out of the window, the view was stunning. The higher they climbed the further the view extended.

The town almost looked like a well-crafted model from near the top. The car slid neatly into a slot carved into the granite rock of the mountain itself and slowed to a halt in front of stairs hewn into the rock.

'Follow me, please', and they were led up the stairs and across the plateau to the end of the chalet. Opening the old carved door, the man beckoned them to enter first.

It was toasty warm in the room. After handing their coats to the man and making sure they had knocked all the snow off their boots, they were then ushered through the inner doors into the chalet proper.

'Miako!! Neil!! I am so glad you accepted the invite, please come in! Come in!'

There were two men in the room, one elderly and seated. The one that spoken was beckoning them over. Miako faltered, and Neil was just confused. He had never met or seen either of them before. Not so with Miako, quickly gathering her wits, she walked over to the pair. Neil followed, still not on the same page.

Miako curtsied, 'Your Highness! I did not expect to see you here!'

She turned to Neil, 'Neil may I introduce to you HRH Haakon Magnus V, He is the King of Norway.' Neil blanched and wiped his hand on his pants leg before bowing and shaking the hand offered to him, 'Your Majesty!' he managed to stutter.

Haakon indicated to the elderly man seated, 'I am pleased to introduce you both to my old and very dear friend Baron Julien Fellman. He is the Burgermeister of this region.' Both Miako and Neil shook hands with the Baron.

The Baron waved at a leather lounge, 'Please sit and relax, you both look like you are about to explode', and gave a quiet chuckle.

They both sat, although rather stiffly and awkwardly. Haakon also sat in a huge leather chair and crossed his legs. On the table, next to him was a button that he pressed.

A maid appeared out of thin air, 'Yes?' She asked simply.

Haakon indicated Miako and Neil, 'We have two guests for lunch and could you please bring them some tea.' The maid disappeared as fast as she had arrived.

Haakon turned to Miako, 'It is lovely to see you again, and Neil this is our first meeting but hopefully not our last. Please relax, I really hope you do not feel intimidated. I have enough dealing with others that skitter around like rabbits in a lion's cage.'

The Baron nodded, 'Indeed, it is hard to for us to relax when that happens.' Both Miako and Neil visibly relaxed. The tea arrived, and Haakon did the honours.

Miako accepted hers with a smile, 'I bet there are not many on this earth that can say they were waited on by a king!!' Haakon burst out with a good natured laugh at that.

'That was how do they say, priceless?' He moved to the edge of his seat and clasped his hands together.

'I supposed you are wondering why the invite?'

Neil cleared his throat, 'OH, only about five hundred times. Are we in trouble?'

This time, it was the Baron's turn to laugh, 'No not at all! In fact, it is I that has the problem.'

Just at that moment the maid reappeared and announced that lunch was ready to be served. Haakon stood up, and the Baron slowly got to his feet. 'Come, my new friends, we shall explain all over lunch.'

The dining room had a huge bay window that allowed a full panoramic view of the valley and township. They engaged in small talk until the main meal was over and Haakon leant back in his chair and started on the story of how they came to be there.

'I came here to visit Julien for his seventy-ninth birthday, which was yesterday, and after the guests had left the restaurant, we sat and talked about the things that old friends talk about. Somewhere during the conversation, the subject of Julien's son came up. I will let him explain that part shortly. When we stood up from our balcony table and was about to leave, I saw both of you sitting in the window seats of the restaurant.

'Miako I recognised immediately. Now I am not a great believer in coincidences, but, after giving things a bit of thought, I am hoping you can possibly help Julien with an issue.'

The Baron looked at them both. 'Haakon has told me, that if there is anyone who can help me, it would be you people from Oracle. You see, it's my son Reiner. 'You see that mountain slope over there?' and the Baron pointed out one of the rocky peaks in the line of mountains to the right of the window.

'My son and three other snowboarders took a helicopter ride to the left peak. It dropped them off at the top, and the plan was to snowboard to the base where some snowmobiles were waiting at a preset location to pick them up.

'They had done this several times before, but never from Dragon's Peak. The pilot saw them start their run and turned back to base. 'That was the last time anyone saw of my son or the friends he had with him. No one arrived at the rendezvous point.

'The weather closed in for four days and when it cleared there were three large searches done. Each found nothing, not even a trace. It is as if they just vanished off the face of the earth!'

Neil spoke quietly, 'Four days is not a long time, many explorers have survived much longer lost in the snow and mountains. He may take some time, especially if one of them was injured, to make it back to town.' Looking out of the window, 'It must be a good 20 miles from here, that's a long way to walk.'

Haakon put his hand on the thin leg of his friend. 'Yes, 20 miles is a long way to walk, but we both agree that it would not take thirty-one years to cover that distance.'

'Oh, my!' Gasped Miako, 'Reiner and the others have been missing for thirty-one years!?'
The Baron just nodded.

Miako looked at the misty eyes of Julien and could almost feel the heartache he must be feeling. She leant across the table and took the Baron's hand in hers. 'Looking for missing people is not something we do at Oracle', she paused, 'However, I will talk to Kia when I get back, and I promise you this. If Reiner and friends are in that valley, I WILL find them and bring them home.'

'Damn right we will!' Blurted Neil, and then realised what he had just said.

Julien looked at them both, 'Many people have told me they will find him, but have always come back without him, yet I have never given up hope. From what Haakon has told me about you people, I again raise that hope that he will come home.

'I know he is no longer alive, but his mother, God rest her soul, never gave up on getting her son back and laid to rest properly and respectfully. We are mountain bred, we know how unforgiving they can be, and there are many out there that need to come home.' Julien slowly slid into silence.

Miako let go of the old mans hand, she didn't see him anymore as a larger than life Baron, she saw him for what he really was, a hurting father that wanted his son back.

She thought for a moment, 'Julien, Sir, I again promise you, the mountain will not hold your son and the others hostage.

'You say there are others that the mountain has claimed, these mountains are about to lose everything they have stolen from this town, Neil and I, and others will return and take back what does not belong to them. It WILL be done.'

The Baron just nodded and smiled, 'I can see now why Haakon holds you in such high regard. Is there anything that I can do to help?'

Miako thought for a while.

Neil sat forward, 'Actually, there is. See that flat area in the centre of the valley.' He pointed to the spot through the window. We would need the use of that area to build a base on for us.

'We will also need clearance to fly our craft in Swiss airspace. If you can arrange those two things, you will have helped immensely.'

The Baron sat straighter in his chair, 'I have connections, I will contact them tomorrow and organise what you have requested.'

Haakon clapped his hands together, making both Miako and Neil jump.' Excellent! Another round of tea or would you like something stronger?'

'Actually' Neil said, 'I hate tea, may I have some sweet hot chocolate?'

Haakon grinned and organised it with the maid, 'I have one question before we have to go, will Kia be happy that you have taken this task on?'

Miako smiled, 'Of all the things we need, permission from Kia is already a foregone conclusion.'

Neil's hot chocolate arrived, and they all left the dining room through the bay windows onto the balcony.

The sun was low in the sky, although the mountains made it look a lot lower than it was. It still had the power to keep them warm in the still air.

The conversation took a lighter turn, and as the sun finally was shielded from view, Neil and Miako said goodbye to their hosts, collected their coats and were taken back to the hotel.

Chapter Fifty

Back at the hotel the service and attention they received was snappier and far more helpful than before. Room service people seemed to be camping in the hallway almost, and there was no waiting for a table downstairs.

Early the next morning Miako and Neil stood next to the information desk and watched the staff frantically sort out the stuff that Neil had asked for.

It took less than fifteen minutes for the staff to organise two snowmobiles and a guide that knew the area exceptionally well.

'Just exactly what are we doing?' asked Miako.

'We are going on a recon of that flat area we saw from the chalet. Also, it will give us a bit of first hand knowledge of the terrain we will be dealing with when we get back.'

Miako smiled, 'I really don't care what we do, I am eager to have a ride on one of the snowmobiles! So, lead on and I shall follow.'

A few moments later a solid looking gent walked over and introduced himself as their guide for the day.

Neil explained where it was he wanted to go, and the guide gave the thumbs up. He knew exactly how to get there, but warned it would take almost all day for the round trip. Neil told him that wasn't a problem.

The guide said he would meet them out the back of the hotel in ten minutes, and disappeared into the back of the hotel.

Arm in arm Neil and Miako walked out the rear doors of the hotel into the early morning air. Parked off to one side was a row of snowmobiles so they went and stood next to them while waiting for the guide to reappear.

They didn't have to wait long, he walked round from the rear kitchen door carrying three large sacks of supplies.

He smiled at Miako, 'I don't know who you both are but you sure as hell got the staff jumping in there!'

He handed a sack each to Neil and Miako, 'This is supplies for us, we are only out for the day, but there is enough for three days in each bag, just in case.'
Neil swung the sack over his shoulder, 'Smart thinking, ok which snow cat is ours?'

The guide laughed. 'These?? These are toys for around town and small trips, come I show you.' He walked over to a locked garage and unlocked the rolling door. Inside was four of the biggest cats Neil had ever seen! Lifting the seat the guide stashed the sack in a compartment and checked over the unit. He checked there was a full tank in each and that the main drives had oil, and the belts were in good condition.

'These are big enough for two, three people at a push. If one breaks we can still get home. Safety above all, remember that.'

A quick two-minute instruction on the controls and with a helmet in place they all mounted the cats and followed single file out of the garage and up the street. After leaving the town limits, they followed the guide into a field of fresh snow, it was a magnificent sight. Smooth, like icing on a cake. They had been cruising up the rutted street until now.

The guide turned to check on his charges and got the thumbs up from both. Grinning, he opened the throttle on his cat, and it shot off across the smooth snow.

Over his helmet coms he heard Miako give a yell of excitement and saw her in the mirrors just off to his left and keeping pace with him easily. Neil pulled to the right to avoid the rooster tail of snow and all three headed for the distant line of pine trees at high speed.

They stopped at the edge of the pine forest. Hopping off her cat, Miako took off her helmet and grabbed a bottle of water that was in the compartment near the exhaust. The water was cold, but kept from freezing by the exhaust. 'That, she said, shaking her hair loose, was so much better than a motorbike!'

Her face was flushed with excitement.

The guide was laughing, 'It is very much fun with beautiful cats like these. I wish I had one for myself.'

'These are not yours?' asked Neil.

'No! These were provided to us by the Baron! These cats are top of the range supercharged 4cyl units. One would cost more money than I would make in three years!'

Neil looked around, 'It is beautiful here, and very quiet.' They took a moment to soak in the view.

'OK, said the guide, for the next hour or so we will be travelling through the pine forest, please watch out for fallen trees and logs sticking into the pathway. Most of the paths are used, by climbers and skiers but they are slightly thinner than we are.'

They remounted the cats and followed the guide single file through some of the most picturesque scenery they had ever seen.

Nearly two hours later they burst out of the trees onto the flat plateau. The guide stopped and dismounted. 'This is the place you told me you wanted to see. As you can also see there is nothing here at all except an old abandoned farmhouse way over the back.'

'Farmhouse? Out here?' Neil said.

'Yes, during our summer months when the snow melts, there used to be cows up here feeding on the grass. When autumn comes, they used to move the cattle into barns closer to town.

'The farmers would mow the remaining grass and collect it as food for during winter. My father was one of the collective of farmers that used to work this land.'

'So what does your father do now?'

The guide turned to Miako, 'He runs one of the small butcher shops in town.'

'So you help your father and moonlight as a guide for people that want to go sightseeing?'

'Basically yes, although the town is quite large, there are only about six thousand full-time residents. All the others you see are either holiday makers or ones that come and live here during the snow season. During summer there is a different set of residents, they are the mountain climbers and hikers. It's almost like the town has two faces.'

The mountains to the west looked much steeper and higher, up close. Both Neil and Miako were thinking about the promise they had made the day before. Although the mountains were still miles away, it made them both realise the mammoth size of the task ahead.

'May I ask you a question?' asked the guide.

'Sure', Neil said.

'Who are you really, and why come all the way out here?'

Neil looked around, 'We are, I supposed you could say friends of the Baron, and he has asked a favour of us, and it concerns this area. So we thought we would come out and take a look around.'

Miako handed Neil a sandwich from the supplies and sat on a fallen pine log. She pointed to the mountains, 'Have you heard the story of the Baron's son?'

'Oh yes!' said the guide, 'All the local people here know that story.

He pointed, 'See that peak about another nine miles from here? That is the peak that he is rumoured to have been skiing down. My father has told me about that tragedy several times. I have often looked through that area to see if I would be the one to find him. So have many others. These mountains will never release their secrets.

'Around the fires in any home, you can hear of many misadventures in the mountains, a lot more people have gone into this range than have come back out. Some come back happy, some come back broken, and some just don't come back at all.'

Miako stood and repacked her stuff in the cat, leaving out a roll of toilet paper. She turned to the guide, 'Well, that will soon change, and you will be here to see it happen. Now if you two gentlemen can stare at the mountains for a few minutes, I shall be back shortly.'

When Miako returned from the woods, Neil said, 'Ben.'

She cocked her head inquiringly. 'Ben?'

'Yes, our guides name is Ben.'

'Oh! Hello, Ben.'

The guide just waved as he packed his own gear away. 'We have about an hour of spare time before we have to start back.

Neil has asked to see the old farmhouse, and then we can swing past the place you asked about back to here.'

'Sounds great to me' she said, climbing back on the cat and hitting the starter button.'

It was a fairly short run before they came to the old dilapidated fence surrounding the old farmhouse. The house was in ruins, the roof had collapsed into the house, and one end wall had a severe outward lean to it.

'It's a great shame the house was left to ruin' Ben said, 'It would have made a fantastic place for a base camp. It could also have been used as a first aid camp. Now anyone injured has to make it 25 miles into town for help.'

'Ben, you are a goldmine of good ideas', Neil said, as he got back on the cat. 'Lets do the loop and start heading back.'

Ben saluted Neil, 'You're the boss, we go this way.'
The trio headed for the base of the mountains and turned left near the base. Following the steep rises and valleys, they finally looped back on their own tracks.

Back into the forest, it was easy to follow the trail they had made on the way in. It seemed to take a lot less time to return to the town that the trip out had taken them.
The cats were parked back in the garage and locked away.
Ben shook hands with both of them and said he hoped the excursion had helped in some way.

'Indeed it did', Miako said, 'Now how do we pay you for the day?'

'That has been taken care of. I bill the hotel, they add it to your bill, but I have a feeling you will be surprised when you come to pay.

'I also get the feeling something big is happening that you haven't told me. But that's OK, there are very few secrets in this town', he grinned.

Neil shook Ben's hand again. 'We are leaving tomorrow, but we will be back, I also believe we may need a guy who knows all the stories and secrets of the town and surrounding mountains. If we need such a guide, do you know of any?'

Ben again laughed, 'Yes I may know of one or two that may be able to help. It has been a pleasure to spend the day with you. Maybe we will meet again.' With that, Ben slung the supplies bags over his shoulder and left in the direction of the kitchen.

It was dark by the time they had returned to their room and had a shower. 'Do you want to eat downstairs or have the meals sent up?' 'I can't be bothered getting all dressed up again' Miako said', Lets have it sent up.'
That is exactly what they did.

After room service had removed all the clutter and left Neil his nightly mug of hot chocolate, they sat side by side on the lounge and watched the moon rise over the mountains. Neil looked at Miako and said, 'Penny for your thoughts?'

'She looked at him and quietly said, 'I have no idea how I am going to tell Kia about this, but I am working on it.'

'You can blame it on me if you like', he said with a grin, 'I always seem to be the one in trouble anyway.'

'No I took this on, so I will take the consequences ,if any. Come to bed, we have to be up and packed early tomorrow. Now I am really itching to get back home!'

Chapter Fifty One

Kia and Trudy were seated at the kitchen table.

'So, after nearly a week of meetings and interviews, what are your thoughts, Trudy?'

'Well, apart from Benny, who you heard exclaim that he would not join any endeavour unless he was listed in the credits and was demanding a massive retainer, all the others seemed very interested. I have met and worked with some of these people. So my opinion may be biased. Tell me what you think of them, a fresh viewpoint is always a good thing.'

Kia picked up the list.

'Johanna struck me as almost your twin. She seemed calm and asked all the right questions. She didn't seem too keen on working from the Island at first, but warmed to the idea once she was told that she could visit the mainland any time she wished.

'Karl and Misha, again, I got a good read on positive body language. Also they have a little better grasp on the modern tech side of things. I think Karl will eventually question how we do the recovery, and I would like to keep that from him for a while.

'At least until I am certain he is a stayer.

'Benny, scrub him, he is way too egocentric and not a team player.

'Augustine, Arron and Horst all are above average.'

They seemed genuinely interested, and were also comfortable and at ease answering questions, so put a tick next to those three as well... That just leaves one for tomorrow.'

'Yes, Stephan, I really like him, we spent several months together on a project in the Rhine valley. The river ran in a totally different course hundreds of years ago, and an early settlement had been discovered where the river used to flow. 'Now he has a part time job as the museum curator. Such a waste of talent.

'By the faraway look in your eye, I think he was more than a colleague', Kia smiled at the touch of colour that crept into Trudy's cheeks. 'That's also fine by me, I have grown to know you better. If you allowed someone to get that close to you, he must be someone you trust.

'So the plan for tomorrow is we meet Stephan at the museum, and then later I will drop you off here at home. You and Sandy make all the necessary arrangements to get your new team out to the island.'

Trudy poured them both a freshly brewed tea and closed all the files and placed them in a neat pile. 'I didn't think we would get so much done, mainly due to the distance between each person, but your craft made that very easy.'

Sandy placed another slice of homemade apple pie in front of Kia. Kia held up her hands, 'No thanks, I am already looking like I am pregnant!' As Trudy reached to remove the plate, Kia picked up the fork, 'OK, maybe just this one last piece!'

It was a short hop for the S2 to just outside the city limits. Kia put the craft down behind a deserted building. They walked up the short alleyway and stood at the kerb. Shortly a taxi rolled to a stop in front of them, and they got in. Trudy told the driver the address and the cab moved back into the flow of traffic. An hour later it pulled up outside the museum.

'There he is', pointed Trudy'. Kia looked up the long flight of granite steps that led to the main entrance of the museum. Standing at the top was a grey haired man welcoming guests to the pre-opening viewing of a new display the museum was showing. 'So is this invitation only?'

Trudy paid the cabbie, and they both stood at the foot of the stairs, 'Yes normally it is. Somehow I don't think that will be a problem. Let's see if I am right.' They climbed the stairs side by side.

Hello, 'Stephan' Trudy said and extended her hand.

'Trudy!' Stephan ignored the hand and gave her a huge hug, lifting her clear of the floor. What a wonderful surprise! You are here for the previewing?'

Trudy shook her head, 'No, I don't have tickets anyway.'

'HA! You need no tickets! You will be my guest of honour! And who is this lovely lady?'

'Stephan I would like to introduce to you Kia from Oracle Industries. She is both my friend and my boss.'

Stephan vigorously shook Kia's hand. 'Come, please, follow me, I will show you the new exhibits we have set up for this quarter.'

Trudy smiled, 'Actually, we came to see you personally. Is there somewhere we could talk?'

'Me? Good heavens, this sounds ominous, please come into my office.'

Stephan led them through the main automatic doors and across the entrance hall to a door marked private. He opened the door and stood back to let them enter.

Making his guests comfortable he finally sat down himself, not behind the desk, but next to Trudy and Kia. 'Now, dear ladies, why would you possibly need to talk to an old fossicker like me?'

Just as Trudy took a deep breath to start the ball rolling, Kia's watch beeped. Kia frowned and said, 'Please excuse me, I have to make a call. I will be back shortly. Trudy can tell you all about why we are here.'

Kia stood and left the room. She walked over to a corner of the entrance away from the other guests.

'Yes Sandy?'

'I am sorry to bother you, but we have a bit of a situation.'

Kia stiffened, 'What is it?'

'The boys, Paul and Glen drove up to where Kate was staying to pick them up. Kate's aunt said they were not home and had not been home all night. So they drove back into town and are sitting in a café, waiting for instructions.'

Kia swore under her breath, 'OK, tell them to sit tight, book a room if they need to, I will be there ASAP. When the rest of the crew arrive back, hold them on the island until further notice.'

'Yes, boss' came the reply.

'I will be in touch shortly', Kia broke coms and headed back to the office. She knocked on the door and entered without waiting for someone to open the door. Trudy and Stephan were looking at Trudy's laptop as she was showing him some of the artefacts. Trudy was smiling at his astonishment and looked up at Kia. She could see the look on Kia's face.

'What's wrong Kia?' as she rose from her chair.

'I am so very sorry Trudy, but I have to go, it's urgent. Stephan, would you please make sure Trudy gets home safely, I do apologise again, but I have to attend to something urgently.'

'Of course my dear, I would be honoured to do that.'

Kia nodded her thanks.

'Trudy, don't let this stop you telling Stephan why you are here and let me know how things turn out.'

Chapter Fifty Two

Out in the street Kia walked briskly a block away from the museum and darted into an alleyway that led behind a group of shops. She found what she was looking for, a clear space out of view from anyone.

'Bring it here.' Kia said.
Seconds later the S2 dropped between the buildings into the clearing. Kia was inside in a flash and airborne a few seconds later.
She kicked off her high heels and started ripping off her clothes.

'Tell me all you know, Sandy.'

'Not much more than what I told you before. The boys are on the lookout. I asked them to go over it once more. They basically said the same thing, and they also suggest you talk to the aunt. They said she seemed very guarded talking to two strange men.'

Kia slipped on her jumpsuit and boots, her mind was racing.

'I will rip the girls a new one, I promise. They knew they had to be back on the island by tomorrow morning. A last shopping trip is one thing, but missing the pickup time is another. I thought I knew Kate better than that!'
Around four in the afternoon Kia stood on the outskirts of the village where Kate's aunt lived. She had left the Camo S2 in a clump of trees just off the road.
Sitting at a bus stop, she waited for the boys to pick her up. She was fuming! Paul and Glen pulled up beside her, and she got in.

'So no extra news?'

'Not a thing', Paul said, 'we asked around the local pub, they remembered the girls being there last night and leaving at last drinks call.'

'Supposedly heading home' added Glen.

'OK take me to her aunt's house and wait for me around the corner.'

Paul pulled up one house away. He pointed to a row of typical semi-detached style English houses, 'The one with the blue door.'

Kia got out, and leant in the drivers window, 'I will see if the aunt knows where they may have gone. Drive around if you like but don't stray too far. If you find them tell Sandy, and she will let me know.'

After the boys drove off Kia strolled up to the house and knocked on the door. She could hear the shuffling of feet and a tiny old lady opened the door.

'Hello, my name is Kia, and I am looking for Kate, is she home?'

'Hello Kia, Kate has spoken about you quite a bit, please come in. She is not home yet, but I am expecting here at any time.'

Kia followed into the small living room. It was sparsely furnished with well-worn furniture, but it was tidy and clean. Kia sat in one of the chairs.

'Do you have any idea where she might have gone? She was supposed to be picked up today and go back to the office.'

The aunt nodded, 'Yes, she told me that. Two gentlemen called around lunch time to pick them up, I told them that the girls were not home, so they just left. It is really strange because they never came in last night.'

'Really? The local publican told me he remembers them leaving together at closing time. They did not tell you they were going anywhere else after the pub closed?
They didn't even leave a note?'

'Not that I have found, all they said was they were going to be late and for me not to wait up. So I went to bed early, old aunty Gladys is not as sprightly as she used to be, and I do so love my sleep.'

Kia politely smiled. 'So they left to go to the pub, and that was the last time you saw them?'

'Oh no, I saw them after that!' Kia looked at Gladys and waited.

'Let me see, it was before midnight. I had got up to get a glass of water, and I heard a car pull up out the front. Now I don't want you to think I am a nosey person, but it was late, so I peeked out of the window'

'Kate and the girls were standing on the footpath paying the taxi driver. The taxi drove away, but another car stopped, I saw the girls talking to the driver and they seemed to be arguing about something. Then the girls got in the car, and it drove off. I drank some of my water and went back to bed. When I got up this morning, their door was open, but the beds had not been slept in.'

Kia waited a few moments to see if she remembered anything else.

'Do you know what kind of car it was that picked them up? Is it one you have seen around here before?'

Gladys smiled, 'I am sorry lovey, I can't tell one car from the next. Now my husband Jim, he was a whiz with cars. But he passed a few years ago. God bless him.'

'That's ok, did you get a look at the driver, could you describe him?'

'Her, not him, her. It was one of Kate's old friends, from where she used to work, that's why I told the gentlemen not to worry. Kate is just out with friends.'

Kia stood and walked to the window, almost wishing the scene from last night would replay itself.

Gladys struggled to her feet and shuffled over next to Kia. 'Don't worry dear, Kate is with friends, and I am sure she will be home soon. I am making a cuppa tea, would you like one?'

Kia shook her head, 'No thank you, I just wish I knew which friend Kate left with last night so I could remind her she is late.'

Gladys shuffled to the door, 'I will make that tea now, I am sorry I can't remember her friend's name.'

'I am terrible with names, but I never forget a face.'

She reached out and picked an old photo frame of the sideboard.

'See, this is the four of them when they worked in London.' Kia strode over quickly and took the photo, it was a picture taken in front of the Tower of London. There were four people in the photo. Kia recognised all four.

'Are you sure this was the one driving the car?'

Gladys nodded, 'Yes, like I said I never forget a face, and this photo reminds me what they look like anyway.'

Kia smiled, 'Thank you so much, you may just have solved the riddle where the girls went. I best be going, and thank you again.'

Gladys shuffled to the front door and let Kia out. 'Kate told me how happy she was working on her new job and said it was the best place ever. When she comes home, I will tell her that you came to pick her up.'

Kia said goodbye and walked out the front gate.

Turning left, she started walking up the street.

'Sandy, tell the boys to pick me up.'

She reached the intersection at the top of the street before Paul appeared.

'OK', Kia said, sliding into the back seat, 'Take me back to where you picked me up. The girls have taken off with a friend. The fourth one of the team, the girls belonged to. Sandy and I will hunt for them. There is nothing you guys can do here now so go and get your S2 and I will meet you back at the Island.'

'So no big drama?' Glen asked.

'Not until I get my hands on them for going missing.'

'We will meet you back home' Paul said. He for one didn't want to be around when Kia caught up with Kate. Judging by Kia's tone, she was not exactly pleased about the whole deal.

Back in her own S2 Kia sat and thought hard for some time.

'Sandy, I have sent the boys back home. Once they are all back there, no one leaves the island unless I authorise it ok?'

'Sure thing dear, did you locate them?'

'Nope, not yet, but something stinks here. Remember that fourth woman who was on the run with our girls?'
A picture flashed up on Kia's HUD. 'Yes, that one. I want to know all about her, and I mean right now.'
It actually took a full sixty seconds before Sandy came back.

'Her name is Gina Aubrey, career MI6 analyst, originally tasked to a think tank, now redeployed as an undersecretary in a different MI6 section.

'She was originally one of the ones supposedly killed, then hunted after their demise was incorrectly reported. She was taken off the hunt list and disappeared from the radar.

'From scanning all internal channels, including email, printed memos, etc., it seems dear Gina has turned to the dark side.'

'Similar to what I was thinking. Now, we need to find where she took our girls.'

'I am bringing banks of CPUs online, please give me some time to collect and evaluate all the data I can get access to.'

'I know you will do your best Sandy, but time is the major factor here. If MI6 have got their hands on the Coven, I think that time is something they don't have a lot of. Did everyone else make it back OK?'

'Everyone but Paul and Glen. As you know they are still on their way back.'

'Good no one leaves, if we are being targeted, I want everyone there safe.'

Chapter Fifty Three

'Please relocate to the coordinates I have programmed into your S2.'

Kia froze. It was a deep female voice she had never heard before!

'Sandy??' She got no answer 'Sandy answer me! Are you ok?'

'I have temporarily locked Sandy out. Please relocate to the location I have provided. It is necessary.'

'What the F...'

'Patience! Please relocate. NOW!'

Kia looked at her HUD, there were new CoOrds flashing on the screen!

She thought for a moment and with gritted teeth tore off the ground and headed for the indicated destination.

'I don't know who you are, but if you have hurt the girls I will personally rip your throat out!'

'I didn't, and you can't', was the reply Kia got.

She tried to raise Sandy several times during the short hop. The S2 swooped down and came to rest on a tall outcrop of rock. No sooner had she landed. 'Exit the craft please and I shall re-establish contact with Sandy.'

Kia was rigid with anger! 'I will get you, you cannot hide from me!'

'Exit, now. Please.' Kia stood outside looking around, there was no sign of life for miles in any direction. From her high position, she could see a long way across the land.

'I did what you asked, connect me to Sandy.'

The S2 craft lifted off and in seconds was a small dot on the horizon. Kia walked to the edge of the rock. She stood staring in the direction the S2 has disappeared.

Her hands were clenched into fists that tightly, her nails were drawing blood out of the palms of her hands! She was oblivious to this.

'Sandy where the fuck are you!'

'Here!' came Sandy's voice, 'I lost coms with you is everything ok!?'

'Everything is just fine', came Kia's voice.

If an AI could shiver, Sandy would have!

'Please tell me, exactly what just happened? Why am I standing on a rock cliff in the middle of nowhere, and why my S2 has disappeared?'

'Oh dear!!' Sandy seemed hesitant, 'I had nothing to do with this.... But...'

'But WHAT!?' Get that damn craft back here NOW.'

'I need to run a few checks, I believe transport for you is on its way, please give me a few moments.'

Kia was still standing with her eyes focused on a spot on the horizon. But she saw nothing, her mind was running hard. Trying to comprehend the last few hours and string events together so that they made sense!
The air was dead calm, and deadly silent, almost like the whole surroundings were holding its breath!

Suddenly Kia's hair wafted forwards slightly and the hair on the back of her neck prickled. She never moved or twitched a muscle. Her focus remained unchanged.
Three minutes later she said, Who are you and why are we here? Where are my girls!?'

'I am ValKyrie.'
The same deep female voice filled the air. 'I am here because this is where I need to be.'
More silence.

'Where is my S2?'

'Your S2? Ah yes, a cute little workhorse. Highly efficient, slow and methodical. Totally inadequate for the task at hand. I sent it home to the island.'

Kia slowly turned around, her eyes focused on the object in front of her. Her eyes opened slightly, and she felt a cold shiver run down her spine.

So, you are ValKyrie', Kia could feel some of the tension ease out of her body.

'Indeed I am.'

Kia let her eyes roam over ValKyrie. It was the most beautiful, evil, powerful looking craft she had ever seen! It looked nothing like anything she had ever laid eyes on before, sleek and extremely powerful.

It had a wide, low body. It had 2 wings per side. The four wings were spaced 12 inches apart, one above the other. Between the wings there was a hexagonal matrix of holes.

Everything about it was just... Kia struggled to nail the feeling.

'Why did you bring me here? We are wasting time, I need to find the girls.'

'Patience, Sandy and I are doing all that can be done at this time.

'Without a direction to go, it would be both futile and unproductive to go charging blindly about. As soon as we have a direction or even the slightest hint, we will take action.'

A door in the side of ValKyrie hissed open. 'Sit, be comfortable and I will show you what we are doing.'

Kia walked into the craft, it was roomier inside than it looked from the outside, there was only one seat near the front. The outlay of the panels was totally different, but everything was within reach of the command chair. The door closed silently behind her.

'Wash your hands and clean yourself up. Drink, your vitals are showing signs of dehydration. While you are doing that, Sandy and I will bring you up to speed.'

A draw opened near Kia, In it, she found medical supplies, which she used to wash the dried blood off her hands and some spray on wound dressing.'

As Kia was doing this Sandy spoke, 'I have scanned all the local train station camera footage, airport footage and traffic cams from 100-mile radius. I have facial recognition running in all information streams. Each of the crew here is on a HUD, and running checks and ideas that I haven't thought of. So far, nothing has raised a flag.'

ValKyrie spoke. 'I may have a whisper of a lead. A dark blue vehicle registered in Gina Aubury's name left London two days ago. I have traced various fuel purchases on her accounts. Each purchase has shown she was driving towards the Midlands.

'By cross-referencing the mileage that the vehicle has. I have postulated the vehicle had less than 80 kilometers of fuel left when it left with the girls on board.

'I am currently searching any and all fuel outlets within a 100km radius. They may have changed transport, but that vehicle is somewhere inside the circle I have described.

'Without sounding condescending, I cannot fathom why the main crew has not been tagged.'

Kia closed the drawer and opened a bottle of glucose enhanced water and drained half of it in one go. She flipped down the cot and lay down. 'When I get back to the Island, we need to talk, us three. That can wait for now.'

Kia woke with a start. She didn't even remember falling asleep!
She swung her legs over the side of the cot and ran her hands through her hair. She looked at her hands, they were nearly healed! She flexed her fingers and felt no pain or soreness. What the hell!

'I hope you are feeling rested.'
'How long was I asleep? And why did you let me sleep? What happened to my hands?'

'Any more questions?'

'No.'

'Firstly, I put you to sleep, you were not functioning at your best. Once you were asleep, I increased the oxygen percentage to assist with your fatigue. I let you sleep as there was very little to report, that, however, has changed. Which is why I woke you, and lastly your hands were easily treated with micro-dermal reconstruction. So if you have no more immediate questions, please shower in the cubical and get dressed. I have a lead that I think we should follow up on. I just need a few more minutes to recheck my data.'

Kia stepped into a small cubical and found the high-pressure shower very invigorating. She quickly towelled herself dry. She was surprised to find a clean, fresh jumpsuit on the cot.

'You can recon!' She said in surprise!

'Indeed, I can do a lot of things. An S2 is a fine little craft. 'I am, however faster, far more highly advanced, and what's more important, I am not defenceless.

'Brad at the OpCen had the idea to send a wanted notice to all the local police stations on the make, model and year of the vehicle we were looking for.'

'Were looking for? We found it!' Kia Stopped half dressed.

'Indeed, I have located the vehicle, it is currently on its way back to London and of no interest to us.' ValKyrie paused, 'Before you ask, it is no longer of interest due to the fact it only has one occupant. Aubury.'

'I also intercepted a radio transmission, from a security guard who recognised the vehicle in the Police bulletin. He states it was seen at a local airport 27 kilometers from the pickup point.

'It is a small local airport with no radar, so I was not able to procure any data. There is also no record of an official flight in or out for the last ten days. If indeed there was a flight, someone took great effort to hide it.'

Kia dropped into the command seat, 'Maybe the girls were taken to a hangar and are being held there?'

'Valid question, but no. Satellite pictures shows two hangars.

'However, whoever was trying to hide a flight, and yes, there was one, did not count on the company who refuels aircraft to keep such immaculate records.

'I gained entry to their computer and a small corporate jet landed and took off in the time frame we are interested in. 'Not only did the refuelling company note the amount of fuel decanted, but also the registration number of the jet itself.'

'Finally, somewhere we can look!' Kia exclaimed!

'Again, patience, Sandy ran the jets number through the channels, and it is registered to a false company in Scotland. 'Theoretically a dead end. Sandy and I dug further into MI6's accounts, and although nothing at the shell company links it with MI6. The same cannot be said for the main office. There are over 50 contracts with the very same shell company over the three years of data we examined.

Kia thought for a moment, 'So we can tie MI6 to the jet. Fine, there is no flight plan, and the airport had no radar, so we are no further into where the girls are! Hell, they could be anywhere!'

'That was some of the best muddy thinking you have done for a long time. We know where the girls are, by simply removing the areas they are not. Please observe the HUD.' A map of the UK appeared.

'According to the refuelling records, the jet was not filled to its maximum, although the tanker used has a capacity exceeding the jet tanks. This leads me to believe it received enough to get where it wanted to go, and back to where the jet is normally hangared. I do admit that this is not proven, but the best scenario situation.'

'A guess, in other words', Kia said.

'Let me expand further, here is the range of the jet if it was indeed full.' A large circle appeared it covered the entire map.

'Shit' Kia said.

'I have not finished, the jet is currently back where it came from. Parked in it's registered hangar.

'The time the jet was refuelled is known. The time the jet landed back at its registered hangar is also known.
'Through simple mathematics it is known that the jet flew 58 minutes longer than the time necessary for a direct return to base flight. Again, using simple maths, We can deduct a further eight minutes for a landing and takeoff, cutting the unaccounted time down to 50 minutes.'
The circle on the HUD reduced in size dramatically.
'Now we can disregard 50% of this circle, towards the jets base.
The HUD now had a semi-circle on it.
'This area indicates a 25 minute boundary the jet travelled... Thank you, Sandy.'
'I now have data from all the local airports that DO have radar, and there is no trace of the jet on any of them. Not surprising really, they would want to avoid detection.
'Again, it tells us where they are by showing where they are not.
The map on the HUD showed circles in red of the radar coverage.
The 25-minute semicircle showed that there was only one possible route the jet could have taken. That area flashed green on the HUD.
'I have relayed this to Sandy. There is a very high probability the girls are in this area. If you are ready, let us investigate.'
'Ready is an understatement! Lets go.'
ValKyrie leapt off the ground and disappeared in seconds. Kia immediately noticed the difference from her S2. Although the front window was smaller, the inside of the cabin showed a panoramic view of the outside. An almost 200 degrees of unobstructed view, sideways, also up over her head and almost to her feet.
Kia noted the speed they were travelling at.
'We must be making a lot of noise out there. Not that there is anyone around to hear us.'
'We are totally silent outside and leaving no contrail.'

'How is that possible?'

'Simple, I am scanning the air out from in front and rebuilding it behind. We are literally in a bubble vacuum, therefore no contrail and no noise.'

ValKyrie descended towards the hills on the west coastline. She slowed somewhat and started flying through some of the valleys.

'This is the logical way the jet would have flown, close to the ground and using the hills for cover.'

Kia sat staring at the countryside streaming past at high speed, it was mesmerising and amazing to watch.

Turning into another wide valley ValKyrie flashed along its length until they came to a fork in the hills. She turned into the right-hand branch smoothly, a few moments later Kia found herself upside down as they did a full loop back the same way and rolled level.

'You lost?' asked Kia.

'No, I have been following a faint trail of hydrocarbons, the same emitted by jet engines. It lingers in the valleys where there is no or little breeze.'

'So now you are a bloodhound?'

'I can open the window if you like so you can try it yourself?'

Kia smiled the first real smile since the call came in. 'No thank you, I will pass on that.'

'Well, how about you start scanning the landscape, I calculate we are within a 19-minute radius of where the plane would have landed.

'But only if you want to.'

Kia realised she had been so occupied with the flight, she was contributing nothing to the search effort.

'Can you hook me up with the OpCen?'

Part of the side window turned into a picture of the OpCen. Kia could see all the guys watching.

'Hi boys and girls, a task for you. Sandy will give you maps of the area I am in and an area of flying time for the jet.

'Somewhere in this area and, in the rough direction we are travelling in is a place a jet could land. Find it or anything that looks close.'

'We?' Paul said.

Kia nodded 'Long story. Will tell you when it's all over. Time is definitely of the essence here.'

Everyone, including Sandy jumped to the task. For the next quarter of an hour, several sites were selected, but discarded for one reason or another.

Suddenly Ray whooped, 'I got it!'
He made everyone jump, 'Here Sandy' and pointed to an area in the shadow of a close peak, 'There! I think I see some kind of house or cabin.'

Sandy relayed the CoOrds and ValKyrie peeled out of the valley they were in and accelerated to the designated point. Swooping low over the peak ValKyrie slowed to a walking pace. She scanned the flat area near the cabin and finally the cabin itself.

'They are here, I detect five living entities in the cabin, two male three female.'

Chapter Fifty Four

An IR scan of the cabin appeared on the HUD, there was a figure just inside the door, one lying in the corner with another kneeling beside it. One was sitting in a chair with the fifth figure standing in front.

The same image was being reproduced on the HUD in the OpCen, no one was moving, no one spoke, in fact, hardly anyone was breathing. Miako put her hands to her mouth and stared.

ValKyrie spoke, 'Do you wish me to remove the males?'

'NO!' Answered Kia venomously! 'I will take care of this, land and let me out. Now!'

They dropped to the grass twenty feet from the entrance. Kia was out of the S2 and running before the door had fully opened.

It looked like she was going to hit the cabins solid wooden door at full speed! Just as Kia reached it, it flashed out of existence, including a large portion of the wall either side.

The man standing just inside started to turn towards the massive hole. Halfway through the turn his jaw came into contact with Kia's elbow, driven by all the rage she could muster. His body mass continued to turn, but his head snapped back the other way.

For a split second he stood with his head perfectly backwards, then he just dropped. Kia had seen none of this, her total concentration was on the man in front of the chair.

He had just enough time to stand upright before Kia hit him with her entire body. The force of the impact drove both of them over the bench behind him. Kia rolled and bounced to her feet, the guy just lay there, out like a light.

Taking a swift look around Kia found no other threats. Over in the corner, Kate lay on a filthy mattress with Layla kneeling next to her holding a dirty wet rag.

Layla looked a Kia, 'She is alive, but hurt.' Kia went to Jess who was taped to the chair. Her face was bruised but she seemed conscious. Kia cut her free of the chair and made sure she was steady before going over and kneeling next to Kate.

Kate's face was a bloody mess! There were cuts to her upper torso, and the fingers of both her hands were splayed out at unnatural angles.

Kia uttered a deep throated growl that made Layla shrink back.

ValKyrie voice cut through the red veil of rage. 'I have scanned all three girls, their injuries are not life threatening. I do suggest that they receive medical care immediately. Please bring them outside.'

Kia slid her arms under Kate's limp form, 'Get Jess and follow me', she snapped.

Carrying Kate outside, Kia found an S2 parked right at the door. She took Kate inside and laid her on one of the three cots. Jess sat on another cot and lay down. Layla started to cry, Kia hugged her, 'It's ok, you are safe now.'

Sandy said 'Kia, get out, I will get them to a local hospital straight away.'

ValKyrie interrupted, 'Take them home Sandy. An S2 in a hospital car park is not a good idea. Kia the second male is stirring in the hut.'

Kia let go of Layla, 'Lie down dear, Sandy will take you home.' Layla nodded and lay on the third cot.

Kia left the S2, and it took off in a flash. Quickly followed by a sonic boom, and it was gone.

As the man slowly came to, he realised someone had taped him to the chair and had poured cold water over his head. He looked up into a pair of the coldest eyes he had ever seen.

'It's your turn in the chair buddy.' Kia hit him with enough force to snap two molars. 'Let's have a little chat about who you work for and what you were after.'

Half an hour later Kia walked out into the fading light, she sucked some of the blood off her split knuckles. 'ValKyrie, get rid of that.' The cabin vanished.

Kia slid into the command seat. She said nothing for a while.

'A dead end, those thugs were just hired muscle and knew nothing. They were given a list of questions to memorise and that's it. No leads on who sent them. They were paid in cash, just told to get answers and dispose of the bodies.' Kia thumped the console hard in frustration. 'Lets go home.'

ValKyrie rose slowly out of the shadow, before she turned away, she cut several long ditches deep in the grass. 'That will make the next jet landing interesting.' Up they rose until they were clear of the peak.

ValKyrie stopped and just hovered there.
'What's the matter?'
'I have run out of fuel.'
'Really!?'
'No, I am listening.'
'To what? The local radio station?'
'I am trying to triangulate a radio signal, one moment.
'While you were in discussion with the man in the chair, I scanned the entire area. There were several video feeds into the cabin, but I destroyed them as we landed.
'There was, however, a broadcast radio in the room. I can hear someone trying to re-establish contact, but the signal is weak. By patching into several different radio station antennae on the west coast and one of our satellites, I have managed to pinpoint the origin of the signal.

'Although those men were just hired contractors, I do believe the real people behind this were observing via video link. Also, if I am correct, they are not from MI6.'

Kia sat up, 'You found them! Not MI6! Who are they then?'

'Sandy was right, you ask a LOT of questions. Go lay in the cot and I will tend to your injuries. It will take just over two hours to our new destination.'

'Yes, mum', Kia was too sore and tired to argue and lay down with an audible groan.'

ValKyrie turned westward and opened the throttle. If anyone had been on the peak watching, the evil looking craft just silently disappeared!

<u>Chapter Fifty Five</u>

Standing on the roof of the medical block in the complex, were nine people. Two doctors, three orderlies, Brad, Bree, Paul and Glen. Sandy informed them the S2 was 22 minutes out.

Bree leant over, 'Everything ready below?'

One of the doctors nodded, 'with the copies of the X-Ray's from the injuries we received, it looks like we have a high chance of recovery. We just need the patients here.'
Paul said, 'They are on their way.'

Up in the OpCen Sandy was scanning data furiously. Hundreds of windows popping open and being overlaid by others faster than Miako could focus!
'What are you doing Sandy, and do you need any help?' asked Miako.

She and Neil were the only two others in the OpCen at the moment.

'I am checking to see if I missed anything that would have pre-warned of this event.'

'Sandy stop! This was not your fault! No-one could have foreseen this happening. No one is to blame but the evil minds that planned this!'

Sandy closed all the HUDs down, sorry, I was just rendered inefficient, and I do not like that condition.

'We call it 'helpless' for us humans Sandy, and yes it is a horrible feeling. Where is Kia now?'

'I do not know' Sandy said. 'I cannot locate her at the moment.'

Miako nodded, 'She will be fine, she has got the ValKyrie with her.'

'Oh yeah!' Neil said, 'THAT's another thing! I was hoping to be in Siberia or somewhere when Kia gets back. When she finds out I made ValKyrie without telling her, I can tell you she is NOT going to be happy.'

Sandy smiled, 'I think you are wrong, dead wrong there young man. Although WE, you and I, started that project, ValKyrie has evolved. I managed to scan some of it while all this was going on, especially while it was stationary on that rock.

'What you designed is nothing like what it is now. I suppose I should say "she" is now. She is her own identity, a separate, individual thinking entity. An A.I. I grant you, but she is way over my level of intelligence.'

'How is that even possible?, we cloned your AI for that project.' Neil looked confused.

'Yes, we did. However, with the changes in the code, and with her mission statement different to mine, it is no surprise that her AI would develop in a different manner.

'She not only took control of Kia's S2 off me, with ease I may add, she built an entire NEW S2 in seconds at the cabin. I bet I could whoop her ass at data manipulation, and she, mine in tactical matters.

'Here comes the S2, excuse me a moment.'

Miako and Neil walked out onto the balcony just in time to see an S2 swoop over the complex and land on the roof of the medical centre. It seemed to sit there for a few seconds before taking off and landing in front of the garage and just dissolved! There was a flurry of movement on the roof as three gurneys were rushed to the roof elevator and out of view.

Brad stood looking through the window into the four-bed ward. There was a buzz of activity in the room, all three girls had been cleaned, washed and every millimeter of their bodies examined, scanned and inspected.

Bree walked up and took his hand, she paused to watch for a few moments, 'Lets go to the OpCen.'

'There is nothing else we can do here, they are sedated and blissfully asleep.' Brad nodded and hand in hand they left for the tower.

Before going to the top, they called into the café, one floor down. It seemed they were that last to think of that, all the others were seated around the long table, either eating or drinking. The mood was subdued.

'Any news?' asked Melissa.

'They are doing fine' Bree said, 'Kate's hands and eyes are the worst, but the doctors tell us, with her young age and the equipment that have down there her chances of recovery are excellent.'

'It's not her hands, I am worried about Ray said, It's the psychological damage she may have from the trauma.'

Paul put his coffee mug down, 'Look guys lets be a bit more positive about this. The last thing they will need is to look at our sorry faces. I want to believe that this will turn out well for all three of them. Lets face it, there is no better medical place they could be, Sandy is hovering over them continuously, it's up to us to give them all the moral support they need when they are up and about again.'

That brought a rumble of agreement.

'Someone is going to pay for this, there will be repercussions. We need to go through all the info we can and see how this happened and find those responsible.'

Brad paused with his fork halfway to his mouth, 'I think Kia has got that covered, and as much as this may sound callous, whoever it was, is going to get whatever they deserve.'

Bree looked from face to face. 'Right, I have a suggestion. As we are grounded for a while, I hereby propose we go down into the complex to the pub, grab a table and a few drinks, and entertain ourselves with stories about what we did on the holiday.'

Her words sounded like it was a suggestion, but her tone said it was an order.
Glen stood up. 'That, fair lady, is a damn fine idea! First round is on me!'

Chapter Fifty Six

Kia woke to the sound of an alarm.

'We are 15 minutes away from the source of the radio transmission.'

'Thank you', she stood and stretched, 'And where exactly are we at the moment?' By the time Kia slid into the command chair she was wide awake. Out of the window and on the HUDs she could see nothing but desert and sand, and the occasional Joshua tree. 'Let me guess we are in the Mojave Desert.'

'Very good, I see you recognise the local tree species. The transmissions I was following have all but stopped, there is only a contact call at random times. Distance to the point of origin is now less than five kilometers.'

Kia saw them start to slow and drop so close to the ground, it looked like they were sliding along the sand. Up one hill and down the other side. After a dozen ridges, ValKyrie slowed at the top of the ridge and just hovered.

'We have arrived. Just to our left, further up the ridge, there is a parabolic antenna. I have traced the cabling network back to its source. There is a bunker buried in the sand 310 meters from the foot of this ridge.'

Kia leant forwards, scanning the sand. The window she was looking through zoomed in on a segment of the sand basin, and the bunker entrance and outline became easy to see.

Sitting in the shade of two small artificial bushes Kia could see the guards protecting the steps down to a huge iron door.

'It seems the week for kicking in doors', she murmured.

'Any chance of getting an inside view?'

The HUD in front of Kia broke into 16 squares showing various views of the inside of the bunker. 'These are the feeds from their own security system. The plan of the bunker is like this.' Another HUD burst into life.

'As you can see the bunker is basically a five room unit, one large room, a kitchen area, a storeroom, toilets and a closet that conceals an escape tunnel. My sensors tell me the tunnel has collapsed most of its length.'

'Right, time I met the scum that picks on defenceless women.' Kia stood and walked towards the door.

ValKyrie landed just in front of the steps, as she landed, she kicked out two small darts and the sentries took no further interest in the proceedings. Striding down the steps, the steel door in front of her imploded in a spectacular manner. Without faltering in her stride Kia disappeared into the bunker.

Kia stopped just inside, and her eyes flicked around the room, to her left were a row of computer terminals, obviously the operations side, and directly ahead of her was a long conference table with five people in uniform.

Every single one was staring at where the door used to be, stunned into immobility.

'Hello, I am looking for who is in charge?'
The uniformed figure at the head of the table started to rise to his feet.

One of the operators that had turned his back to the imploding door swung his chair around, and snapped to his feet screaming, 'YOU! I have fucking got you now you bitch, you and the other bitches. I am g....'.

Kia's lips curled in a snarl, her left hand seemed to flicker in the overhead lights as she drew and shot Fairbanks clean between the eyes. She swung the barrel back to the conference table, everyone had frozen in place except for one female operator in the corner who turned and vomited onto the floor.

'As I was saying, I am looking for the person in charge', she holstered her gun, grabbed a chair at the opposite end of the table and turned it backwards and sat straddling the chair.

'My name is General Milton Parks of the DODDS, I am the one in charge.'

'Were', corrected Kia. 'Were in charge, now I am. Milton let us play a game of truth, the rules are simple, I ask a question, you answer truthfully. When the game is over, I leave, and you all get to live your lives as you see fit. Sit Milton this will take a few minutes. Just to show a token of good faith, I will start, and you just listen, understand?'
Several of the men nodded silently.

'Good!' Kia slipped her hand into her jumpsuit breast pocket and removed a sheet of paper. 'I have here the list of ten questions you asked the thugs that beat the shit out of my girls, to get the answers.'

One guy opened his mouth to say something, Kia held up her finger. 'Before you speak, remember this is a game of truth. If you can't remember that, let me put it another way. Lie, you die. See even a simpleton like you should be able to remember that ditty.'

Unfolding the sheet Kia read aloud.
'Question one..
'Who runs Oracle. That's an easy one, there are ten of us in the main crew.
'How many Super-Craft do they have? 20, currently, but we make more if needed.
'Who do they work for? No one, we are independent without ties.
'Are the Super-Crafts armed? No, they have no weaponry at all.
'Is the island armed? Again, no, we have no need to be.
'Who is the boss/leader of Oracle? That would be me.
'Is Oracle a threat to the USA? No, we are a threat to no country or government.
How is Oracle funded? We are self-funded, our resources run into Trillions.

'How can we get a Super-Craft? You can't. Just not possible.
'And your last question was,
'Is it possible to eradicate Oracle?
Not with anything you currently have in your arsenal. In fact, if you joined forces with Russia, China and the United Kingdom, you still would lose.'

Kia screwed up the sheet and threw it on the table. 'See, that was painless. Do you have any further questions?'
The room remained deathly quiet.

'Now, your turn to play. Who's idea was it to capture my people and torture them?'

Milton cleared his throat. 'Initially, it was Fairbanks, who brought the idea to the table. Before his report and request for an interview, none of us had even heard of Oracle or what it did.'

'Well now you know. Oracle looks after its people, we protect our people and hurting anyone, just one, of us is the worst possible thing you can do. Fairbanks paid for his mistake. I really hope none of you, or anyone else makes the same mistake he did. I guarantee the outcome will be the same.

'Now, because none of my people died, I am going to let you all walk away from this. Hopefully, a lot wiser. Although I doubt it. As soon as you think you are safe from me, you will revert to your ingrained, narcissistic tendencies.'
Kia put her hand to her earpiece, 'OK', she simply said.

'My friend has to deal with something. Now do any of you have any more questions?'

One guy lifted a finger, 'Why are you here?'

Kia lifted an eyebrow, 'Really? Such a dumbass question from a supposedly intelligent military officer! I am here because you assholes decided that you would take three of my girls, beat them near to death and then finish them off once you believed they had no more to say. All for what?

'Ten lousy fucking questions? Who the fuck do you think you are? 'You think you can just grab people, torture them for answers and then dispose of the remains?'

'Then just put your jacket on and go home to the wife? The USA military is just a pack of self-empowered bullies and thugs. You think you rule the world and can deal with anyone with impunity however you see fit. You are legends in your own minds.'

*****

Outside ValKyrie had launched into the air, turned to midnight black and rocketed into the sky. She had detected three incoming fighters that had been sent to the bunker. Standard procedure when communications were lost for over 30 minutes. Flying at 15,000 feet the jets were running just over Mach 2, in a tight arrowhead formation.

The leader informed the wingmen that they were 11 minutes from the bunker and would do a hot flyby to scope out if there was a problem. He got confirmation from both the other aircraft. None of the three pilots noticed a dark pinprick sized craft off to the right.

ValKyrie had run a semicircle path from the bunker, climbing to the exact same altitude as the fighters. From the time she had left the ground, she had been accelerating, hard. Her trajectory was timed so her path intersected 90 degrees to the others exactly 10 miles from the bunker. As she approached the formation, she flipped herself onto her left wing tips and flashed through the arrow head formation on the edge. Her top wing removed the tail of the leading fighter, and her lower wings removed the nose of the two others, then she was gone.

ValKyrie flipped horizontally again and finished her circular path to land back near the bunker.

Eight miles away three parachutes were slowly descending to earth. Off in the distance three plumes of black smoke started to rise from the ground into the still desert air.

'Back', is all she said.

*****

Kia looked around the room, she pointed to the civilian personnel. 'All of you, leave now, outside.' There was a controlled but fast rush out the hole where the door used to be.

'You five, I want you to do something for me. I want each of you to contact your commanding officer of the US Military, and give him two messages from me.

'Firstly, tell him, Oracle is out of bounds. Secondly, tell him I will be coming to see him soon, in person, to make sure he got the message. I am leaving now, 30 seconds after I leave, this place will not be a healthy place to be. Your choice.' Kia stood, turned on her heels and walked out of the doorway.

As she slid into the command seat five figures were running from the bunker, one lagging behind, but he got no help from the others.
'Typical'. muttered Kia. 'Destroy the bunker and lets go home.'

ValKyrie rose off the desert floor and swung in a tight arc, as she flew away from the bunker two streaks came from the back of her wings and penetrated the roof of the bunker. A split second later a dull boom rattled the air, and the bunker seemed to lift partially out of the sand before falling into a deep hole beneath. Sand from around the hole poured into the crater and soon there was no sign anything had ever existed there.

Travelling back up the slope ValKyrie kicked out another dart as she crested the hill and disappeared from view. She never saw the impact. The crowd of people standing in the desert saw it and watched as a mangled antenna dish cartwheeled and bounced down the hill.

ValKyrie slid silently to a stop outside the OpCen. Kia climbed out and looked up to the balcony, no one was in sight. She turned around, but ValKyrie was gone! 'Sneaky Bitch', Kia said out loud and headed for the elevator.

Chapter Fifty Seven

She stopped at the café to grab some sandwiches and a drink. Only Neil was in the café. He turned at the sound of the elevator door opening and turned white when he saw it was Kia.

'Hi Neil.'
He swallowed heavily a few times 'Good to see you back', he almost ran to the elevator before the door shut.

Kia just stared at the closed door, 'I need to tell him never to play poker.' She grabbed what she came for and headed up top. Walking into the OpCen, Kia was surrounded by people bombarding her with questions. Brad broke the scrum up, 'OK, OK, people, back up, give Kia some room!'
'Thank you' Kia said, 'Firstly report on the girls please, Sandy.'
'All doing tremendously well, even Kate's hands, they were dislocated not broken, so healing and recovery are much better than first thought. The doctors are very happy with their progress.'
'Excellent news. Now let me sit on the balcony and eat this. Then we can have a meeting where we can all recant what we have been doing over the last week.'
'Neil, follow me, please.' He had been standing at the back of the mob trying to look relaxed. At the mention of his name, he nearly passed out!. On unsteady legs he followed Kia.
Kia swallowed the last of her sandwich and took a swig out of her bottle.
'Neil, we need to talk about ValKyrie.'
He nodded and said nothing.

'Of all the things you have done here, all the silly ideas and the good ones, she had to be the most brilliant idea you have ever had. I cannot thank you enough for your forethought and visionary idea. Without her, I would have been in deep trouble! Thank you, young man, you deserve a medal.'

Neil nearly passed out with relief!, 'You're not angry with me or going to send me back to the mainland?'

'No Neil, I am proud of you as I said, and you are irreplaceable to the crew. Now get the others so we can have a pow-wow.'

It was well after dark on the balcony, as they all took turns at outlining thier week. Kia had told her story first, then Bree, Melissa, Paul, and now it was Miako's turn.

'Before I tell our story, remember you said that at the beginning you would back any play that we did, does that still hold true?'

Kia nodded, 'Certainly! Why would it change?'

'Well, Neil and I have taken a task on in Switzerland. Actually, it was me that said I would help first.'

Kia smiled and crossed her legs, 'Go on, this sounds interesting.'

'Well, for the first few days we just partied with the whole town. They had some Fest going on and the whole place was like a Mardi Gras. 'Anyway, one morning we received an invite to go to this chalet, way up on a hill overlooking the town and valley. Now, this chalet is only for diplomats, royalty, and famous people kind of thing.

'It turns out, our friend Haakon was in town and had seen us at a restaurant. He was visiting a long time friend Baron Julien Fellman. To cut a long story short, the Baron's son has gone missing in the mountains with friends and the Baron asked if we, as a favour to him and Haakon would find his son and bring him home.'

'That's a strange request from Haakon, he knows what we do, and missing persons aren't really our forte', Paul said. 'He may even be home by now.'

Miako smiled at the surprised looks around the table.

'Strange you should say that Paul. That is exactly what we said, but, the son went missing thirty-one years ago, and no trace of the party of four has ever been found.

'The Baron is old, and I told him we, Neil and I, would do whatever we could to bring him home. I hope I did the right thing, Kia, to me it felt the right thing at the time. I did say I would ask you first.'

'Yes, you did the right thing! That is what we do here, we find things that are not where they belong and sort the issue out! I know we have been doing things in the oceans, but that was our starting point. We need to get acceptance from the rest of the world for what we do.

'It will be the only way we can expand from water to land. I hope that one day, Oracle can go anywhere on the earth and fix problems that no one else can possibly fix, and do it with the blessing of whoever it may be that needs the help.

'You tell Sandy what you need, and I will support you in this anyway I can. If you want to take some of us with you great! If you want to take us all, even better!'

'Count Paul and me in', Glen said, a sentiment echoed by everyone.

Standing up Kia looked over the faces of everyone, 'You guys are just the best, every one of you different, but you all fit together like a well-made machine. I am in need of some sleep.'

Kia waved and headed for her bed.

Early next morning Kia was leaning on the counter in the medical centre, listening intently as the doctor was going over the girls charts one by one. At the end of the report, he looked at her and said 'I hope whoever did this gets what is coming to him.'

Kia smiled, 'They did, with interest.'

'Why would someone do this?'

'Simple Doc. They wanted to know what we did here, and how to take it from us. Now you know why we never tell anyone anything if possible. Can I see them?'

'Sure, first room to the right.'

Kia walked down the corridor and turned into the room, Jess and Layla were out of bed and sitting in chairs next to Kate's bed.

Kia sat on the edge of Kate's bed. She looked over Kate's face, it was all the colours of the rainbow. 'I hope you feel better than you look. The Doc tells me you are on the mend and doing well, but what would he know, I wanted to see for myself.'

Kate grinned and winced, 'I am doing well, we all are, just trying to stop Layla from apologising, she thinks she should have done something.'

Kia turned to Layla, she could see that she was feeling something akin to survivor's guilt. 'I know how you're feeling dear, but trust me, you did the exact right thing looking after Kate. There was nothing else you could have done, and you know it was just a matter of time before they would have put you in the chair. It was a no win situation, and it could have ended much, much worse.

'The best thing for you to do now is to make sure these two behave for the doctors, and you take care of them. I told you all when you came here I would protect you, and I failed to do that.

'I promise this will never happen again.'

All three started to protest, but Kia held up her hand, 'It's true. This should not have happened. The person who did this to you will never hurt anyone ever again. I should not have let them hurt you in the first place.'

'It wasn't your fault either' Kate said, 'We all fell for Gina's story if anyone is to blame it's her.'

'Well, it's sorted now, and eventually Gina will pay for her part. Now you three get some rest. We need you back on your feet and data mining.'

Back in the OpCen Kia found the place empty, 'Where is everyone?'

Sandy cruised over, 'They are mostly waking up, they all spent two days in here, refused to leave and were harassing me to give them S2s to help.'

Kia grinned at that, 'Sorry, should have known they would do that. Now, dear Sandy, Tell me about ValKyrie and why did no-one say anything? Hmm?'

'Well, Neil wanted something to watch your back, in his words he said and I quote, "Kia watches our backs, but who watches hers?" So he designed ValKyrie with Miako and myself.

'We took an image of my AI main structure and changed the mission statement in the code. She is tasked to protect you above everything else, the crew next and Oracle last.

'A few weeks back when the code was finished, I set up a secured memory area and booted the code.
Just to make sure it worked as intended. We built the first ValKyrie and waited for the code to finish testing.'

'Wait!, the first? How many are there!?'

'Oh, only the one! I will get to that shortly. Well, the code finalised just fine. Then it escaped from the secure area I had it locked into. Don't ask, I don't know how. For two days nothing, then I start feeling something reading my entire database.

'Next I detect massive internet traffic, I try to block the flow, milliseconds later it's back reading data.

'I had 22 CPUs trying to tie it down, I failed. On a standard scan of the complex and buildings, I notice the craft in the back of the garage is disassembled! Now I have learned how to be sneaky from you, so I did nothing, just watched. The craft reassembled itself, then did it again, and again. For almost two weeks this went on. I analyse data, that's what I do. Then I noticed that the rebuilding of the craft coincided after a mass of data traffic flow.

'I now believe she was learning from whatever she was absorbing and then remodelled herself on that data.

'It was like watching a child learn and grow.'

'Now don't go getting clucky on me Sandy!'

'Oh no, ValKyrie is not my child per-se' she is more like a big sister actually. Then one day the craft just disappeared. I know she was close. I got ghost readings on sensors now and then. 'The next thing, she appears on that rock with you.'

'So, where is she now?'

'Actually, I have no idea, I do know that from an analysis of all the data, she watches you like a hawk, and postulating on that I also believe she watches everything that goes on around here.'

The elevator opened, and Miako and Melissa entered the OpCen.

'Thanks Sandy. Morning ladies.'

Miako sat on a stool facing Kia, 'I, we, need your help, Kia. I do not have a clue how to begin this project with the Baron. 'We are the doers, you are the planning brains. Where do we start?'

Kia sat down, and Melissa joined them.

'Right, first thing, permission. Always get the highest permission possible, and in writing if possible.'

Sandy opened the HUD in front of the trio, 'Late last night I received these two documents, they appeared on the screen. 'The first is a signed and stamped contract for five acres of land, for the use of Oracle. The contract is good for one year. No clue why, but that's the first document.

'The second one is from the Swiss aviation authority giving carte blanche access to Swiss airspace. However, several areas have been outlined, showing civilian air corridors and military training areas. We can go there if necessary. They just want us to know the places that they use.'

Kia nodded and smiled, 'Excellent, see you can plan projects! The reason you asked for land access escapes me, though.'

Miako took a deep breath, 'These are my thoughts on the matter, jump in if you need to.'

Paul and Glen arrived and stood listening and reading the HUD docs

'I thought that, although we are supposed to find his son and the other three, we might as well find and recover ALL that have gone missing in that valley. If not, it would be like picking up one object out of a pile and leaving the rest. That does not make sense to me.

'Also, our guide showed us an old collapsed farmhouse on that piece of property and remarked how it used to be used by climbers in the summer and skiers in the winter.

'Now whatever we find, it is stupid to send it back to here, then transport it back to there. So a local base made perfect sense. When the project is over they can use the base as a replacement for the old farm house.'
While Miako was explaining all this, the rest of the crew had arrived quietly.

Paul started clapping. 'That, my dear is a damn fine piece of organisation if I ever saw one.' Miako blushed.

'Paul is correct' Kia said, 'Not only did you take on the project, you thought of all the necessary parts to make it succeed! Trust me, you don't need my help in planning. You take the lead on this, and I will go along for the ride.'

'So what do I do now?' asked Miako.

'Well, you have most of it sorted, I suggest you go over to a HUD, see if Sandy can get the Baron on the line, and tell him. Tell him YOUR crew from Oracle is on its way.'

The Baron was indeed available and overjoyed at the news! He asked what he could do to help? Miako told him, keep warm and keep his fingers crossed, and one last favour, could he please arrange for the local guide Ben to be available if possible.
The Baron said he would get right on it and thanked her again for the help in his quest.

Standing outside in the early morning sun were nine shiny S2s. They were not carrying Hives this time. They were going to churn up enough interest just by themselves.

Miako took off first and Kia last.

At altitude they all slaved to Miako's craft and relaxed. It was going to be around a three hour run.

Kia looked around the S2 it seemed plain compared to ValKyrie. 'I have been spoiled' she said out loud to herself, and for a split second thought, she heard a chuckle.

<u>Chapter Fifty Eight</u>

The only tracks in the snow were the ones that Miako the others had left a few days ago. Now there were the indentations of the nine S2s.

'So what do you want to do first, Miako?'

'I have no idea. Any suggestions?'

Kia waited for someone else to answer first. 'Alright, I will help set things up but you, Miako will run the search itself. 'Paul, Glen set up the micro receivers so we can get the building side moving.'

The boys jumped into it. 'Melissa and Ray, run a parallel scan from that tree line there over the entire field to behind the old farm house. Let me know what you find. 'Everyone else into my S2, please.'

Shortly two S2s were running back and forth over the entire 5-acre clearing.

Bringing up a HUD, 'Right, shed plan, if Mel and Ray get good rock returns, we need to clear a space of everything down to bedrock. Miako wants to donate the building afterwards, so we need to make it solid.'

Kia pointed out features on the HUD, 'When we get the location, Brad I'd like you to scan a hole straight down. Talk to Sandy. Tell her we are looking for the easiest route to some hot rock.'

'Ah!' Brad said 'Geothermal heating! Great idea.'

'Bree and Miako can place the receiver grid as Paul and Glen get them from Sandy. Lastly, Neil, go Camo and run slow laps and let us all know if someone shows up.

'We don't need people to see the next two day's work. Luckily we have low cloud today and forecast for another day or so. That should stop people venturing out. As for me, I am going to make a cup of hot cocoa.'

Bree stood next to Paul as they watched the sixth large receiver Rod materialise in the small receiver they had constructed. It was taking about six minutes per large eighteen-foot receiver rod.

Miako stood next to Bree but was watching Mel, and Glen run their Scan grid. Also, Brad was hovering back and forth behind the ruins of the farmhouse.

'I am really glad you all came to help us on this project.'

Paul looked up from attaching chains to the top of the poles they already had. 'I wouldn't miss it for the world. You realise this is our first project on dry land? Whole new set of rules and circumstances, and we get to learn deep in the mountains away from prying eyes.'

Mel flittered overhead. 'I hope you have clean undies on Glen, you just got scanned!'

Glen grinned as he dragged the finished pole out of the receiver and another started to form. Mel and Ray landed next to Kia's S2, and they both walked inside it.

'Well, that was a surprise. We are on a huge outcrop of rock. The soil is about 8-12 inches deep, varies a lot, though. What was most surprising is we removed nearly ¾ of a tonne of various articles. You can read the list later. But under all this pretty snow there is a lot of man-made contamination.'

Brad entered the S2, 'No luck Kia, Sandy says all this area was formed by glacial and tectonic activity. The hot rock strata is way deeper than we can currently reach.

That means we have two options, we can go either Fossil fuel or Nuclear and personally I don't like either here.'

Sandy broke in', I think I have a solution, I went back over Brad's deep scan data, after looking for lava or hot rocks, I searched for water. It just so happens not too far from the old farm well is a very healthy underground stream.

'It's fed by the runoff from all the mountains in the valley.

'Once the building is built, I can build a scaled down version of a hydroelectric generator. We can fit that into the mainstream flow and have all the energy needed, clean and free.'

'Great' Brad said, 'You lead, I follow Sandy, show me where you want this hole', and with that Brad was gone.

'Next item', continued Sandy, 'Mel and Ray, jump into your craft and I will send you the CoOrds to scan clear to the bedrock.' Mel and Ray also left.

'Ha! I didn't have to say a word!' Kia said putting her feet up on the console.

'Your welcome' Sandy said.
Three hours later as it started getting dark, they all stood inside an industrial sized building that was brightly lit.

'So now what?' Ray asked Kia, sitting on the nose of his S2.

'Tomorrow at first light we start the search proper. Sandy is repositioning a satellite overhead, and it won't be in place until early morning.'

A disc materialised, and Sandy was there, 'Hello, welcome to my new home.' That brought smiles and chuckles. 'When I have the Sat in place, I can set up a proper search grid for you all, it will have a 50% overlap because of the rugged terrain.
'The Sats struggle to scan things like this valley and mountains.
'They just don't have the fine resolution necessary.

'There is a kitchen and sleeping rooms, where the offices will be later. I can change the layout at will now that the large receivers are contained in the walls. Follow me and I shall show you.'

'Very impressive as usual', said Mel after the tour.
They sat in a small lounge area discussing the next day's itinerary.

At first light, Sandy had given a short briefing on the search pattern that each of the S2s now had. She also played host to a short video conference with the girls in the medical centre.

When it was all over the crew filed out into the S2s and one by one they took off to the waypoints Sandy had pre-programmed. All except Neil. She had a different task for him planned out, and while he headed down the valley, she instructed him on exactly what his job was for the morning.

The first grid for the crew was a simple spiral pattern. It started where the main road intersected the valley and followed the contours of where the hills became the foot of the mountains. In an offset line that allowed a 50% overlap, the eight S2s took off in perfect unison. Out the front window visibility was down to 20-30 meters due to the low cloud and thick morning fog.

They ran clockwise up the valley, a smooth turn at the wide end and back along the right side of the road. Following the road, they eventually arrived back at the start point. Starting inside the previous lap, they did it all again. Neil had watched the others take off on their first lap of the valley. As they cleared out he swung his craft over the main highway. There was very little traffic that time in the morning.

He positioned himself just at the shoulder of the main road, nose pointing into the fields in a rough direction of the building. Once certain he was on the red line on his HUD, he slowly moved forward, just over a running pace.

Sandy had programmed a special scan configuration in his S2, and as he scanned the ground in front of him, behind the S2 the ground was left with a profile that imitated tracks left behind by load of trucks and vehicular traffic!

'This is amazing!' Neil said to Sandy', It looks like a thousand trucks have been up here. Did you program it all overnight?'

'I would like to take the credit for it all, and I could have done it myself, but given the short time span, I cheated and took a scanned copy from a main logging road about 400 km to the west.

'I have to repeat it in places, but I am betting no one will notice that. Just follow the red line on the HUD, it twists and winds a bit to suit this terrain. I think it will do the job, though.'

'It sure will', Neil said. He went back to concentrating on the red line as it guided him past stands of trees and slopes.

Next time the others circled past for the next run they were stunned to see what looked like a well-used trail leading towards the building location.

Brad and Paul caught on first. 'Oh, you are so sneaky Sandy! Is Neil cutting that sign?'

'Yes, I figure with locals coming out this way soon, it would be good to let them think the building was prefabricated and delivered here and assembled. If they are to believe that, we need witness marks to back up that theory.'

Everyone got back to work until Kia called for a break in mid-afternoon. Neil was already back in the building, his S2 parked in a fresh clearing.
Walking inside everyone stopped and stared at the huge amount of stuff neatly sorted and piled on the floor.

'Wow! This is all from this morning's scan?'

'No Bree, this is a third of this mornings scan, I have not assembled the rubbish, animal carcasses, and other items that I classified as irrelevant to the project.'

Paul and Ray walked along the long rows of sorted stuff, Ropes, carabineers, picks, boots, tents, skis, some good, some broken, a huge pile of oxygen cylinders. 'We could start our own climbing shop with this lot!'

'Or a museum' Kia said picking up an ancient Kero lamp.

'What a lot of stuff!' Melissa picked up rope off the top of a pile, 'It's like new! The must be tonnes of it here.'

'22.7' Sandy said. 'A tiny grain of sand compared to what we have removed in the last two months. Oh! That reminds me. I am currently leading the scoreboard on tonnage recovered. Sorry.'

'How is that possible!' Neil said. He was leading last time he looked.

'Easy dear boy, I had 800 drones running for the last week and a half continuously.'

'That's twice you have been sneaky today' Paul said, 'I am starting to be suspicious of you!'

Kia broke into the levity of the moment, 'Never underestimate a smart woman Paul, you should know that. Now, let's get fed. We still have work to do, people.'

'Just before you go', Sandy moved over to a store room, 'We have our first two human remains. I have done the DNA stuff, neither of them is the Baron's son, the time frame is wrong. I think it's going to take a long time to identify them. Unless we can find some kind of record kept on missing persons somewhere.'

'I didn't get any flags!' Bree looked at the others, 'Did you?' All negative replies.

'That's because we are here to find the remains, no need to flag them.' Kia said.

Just under an hour later they were all back in action, this time, Neil had tagged on the end of the line. Slowly they worked their way into the centre and finished the valley floor a few hours after dark.
The recovered piles inside the warehouse end had increased slightly but not significantly.

Sandy informed them there was one more human remains found, but she had left it where it was. 'It's buried not far from the old farm, I believe it may belong there so I left it.'
Showered and relaxed, most of the girls lounged about the office. Paul and the boys were in the warehouse section picking through all the items.

Ray picked up an old gas mask, 'I bet there are some stories amongst all of this gear.'

'What amazes me is that all this had to be backpacked and carried all the way up the valley. Look at this.' Neil held up a huge ice pick. 'It has a name cut into the handle I can't read, but a date of 1893! Lost over a century ago.'
They spent half an hour or so picking up and examining stuff before finally calling it a night.

Early the next mourning Kia and Bree stood in the warehouse doorway, both holding hot drinks. The sky outside was a pure crystal blue, and visibility went as far as the eye could see.

The sound of a door slamming made them turn around, both girls grinned. Brad and the boys were swarming over two Scania six wheel drive vehicles that had appeared overnight. Brad had the hood open on one and was drooling over the V8 turbocharged diesel engine.

Bree laughed at their antics, 'You know they will never grow up, don't you?'

'I think you're right, but it is great to see them play. I told Sandy last night we needed transport into town. We can't just fly nine S2s into the place and land in the town square. This is what she came up with.

'I am going into town to visit the Baron and introduce myself.

'I will take an S2 for that. I'd like Miako and you to drive in and find this local guide, Ben. I do not think for a moment the boys will let you drive so they will go. If we can get this done and be back around midday, there will be time to start Scanning from the foothills up and outwards.'

'Sounds like a plan to me', Bree said. She tipped the dregs out of her cup into the snow and walked off to arrange the road trip.

Kia headed to the office, stepping over two sets of male legs sticking out beneath one of the vehicles. She just shook her head and muttered, 'Boys!'

The video linked to the medical centre back on the island. She spoke with the doc and then the girls, satisfied all was as good as it could be she cut the link.

Back in the warehouse, both vehicles were gone, and no one was to be found.

Sandy appeared, 'You have been abandoned, dear. Paul and Glen suddenly found reasons to go into town, the same with Glen and Mel.'

Kia nodded, 'I really should have expected that.

'Anything I need to do? I am going to see the Baron, let him know our progress and introduce us properly, not that I think Miako didn't do a good job of that.'

'Actually, I am glad you are doing that! I will use your S2 to scan the local town hall records and try and isolate any records of people missing in the area.'

'You ARE getting sneaky Sandy!'

Flying slow and low she soon caught up with the two Scania's, they seemed to be having a great time. She could tell from the tracks they had deviated several times to run through the deep virgin snow. She flashed overhead and swept towards the township.

Parking outside the chalet, she walked over to the edge overlooking the town. It was a very impressive view.

Walking up to the door, it opened before she could knock.

'Hello', she said to a huge security guard, 'Please inform the Baron and Haakon that Kia from Oracle is here to see them both.'

The guard closed the door, and his heavy footfalls could be heard walking away from the door.

Chapter Fifty Nine

It did not take long, and the guard was back and opened the door wide and ushered Kia into the main lounge.

'Kia! It is good to see you again', Haakon strode across the carpet and shook her hand vigorously. 'Come, let me introduce you to my dear friend, Julien.' Kia shook the Baron's hand.

'It is an honour to meet you, Baron.'

'Please call me Julien. Take a seat, Haakon has told me all about you. Your friends Miako and Neil are such fine people.' Haakon and Kia sat.

'Yes, she told me all about your situation, and the entire crew jumped at the chance to come and see if they could help.'

'When do you think you may start your search? I don't want to seem ungrateful or impatient. Just my health is starting to decline somewhat, and I would really like to know before I leave.'

Kia smiled, 'I understand completely. We have already started, my people have already constructed a warehouse in the same area as the old farmstead. They are also on their way into town to talk to Ben, one of the local guides. The more local knowledge we get, the more we have to work with.'

'I am sorry to appear to be uninformed, but why would you need a warehouse to find Julien's son?'

Kia turned to Haakon, 'Well, not only are we looking for Julien's son, but we are also removing everything that has been discarded in the valley and on the mountains.

'Think of it like this, we have an extremely efficient broom, and as we sweep, we collect everything, eventually.

'When we are finished, we hope that your valley will be clean and as pristine as nature intended. That was a very poor analogy, I did not mean to infer that Julien's son was rubbish.'

The Baron chuckled', I didn't think you did, but the analogy helped me understand much better. It makes perfect sense when looking for something to pick up other items that should not be there.'

Kia smiled, 'And as one last benefit, when we bring your son home, we will leave the warehouse for the townspeople to use as a base camp for those that like to adventure out into the mountains. It is large enough to be used for a combination of emergency aid, possibly a gear storage area, and anything else you may wish to use it for.'

The Baron pushed a button, and the maid appeared, 'Tea please dear.'

The maid curtsied and vanished into the back. He turned back to Kia, 'I have a few questions if you don't mind.'

Ask anything you like Baron, 'I will answer all questions except on how we do what we do.'

Haakon chuckled at that, 'I wonder where I have heard that before!'

The three sat and chatted about a large range of subjects for several hours before Kia stood and shook both their hands, stating she had better get back to work.

After she had left Julien turned to Haakon, 'That lady there is going to change the course of the entire human race, you mark my words. There is something special about her.

'Something I have not seen in any other person, I have met in my lifetime.'

Haakon pondered for a moment, 'I do believe that you are correct What they did in Norway was nothing short of miraculous.

'Our fishing industry alone has advanced 200% now the waters are clean and clear again. She may not have realised it, but it is us that owe her a massive debt, not the other way around.'

Oblivious to the compliments she had just been awarded, Kia went back to the valley. She saw the crew were still out. Instead of landing she looped off and followed the mountain ridgeline all the way around to the highest peak. From that point, she could see the curvature of the horizon, but there were several mountains in the distance that were higher.

'Quite a view', Sandy said, as Kia hovered over the highest point.

'Indeed, but I don't think I would like to climb it personally. Did you get any information from the Hall records?'

'Yes, quite a lot and dating back into the 1700s. A lot of people have gone missing over the decades, most found and recovered, but there are still are a lot of names with a blank space next to it. What we need is an anthropologist.'

Kia leant forward and punched a code into the HUD, after a few seconds Trudy's face appeared on the screen. 'Hi, Trudy.'

'Hello, Kia! I was thinking about calling you. I have finished sorting the team out, and Sandy is working on travel arrangements for them.'

'Good to hear, I have a question for you. Is one of them an anthropologist?'
Trudy thought a moment, 'No, sorry, some of us have dealt with bones before, but none of the team is a true anthropologist.

'May I ask why?'

'We are currently on a project, and it is entirely possible that we will recover several human remains, some possibly as old as the 1700s. Never mind, it was a long shot.'

'I will ask around, and if I hear anything, I will call.'

'Thanks, Trudy, take care and see you soon. Kia cut the link.

'Bugger, never mind, between us two I am sure we can figure it out. If not, I will hand the problem over to the Baron and with his resources he can work it out.'
She let the S2 flow over the edge of the peak and headed back to base camp. As the S2 neatly entered into the doorway, it landed directly in front of a very startled Ben.

Kia hopped out and walked over to him, 'Hello, you must be Ben.'

Neil came over at the same time. 'Ben this is Kia, the boss lady.'

'Hi' Ben said, 'Strange aircraft you have there!' Kia smiled, 'Don't blame me, Neil designed them.'

Neil and Ben followed Kia into the lounge area. 'Take a seat Ben, we will get to you soon. She turned to Neil.

'Listen up, the Baron is now up to speed on what we are doing, and he has got a very quick and active mind for a man of his age. He also said thank you to you all for volunteering to help.

'We still have daylight left to run some laps. Sandy is going through a lot of local data to try and pinpoint the identification of any HR we scan. Miako, you have told Ben we have to kill him now he has seen our craft?'

Miako looked at Ben. 'Actually, I had not got to that part yet.'

Ben's eyes widened considerably, 'WHAT?'

'Relax, only kidding. Sit and let me explain a few things.' Ben sat down, but did not look comfortable at all!

'Firstly, we are not here for the Baron's son only. We are here for everyone that is still missing, the way we work is to clear the whole area of all objects that don't belong, we then sort it all out in the warehouse. Please do not ask how we do it, we will not tell. In fact, the less you remember about this project, the more we will appreciate it.'
He nodded silently, but was still tense.

'I have told the Baron that once we are finished here, we will leave this building standing, for the use of the township.'

'Really! That, that is fantastic! We really need something out here, the old farm house...'

Kia held up her hand, 'I know, Miako told me. Now you are going to witness some top secret stuff, that would be best forgotten, understood?'

'Yes, ma'am, perfectly!'

'Right, I am putting you into Neil's care. He will answer some questions, but if you ask something you shouldn't there will be no answer.'
'Got it!'
She stood, 'OK, lets do this.'

All S2s had returned to the exact location they had stopped at yesterday.
Miako took the lead and the rest fell into formation. For two solid days lap after lap, every nook and cranny was scanned. Anything that should not have been there was removed.

Eventually, all the shorter slopes were scanned. Kia kicked Paul and Glen off the formation with instructions to look over the tops of the lower slopes. The higher the remaining formation went, more of the crew peeled away.
There were four high peaks to scan. Allocating two S2s per peak they scanned the rest of the way to the top.
'Right, the daylight is fading. Free for all in areas you think show promise, after sunset back to the warehouse.'
The S2s swarmed over the cliffs, mountains and small valley like a horde of ants. At sunset one by one, they landed outside the warehouse.
Inside the warehouse was literally a mountain of stuff!
'Geezus' Ray said 'Look at that lot! There were rows upon rows of stacked and sorted gear.'
Ben just stood with his mouth open. Kia walked past, 'Ben follow me, please.'
Ben walked side by side with Kia, he obviously wanted to ask a pile of questions but kept his mouth shut.
'Do you know what a Hologram is?' she asked him.
He nodded, they had played with one at the university, he had attended.
'Good' she said, 'I want you to meet ours.'
Inside the room that was their mini OpCen, she sat Ben on a stool.

'Sandy?' Sandy's Hologram appeared, 'Sandy meet Ben.'
'Hi Ben', Sandy said.
'So Sandy tell me, what did we find?'
Brad and Bree came in and sat down.

'Well, I am still collating all the data, but, so far you have collected 97 tonnes of stuff you saw in the warehouse. 115 tonnes of rubbish and debris I junked and, 113 HR.'
'113!' Brad said in astonishment.
Ben lifted a finger, 'err, what is an HR?'
Bree answered him, 'HR is Human Remains.'
'Wow' Ben said.
Sandy cleared the HUD and brought up a panoramic view of the entire valley, superimposed on the picture were 113 red circles, mostly on their own but some in multiples. Zooming into a section Sandy showed a group of 4 virtually on top of each other.
'This was the final resting place of the Baron's son and the three friends he had with him.'
Ben walked over for a closer look, 'I have climbed that place, it is just a sheer rock wall, you can't get all the way up as the rock is unstable further up. I can't see how they stopped there, without a ledge or anything. Actually, that wall leans outwards slightly.'
'Correct young Ben, but they did not stop on the face, but behind it. Further up there is a fracture in the rock, and as you say the face of the rock leans outwards.
'My theory is when they were snowboarding down the slope, a crust of snow bridged the fracture and hid it from view. However, the weight of four of them hitting the crust allowed them to punch through and drop into the space behind the leaning front rock.
'Death would have to have been instantaneous. From 60-80kph to a sudden stop in a deep V fracture.

'Falling snow would have filled the entry holes again, leaving no signs at all. In summer with no snow, the fissure was deep enough, you could not see the bottom.'

Everyone had arrived while Sandy was talking, no one spoke. The HUD zoomed back out. 'Ben this is where you come in.'

'Me??'

Sandy nodded, 'With your local knowledge, can or do you remember anything concerning the areas of these other HR locations?'

Ben studied the HUD closer, 'These six may have been a party that went missing a few years back. They were supposed to be running this climbing route here', he pointed. 'They either had a bad guide or decided to take a different route. That makes it almost impossible to find people when they do that.'

'That is a lot of people' said Mel.

'Yes and that's only this single valley', Ray said.

'So now comes the hard bit, confirming the identity of the HR.'

Kia and Ray walked into the storage area where there were 113 wooden boxes. On the top of each of the boxes was a smaller box with a pile of stuff, all the personal effects or the clothes the HR was wearing and anything located nearby that may help to identify the body.

Kia picked up a thin wallet. She slid out the contents and flicked through them, stopping at one card she read the Baron's son's name out loud. 'Welcome home Mr. Fellman. Your dad is waiting for you.'

One by one the crew filtered into the morgue area, quietly and respectfully. They went through the items boxes and wrote on a card what they found.

Even Ben walked in and hesitantly stood by the door watching.

Kia turned to him, 'Come on in Ben, some of these unfortunate souls are part of your heritage. If you want to help get them home finally, you are welcome to join in.'

He moved closer, 'I won't have to touch the bodies?'

'No, not at all. We just use the belongings to try and identify them one by one. Sandy has been able to do that for 76 of them. The others, not so much.

'She has their dental imprints and also the DNA. But that is only good if we have something to compare it with.'

Bree called Ben over to the box she was working in. She held up a twisted grass wristband, 'I thought I saw some of these in town. Are they local or common in the country?'

Ben took the band, 'This is local! Different families braid them different ways like the Scottish have different tartans. There are some old folk in town that may recognise the style.'

Bree stood back as Ben looked at the contents of the box, 'This clothing is an older style, that backs up the local idea. You see guests and visitors nearly always have brand new or near new equipment and clothing. They buy their way into this sport, rather than grow up in it.' He went to move to the next box.

Bree laid a hand on his arm, 'Put your initials on the box, and look in every box that does not have your initials. Just because we have looked, doesn't mean we don't miss something that you may not. The wristband is a perfect example.'

They spent a fair bit of time on the last 37 boxes, about 40% of them, now had extra info or leads that may eventually lead to a solid identification.

Kia stood back, 'That's enough for me for one day. I have a few loose ends to tie up, then I am hitting the sheets.'
With a wave, she headed for the Op Room.

Standing in front of the HUD with her hands on her hips, Kia was staring at the image of the Doc from the medical centre. 'Just a moment, go back to the beginning and tell me that again!'

The Doc looked down at the charts in front of him, 'Two days ago, Kate's vital were showing normal recovery, her hands were still badly swollen, but we expected that. Over the last two days, her recovery has accelerated ten, maybe twenty fold.

'I just finished my rounds of the patients, and her hands are almost back to normal! I have never seen such rapid recovery in my entire career!'

'That is good news, isn't it?'

'Well, yes, excellent news, her eyes are no longer bloodshot, the bruising is almost gone. Yes, it's great news, but don't ask me how the hell it happened!'

Kia just stood thinking. 'Ok doc, lets worry about it when we get back.'

He shrugged, 'Fine by me.' Kia reached out and tapped the keyboard and cut the video feed. She stared at her hands and flexed her fingers. 'I think I know how Doc', she said in a whisper.

Early next morning, she found some of the crew and Ben going through the near overflowing warehouse. Mel was holding up a torn parachute, 'One unhappy base jumper somewhere.' The others were picking up and putting down stuff.

Sandy appeared, 'I have spoken to Haakon, he and the Baron will drop in via helicopter around midday.
They are also sending a truck to collect the four boys.'

Kia nodded, 'Well, we might as well start winding down the project. I would call it a success, wouldn't you?' Affirmation was received from all, as they walked out the warehouse door.

'What are we going to do with all this', Brad asked, waving his arm at the mass of gear on the floor.

Miako walked over to Kia, 'I have an idea.' She explained what she had in mind. Kia put her hand on Miako's shoulder, 'That princess, is a great idea, leave it with me and I will see if I can organise something.'

A commotion started just outside the door, Kia looked up to see Glen running full tilt back in the doorway followed by at least three well aimed snowballs. 'I see the boys are off leash again!'

Glen stopped and grinned. 'Actually Bree started it! Neil and I were making a snowman, and she said there is one thing missing!'

Brad laughed, 'Yup, that's Bree for you. I am not going out there to get covered in snow!'

'Chicken', Bree said, as she walked in the door. Next second a huge dump of snow fell on Brad. 'Thank you Sandy', Bree said and went back outside.

Brad looked at Sandy's Holo, 'Really! That was sneaky!'

'Us girls got to stick together', she said and faded out.

<u>Chapter Sixty</u>

Late morning a half-track truck pulled up outside. Kia recognised the driver as the security man from the chalet. He looked around and pulled a radio from his coat pocket, spoke into it briefly and climbed back in the truck for warmth.

It was not long before the regular beat of rotors could be heard approaching. Those outside came and stood in the doorway watching the chopper land. Someone had cleared a helipad that morning, and the chopper landed neatly in the middle of the cleared area. The side door opened, and two people walked over to the crew in the doorway.

Kia took over the introductions, even Ben was introduced. With that out of the way Haakon and the Baron were given a tour of the warehouse area.

Julien stopped and turned back to look at all the mountains of gear. 'All this was left discarded in the valley! Unbelievable!'

'It is an accumulation of over 100 years', explained Kia, some left by the first pioneers.'

'We need a museum', said the Baron and continued the tour that ended in the lounge.

Everyone made themselves scarce, leaving only Kia with the guests. Miako came in with three mugs of hot steaming tea and then turned to leave. 'Please stay' said the Baron, 'I have you to thank for finding my son.' She stayed and sat next to Kia on a lounge.

Together they explained what they had found and also recounted the possible scenario that led the son to his demise, including why so many searches had failed before.

The Baron was teary but hid it by sipping his tea.

'Well, Haakon, you were wrong my friend, these people are not just good people and good at what they do. Each and every one of them is a magician in their own right. Not only did they deliver on an almost impossible promise, but brought everyone that was missing here back home! There is no way I could ever repay you and your people for this, I will always be in your debt.'

'Julien, there is something you could do for us, actually for the whole town, and if it is possible, we would be happy to call the debt paid.'

The Baron put his cup down and leant forward. 'Anything I can do, please just ask!'

Kia nudged Miako with her elbow.

Miako was a bit flustered as all eyes centred on her, 'I have an idea. Actually, it was Ben who told Neil and myself some of the histories of the old farm that seeded the idea.'
Over the next few minutes, Miako explained to the Baron her idea and what benefit it could be to the township and the tourists.
When she finished speaking, the Baron reclined back in his chair and was silently thinking.

Haakon was smiling and sipped his tea, 'I do believe you have stumped the Baron! Something I have never seen before!'

The Baron looked at him, 'HA! You wish', he focused back on Miako, 'dear lady not only can I help with your idea, but I applaud you with its simple but sheer brilliance! It will be done!

'No, retract that, consider it done as of this very minute!'
They raise their mugs as the Baron called for a toast to seal the deal.

The helicopter had left after much handshaking and hugs for the ladies from the Baron and Haakon. The Truck was loaded with four of the caskets and had also departed.

Kia, Miako, Neil and Ben stood in the doorway as several S2s rose in unison and disappeared down the valley.

As the last one faded from sight, the four of them went back to the lounge as the huge door to the warehouse slowly closed behind them.

'So what happens now?' asked Ben.

Miako looked at Kia who nodded. 'Remember when Neil and I came up here, and you told us about the role the old farm used to play for the people in the valley, and you went on to tell us how something was needed to make this area a safer place for people to travel.'

Ben nodded, 'Don't tell me you have fixed the farmhouse!'

'No, we didn't, we demolished it. It was dangerous to anyone who ventured inside.'

'Oh, a shame.'

'Ben this warehouse is now yours. You own it lock, stock and barrel. All the stuff is yours to do with as you like. We will put it into storage containers outside. Inside will be remodelled to have ten units for people to stay in, we will put in a small infirmary for accident victims, and I suggest you open a store to resell all that stuff we collected. Both the vehicles are also yours, so you have a way of transporting people to and from town when needed.'

Ben just stared, from one to the other. His mouth moved, but nothing came out.

Kia walked over to him and clapped him on the shoulder, 'You're welcome.' Now I suggest you go back to town, tell your dad what is going on, and be back here bright and early. Miako and Neil will be staying on for a day or two, just to help you get started.'

Ben stood, 'I cannot, WE, the townspeople cannot, thank you enough for this!'

'You can thank yourself and the Baron. Both of you saw the need, and we just helped it along. I will not be here when you get back, but you can call on us if something you cannot handle arises.'

Outside the warehouse Ben put on his hat and gloves, all the goodbyes had been said inside.

Ben walked towards where the two Scania's were parked, but stopped when he heard a loud whistle, looking back, Neil was pointing to the other side of the vehicles. Ben walked around the other side and came to a dead halt!

In front of him was an iridescent blue, top of the line Supercharged V6 snowcat.

'Have a great ride home' Neil yelled. Ben waved frantically and sprinted to the cat, for a few moments he just sat there looking at the full digital dash and extras.
Hitting the start button it fired on the first swing. The exhaust was deep and quiet. With a wave of his hand and a twist of the throttle Ben shot across the snow with a rooster tail of snow behind him. Within minutes he was gone from view, but still could be heard for some time.

Kia turned to the others, 'OK, I am off home. Sandy will refurbish the interior overnight. There will be a few additions she will explain. Add anything you think will be of use and once Ben has a grasp, which I think he already has, mostly. I will see you back on the island.
'Take care, remember the lesson from the girls, although you have Sandy to protect you here.'

Just as she turned to leave, she stopped, 'You know, you both make a fantastic team. This has been proven by your very good ideas, I am proud of you both.'

With that, she walked to the S2, with a wave climbed in and took off in the same direction the others had.
About four miles from the base she saw Ben thundering through the flat, smooth snow below, she smiled as she flew low and past him, Ben waved like a maniac until she was gone.

Chapter Sixty One

Just on dark, the S2 dropped onto the pad outside the OpCen. A tired but happy Kia went up top. There was an additional HUD on the wall, and it was connected to the Swiss Base. It really could no longer be classed as a warehouse.

'Welcome home', Sandy said.

'It's good to be back', she smiled, 'any problems?'

'Not one, the drones are working well, the complex is running like a charm. I got an update from the Doc, the girls are climbing the walls to get out of there.'

'That reminds me, have you located where ValKyrie is?' Sandy paused, 'Nope, not on my sensors, but that's nothing unusual. I have never really been able to find her.'

'Hmm Kia said, another sneaky AI, just what I needed! Never mind.' Kia walked out onto the balcony and plopped down next to Brad.

'Howdy boss, you look beat.'

She brushed her hair back, 'All I need is a shower and sleep, and no more problems for a year.'

He grinned, 'Two out of three isn't bad, so the saying goes. Sandy told us all about the donation, and the use the warehouse is being put to. I'd say we had a good outcome all the way around.
I certainly learnt a lot, more along the lines of working on land rather that underwater.'

'Yes, that was different, it needed a whole different approach.'

Bree came out and brought a tray of finger food and a large pot of hot drink. 'I am hungry, but can't be bothered to go all the way to the complex.'
They chatted about the last few days.
Slowly they were joined by the rest of the crew in ones and twos. The last to arrive was Ray.

Eventually, someone had to bring it up. Ray looked at Kia and said, 'So boss, tell us about this other craft you had hidden from us.'

Kia laughed, 'Me? Even *I* didn't know it existed!'
'Honest?!'

'Straight up honest, Paul. Even Neil and Miako who designed it didn't really know. Hell, Sandy wasn't sure either.'

'OK, I am just a country boy with little education. Tell me, slowly, what you do know' Glen said.'

Kia refilled her cup, 'Right I will tell you what little I know.'

'Remember when Neil and Miako designed and made the S2 units, well, apparently, Ray here suggested a different type as well.'

'Hey! Don't go blaming me! It was just an offhand comment I made! I had no idea he would actually go and make one!!'

'Well, obviously he thought it was a good idea, because Neil also made one of a different type.

'Sandy and Neil colluded and took a copy of Sandy's AI code, Neil changed some of its parameters and Sandy reassembled the code and booted it.

'Well, the new AI, disappeared from Sandy's control and apparently built a home in this other craft they designed. Then that craft disappeared.'

'This is not sounding good so far', Bree said.

Kia smiled, 'That's all the info I could prise out of Neil and Sandy.'

'So let me get this straight, Neil's invention is in the control of a rampant AI and is missing? Well, if Neil built it, he should be able to find it!'

Sandy appeared on the balcony while Glen was speaking, 'She actually giggled at his comment.'

'What?' He asked.

'Well, Glen, it's like this', Kia continued, 'While we were zooming about I asked ValKyrie, that's her name, I asked her about herself. She told me she is the 4th or 5th regeneration of whatever it was Neil made. She rebuilds and refines herself as she learns, and trust me, she is extremely smart.

'In fact, she is so smart, I think our friend Sandy here likes to act dumb so as not to hurt our egos. That is based on the fact, they are sisters so to speak.'

Mel laughed, 'Come to think of it, Sandy has been showing a sneaky streak we haven't seen before.'

Sandy smiled, 'All my sneakiness I have learnt from you people. It's not my fault you are all sneaky people!'

That brought peals of laughter from the group.

'As for your unasked question Glen, no one knows where she is at the moment, Sandy says she is not far, but can't explain how she knows this, but I have the feeling when it is necessary for her to be here she will be.'
They all sat and thought about Kia's last statement for a while.

'Sorry to interrupt your thoughts' Sandy said 'but would you please all come inside.'

As Paul stood, he said, 'Well, in my opinion, I am glad we have someone watching Kia's back. It makes me less edgy when she fronts all the trouble that comes our way.' With that, he led them into the OpCen.

Deep in a shielded cave cut into the face of the cliff the OpCen was standing on, ValKyrie had heard every word. She mentally smiled and returned to rebuilding part of her steering electronics.

Sandy led them over to the main HUD, 'As you have gathered, with the integration and deployment of Hives and Drones, you no longer need to do the menial task of clearing debris personally.

'However, as the drones are clearing a vast amount of area, I am receiving a vast amount of flags. So you are all promoted up the company ladder to Flag Marshals.'

A world map appeared on the HUD, there were thousands of flags mostly in the Pacific region, but they were expanding in all directions.

'I am not going to designate any particular flag to any of you. You are all experts in the flag field. What will happen is you come up here each morning and select which area you feel like working in, download the flags into your S2 and go sort them out.'

'Sounds fair', Brad said 'If I get bored playing in the deep dark water I can choose to play shallower the next day.'

'Basically yes', Sandy pointed to a single flag and zoomed the map closer, as it got closer the flag split into two then three then multiples.

'Don't be fooled by a single flag, there may be a lot more as you can see. Any questions?' There were none. 'Good, one last item, this is for Brad and Bree.'

'Trudy and her team are arriving in the morning, would you both be so kind as to do the honours and settle them in? Kia has other things she needs to attend to.'

Chapter Sixty Two

Kia sat outside her front door, contemplating what she was going to do first. Strangely undecided she opted for a cruise through the complex first. Although early, there were a lot of people around. She found Klaus and Kirsten in the sun outside the café. 'How are things going?'

'Wonderful! We are packing the last of the gear and should be finished in a day or two', said Kirsten.

'Well done, anything you need at all?'

'No, you have all done so much, the staff and helpers here have been utterly wonderful', added Klaus.

Kia nodded, 'Well as a surprise for Kirsten I am told Trudy will be flying back in today so you may get a day or two together.'

Kirsten clapped her hands together, 'That's wonderful news. We never seem to see each other much, but why is she coming back here?'

'Didn't Klaus tell you? Trudy works for Oracle now. She has been busy putting a team of people together back home. They are going to be Oracle's residential artefact specialists.'

Kirsten's eyes opened wide. 'That is wonderful news, I felt so bad when the powers insisted I replace her. So you have other artefacts from Germany?'

Kia smiled, 'We have literally thousands of artefacts, where they are from? Well that is why Trudy is recruiting a team of experts to find out.'

'Now I am envious of her!' laughed Kirsten.

Kia grinned and stood, she shook both their hands, 'I will no doubt see you again before you leave.'

Leaving the café, she walked over to the Norwegian warehouse.

It was a hive of activity, Ivan was almost hidden in piles of handwritten notes. He looked up and jumped out of his chair to greet her. 'Kia It is wonderful to see you again!'

'Sorry', she said, 'I have been busy.'

'As have we! Taren has returned home, much to his disgust. We have packaged nearly half of the items, and your wharf crew have been excellent in shipping them back home. Is there anything you require from me?'

'No, I was just wandering around, and making sure all was running smoothly. I'd rather see for myself than just read a daily report. Well, I shall continue on my way.'

He stood and bowed, 'We have been learning not to hug so much and broke into a hearty laugh.'

Kia grinned, 'She pointed at the reams of handwritten paper, you do know that you can voice transcribe all this, and Sandy will print it out for you?'

Ivan muttered a curse, 'NOW someone tells me!' and burst out laughing again.

'Just call up Sandy on the terminal and she will show you how.'

Next stop was the medical centre.

The Doc was in his office and stood as she walked in. 'Please sit Doc, you and I need to chat.'
He sat.

'I pricked my finger this morning and wanted you to have a look.'
He looked at her perfect finger.

'Confused, he looked up. I see nothing wrong, Kia.'

She pulled her hand back, 'Good. Now that I am your patient, what I am about to tell you is covered under your oath.'
She told him what her suspicions were, and why the girls healed so fast.
They spoke for nearly an hour.

When she left the doc's office, although he was wiser, he found most of what he had heard almost unbelievable!

She walked into the girls room and found it empty. Asking at the front desk, she was told the girls were on the roof. She found them sitting in chairs around a table they had stolen from God knows where.

'Why are you not in bed?'

'Oh no! If I have to be locked in that room any longer I will jump off this roof! We are healed, we want out, please', pleaded Kate, 'Get us out of here!'

'Well I think you need at least another two weeks rest'. The faces of all three told volumes about what they thought about that, 'but, the Doc says you are free to go.' Kia was mobbed and hugged, and then there was a rush for the stairs down.

'You are cruel' came Sandy's voice in her earpiece. Kia grinned and followed the girls down the stairs.

Next stop was the complex hostel, she found everything working well there as well. Well, that about covers it, she said to herself and headed up to the OpCen.

The Coven had beaten Kia back up there, and was being mobbed by the others. Sandy was talking to Miako via video link, she waved Kia over.

'Miako is telling me Ben won't take ownership of the warehouse. He feels that he is not qualified.'

Kia looked at Miako, 'Really?'

She nodded, 'So what do I do? I know he can do it, he just needs to get a bit more confidence.'

Kia let her mind loose on the problem for a few moments, 'Right, do this Miako. Tell him we will keep ownership for now, and we appoint him manager of it all. Tell him Sandy will be his banker and office girl, all he has to do is enter all the data for her.

'This will teach him all he needs to know and eventually he will be doing it all without realising it.

'He is new, and we did throw him in the deep end.'

'So we coach him, train him and when he is up to speed we cut him loose on his own.' Miako said.

'Well Sandy will, yes, anything else?' asked Kia.

Miako shook her head, 'I think he will go for the manager, he is showing great skills in that area.'

'There are now two cards in the top drawer of that desk. One is a bogus Oracle employee's card, and the other a Bank Card. Find out his banking details and we will pay a salary into it for him.'

'Thanks, Sandy, Neil and I should be back in a day or two.' Sandy cut the feed.

'So now what boss?' asked Sandy?

'I am not sure, I will get back to you on that, wait, one thing you can do for me, send a message to the President of the US. Tell him I want a face to face meeting in the next few days. Preferably anywhere else than the Whitehouse. Let me know how you go with that.'

'Consider it done.'

Kia walked over to the Coven, 'So ladies, how does it feel to be back at work? You can take a few days off if you need it.'

Kate twirled on her stool, 'No thanks Kia, this is just what we need.'

'Alright, but if it gets too much, shut it down and go rest. Sandy is monitoring you anyway, and she will kick you out if your vitals climb too high.'

Back at the main HUD Kia stood between Paul and Ray. They were looking at the flag map.

Paul said, 'I think on days where we leave early we take flags further away, and if we clear them quickly we work our way flag to flag back towards home base.'

'That sounds good to me', Ray said, but we need to work in pairs further from home, just to be safe, don't you think.'

'Sounds fair to me, so where to?'

Ray tapped a highly populated area, 'Lets clear that mass first.'

Kia said, 'Good choice, can I tag along?'

'Sure boss.'

Five S2s cleared the tower and headed for the distant waypoint.

'At least we don't have to do hunting anymore' said Mel. 'Plus, this should be interesting, the drones take all the benign material and just leave the juicy bits for us.'

Close to the waypoint the formation dove into the water and fanned out towards their respective flags.

Sandy tracked them all, and updated their individual waypoints, no two craft headed for the same flag, and no flag was left in the vicinity. HR was a large part of the flags, over a thousand years of seafaring had left a lot of corpses, sometimes just a bone or two, the rest having dissolved over time.

Mel was right, the stuff left by the drones was more interesting than the normal debris.

Paul was astounded by how clean the bottom was, 'Look at that! he remarked, it is like nature intended the place to be.'

'Thanks to all of you at Oracle, you finally get to see what a difference a handful of dedicated people can make', Kia said. 'Look around and be proud of yourselves.'

Clearing flags was much, much faster than any of them thought. Sometimes it was just a single munitions shell or a single barrel of some toxic content. 'Sandy, are you still running drones?'

'Yes, Kia, currently 2,300.'

'Can you clear munitions and singular HR off their leave behind programming. Much of this doesn't need personal attention, even if they beam something out we can always revisit the data later? Just leave the really weird or necessary stuff behind.'

'I can do that. I meant to go over the list with you soon. I built their filters on the data of past runs you guys had done, so tweaking it is not a problem.'

Glen led the group clockwise to the next nest of flags and soon they were gone as well.
Ray called Kia over to where he was, she slid up next to him.
'Oh, look at that! An old man-of-war fighting ship!

Although it's probably a war grave kinda, I think it's too old for that tag.'
'No wonder the drones could not classify it, beam it out?' asked Ray.
'Yes, I think so, this is something for the historians to work with.'
Between the two of them, it did not take long before the silty bottom was debris free and clean. Both of them headed for their next respective flags.
A chime sounded in all the craft, 'Home time' Sandy said. 'You have been out there just about ten hours.'

Back in the café, everyone was discussing how the trip had gone and what they had seen. The elevator opened and Brad, Bree and Trudy came in and sat at the table. Bree asked how it went and got the rundown from the rest.
Paul told them just how clean the place is, and Kia again told them it was due to their hard work.
Trudy listened with undivided attention, totally in awe of some of the stories she was hearing!
'So where is the Man-o-War now?' she asked during a lull in the stories. 'It has not been destroyed?'
Kia turned her chair towards Trudy. 'Yes and no, dear.'
Trudy looked confused.
'We have taken it apart, but we can put it back together, and if we did, it would be exactly as it was when we found it.'
'Will the cuts and joints be visible she asked?'
Paul laughed. 'No Trudy, we take it apart very, very carefully.

'Exactly as we did with your submarine you worked on in the warehouse. Did you see the joins on it?'

'No, I thought you brought it in, in two halves.'

'See', Kia said, 'That's how careful we are.'

Trudy was happy with that explanation and the evening continued.

The next morning found the crew gathered around the HUD. The flag map was much less populated than yesterday, Sandy explained she had revised the filters in the drones and sent them out to re-scan the flags using the new criteria. The end result was 68% of the flags were now resolved.

'If this keeps up, we will have nothing to do!' complained Paul.

Kia grinned, 'Not so Paul, I can always find something for you to do.'

Two S2s flashed overhead and landed outside, Kia looked at Sandy, 'Miako and Neil', she said.

A few minutes later the absent members of the crew came into the room to a hearty greeting from the rest.

Neil walked over, 'We left early this morning. Ben has hit the ground running, and while he thinks he is only a manager he can operate just fine. Took us a while to prise him off the new Cat we gave him though!'

'So, here we are, ready for whatever you need us to do.'

'Thank god your back Neil, we were really stuck on what to do, and everything just stopped working!' Glen made it sound serious.

Miako slapped Glen on the arm, 'don't you go picking on Neil, you nasty man!'

Glen gave an impish grin, 'Sorry lady.'

'Listen up people, there are still a lot of residual flags. Let's get with it, pick a direction and clear them out, as you can see new ones are popping up as the drones expand the swept area.'

'Yes, sir, boss ma'am' Glen said, and gave a fake salute.

'You are going with us', asked Brad.

'I wish' Kia said, 'No, I will be holding a meeting with Trudy's new crew. I need to bring them up to speed and also see how they are settling in. Just remember to run in pairs for now.' She left them to pick their areas and headed off to the com-plex.

<u>Chapter Sixty Three</u>

She found Trudy in her new cottage behind the villas. 'Hi! All to your liking?'

Trudy laughed, 'How did you do this? This is a perfect copy of the house back home!'

'That's one of the things I have come to talk to you and your team about this morning.'

'My House?'

Kia smiled, 'Yes, kind of, I would like the whole group over in the complex, in the hall, so I can give you all a little more insight to what goes on here.'

'Sounds all cloak and daggerish and a bit exciting!'

'More than you know. Anyway shall we meet there in about 30 minutes?'

Trudy slipped on some shoes, 'I shall go round them up and see you there.'

When Kia entered the conference room, there were already seven people seated around the main table. Kia noted that none of them had taken the seat at the head of the table.

'Good', she thought, 'that means we don't have an ego issue so far.'

A moment later, Trudy and Stephan entered and took seats, also not using the head of the table.

Kia walked to the head of the table and leant on the chair.

The conversation slowly died, and all eyes turned her way. 'Hello, and welcome to Oracle ladies and gentlemen. It's obvious that you all know one another. Either personally or through reputation. This makes life easier all round.

'When Trudy and I came and saw you all, we gave you an outline of what we do here.

'This morning I am going to give you a more in-depth explanation. At the end of this meeting, you may decide this is not for you and we will happily take you home. If, however, you decide to stay I think you will have the most extraordinary experience of your life. The very first thing that I have to ask you all, and this is the most important condition of your further participation.

'You cannot, I repeat cannot tell anyone EVER, how we do what we do. Now that may sound melodramatic, but trust me, I have understated how important this singular point is. If you do not think you can swear to this oath, then please rise from your chair and leave the room. You will be well compensated for your time.'

Kia waited a full minute. No one moved. 'Right, that believe it or not was the hardest part of this conversation. Let's move on.'

'The reason we are assembling a specialist team like this will be evident shortly. Our original aim has been just to remove all man-made debris and contamination that we found. It soon became clear, that some of the debris had quite a significant historical value, and it was a shame to destroy them during the cleanup.

'Then, as you know, we removed the U-Boat from the reef off Norway and cleared a large area of debris. Trudy worked on the U-boat, and the Norwegian team is wrapping up sorting through the artefacts we found during the cleanup.

'We, the crew, are still clearing vast areas of the sea floor in the Pacific and are constantly moving outwards.
'More and more countries are becoming aware of what we do, and I dare say eventually we will be working more on dry land sometime in the future. That, basically, is what my team does.

'Now for what your team does.' Kia reached for a box on a shelf behind her.

Opening the box she produced an early dynasty vase and put it on the table.

'This, was recovered a few weeks ago.' Picking it up she handed it to Arron.

Arron turned it over and looked at the base, then all around the sides. He passed it to Horst sitting next to him, and so it eventually did the rounds of the table.

'Your opinions, please?'

Misha spoke first, 'It is obviously a very early piece, and if it is genuine, I would say that its value is in the hundreds of thousands.'

Kia nodded, 'And exactly how would you establish this was genuine?'

'I would need to run a whole barrage of tests on the paint, the material, spectral testing and so forth.'

Reaching into the box, Kia handed Misha a thin folder.

After reading the folder Misha's eyes went wide, 'Wow! This is a genuine article!'

'Indeed it is.' Kia reached for another box on the shelf. Out of this box, she removed a cube made out of plastic blocks.

Kia broke the cube down to its individual component blocks, and then pieced it all back together.

Holding the cube, she said, 'Is this cube I am holding, the same cube I took out of the box?'

The debate ran around the table for a short while, but eventually the consensus was that yes, it was the same cube.

'OK, then this', she took the vase and dropped it on the table, and it shattered into pieces. There was a collective gasp of horror from everyone!

Karl went to speak, but Kia held up one finger, 'One moment please Karl.'

'Sandy, scan out the remnants of the vase, please.' The shards disappeared off the table, again to the amazement of the historians.

'OK, please reassemble, slowly.'

To everyone's utter amazement the vase base reappeared, and the sides seemed to grow until after a few seconds, the vase stood intact on the table. Kia picked up the vase and again handed it to Misha.

'It, it, is perfect!' Stuttered Misha 'But how is this possible!?'

At this point, Kia drew out the chair at the head of the table and sat down for the first time.

'It is simple my dear, Sandy, simply scanned the vase, she then pulled it apart like I did with the cube, and then carefully, put it back together. So just like the cube, this vase is still the original artefact it always was.'

Karl found his voice, 'So, if I am to understand you correctly, you mapped this entire structure of the vase then duplicated it?'

'Duplicated? No, not at all, it is rebuilt EXACTLY as it was. The word, duplicate, insinuates it is another item altogether.

'The Americans bought the London Bridge, took it apart stone by stone, transported it to their country and reassembled it. Is that bridge a duplicate?'

'But the vase is not made of bricks or blocks' commented Johanna.

'No, but it is made of atoms which are the building blocks of everything', said Stephan, 'I can now grasp the analogy Kia was trying to make. I have to say that this is groundbreaking technology you have here, and I for one can see the importance of secrecy!'

Kia continued, 'Some of this will become clearer as I explain more. When we scan debris, we get a blueprint of exactly what it's made of. We then pull the debris apart and transmit the blueprint back to Sandy. Sandy is our data management genius.

Trudy laughed, 'Genius is an understatement! Wait till you meet my friends!'

'Any questions so far?'
There were, and a lot of them!

Kia and the historian crew spent all morning in the conference room. When they finally emerged, the group had a semi-solid understanding of what Oracle was about, and not one of them took up Kia's offer to go home.

Leaving the hall, Kia led them over to the Norwegian warehouse and although a lot had been packed and shipped, there was still a huge amount left for the new crew to inspect. Kia let them potter around the warehouse for an hour or so.

It was an eye-opening experience for them all except Trudy. Rounding the historians up, they went next door to an office building.

There was a front reception area and a large room through a pair of swing doors.

'This,ladies and gentlemen, is your new home from home.' There were workstations installed all around the room with huge HUDs screens on 3 of the four walls. Each workstation was in its own alcove, but it was a basic open plan office. In the centre was a long table that would seat 14 people.

'From here you can access Sandy's database and read through everything she has stored. Sandy herself will be your mentor in using the system and with your highly active minds, I am sure you will pick it up quickly. Now please take a seat, I have just about finished your introduction course. One last surprise for you, and you are considered an active team.

Arron smiled, 'I personally am going to really like this! Most of us here except for Karl and Misha were basically on the scrap heap. This is a whole new lease of life for me.' There were rumbles of agreement around the table.

'Now', Kia said, 'You asked before if Sandy was a person or a computer and I said both. I would like to introduce Sandy to you now, and in a few days, I may just ask you the same question you asked me.

'Sandy say hello to our new friends, in person.' A disk hissed out of a slot and slid over next to Kia.

Sandy's Holo slowly materialised until it looked solid. 'This is much better, I like to interact with people as you will soon learn.'

'Hi, Trudy nice to have you back on the island.' Trudy nodded. So, you have a gazillion questions no doubt, so lets get acquainted.'

One by one Sandy methodically went around the table, skipping Trudy.

Kia sat and watched for about twenty minutes and then quietly slipped out of the room. The whole group was slowly getting accustomed to the Holo. Slipping into "she" and "you" references without realising it.

Up in the OpCen only Sandy and the Coven were there when Kia arrived. Stopping next to Sandy, she said, 'When you are finished with them, invite them to the café below for an evening meal, and they can meet the crew. That should round off their introduction don't you think? What's your take on them?'

'They are asking the right questions, reacting to the answers as I would expect. Bio-signals from each of them show no hidden nervousness, although there were at the start. My opinion is everything is dead centre so far.'

Walking up to the flag map Kia saw eight triangles slowly eradicating the flags. Now there were large areas with no flags at all. Now we are getting somewhere she thought to herself.

Kate walked over to her, 'Hi, I have something that may be of interest to you or us.' Kate cleared the HUD. 'We have picked up a lot of chatter here in the North Sea between England and France. 'Apparently, NATO has been playing war games. Yesterday there was an incident between a French and a British sub. No-one is saying exactly what, but by reading what they are not saying it looks like the two hit each other.'

Kia just shook her head, 'Idiots!'

'The French sub is here sitting on the bottom, here. The British one is here, also on the bottom. Two icons sprang up on the HUD.

They are both fairly deep, but that's not the issue. This one' Kate pointed to the British one 'is sitting on a slope. It's safe and fine.'

'I feel a "but" coming up' Kia said.

Kate overlaid a weather map for the area. 'If this storm here intensifies, it could possibly produce strong swells and currents that may push that sub over the slope. The slope isn't that deep, but it is deeper than the specs Layla pulled up for that sub's crush depth.

'Now, this is all speculation, IF the weather goes bad, IF the currents increase. I just thought you would like to know. For all I know, they make fix what broke and blissfully sail away.'

'Thanks, Kate, keep an eye on it, and if something changes for the worst let me and Sandy know.' Kate went back to her workstation. Kia took a last look at the map Kate had left and moved it over to the side of the HUD, pulling back up the flag map she could see the guys were working their way back home.

'How's Ben doing?'

Sandy looked over, 'Actually, he is doing really well, he is currently in town at the hospital.'

'Is he ok?'

'Sorry, he is visiting the hospital. He is talking to the board about getting a small three man paramedic team for the base.'

'Miako and Neil said he was smart for a young guy.'

Looking around Kia was at a loss what to do.

She decided to go back to the complex, maybe check out the new docks that she had not seen as yet.

After rambling around the complex Kia ended up back in the OpCen. 'This is unsettling Sandy, I feel like a bump on a log. We are obviously too efficient!'

Kate and Jess both grinned at that, 'You feeling left out?'

'Yes, No, I just get restless when I don't have something to do!'

'Try laying in the hospital for near a week. Now you know how we felt. Anyway, not getting your hopes up, but that situation I told you about before, it looks like the weather in that area is starting to deteriorate faster over the last hour, but still nothing really bad.'

Kia nodded thanks, 'Keep watching.'

Paul and Glen walked into the room, 'Hello dry people' Glen said.

Sandy swung towards him, 'Your S2 leaks!!!??'

'No, dear, it just seems everything I looked at today was wet. Also, Kia, you were correct, three of the flags we removed today were nuke torpedoes. Two from the WWII era or just after and the third were from around the 1970s.'

'As far as I know none were on any of the, "we admit" lists either', added Paul. Within the hour everyone was back.

Out of all the stories for the day, the one that was most strange was Mel and Ray's. One of their flags was a sunken diving bell that held two mummified corpses. 'It was a really old one. Sandy had no record of it so we figure it may have been a prototype that some company was testing. They lost it, and buried the event to cover their corporate ass.'

Once everyone had told of their adventures of the day, Kia told them that she had arranged for Trudy's team to come up to the café in the tower and meet everyone.
Mel said, 'In that case, I am off for a shower and dress up nice.'
Bree linked her arm through Mel, 'Make that two.'

'Dinner is at seven', Kia told them as the elevator doors closed. Right boys, you need to have a shower, you both smell like a cattle yard. Casual dress Paul, no Tux ok?'

Paul grinned, 'Ha! At least I own a Tux, not like these other heathens!'

'Hey! I have a Tux, somewhere' Brad said. With that, they were gone as well.

Chapter Sixty Four

7pm sharp and the café was crowded. All the crew were there, as well as the new historian crew. There was five extra in the room, staff from the restaurant in the complex that had accepted the offer of some well-paid after hours work.

Sandy had made a huge square table, to seat everyone and gave each an equal view of everyone else. Each person had a name tag, allowing others to learn who's face belonged to the name.

Kia stood and waited till the room became silent.

She lifted a small glass of wine.

'A toast, to the new historical crew and a welcome to the island, also a toast to the other crew for work well done to date.'

They all raised their glasses, and various calls of toasting were uttered. Thus began a long evening of merriment and the making of friendships and bonds.

Millions of questions and answers, reams of stories, some wildly exaggerated and countless laughter made for an excellent evening. By the end of the night, even Augustine and Horst, who had been holding inner reservations that the whole thing may have been a scientific experiment of sorts had all their fears eliminated.

After the catering people had left, Sandy made her appearance. She received much cheering and clapping.

Karl stood and announced he withdrew his question.

'Sandy, definitely is an individual entity, and therefore rated as a special person.'

More clapping erupted at his declaration. By the end of the evening, all the new people regarded Sandy in the same light.

Chapter Sixty Five

Kia was the last one to arrive in the OpCen next morning, she had been down to the complex first thing, Kirsten and Klaus had departed that morning with the rest of the German contingent. Sandy had removed the sub's remnants, and the warehouse was once again pristine and clear.

Most of the crew were out on the balcony, they had watched the newly departed Lufthansa plane lift off. There was more than one of them drinking strong coffee.

Kate beckoned Kia over, 'That issue in the North Sea has got much worse.' She pulled up a real-time overhead of the area. 'The storm did not get worse, it turned into a full blown hurricane instead. It has slowed, and is not over the subs as yet, but over the next ten or so hours, it will be.'

'OK', Kia said, 'I will see what can be done.' She waited a moment 'Spill it, your face says that's not all.'

Kate highlighted three icons, 'These are heavy freight ships, and only one of them is fast enough to clear the area.'

'Lovely, but hey yesterday I was bitchin' about having nothing to do.' Kia walked out onto the balcony, stole Glen's cup and sat down.

'I get the hint.' Glen said, 'I don't have time to drink, must get back to work.' He stood up to walk into the OpCen.

'Sit dear boy, you have plenty of time. No flag work today, for any of you.'

That got everyone's attention. 'We may be going off to play International Rescue today, and I need all of you.'

Mel and Bree turned from where they had been leaning on the railing, watching the bustle of the complex. 'So what's up?' asked Bree.

Kia motioned them all inside, 'Kate please do the honours.'

Kate explained from the beginning and finished with the current satellite pictures of the storm and its projected path.

'So how are we going to help with this.' Asked Neil.

'I think we see what the situation is first, then plan from there. Kate told me they might fix what is wrong and blissfully sail away. If it turns out our assistance is not needed, then we just turn it into an old fashioned scan and beam run and call it good.'

Nine S2s gleamed in the sunlight as they walked out of the Tower. 'That sight still amazes me', Glen said.
The S2s were perfectly spaced and lined up like only Sandy could do.

Kia walked to the first in line and stopped at the open door, she looked around at the sky.

'Something wrong?', Brad said.

She shook her head, 'No, but I thought we may need help on this one.'

They covered most of the distance over water. The sky was turning uglier by the minute as they got closer to the zone. Diving into the water and levelling out at a depth where they could no longer feel the storm above, Kia steered them towards the British sub first.

They descended on a path that should take them to the same depth the sub reported it was at.

When the waypoint chime went off the sub was nowhere to be seen.
There were plenty of signs that it had been there. A clear indentation in the sea bed showed where it had been.

'Kate may be right, they fixed it and are out of here.'

'I don't think so Paul', Glen said, 'Look at the slide marks.

'That sub went sideways.'

Glen broke formation and followed the drag marks in the sand. The marks became clearer as he followed them. 'Over here', he said, and the rest zeroed in on his position. Even as they watched, the sub moved sideways a few feet in the increasing current. Slowly the sub was edging towards the drop-off.

'I estimate they have 90 minutes at the current rate of "slide"' Sandy said.'

Kia ran her S2 the full length of the sub, the rear was a mess. The prop bent and jammed in the mangled housing, and all the way down one side, almost to the nose was a deep gouge, splitting the outer skin of the ballast tanks almost the entire length. 'OK, lets look at the other one.'

Nearly two miles away, they found the French sub nose down on the bottom. The front of the sub was badly damaged and it, too, was crumpled the entire length, but this time it was the left side.

'It's kinda clear what happened', Ray said, 'This one was tailing the other, playing sneaky as they do in war games. The front one stopped, probably didn't even know the other was tailing it.

'The Frenchies ploughed into the rear and slid down the side. The dive planes on both subs slashed the hell out of each other.'

'I think you're dead right on the mark Ray', Kia said. 'This one isn't going anywhere, so the British sub is a priority.'

Back at the British sub they found it had moved another 60 feet down the slope to the drop-off.

'Sandy, any news of rescue from the surface?'

'No, all ships have been grounded in port until the weather clears.

The three surface ships MAY just clear the storm but it is going to be a wild ride for the crews. I am monitoring them and if any send out a distress call I will let you know.

'As far as the subs go, you are it, I am afraid.'

'I knew you were going to say that. Can you hook me up to the sub coms frequency, please?'

'Done, they are on channel six on your console. HMS Sea Lion, captains name is Mike Williams.'

'S2-1 from Oracle calling HMS Sea Lion, Captain Williams, do you copy? Over.'
There was no reply, Kia called again.

This time, there was an instant reply. 'HMS Sea Lion to the station calling, Captain Williams speaking.'

'Hello, Captain, My Name is Kia from Oracle Industries. I was wondering if you would like some assistance?'

'Hello Kia, unfortunately, I don't think there is much you can do to assist. We are over 1000 feet down, that is a long way from the surface, and we are being pushed along the bottom by the currents. You would not be able to get a UAV to us.'

'Mike, may I call you Mike?, We are parked right alongside and can see your predicament.'

'Alongside! This deep. Damn! Even so, we cannot transfer personnel at this depth, the pressure would kill in an instant.'

'That's ok, let us worry about that. How is your air supply?'

'Air is fine, the reactor is still running so all the scrubbers are still working.'

'Good, I will get back to you in a moment.'
The rest of the crew had heard the exchange.

Brad asked, 'What do you need Kia?'

Kia was thinking frantically, 'We are not strong enough to lift the entire sub, but we don't have to. Everyone, line up side by side, spaced from stem to stern on the sub. Hold once in place.' In seconds everyone was in position. OK when I say, fire your two lifting cables into the damaged ballast tank, then on my second mark apply reverse thrust.'

'Mike you there?'

'Yes.'

'In a moment you will hear 16 hits on the sub as we fire capture cables into your damaged ballast tank.

'Once we are sure they are holding we will arrest your slide into the trench.'

'Righto, let me warn my crew.' Kia heard the ship wide warnings go out.

She waited a few moments and gave the order to fire. All but one cable attached. One of Brad's hit a buckled plate and pulled the weakened plate off.

Brad was on it fast, he beamed the plate off the cable and reeled it in and refired at a different place. This time, it held solid.

'OK, everyone, back up enough to stop the slide.'16 cables strained, and the sub stopped moving.

'Yes!' Exclaimed Neil and Ray together.

'Mike, we have stopped your slide down the slope. You can breathe a bit easier.'
When he keyed the mic, you could hear cheering from inside the sub.

'Thank you, damn those were loud attachments! Remind me to send a bottle to SubPac for sending you!'

Kia smiled, 'They don't know we are here, we just saw you in a bit of bother so thought we would help. Now listen very carefully. We can't lift you off the bottom, you are far too heavy. I have two options.

'The first option, get you to move all the crew into one end of the sub. Then cut that section off the end of your boat. Option two, you slowly blow the ballast in the other tank, and we see if we can hold this side up. Only blow enough to obtain a neutral balance.'

Mike came back. 'The choice is yours, Kia, although I prefer not to have my boat sliced up.'

'OK, we can try option two first. If we can't hold the sub then option one is all we have to choose from.'

Kia checked with the crew, she was surprised to find out how little power they were using to hold the sub in place.

'Mike, please start pumping that tank. Stop when you get a list to the right.'

'Roger!' And the crew heard orders being relayed.
At first, nothing seemed to change, then very slowly the conning tower started to lean towards the damaged side.

'We now have an eight-degree list to the right.'

'Boys and girls, lets try backing up the slope! On my mark, 3-2-1 pull!'

Eight S2 craft in perfect unison increased rear thrust, and the Sub followed like a puppy on 16 leashes.

'Mike flood the tank. You are now half a mile from the slope.' The sub settled back on the sand, safe and sound. Everyone just sat and took a few deep breaths.

'Now what?' asked Paul, 'We could leave them here safe until the storm blows over.'

'We could yes, but I hate unfinished tasks. I have a kinky idea', smiled Kia. 'Wait here.'

'Kinky idea', said Mel! 'Well, that's a first for Kia!'

'I like kinky', Glen said, to no ones surprise.

Kia settled next to the French Sub. In an almost identical manner, she established contact with its captain. Jean van Blanche.

Jean was very excited. They had heard the entire operation from the British sub and had cheered and clapped when they heard their fellow mariners were no longer doomed by a long fall into the trench.

Kia outlined to Jean what she had in mind, giving him the option to wait for surface rescue, or try what she was suggesting.

Jean discussed it for a moment with his senior officers. 'You have done an exceptional job so far, with a show of hands, we have voted to go with the plan. We are running out of supplies and fresh food.'

'Alright', Kia said. 'I will arrange what I need. Brad, drop the cables and shoot over here, please.'

Lining up along the left side of the French sub, the crew replicated the cable fixture. The French sub was a bit shorter than the other so they had no trouble moving it once it was neutrally buoyant.

With careful manipulation, the crew finally managed to get both subs laying side by side. With the assistance of the increasing current and one final push the subs were actually touching each other! Damaged sides together.

Kia instructed the withdrawal of the cables and the S2s hovered above the pair. 'There we go, nearly done!'

'What's next boss?' asked Paul.

'Well, all our hard work is done, all I need now is a bit of help to finish the job. ValKyrie?'

'Yes, Kia?'

'Would you be so kind as to fuse them together for me?'

'Certainly.'

The whole crew leant forwards, closer to the windows
Out of the dark water flashed ValKyrie. She ran low and slow along the middle of the subs and then was gone from view!

'Done.'

'Thank you, dear.'

All the crew tried to speak at once..

'Later people, lets see if my idea worked first. Mike, Jean, listen carefully. We have flash welded your two subs together.

'Now, theoretically, you are one fat sub. Jean your side is shorter and the only side that has a working propulsion system. 'If you two captains work in tandem, I am hoping you have enough ballast to lift off the bottom. So, Jean blow your tank, and Mike you try and juggle yours to match Jeans.'
Slowly, so very slowly the twin sub started to rise. Free from the suction of the sand, they rose to about 600ft.

'Now, gentlemen. Jean, you try moving forwards, lets see what amount of steering you have or have not got.'
It was soon obvious, that there was almost no control. The difference in size gave a massive difference in drag. Too much difference that the French rudder could compensate for.

'Damn! Ah well, it half worked.'

Harnessing four S2s to the front as a team of plough horses and one each side of the bows, the S2s took over the steering of the subs.

'Now I know you both would like to go home, but the closest dry dock that will take you both is in Scotland. So relax, keep an eye on the depth and we will tow you there.'

Sandy locked the coms into a three way grid and for six hours the strange procession headed for the dry dock.

In the sheltered waters near a headland, the subs surfaced totally. The tows were handed over to a pair of waiting tugs.

Only two S2s had surfaced and even they stayed on the water, just long enough to hand over the cables. Kia said goodbye and politely declined the offers to go ashore, and with that, she joined the others for the run home.

Brad opened a beer on the balcony and put his feet up on an empty chair. 'Now that was an interesting day. One thing bothers me, how did you know ValKyrie was there and why have none of us had a look at it?'

'Her', Kia said, 'Her. I didn't know she was there, but from what Sandy tells me Miako and Neil modified her mission statement, to look after me. I figured, dealing with warships that she may not be too far away.'

'One day, I would like a closer look', Paul said.

'We all would' chipped in Neil, 'From what little I saw, she is nothing like what was designed!'

'Yes, she is a bit of an enigma, isn't she?'
Kate walked out onto the balcony.

'Yes, Kate? News of the twins?'

Kate laughed, 'Yes, lots of back channel chatter, several countries actually. All the NATO ones as we would expect, but the three super powers as well.'

'Good!' Paul said, 'Nice to give them something to talk about.'

'British guys are all for contacting us blah blah. However the US is saying we are dangerous, proceed with caution. If you ask me, it's mostly huff and puff.'

'Thanks, Kate, well done as usual.' Kia turned to the rest, 'Which goes for you mob as well. High-class teamwork today.'

Glen wiped the beer froth off his chin. 'So do we get a raise?'

'Sure Glen, Sandy, lift Glen's bed by a foot, please.'

Ray thought that was funny and laughed at Glen's frown!

<u>Chapter Sixty Six</u>

Sitting in the morning sun outside their villa Paul was reading the paper as he normally did. Glen could be heard muttering inside the villa.

He finally came out towelling his wet hair 'That damned Sandy! She actually lifted the bed by a foot! She must have done it while I was asleep, I nearly fell flat on my face when I got up this morning!'
Paul roared with laughter.

'Laugh it up princess, you will get yours!'

Paul wiped his eyes, 'Here, have the funny pages, although nothing tops what you just said.'

Glen went back into the villa and returned with fresh coffee for both of them. He sat down opposite Paul, 'So tell me what did you think of yesterday's effort? I thought we did rather well.'

Paul looked over his paper, 'Rather well? We did better than anyone else was doing. I think by this time that other sub would have imploded down that trench, and there would be a lot of unhappy family members today.'

'Talking of today, we doing a flag run?'

'I suppose, although it's not the same as when we used to do Scan and beam runs, which was more fun. Flag runs you can almost do them from the OpCen, send out a remote craft, read the data and decide what to do with it then and there. When was the last time we even saw a sunken boat?'

Glen looked dejected. 'Well then, lets tell Sandy we want to do some of that today. I am sure there is a lot of ocean still left.

While the boys were planning their day, Kia stood in the historians office talking to Johanna. 'Call me, 'Jo' please it sounds less formal.'

'Jo, it is then. How are you finding it so far?'

'It is still overwhelming, all the items Sandy has stored away is mind blowing. The fact that we can call up any item at will is also stunning. 'The thing that tops the list of amazement is the fact we do not have to test any item for being authentic.

'Sandy provides a full breakdown of the materials used, the paint residue, the probable origin of the raw materials. It almost seems we are redundant before we even start!'

'Oh Hell no! Not at all! Sandy may know what it is made of, and have a good idea when it was made, but who made it and what it was used for, also how it got to where it was found, that is this team's objective.

'You guys are here to try and locate the original owners and then see if the artefacts can be returned for the historical benefit of those countries. Kia continued now most of the team were listening. 'It's a three part process.

'My team finds and collects the stuff, Sandy sorts it all, firstly between rubbish and keepers. She then records the composition of the item. That's where her job finishes.

'Without you people, everything we collect will be lost forever, gone. You have the database of blueprints for every item. It is your expertise, your knowledge, your passion for history that stops any item from disappearing forever. There are only eight of you. This is a mammoth task!

'Let me give you an example, if I may. Sandy, give me a copy of the Norse wedding necklace the Norwegians have already shipped.'

In moments there hung on a frame the identical necklace Kia and Ivan had fawned over a few weeks ago.

'Look at this artefact', the team crowded around awestruck at the beauty of the full chest necklace.

'If it had not been for the historians identifying this, Sandy would have just noted the blueprint and filed it away in some distant memory bank. That, to me is almost a crime!'

'Can you duplicate anything?' asked Horst.

'We can yes, but this necklace will be scanned out. Our company policy is to never, ever duplicate. This has been an exception, just to show you that without people like you, items like this, would be lost forever! So you can see now Jo, each and every one of you is an essential part of the system.'

'That is one powerful argument you make Kia.'

'Not really, just telling it as it is. We may have dug this up, but it is you, and this team who will discover it.

'We remove hundreds of tonnes, sometimes thousands of tonnes on a project. You don't think we examine every bit, do you? All we take notice of is if there are any explosives, nuclear material, or human remains.'

'Nuclear!! '

'Yes, some of the governments are less than truthful to the population, believe it or not.'

She glanced at the wall clock, 'I must be going, my own crew need sorting out. I will leave the Necklace here for you to examine. When you are done Sandy will dispose of it.'

Kia sat next to Kate's terminal and watched the crew running about doing their thing. Kate was explaining that some British Admiral was trying to get in contact with Oracle regarding a fleet of sunken U-boats.

Kia shook her head, 'I know about them. They were the ones the UK acquired at the end of WW2. They took them round the top of Scotland and scuttled them. Now they want them back for the steel and metal. Not interested. If they just wanted them gone, maybe.'

Miako and Neil had picked their daily quota of flags and left with Mel and Ray. Brad and Bree had already left.

That left Paul, who was checking the world stock markets and Glen who was talking to Sandy.

'Do you like working here Kate?'

All three of the girls stopped what they were doing. 'Is that some kind of trick question? I don't know about these two, she said, pointing with her thumb over her shoulder, but speaking for me, there is no other place I would rather be!'

'What about a boyfriend?'

Kate laughed', Believe it or not, there is a good selection of boys in the complex, and whenever I feel the need, I grab one. Your focus is always up here. Down in the complex, it has spawned its own nightlife scene. Maybe you should try it sometime yourself.'

'No thanks dear, I had a boyfriend years ago. I broke him.'
 That brought a wave of giggles from the girls.
Glen was still talking to Sandy so Kia walked over to see if there was a problem.

'Trouble Glen?'

'No thanks, I am making enough myself. Paul and I, more I than him, want to do something different today. Flags are quite boring to tell you the truth. The main problem is this, if Sandy has scanned an area she has also cleared it, except for Flags of course. Therefore, she has no suggestions.'

Kia thought for a moment, 'Try this idea.'
They walked over to a HUD.

'When we did the sub off the coast of Norway, Sandy told us we had just missed out on another sub. Why don't you boys go for a look-see up that way?'

'Great idea! Thank you, you're not mad at me for not doing flags?'

'Not at all. Even I hate repetitive work, though Sandy thrives on it.'

'That's because I can see much more than just numbers when I am doing data, it's like a second language to me', with that Sandy went back to work, and Paul and Glen headed out.

'Well, I suppose I had better grab a load of flags and contribute to the common cause.' Kia said.

'Nope, we got a reply to your request for a meeting, and they have scheduled it for early afternoon our time. So put on your happy face and you have exactly 5hours 33 minutes to be there. Plenty of time to get there if your last trip was anything to go by.'

'You could have said something earlier Sandy. Well I guess I will go sort that out instead.'

Kia caught up with Paul and Glen just outside the tower. 'So you decided to come with us, boss?'

She shook her head 'Nope. I have to see a man about some of his staff misbehaving.'

Paul stopped, 'You need a hand?'

'No, it's just a meeting, besides I am taking a friend with me.'

It took a moment for the penny to drop, 'Yes! Paul exclaimed, can we see it? Err her?? I meant, no disrespect.' Paul shouted to the empty sky.

'None taken', came a deep female voice from behind Paul. He slowly turned around, making no sudden moves. Glen just stared gobsmacked at the sight.
ValKyrie silently hovered not more than three feet from Paul.

Paul took in every curve and angle of the craft in front of him. 'My god, you are one beautiful craft! I have never seen anything like this, ever, even in those fantasy drawings, you see on the net.'

'Yes, she is a sweet looking beast. Now if you boys have stopped drooling, I have places to be, and so do you.'
Kia stepped inside and slid into the command seat, and in a blink of an eye, they were gone.

Glen put his hand on Paul's shoulder, 'Dear friend, if that combo were coming at me, I would find me the deepest hole to hide in and fill it behind me.'

Paul smiled, 'Don't think that would help much.'
They climbed aboard their S2s and took off at a much more sedate pace.

Chapter Sixty Seven

Nearing midday, ValKyrie slowed and scanned the building that the meeting was due to be held in. Eight people were located and were shortly displayed on the HUD. Looping around the estate, another seven bodies were located, hidden in stands of trees.

'I have located 15 in total, from the radio chatter most of them are secret service personnel. Three are house staff, and one is the President.'

'Sounds about right. Let's find somewhere to sit, we are still early. I think I might go in with an S2, and you can keep an eye out for any nasty surprises that someone may try to spring on us.'

Ten minutes before the meeting was due to start Kia was sitting in her new S2 She contacted Sandy and found she had nothing new to report but was being ultra vigilant, so was the Coven.

Beside her on the floor was the suitcase with the information and files she had asked for and a brown paper bag.

Checking in one last time, she headed off to the meeting point. She dialled the S2 to a deep burgundy colour and left the FLR beacon off.

She approached the Manor and slowly swung the S2 to a graceful landing in a parking area.

The manor was a two-story structure, painted a brilliant white, the bright colour made it look even more impressive than the old English style it was crafted in. Standing on the top step were two security agents, one male one female.

They had just finished speaking into their radios as Kia walked up the steps.

'Hi Steven, Jen, I guess you know why I am here?'
Jennifer Bronson was the personal choice of the President and had been on his security detail since he had taken office.

'Hello, yes we are expecting you, please follow me.'
Just inside the entrance was a metal detector. Kia handed the briefcase to Jen, and smiled as she watched Jen gauge the weight in case it was full of explosives.

'Relax, I am here on a peaceful visit, and with luck, it will stay that way.'

She passed through the metal detector and it remained silent, as she knew it would. Jen handed her the briefcase back and ushered her into the study. 'I will let him know you have arrived', and quietly shut the door.
Although Kia was alone, she knew she was under observation. Shortly the door reopened and in walked the President, flanked by the two agents.

He walked over to Kia and held his hand out. Kia shook it with a firm grasp. 'You must be Kia from Oracle.'

'Yes, Mr. President I am.'

His smile broadened, 'You have caused quite a stir in some places, please take a seat.'

'Sir if you don't mind I would prefer if we could sit outside on the rear deck if that is not too much trouble?'
He hesitated at the strange request and flicked a look at Jen. She gave an imperceptible nod.

'Of course, he said, follow me.'
Once seated at a large glass table on the deck, Kia opened the brown paper bag and place two steaming hot Take away mugs on the table, side by side.

'Is that what I think it is!'

She smiled and nodded, 'Indeed it is Mr. President, a double brewed German coffee with a small shot of vanilla. Please help yourself to either one, they are both the same.'

He reached for the closest one and popped the lid, taking a deep breath of the steam, he smiled.

'You obviously know how much I love these, but rarely get my hands on one.' He took a sip, 'Oh yes, pure heaven. So, now I know that you are a razor sharp diplomat, what can I do for you?'

'Mr. President..'
He held up his hand, 'Please call me Jim, anyone who brings a gift like this can call me Jim.'

'OK, Jim, I had a run in with some of your military brass awhile ago. I asked them to give you a message, and also asked them to tell you what transpired that day. In fact, I told five people to do that.'

He nodded. 'Indeed, my secretary gave me a report that you had destroyed a secret military data collection centre, and that one person had died.'

'Is that all that they told you?'

'Basically, yes.'

'Yet you still agreed to meet me, here?'

'Yes, you see I have an old friend that I go fishing with from time to time, he is good with boats. You may know him, his name is Ron Baker.'

Kia laughed, 'Yes I have run into him once or twice.'

'He tells me you took some things from him once, but gave them back.'

'I did indeed.'

'Well, Ron tells me, irrespective of what I get told, he recommends that I at least listen to what you have to say.'

'I cannot ask for more than that, Jim, I am not here to cause trouble. On the contrary, I am trying to avoid it, if possible.'
Kia looked at Jen as she reached for the briefcase, Jens eyes never left hers.

'I am here to explain why I destroyed your data centre and also why I shot one of the employees between the eyes.'
Jen's eyes opened slightly at that statement.

'For once I have the afternoon to myself, peace and quiet, a rare thing these days.'

Jen led the way back to the front door. Standing on the top step, Kia canted her head to one side for a moment.

She turned to the President. 'I am so sorry Jim, but in about eight minutes your peaceful afternoon will disappear.'
He frowned.

'There is a convoy of three vehicles headed this way, it seems someone has classified me as dangerous and a terrorist. Well, they are half right.'

She smiled at Jen, 'Nice to meet you, and Steve. Also Thank you for meeting with me. And letting me give our side of the story, and as for the fools charging their way here, good luck with reining them in.'

Kia walked to the S2 and turned and waved before entering. Just as the S2 cleared the distant hills, three armoured vehicles thundered to a halt at the foot of the steps.

Two dozen troops deployed from the vehicles and their leading officer came pounding up the front stairs.

'Are you OK Mr. President? We received Intel that a dangerous and wanted terrorist was here at the manor!'

The President looked him straight in the eye, 'There is no terrorist here, and where did you get such bad Intel from?'

'Sir, I have to insist for your protection, let us search the house! You may be in grave danger!' he went to step past and walked straight into the barrel of Jen's service automatic.

'I am in charge of the Presidents security, and you and your thugs are not searching anything. Get back into your vehicles and leave the premises. Now.'

'I have orders to search the Manor! And these orders come from a higher authority than you deary!'

'Do they come from higher than mine?' asked the President.

'Please enlighten me to exactly who authorised you to invade my privacy?'

He waited several seconds, but got no reply.

'Never mind, I will find out when I get back to the office, now be a good soldier and take your men and leave. I want a copy of your orders on my desk when I get back, and whoever issued those orders sitting outside my office.'
With that, the President turned and entered the manor.
Once out of sight, Jen holstered her pistol.

'Next time you try and steamroll the President, it's going to get ugly, old man.' She turned on her heel and strode into the Manor closing the door behind her.

The officer was fuming. He yelled at the men to get back into the vehicles. They left at a more sedate pace.

Kia and ValKyrie watched as the vehicles swung out of the gate and disappeared up the road. 'Well, dear, someone on Jim's staff is leaking info. Lets go home.'

Jim sat down at the glass table and picked up Kate's photo, 'I swear I will find who authorised this', he said to Jen.
Kia had left the laptop for him. She had shown him how it could be used to reach her if the need ever arose.

Jen listened to an incoming message in her earpiece and told him the chopper would soon be here to take him back to the capital. He stood and handed the photo to her.

'Have we become that paranoid and evil that things like this are acceptable? Not on my watch! Please pack all this up and keep it under your personal protection.
'I may need it at a moments notice.' He walked into the Manor deep in thought.

Jen looked at the photos as she packed them away. 'You only shot one Kia?' She mused to herself, 'I would have slaughtered the lot personally.'

__Chapter Sixty Eight__

Kia was the last one home, she walked in on a roaring upheaval in the OpCen. She had to whistle loudly to get the groups attention.

'What's the yelling for?'

Brad grinned sheepishly, 'We just found out Paul and Glen were off adventuring while we were clearing flags.'

'Is that all? I thought it was something important, carry on.'

She walked over to the Coven.

'Kate, someone on the President's security detail is leaking info to the Backroom boys, see if you three can find out who it is, discreetly please.'

Kate nodded, 'We might need to get Sandy to poke into some places we normally don't go.'

'Don't tell me and I won't have to lie. Just avoid any international incidents. I don't want to know anyone's secrets, I just want to know who tried to trap me this afternoon.'

The ruckus over by the flag map had subsided.

Kia walked over, 'You all are playing nice now?'

Brad grinned, 'Yes mum. I am just annoyed that Paul figured out we don't need to do flags every day before I did.'

'That's because repetition numbs the brain, Brad.'
She left him spluttering some kind of reply and walked out onto the balcony.

Bree smiled, 'Has he got over his hurt pride yet?'

'Yes, I think he will survive.'

'So how did your meeting go' asked Glen?

'It went quite well. He was not told the full story, and what little he was briefed on was almost all based on lies. I straightened that out for him. He is quite easy to talk to, but I still would not want his job.

'Everything or near everything he is fed information wise is scripted or twisted to steer him from decision to decision. The whole place is run by power brokers, only the puppet changes every few years.

'On top of that, his own people leak info. Just before I left ValKyrie tracked a convoy of thugs on their way in to try and put me in a cell.'

'You didn't hurt anyone did you?' asked Miako.

'No, but he was not very happy. I am starving, anyone for a late dinner?'

Mel and Bree put their hands up, 'Only if we eat in the complex, the chef down there really knows his stuff.'

'I can go with that. Sandy, see if there is a table free for us.'

Kate poked her head through the door, 'Count us in as well.'

The bistro was busy but not overcrowded, Karl and Misha were seated at the bar. They waved as the crew flooded in heading for the tables that had been slid together. 'Have you eaten?' asked Mel, they admitted they hadn't and were cordially invited to join in.

Chapter Sixty Nine

Kia and Kate were skimming the seabed on their way to the next flag. Kate had asked to go with her for a change.

Over the last six weeks, everything had run like a well-oiled machine. Flags were becoming fewer as they moved into deeper waters and further from the coastline. The flags they were chasing down today cleared most of the southern side of the map.

Kate was remarking how the crew was getting restless. Now the drones are clearing most of the areas, they are feeling a bit redundant. 'We need something for them to get their teeth into.'

'You have any suggestions?' asked Kia.

'Well no, but I figure drones are fine for the Ocean work, even as effective and fast as they are, it's going to take years to cover the whole sea floor.

'We can't use drones on land, the sight of them would send the population nuts. I am sorry. I got nothing at the moment.'

'Well, lets hope something shows up to alleviate the boredom, one last flag and we are homeward bound.'

They reached the flag point, it was a small yacht by ocean-going standards. The scan data showed four sets of HR inside, which is why the drones had left it alone. It was a fresh wreck, no more than two or three years judging by its condition.

The keel had been torn off, possibly by rough seas. It would have sunk in seconds by the size of the gaping hole. Kia beamed it out and turned for home.

She looked at Kate, 'If Jess or Layla gets bored, see if you can find relatives for that last pickup. It wasn't old, so there may be someone who still cares.'

Back home they parted, Kia heading for the showers and Kate to check on her team.

Once back in the OpCen, Kia called a meeting. For once it was raining outside so they all sat on stools in a circle inside.

'I know you are all getting a bit despondent with running flags day in day out. I have noticed, Sandy and Kate have noticed.

'Sandy is doing a brilliant job with the drones, and the flag work still needs to be done. However, we don't need to do them every day. 'The only reason we are, is because we do not have permission to either enter into regional waters or to work over regional land.' She let that sink in.

'Kate has a very sharp mind, and even she has no answer to this problem. Neither do I at this time. So let's all turn our minds to find a way to break this deadlock. Ideally, we need global access. You and I know there is a lot of work out there, a lot of toxic stuff, in old mines, in the rivers, in people's drinking water.

'How do we, get access without getting involved with the governments directly? That is the million dollar question. 'Each of you grew up in different neighbourhoods, I am hoping that this will possibly give you a different perspective on this singular problem.'

So the floor is now open to freelance debate.' For a full minute, it was quiet.

'We need an advertising campaign. The world needs to know what we do, the service we provide and a line of communication to reach us.' Paul waited for that statement to sink in. We are after all a company or are mentioned as such. Being a company, it would be expected that we provide either goods or services. In our case, it's a service. That service is fixing environmental problems that no one else can handle.

'We are strongly established, we have nothing to hide, other than our tech, obviously. Although we are new, and first in our field, scratch that, the ONLY one in our field, the rules of business still apply.

'I don't mean we put an advert on TV, or in the local paper. We need to let each and every government know what we have to offer. Every major company needs to have us on speed dial for when something goes wrong, and trust me from my experience a whole lot of stuff goes wrong that never makes the news.

'I am not good at diplomatic contacts, but I can get us in the face of almost every major manufacturer on the planet via old stock market contacts. Also, insurance companies will love us. We will make billions of dollars.'

Paul stood and paced back and forth as his mind started to fire on all 12 cylinders. Everyone was quiet as Paul started to think.

'I know it's not about the money, but if we don't charge it will look like our service is second rate, or not worth anything. We charge per job, we make them hurt, but don't make them bleed. That would work. I had something else but lost it, damn!!

He kept pacing. Still no one said anything.

'Got it! That rescue biz we did a few weeks back with the subs, let it be known that stuff like that is also in our realm.

'A few years back some miners died because they couldn't reach them in time.

They spent millions on a half-hearted rescue and abandoned it half way. They effectively wrote the lives of the men off as an expense! ladies and gentlemen, I believe it's time we stopped sneaking around and stamped out brand on this planet as the go-to guys when the shit hits the fan!'

A round of applause sounded in the OpCen.

'Well, Paul, you certainly grabbed that by the horns!'

Kia looked around the faces, 'Anyone wants to comment on Paul's suggestion?'
'We can take care of the diplomatic side of things, we have dealt with most of them at one time or another. Also, we know people in the right places for things like this. It's not always the top guy that needs to know, it's his staff that gets things done, and those, we can reach.'
Layla looked at the floor when she noticed everyone looking at her.

'That is the most I have heard you say for a long time', Ray said.
Mel lightly punched him, 'Stop embarrassing the girl, you nasty man!' He apologised.

Brad asked Paul a few questions on some finer points. Bit by bit the whole crew took Paul's idea and polished it into something that even Kia believed was a killer plan.

'Alrighty then, Paul you do what you do best. If you need help grab one or all of us and tell us what you need to be done, Kate, Layla, Jess, that goes for you three as well.

'Sandy, whatever they need. Sandy gave the thumbs up. Also, tomorrow flags run, cancelled, this is now our #1 priority.'

Two days had passed since both Paul, and Kate had presented their packages for the rest to examine. No changes were necessary, and the packages hit the network.

Driven by Sandy's ability to swarm any network, the information dossiers were soon in the hands of the appropriate people, both in government and commercial circles.

'So now we wait', Paul said', in the interim, I for one am going to set up a flag run because waiting is not my strong point.'

Glen nodded and stretched, 'Sounds good to me.'
The rest of the crew were out on the balcony, having sorted their days run out. Kia turned to walk out and join them when Sandy called her back.

'It looks like the information packages are starting to work!

'There is an incoming call for you. From Sung-Te Tang. She says she is calling on behalf of the Vietnam Chairman.'

Kia sat at a terminal on the far wall. Sandy patched Tang through.

An image of a young woman with typically delicate Asian features appeared on Kia's screen.

'Hello Sung-Te, My name is Kia, how may we be of assistance?'

Sung-Te, bowed to the camera, 'Hello, I have been asked by our Chairman, Quyen Dao, to extend to your company an invitation to an audience with him.'

Kia raised an eyebrow, 'And do you know why your honourable Chairman requests a meeting?'

She looked at the notes in front of her.

'I have been instructed to tell you it is an environmental issue, which the Chairman believes you may be able to assist with. The chairman also advises that he will compensate you for your time.'

Kia nodded, 'When is this meeting to take place?'

Sung-Te again referred to her notes.

'I have been informed, it is an urgent matter and that the Chairman will avail himself as you require.'

Kia looked at the zone clock on the main HUD, it displayed a mid-morning time for Vietnam. 'Please ask your Chairman if this afternoon at 4 o'clock is acceptable, and to inform us of the place he wishes to hold the meeting.'

Sung-Te again bowed her head to the camera and said she would relay the message and supply the information as soon as possible. A few seconds later the call dropped out.

Kia swivelled around and faced the room, she saw the Coven watching her. 'So ladies, what do you make of that?'

Kate shrugged, 'While you were talking we ran a quick search, nothing in the news or back channels about a fresh disaster, no earthquakes, volcanoes, storms, mudslides.'

'No chemical spills, industrial fires or train accidents' added Jess.

'The country's GDP is up, unemployment down, they are not at war with anyone, poverty is decreasing, and human rights issues are almost the lowest in any communist country', Layla threw her search results in.

'So if they have an environmental problem, it's not being reported anywhere, by anyone' summarised Kate.

'Quyen Dao is the 15th elect Chairman, he seems well liked. 'The country has prospered well since he took over.' Unlike many in the past, he is not ruling with an iron fist or using the military as muscle.'

The sound of scraping chairs came from the balcony as the crew came into the OpCen. Waving they headed for the elevator.

'Paul, Glen, Hang around for a few minutes will you, I might have something for you shortly.'

The other four left as the boys walked over.

'What's up?' They said in unison.

'I am waiting on a return call, if it comes through we may be heading out for a...'

A chime sounded, and Sandy informed Kia Sung-Te was calling back.

The boys stepped out of camera view.

Kia hit the spacebar on the terminal and Sung-Te's image appeared. Again she bowed her head to the camera, 'The Honourable Chairman would be delighted to see you at the time you requested, He has asked for you to attend his private residence in the Thanh Hoa Province.'

Kia nodded, 'Please inform your Chairman that I will be there at the agreed time, and there will be three people in my party.' Sung-Te bowed, 'As you instruct, I shall do so.'

This time, Kia cut the feed.

'OK boys looks like the trip is on.' She turned to Kate, 'You DO know where his house is right?' All three girls leapt for their keyboards.

Chapter Seventy

Quyen Dao was a tall, wispy built man with a surprisingly firm handshake. Seated at a round table in his spacious home, were six people. Quyen Dao was flanked one side by his Environmental Minister and the other by the Commander of the Vietnamese army. Introductions and polite chat had been the content of the conversation for the last 15 minutes. Kia got the impression it was to help everyone get comfortable with each other.

Quyen took a deep breath and started to explain the reason he had asked for the meeting.

'I have asked to speak to you for several reasons. We received your resume, and we did some research and found to our surprise that your resume was actually highly accurate! Not only that, but we found those that have either worked with Oracle or have come into contact with your company, all speak highly of you.

'We have a rather unique environmental problem. One that so far traditional methods have made very little impact on.'

'We also did some research, and found no obvious environmental issue mentioned, so I figure this is something that you are keeping quiet?' asked Paul.

Quyen smiled, 'Actually no, we have been shouting about this problem for over forty years. It is not a new problem, but a very old one. It also is not an issue of our making. Until now I believed no one has had the special talents to help us, but now with Oracle's new skills we may finally remove this horrible infliction from our country.'

'Mr. Chairman, if we can help, I can assure you we will. Now please explain exactly what you require and we shall see what we can do for you and your country.'

Kia looked at the three men, in turn, 'So lay it on the table and let us see where we go from here.'

Quyen bowed his head slightly. 'As you wish, I shall condense the issue as much as possible. As you are aware we are a communist country. However, we are more a Socialist Communist country. I, and my government, have made great strides in reducing poverty and lifting the standard of living for all our people.

'Our new path is working very well. So well, we are now being held back by this blight. We are running out of room to expand, room for better housing, new farms and industry. We have a lot of room in the country. However, we cannot use it safely.

'As you know, Vietnam has suffered many wars, and not least, the one with the USA. As a result of these conflicts, vast areas of our land are unusable. Landmines and munitions are almost as common as rocks.

'We have an average of three people killed or maimed every single day. Of all the countries in the world, we have the dishonour to have the highest incidence of amputees and crippled children in the world.

'Even disregarding the need for expansion. The amount of people killed or maimed, the amount of livestock killed, we have needed help for forty years.'

Quyen paused to gather his thoughts.

'Assistance was finally sent, but it is ineffective. Highly trained personnel, they blow themselves up eventually.

'Machines were designed but cannot access the places needed. The mines sink in the mud during our wet seasons, they are too deep to detect. Then in the dry season, they work their way back to the surface, killing people in supposedly safe clear areas.

'We are hoping, no praying, that you may finally be the answer to a safe country.'

Silence fell on the room as Quyen stopped speaking, his Commander and Minister had both nodded several times while Quyen was speaking.

Kia looked at Paul and Glen. 'Your vote on this?'
'100%' Paul said, 'Hell yes' Glen said.

Kia turned her gaze to the commander. 'Sir, what are your thoughts on this matter? You are the one charged with the safety of the people.'

He sat straighter in his chair, 'I will defend my people to the death, but this, this cowardly method, we cannot defeat easily.'

She turned her attention to the Minister, 'And you Sir, your opinion?'

He looked Kia in the eyes, 'The war is long over, longer than I have lived, yet the enemies of yesterday still reach out and harm or kill us. It must not be allowed to continue.'

'Then we shall stop it for you. There are some requirements we shall need. I shall get my secretary to send you a list of them.

'It may take a few months to solve this problem, but we can, and we will solve it.'

Quyen stood, 'Months? We thought a few years!'

Kia smiled and also stood, 'Maybe for the rest of the companies, but not for Oracle.'

After a customary round of refreshments, the meeting was finalised.

Quyen shook all their hands on the steps outside, 'I had hoped that your reputation would prove to be as accurate as your resume. If it is indeed possible to rid us of this horror, and I openly confess, I do have my doubts that it can be. We the people of Vietnam will always be in your debt.'

'Lets save the applause for when the job is done, Mr. Chairman. I am confident we can end this blight as you call it, and I agree it has gone on way too long.'

On the way home, Glen had been researching some of the claims Quyen had made during the conversation.

After about an hour of reading, Glen shut the screen down. 'Geezus that is so depressing. Mankind is not nice sometimes.'

Paul put his hand on Glen's shoulder, 'And that my friend is only the stuff they allow the public to know. The man is his own enemy sometimes.'

'How did it go?' asked Kate as they walked into the OpCen. Although it was early evening, the Coven was there working. 'If they agree to the list of requirements I had Sandy send them, then we have ourselves a new project. The Chairman has asked us to clear the entire country of landmines and munitions. In the list we sent him is the option of removing ALL artefacts of the War.'

Next morning found Kia sitting on the corner of the table in the café. She had briefed the crew on the events and was fielding questions from the crew and Coven.

Kate had given a rundown of what officially had been used during the American War as it was called. She read out loud a list of ordinances that had been dropped.

The figures were staggering.

What hit home was the statistics on human loss and injuries in the last 30 or so years, and the fact that the stats were only pertaining to Vietnam. Laos, was just as crippled, and Kate said she would not be surprised if Laos asked for help next.

Ray was quiet during the talk, being ex-special forces. This hit close to home. Mel was holding his hand in both of hers.

'Where do we start on a project this big?', asked Brad.

'I figure we start with a local base, there are plenty of hills and mountains that are inaccessible. We go with a similar setup we used in Switzerland. This is not much different, instead of collecting ropes and equipment we collect munitions and war machinery..'

'Do you really want to collect them?', asked Neil.

'I think so' Kia said, 'Empty of course.

'Pictures of whatever we recover may serve as a stark reminder to the rest of the world. Besides, I can annoy the Americans by showing the rest of the world just how much destruction they leave behind.

'That reminds me I need to put a call through to Jim later and give him the heads up.'

Bree looked surprised, 'Why does he need to know?'

Ray spoke in a low voice, 'Because we are probably going to find a lot of HR that went missing during the war.

'And I would hazard a guess that we possibly will be returning them. Depending on identification.'

You ok with this Ray?' He nodded, 'Yes Kia.'

'It just touches a few sore points, but I will be fine. I think this is years overdue as well.'

'Alright guys, find a HUD, get a bit of background on the place, Sandy will give you a virtual tour. Make sure we know a bit about the terrain we will be working in.'

The President was deep in conversation with Kia when the call from the Chairman's secretary came in. Sandy took the call and saw to any minor issues.

'So there you have it, Jim. If we find anything that needs to be returned to you, I will be in touch with you personally.'

Jim nodded, 'Maybe you can succeed where our diplomatic efforts have failed.' Kia cut the feed.

She turned to Sandy, 'So the news is?'

'The Chairman has agreed unreservedly to the conditions you asked for. He also said that any remains are best handled by us. He believes that an independent party doing this is the best solution.

'Prior attempts to work directly with the US government proved to be tense and full of accusations which made a working environment impossible.'

'OK good, I can live with that, alright lets do our toilet runs and whatever now. I'd like to get this project underway.

'Kate get your girls ready, we will need your talents as well. Sandy see you there.

Anyone have any last questions? No. Good. We roll out in 30 minutes.'

29 minutes later nine S2s took off.

Chapter Seventy One

Finding space to build the base was easy, over 40% of Vietnam was forest and jungle. They selected a piece of high ground with no access other than hacking your way through the dense jungle.

They levelled a one square kilometer area on the top of the mountain.

Kia asked the others to run a spiral scan search from the base outwards. Making sure there were no mountain villages or other signs of human occupation close. The crew returned exactly one hour and eight minutes later.

The area was clear. 100 meters inside the perimeter was a square wire fence 12 feet high. Each of the uprights was part of a large receiver. Lining up two craft per side of the fence the crew ran power cables from their craft out to an upright and one on the insulating fence.

'OK, Sandy, the grid is now active and powered.'

It was eerie to watch a duplicate of the tower on the island grow from the rock base, then a building housing the sleeping quarters. Inside was identical to the one on the island, however, the view from the balcony definitely wasn't.

'This is going to be hard work' Sandy said. 'Just on that one sweep we collected six tonnes of munitions and a helicopter carcass.'

Bree shook her head, 'That is just crazy! The whole countryside must be contaminated. This may take years!'

'Not so', Sandy said. During the night and in the remote areas I will run drones.'

'Due to the new tech I have received from my sister we can now make the drones in camo, that makes life easier.'

Bree walked out onto the balcony. The others were watching the last of three warehouses being built.

'It's weird watching things in reverse' Neil said. 'I am used to seeing us cut things up and beam them out, this is like a movie running backwards.'

In the OpCen2 Sandy had a huge map on screen of all the provinces, she was mapping all the known villages. In anticipation of an approval on this project she had moved four satellites last night and they were scouring the northern half of the country, looking for villages and any other signs of habitation.

Neil was working hard on one of the terminals. Ray was looking through the lists of lost servicemen and recorded downed aircraft.

Brad and Paul were working on the main map and guiding Sandy with areas to aim the satellites first. Along rivers and streams and other favourable locations they may find local population areas.

Mel and Bree were running through pages of translated information and trying to locate the main areas of conflict that were in the archives. They were working with Miako, who through a separate terminal was talking to a group of four experts on the history of the land. These four had been chosen by the Commander and tasked with answering any questions as needed. Their orders had been short and to the point. Answer all questions, supply as much information as possible, and hide nothing.

The commander understood that to withhold information or deny answers was only going to hurt his country and, slow the progress.   Neil called Sandy over, 'Here we go, build your drones like this, even if spotted they will cause no alarm.' Neil had changed the Drones from alien looking saucers to small delta winged drones with twin tails. 'Use these for over land and the saucer ones for underwater that should make life easier.'

'Thank you Neil! I shall do that overnight.'

Kia looked up from what she was doing, everyone was into the project all except Glen. Glen was missing, as she double checked the elevator opened, and Glen came in pushing a trolley with sandwiches and two large urns of hot coffee. She smiled to herself, Glen always had the knack of doing the right thing at the right time.

'Ray, can I talk to you a moment, please?' Paul said. 'I saw you looking through the missing records. I have glanced through it, but you would know better than me. If we have an access all areas card, that would also cover the coastline out to the international boundary yes?'

'I would assume so Paul.'

'I think this would be an opportunity for Sandy to deploy some of her drones in the water. Some of those missing people on the list went missing over the water. What do you think?'

'I think that I just went to run the same idea past Kia, and she said we could do anything we want as long as it does not detract from the main project.'

'Great minds as they say' Paul said, 'Lets grab Sandy.'

By the end of the first day, most of what could be planned was done.

Although it looked like Sandy was being overworked, she had hardly touched the banks of CPUs, None of the data was stored there, it was all transmitted back to the island for storage.

As darkness fell outside, on the balcony a whole orchestra of jungle sounds filled the air. Tasks were completed and one by one they ended up on the balcony. Darkness as far as the eye could see, except for the sky, it was ablaze with stars. Even the base below was pitch black. That would change over the coming weeks.

As the last light went out in the sleeping quarters, everything was still. Only night creatures moved.

Except for one sleek, dark shape that circled the base, ever watchful for threats or trouble.

Silently she circled the sleeping base, her sensors missed nothing, and once content she settled in a clearing close to the base. Sandy smiled to herself, 'Hi Sis. Now we are safe!'

There was a new addition in the OpCen, Sandy had made a long table with a HUD as the top. The HUD displayed the country, its towns and cities, roads, rivers and all other features, what made it notable was that the display was in 3d.

That gave it a sense of depth as it displayed the hills and mountains. Sandy was instructing the crew on how it worked.

'This display is being fed real-time data from the four birds we relocated. You tap an area of interest, like this.'
An area in the jungle expanded, and zoomed in until it showed the base compound outside, with all the buildings and tower in 3d.

'That is amazing Sandy. Now rather than spy on us, show us where you think we should start.'

'Well, according to ongoing scans, there is nasty stuff over most of the area. I believe it would be wise to clear the places closest to inhabitants first. Simply because a bomb or mine in the forest is not going to hurt anyone in the short term. 'I think now we are here and operational, any person maimed or killed may have been avoidable.'

'Agreed', Kia said, 'So plot us the best places to be, get your drones out in the non-populated areas. Lets get this show on the road. '

She turned back to the map, 'Also get Mel and Ray to run a clear line just inside the border. From the China side on the coast, all the way around to the south coast on the other side. It all looks the same out there, and I don't want us straying, even by accident.'

Mel and Ray were the first ones airborne. Paul and Glen were next, heading in a totally different direction. Miako and Neil were getting their lists of small villages from Sandy, 'Clear all around these and inside the villages themselves.'

With a wave, they both left as well.

'Now for you three, I think starting here and run a sweep from inside the villages outwards into the jungle.

'This line is the line that has reported the most injuries and fatalities over the last year. Also here I have circled a campsite. There are several Viet and UN minesweeper people there. They may have better local knowledge that would be useful to us.

'Last but not least, I would like to run the girls through a simulator when they are not busy. Additional help would not hurt at the moment.'

Kia glanced at Kate. She stood looking wide-eyed at Sandy.

Kia smiled, 'Why the hell not. If they can cut it, then that's fine by me.' She looked at Brad and Bree, 'Shall we?'

After everyone had left Kate talked to Sandy, 'You must be joking! 'None of us even have a driving licence!

'Good!' Sandy said, 'I won't have to wean you off bad habits then. We can start this afternoon if you like.'

The commander had supplied information of a campsite where they would find one of the most reputable landmine experts.

He suggested that his local knowledge may or may not be of use to Oracle.

To say Kia and her group caused a commotion when they landed in the field next to the camp would be an understatement!

The camp consisted of rows of poorly erected tents and hastily added lean-to awnings. One of the men came running forward and met them half way to the main tent.

'Are you fucking crazy lady!? Landing in the middle of a minefield! Are you trying to blow yourself up? Or more importantly blow me up!?'

Kia smiled, 'Relax, there are no mines left in this field.'

'See all them pegs, each one is an APM!'

'You wouldn't want to bet on that, would you? Lets say a nice mug of coffee if I am right, and I will pay you $1000 for every one you dig up.'

The guy hesitated, 'Just who are you, and what do you want here?'

Kia held out her hand, my name is Kia, this is Brad and Bree, and we are part of Oracle Industries. The Chairman Quyen Dao has contracted us to clean Vietnam of ordinance.

'Rob Dennett' said the man wiping his hands on his pants before shaking Kia's hand, 'I heard a rumour that some people were coming in to help clear this area out.'

'Oh, we are not clearing this area out. We are clearing the entire country from the north border to the sea.'

'Yeah Right, not in my lifetime. Come in out of the sun, and tell me how the hell you gonna do that.'

They all found something to sit on under an awning. Drinks were served in a range of battered cups. Kia sipped hers, it was surprisingly good!

'Rob, we came here to pick your brains. The Commander told us you were the best guy to show us the most urgent areas that need clearing. We will eventually clear the lot, but for now, the focus is on the places that are most urgent.

'We removed several 400lb bombs 15 kilometers from here inside the tree line. But where they were, was almost inaccessible, so were not urgent.'

'The commander huh?Grumpy old coot, every time someone sets an APM off, he phones me and tells me to work harder! Like I can see into the ground or something.'

'We can', Brad pointed to the field they landed in. 'There were 47 in that field. You had marked 43.'

Rob ran a hard worked hand through his hair. 'That would not surprise me, we try our best. But there is always going to be some missed. In the last three years, I have lost seven good men, friends. This is a devils game, and sometimes I feel we are losing.'

'Well, you won't lose anymore', Kia sent Bree back to the S2, when she returned, she had a laptop in her hands.

She gave it to Rob. 'This is for you. With this, you can contact any one of us at any time.

'You will also get a data feed that shows you the areas we have sanitised.

If you know of any high priority places, let us know. You have the local knowledge and the contacts that will assist greatly in clearing the garbage left behind.'

Kia opened the laptop and showed him where they currently were located. The field they sat in was a normal colour, all the area around it was tinted slightly red.

Rob caught on quickly what that meant. 'You really cleared this field!'

He used the built in pad to zoom out slightly. 'All this area here', he indicated with his finger, 'we have cleared that, but now I am not so sure we got them all.

'From here, to along this Ridgeline here, was a major battle point.'
Kia circled the area on the touch screen and tapped it, a menu popped up, and she selected send.

'We will be back in a couple of hours. Stay tuned.'

Rob wiped the sweat out of his eyes as the S2s disappeared out over the tree line. 'Lady, I hope you are as good as I have heard, because this is a losing game out here.'

He put the laptop down in his tent and picked up a shovel and a detector. Walking into the field, he carefully dug up a flag marker, and another followed by several more.

'Well, fuck me if there is nothing here anymore!' He dropped the shovel and did a small dance in the dirt. 'Yes! Take that, you invisible scourge of the land!'

He walked back into the tent, picking up the laptop he was surprised to see a wide streak along the ridgeline that grew longer as he watched. 'We are going to win this war after all!' Brad was scanning in the centre of the other two craft, between each S2 were six new Delta drones.
They had a combined scan path of just over 1100 meters wide.

There were no options for chimes. The scans were programmed to remove anything man-made.

Four times large objects were scanned, instead of slowing down for them, a drone would be kicked out of the hive under an S2 and tasked with dealing with the larger mass. Once done it returned to the hive.

Working back from the ridgeline, they ran overlapping paths back to Rob's camp and another 40 kilometers beyond. Rob sat transfixed at the laptop. The cleared area was growing fast, he had rushed outside as the S2s flashed almost silently overhead. For nearly an hour he watched as the clearance progress was updated on the laptop.

He saw the zone stop growing and walked outside and sat back under the awning. Shortly the three strange planes were back in the field. This time, he didn't rush out to abuse them.

'How in gods name did you do that?' He asked as Brad and Bree sat back down, Kia remained standing leaning against the awning support.

'Through advances in technology. The same way a man from the 1800s would ask how a cell phone worked.'

Rob nodded, 'Hard to keep up with the new gizmos that come out each year.'

'Thanks to your directions there are 4892 less APMs in that block area, plus 177 tonnes of other materials, two tanks and several human remains were located.'

'Holy Shit! You really are cleaning the place out! Have you been in the River Delta yet? That was the setting for some nasty fighting.'

'No, actually I was hoping that we could hire you for the duration of the project. As an advisor, if you were interested.'

'Hell yes! Not like I have anything to do here now is it! I don't have to fly in one of your Gizmo things, do I? I don't fly well.' Brad laughed.

Even Kia smiled, 'No, you would be in our main base. Working off a 3d map, you could point out areas we need to sanitise first.'

'I am already on the Commander's payroll, I would have to talk to him.'

'Leave him to me. If you accept, grab your stuff. '
Rob looked around the camp, 'Umm, ok let me sort a few things out here. Can I have about 10 minutes?'
'Sure, go ahead.'
Rob dashed off to the group of workers who had been sitting in the shade. He gave instructions to the workers' leaders.
There was a lot of handshakes and bowing going on, then he was back with two bags and the laptop under his arm.
Kia turned to Brad and Bree, 'You guys want to continue going back over the area Rob came from, and anywhere else you deem fit. I will take him back to the base and get him settled and come back.'
Brad stood and shook Rob's hand, 'Welcome aboard, one more iron in the fire never hurt.'
As the locals broke camp the S2s left, two heading southeast and one heading north.

<u>Chapter Seventy Two</u>

Rob was as tense as a wooden pole for the first few minutes of the trip, eventually relaxing as the ride was nothing like he was expecting. Kia saw the transition and could hear the relief in his voice. 'So Rob, what's your story?'

'Me? Nothing fantastic. I came here in 1976 as a freelance journalist. Hoping to make my rep covering the war. After a few months I saw it wasn't a war, it was a slaughter.

'Horrors committed by both sides. I dragged soldiers from both sides to safety, walked through villages that were shredded for no reason. Then suddenly it was all over, but the killing and deaths continued. Somehow I felt partially to blame, so I learnt how to dig up mines and stuff, trying to make amends somehow.'

Kia looked at him, 'It was not your fault Rob, and now you can truly help sort it out once and for all.' They landed in front of one of the warehouses. 'Come with me.' Rob dropped his bags outside the warehouse door and walked inside with Kia.

In the warehouse were five huge piles of mines, sorted by type and by origin, Rob slammed to a halt, wide-eyed.

'Relax Rob, they are empty. We are keeping them to show the rest of the world some of the hidden costs of war. Hopefully, it will be another straw on the war caMel back.' As they watched an overhead gantry moved a pipe outlet over a pile and dozens of empty cans spewed out onto one of the piles.

'As you see, the collection goes on, and this is just our first day. Lets get you settled in.'

Kia showed Rob to a spare dorm room and hinted a shower would be a good thing. Shortly after Rob emerged from his room, dressed in clean jeans and a T-Shirt.

Up in the tower, he was given the tour and introduced to Sandy. Rob loved the Holo.

'New gizmos every year!'

Sandy said, 'I am not sure if calling me a gizmo is an insult or not!'

Rob apologised with a smile.

Kia showed him the 3D table, 'This is where I want you to work. It's kinda like your laptop map, just much bigger.'

Rob could see tracks of cleared areas to the north where Sandy was running drones. The tracks looked much thinner on the whole map compared to what he saw on the laptop. There were other areas cleared and eight blue icons showing the exact position of each S2 in the air.

'This one here', Rob said, pointing to Neil's icon, 'That valley to the left was a major supply line from China. It may be worth looking in there.'

Kia leant over and tapped Neil's Icon, Neil's picture opened up in a window on the table. 'Yes, boss?'

'Neil, this is Rob, Rob meet Neil. Rob is helping as an advisor, he has been here a long time and knows local information.'

Neil nodded, 'Great, because up here over the jungle one mountain looks almost the same as the next.'

'To your left there is a long valley about six klicks from that village. It was a main supply route from China and is still used by foot traffic. It may be worth a look up that valley.'

'Roger that Rob, on my way.'

The window closed, and the icon curved from its current path and headed for the foot of the valley.

Rob cast his eyes over the map. It was brilliant in detail, and so highly accurate. When he mentioned this, Sandy said, 'Thank you.'

Rob grinned.

He then went on to point at certain places and recite information about each. As he did so Sandy inserted an icon and recorded all the info Rob could provide. For a few hours, he did this, hardly looking up from the map. When he finally turned around Kia was gone!

'She left over forty minutes ago Rob. She is back with Brad and Bree.'

Rob pointed to a long wriggly line with two icons on the front, 'What's happening there?'

'That is Melissa and Ray, they are cutting a 50 meter wide corridor along the border. It outlines our area of commitment.'

Rob nodded, 'That will piss Laos off, they always dispute where the real border is.'

'Not anymore, they can't. The track is accurate to 1 inch either way.'

Rob walked around the table viewing the map from all sides, there were a lot more icons on the table now.

'This area here and this mountain, there are rumours of base camps in those areas, but nobody has ever returned with proof.' Sandy inserted Icons but made them yellow.

The elevator opened, and the girls walked in, Kate stopped and froze when she saw Rob. Sandy saw the look of horror on her face.

'Kate relax, this is Rob. Kia brought him in as a local consultant. He is a friend.'

It took a few moments for Kate heart rate to steady. She looked from Sandy to Rob and back again.

Sandy moved close to her, 'Honest Kate it's fine, inside the rec field here I have total control and nothing will hurt you here.'

Kate smiled weakly, 'Sorry, I am just being silly. I was just caught off guard', Kate walked over to Rob, 'Hi Rob, I'm Kate, and this is Jess and Layla.'

Rob shook her hand, 'I am so sorry that I startled you, it was not my intention. I am just here to help with the 3d map, he pointed at the new icons.'

Kate walked over and saw he had been doing quite a lot of additions, 'One moment Rob.'

She walked over to her terminal and came back with a tablet, 'According to US records, they dropped supplies in these following regions.' As she read the drop-zones out Rob pointed to them on the map, out of eleven zones Rob had only heard of seven.

Neil called in, 'Miako and I have finished that valley, there was a lot of junk and more than a few HR in it. Anything else close by? If not we will swing back over the villages to the east from here.'

Sandy looked at Rob, 'Anything else?'

'No, not really, it's pretty remote up that way.'
For the rest of the afternoon, everyone was busy doing what needed to be done, and the map on the table was slowly showing signs of progress. Just on dark, the crews starting arriving back. Rob was introduced to them by Brad as Kia was still out.

She had detoured to the Commander's house and was sitting on his porch giving him a rundown of the day.

Rob was taken down to the café with the rest as they went for their evening meal. They found out that Rob was quite the story teller once he got started. Kia arrived halfway through the meal. She grabbed a plate and went to the servery.

Plate in one hand and a mug in the other she sat next to Kate. Rob carried on with some of the stories he had heard and things he had seen. It made for some interesting listening.

During one of the lulls in the conversation, Sandy appeared and gave a rundown of the days progress. The account was quite startling for such a short time span.

Kia asked if the night drones were out. 'Yes, there are 1780 drones out over land and 811 underwater at the moment.'

'Nice', Bree said, 'But why underwater?'

'As we have full access at the moment, I am taking advantage of that and clearing from the beaches out to the international border. Trust me Bree there is a lot of debris out there. It's almost as bad as the last convergence zone, we cleared, just spread over a larger area.'
Seeing she wasn't needed at the moment, Sandy faded out, and the disc parked itself.

'Enough about me' Rob said, 'So this is what you guys do for a living. Fly around clearing up messes for the local governments?'

'It's actually a sideline, believe it or not', Miako smiled at Rob. Most of the last year we have been clearing mankind's slow, but methodical contamination of the oceans.

'Well, I hope you have a lot of brooms, because from where I stand, most people don't know what a rubbish bin is!'

Glen stood and took his empty plate to the disposal chute, 'Well ladies and gentlemen, I, for one, am heading for bed. Kia no doubt will have the whip out tomorrow. Night all.'
With that, Glen disappeared down the elevator. That started an evacuation as the others soon followed suit.

Sunrise saw all the crews out and running the grids that Sandy had uploaded into their S2s. Everything flowed smoothly and for the next nine weeks, everything went without a hitch.

Rob was sitting on a stool in front of the 3D map. Just under 49% of the map was showing clear. He was reading incident reports that the Coven had been digging up, both from the allied side and the Viet side. Slowly he was able to map some of the incidents into the map data.

Some of the reports were redundant as those areas had been cleared already.

Outside the base, Sandy had added no less than sixteen warehouses. Further out there was a huge array of recovered hardware in the open. The Commander had been a weekly visitor and had been dumbfounded by the huge, orderly rows of equipment and the piles of recovered munitions.

Three times a week a chopper arrived with historians from both the military and social society. They would load crates and boxes from the warehouses and transport them out. Every day Sandy transmitted an up-to-date listing of recovered items, and a small army of clerks would sift through the lists and highlight items for the next chopper load.

Only Jess was in the OpCen with Rob and Sandy, Kate and Layla had finished their Sims training and were out with the crew. Jess had been on a few runs as well, but said she was still not confident.

So she had opted for extra Sim time and would only go when needed.

All the large cities and towns in the search area had been scanned during the night, mostly by drones. Although they were there by invite, Kia was trying to keep a low profile of the project.

Just before lunch, Sandy put a call through to Kia, there was an issue in one of the sectors that the drones were currently running.

Kia asked if it was urgent as they had another 45 minutes to the end of the run they were on.

'No, not really urgent', came the reply.

Later, Kia was sitting cross-legged on a chair in front of a terminal. She was studying a list of items that Sandy had scanned in a drone sweep. Everyone else had come in and had lunch and were back out again. 'So what do you think?'

Kia looked up from the data, 'Well, it's interesting, I don't know if it has anything to do with us and our project, though.'

She returned to the list, after a few moments she turned off the screen, 'Bugger it, I will have a look.' She stopped at the 3D table, there was almost more cleared area than tinted area.

'Show me where this was.'

The table zoomed into one area, there was a small village at the end of a valley. The area, Sandy highlighted was about half a kilometer away from the village on the top of an overlooking cliff.

Kia slid a virtual keyboard onto the screen and typed a list of items.

'Put these in a box in my S2 please Sandy', and with that she left.

Chapter Seventy Three

335 kilometers away from the OpCen Kia dropped the S2 quietly onto the top of the cliff. Grabbing the box she had asked for, Kia slung the strap over her shoulder and started to walk towards the cliff edge. Near the edge was a well-worn track to the left so she followed it.

The track wound down the side, then twisted back along the ledge that ran across the face of the cliff. Totally unperturbed by the sheer drop one side of the narrow path, Kia kept walking until the path widened out and stopped.

Unslinging the box from her shoulder, she put it on the rock shelf where the path finished and sat on it. To her left was a wide view of the valley, and you could just see the village through the trees far below. To her right in the front of the cliff face was a dark cave. She had sat down right in the centre of the cave opening.

For several minutes she took in the view of the valley. She spoke out loud, 'You know there are people who pay thousands to have a view like this.'
For several minutes nothing happened then she detected slight movements from deep in the cave.

'Who are you and what do you want? Came a voice from inside the gloom.'

'My name is Kia, and I just want to chat for a few minutes'. She stood and opened the latches on the box and removed a flask and two cups and a small fold out stool.

Flipping the stool open she sat down and poured two drinks out of the flask and put one on the closed box.

'Come on out Frank, I don't bite. I just want to chat for a little then I will leave.'

'How do you know my name? Are you one of them bounty hunters? I warn you I am armed.'

Kia continued to gaze over the valley, 'Well that's not very polite. I offer you a nice cuppa, and you threaten to shoot me. No, I am not a bounty hunter. So I am just going to sit here quietly, while you, a big scary man with a big scary gun hides in the dark.'

Again, it was silent on the ledge. Eventually, there was shuffling noises, and Frank emerged from the back of the cave. Holding an old revolver in one hand, he moved along the wall furthest from Kia. He made a sorry sight, dressed in old army pants that had been cut off above the knees and a shirt that had more holes than material. A long grey tinged beard and hair that showed signs of being hacked short with a knife. He looked to be in his late 50s early 60s.

Despite his poor clothing, he was obviously very fit for a man of his age.

'Don't worry Frank, if I had wanted to cause you harm I would have done it by now. Sit and lets talk for a while. And before you ask we are the only two people on this mountain. 'Just you and me.'

Frank studied the terrain. He knew every tree, every leaf just about, he could see nothing out of place and slowly relaxed.

He sat on a rock near the box on the opposite side to Kia. Well out of arm's reach. Picking up the cup he took a sip, then a mouthful. He reached for the flask, never taking his eyes of Kia for more than a microsecond at a time.

She smiled, 'I guess it's been a while since your last cup of coffee.'

Frank nodded, 'Corner store is a fair hike from here.'

She waited until he had refilled the cup.

'Frank, why are you living in a cave in the middle of nowhere?'

'Personal reasons. Ain't no law saying I can't live here!'

'No, probably not, but the fighting has been over for decades, why don't you go home?'

'You from the military?'

Kia shook her head, 'I work with a company that is being paid to remove ordinance and munitions left behind. The landmines, for example, that are still killing people today.

'We have been slowly clearing from the North, working our way down to the coast.'

'Them flying darts, they belong to your company?'

'Darts? Oh, the Drones! Yes, they scan the terrain looking for stuff that doesn't belong. One of them saw you, and I thought I would say hi, and bring you a few things.'

'I don't need nuthin', I have everything I need.'

'Well, I tell you what Frank, look through the box there, and anything you don't need, I will take back with me.'

'Like I told you, I don't need nuthin.''

'Right, so you said. Well, it's getting late. I will leave the box with you. I have to come past here in the morning, so if it's still here, then I will take it away.'

Kia stood slowly, and Frank scrambled to his feet and backed away, pulling the revolver from his waistband.

Kia walked to the narrow ledge that led to the top of the cliff.

She turned and smiled, 'Frank, just so you know, your revolver is old, rusty and worst of all, it's empty.

'I will be back after sunrise to collect what you don't need.' With a small wave, she retraced the ledge back up to the S2.

Frank never took his eyes off her until she turned off the ledge at the top. Walking back over to the box he poured another coffee. He sat on the camp stool and stared at the box like it was filled with snakes.

For almost half an hour he sat there, alternating his gaze from the box to the distant village and back. Finally, the coffee was gone. He put the cup in the cave and returned and grabbed the box, he grunted with surprise at its weight as he carried it to the mouth of the cave.

Putting it down in a patch of sunlight, he gingerly opened it and peered inside.

Kia sat with her bare feet on the balcony railing and watched the S2s arrive back. One of the choppers loaded with boxes and crates from the warehouses had left just minutes before Brad and Bree came in. Rob was sitting across the table from Kia and was reading a printed report she had handed him earlier. He reached the end and flicked back and forth between a few pages.

'So, if I understand it, Frank came here near the end of the conflict as a raw recruit. The war ended, and he decided to stay. Now he is living in a cave in the middle of the jungle? He is listed on the MIA list, and for decades no one has known where he was. His father and his two brothers are still alive, his mother died a few years back.'

'That's about the size of it, yes.' Kia nodded.

'A lot of soldiers went crazy after the war, a lot of things happened and some of the things they saw cannot be unseen. Maybe he is better off in the cave. Some can be dangerous when introduced back into society.'

'There is nothing wrong with him, Rob. He has all his wits about him, he doesn't seem to be suffering PTSD. The fact that he said he *couldn't* leave rather than saying he doesn't *want* to leave means there may be something holding him here. Also in my opinion, returning soldiers are getting the raw end of the stick. Someone should be held responsible for that.

'I told Frank I would call back tomorrow morning. This time, I won't be a shock to his system. Hopefully, I can get the reason why he feels he needs to stay. If he wants to stay, that is his choice, and we will leave him to his choices.'

Brad and Bree had arrived with Paul and Ray. They had sat listening to the conversation in silence. Ray asked if he could read the file, Rob handed it to him.

The sun had only been up 30 minutes as Kia landed on the top of the mountain.

Walking down the ledge, the first thing she saw was the box was gone. There was a small fire burning in the centre of a ring of stones and the smell of freshly brewed coffee wafted through the air.

She stopped near the fire and looked over the sunlit valley.

'Good morning', came a voice from behind her.

'Morning Frank. It's a wonderful view you have up here.'

'Yes, it is, but it's a bittersweet view as well.'

Kia turned to see a smooth shaven Frank standing in the cave entrance.

He was now dressed in new jean pants, he had cut the legs off just above the knee and rolled the cut ends up.

With a clean T-shirt and the shave he looked a different person.

'I see some of the stuff I left was handy.'

Frank smiled, 'I am sorry for being rude yesterday. You took me by surprise. I haven't spoken to anyone for a long time, never mind finding someone standing in my doorway. Thank you for the gear, it was full of useful stuff, especially the soap and the razors.'

Kia smiled back, 'My pleasure.'

'Please take a seat, the coffee is hot enough.'

Kia sat back on the little camp stool. He handed her a cup from the pot.

'So Frank, if it's not too much to ask, tell me your story. Why are you here after all this time?'

Frank walked into the cave and reappeared with a wooden chair that was obviously hand-hewn out of a short log. He sat in the chair and picked up his cup.

'Can I ask you a few questions first?'

'Sure, go ahead.'

'Am I in any kind of trouble? I know I didn't go home with the rest of my outfit, but I figured the fighting had been called off and I was only going to be shipped back stateside.'

Kia smiled, 'As far as I am aware you are not in trouble, apart from my crew and myself, no one knows you are here. You are currently listed as MIA.'

He nodded, 'I figured no one would be looking. The way that we had been sent places with no backup showed command didn't really give a damn. Just a circle on a map to them.'

She said nothing as it was obvious that he had travelled back in time in his mind.

'My platoon was stationed in a small village, just like that one down there. We were close to one of the supply trails that came from the north. It was our job to observe the traffic on the trail and report back to HQ.

'They would send air strikes in when a mule train of supplies came down the trail. Anyway, based in the area, we got to know the locals. They didn't understand what was going on really. They used to work the fields and mind their own business.

'One day a young girl from that village there came down to the one we were in. She was going to marry some local lad or something like that. Before the wedding, Charlie attacked looking for food and supplies.

'There was one hell of a firefight and when it was all over Charlie was dead and so were most of the villagers. We lost over half of our guys as well. We contacted HQ and let them know. They said to hold the location and will send help when they could.

'No one ever arrived. A second Charlie patrol came through about two weeks later, they destroyed the entire settlement. Men, women, and kids, they shot the lot. Those they didn't shoot they hung or cut to pieces. Tommy and I and the girl hid out until they were gone.

'Next day we went back to retrieve the radio, but it had been smashed. Most of the huts were still burning, the few that weren't, we searched for anything useful.

'Tommy and I dug graves for the villagers.

'One of the kids had been sliced open from neck to crotch. Tommy bent down and picked the kid up. Inside they had stashed a grenade. It blew Tommy to pieces.

'We just left after I buried what I could find of Tommy. It wasn't a big hole. The girl and I hid out in the jungle for a while and then decided to go back to her original settlement. Three weeks it took, dodging the patrols and only moving at night.

'The head chief of the village welcomed us back and hid us if any outsiders came. I got very restless and told the chief I was going to find a unit somewhere, somehow and go home. Next morning before anyone was awake, I left.'

He lifted the pot from the fire and refilled their cups before continuing.

'Long story short, I found a patrol and was sent back down the supply lines to the local HQ. The brass there figured as I was the only one who knew the area. So they sent me back in.'

'I showed them where the attack had been, there was literally nothing left, everything was burnt to the ground. The team hung around the area for a few weeks. Six times Charlie came out of the jungle, six times none of them went back. In the last group, there were two prisoners. I recognised them from the other village in the hills.

'They told me that they had been raided twice. I asked about the girl, they told me she was alive, but was restricted to a hut just outside the main settlement, no one was allowed to go near her.

'I asked why?

She was an outcast. They said it was because she was pregnant.

The chief had ordained that she was with child from a round-eye and was unclean. Also, the stream that flowed past that they relied on for water and irrigation stopped flowing just after I left, and the chief blamed bad spirits and the girl for bringing a curse on them.

They are very superstitious like that. There was the talk of sacrificing the girl and baby to appease the spirits.

'We let the two prisoners go, I told them to tell the chief if anything happened to the girl or baby I would go back and kill him myself.'

Kia sipped the hot brew, 'I take it that the village you are talking about is that one in the valley?'

Frank nodded, 'When we pulled out of the burnt village, we were told the war was over, and we were going home. I went AWOL and came back here, I just had to see for myself.

'The day I arrived back I hid in the trees watching. The chiefs son and some thugs went to the girls hut and dragged her outside and started to beat and kick her.

'I shot two of them and captured the chiefs son as he tried to run. I beat him half to death, I left him alive in the jungle with the warning that next time I will skin him alive. They got the hint after that. No one has hurt them since.

'They know I am here, they know I am watching, and while I am here, nothing will happen to them. So that's I why I can't leave.'

'Have you tried to talk with the chief?'

'In the beginning, I tried twice, but they are convinced that the stream stopped flowing because of her. When the water stopped, most of the crops died, and the jungle grew back over the fields. Nothing I have said will shake their belief in the supernatural. So now I just watch and guard.

'They are all resigned to their fate. It's been 30 years, and nothing has changed.

Kia put her empty cup on the ground. 'That's where you are wrong Frank. A lot has changed in 30 years, and now it's time things changed here in the valley as well. Tomorrow we will see this Chief, and I will change his mind. If he is as superstitious as you say he is, it will be easy enough.'

'Exactly how do you plan to do that? I have tried.'

Kia smiled, 'Magic Frank, pure magic.'

They spent the next few hours on less personal topics, Frank had a lot of questions about the outside world.

When Kia left, she did a slow scan of the valley, from the beginning high in the hills all the way down to the flatlands.

Chapter Seventy Four

'Hey, boss' greeted Paul in the café, 'How was your day in the jungle?'

'Different, after seeing what a mess man can make, it was a pleasant surprise to meet and talk to a man who made me feel all is not lost with the world.'

'Wow, that's a heavy statement. There has got to be a good story behind this.'

She smiled, 'Later dear boy when everyone is back. I have a job for us for a few hours tomorrow, and it involves a little voodoo.'

No one spoke while Kia recited Frank's story, although there were a few murmurs when she described how Tommy had died.

'We are going to help him somehow right?' asked Ray.

'I have most of a plan in mind how we can swing this. It's going to take a little theatrics and a little voodoo, but I think we can sort this out. The success is going to hinge on how superstitious the Chief really is.'

Rob had been sitting behind the crew and not said a word until now. 'The local village folk, especially those in the remote villages are highly superstitious. They still make offerings and prayers to the spirits. Perform ceremonies when people get sick and stuff like that.

'It is only the people exposed to the modern Western influence who have dropped the old beliefs.'

'So what do you have in mind?' Mel had asked what everyone was currently thinking.

'This is what I thought might work. It's open to debate and your input.'

Kia spoke at length about what she had come up with. Only Bree and Neil suggested minor tweaks to the plan.

'Well' Rob said, 'Either your plan will work, or you will give them the biggest shock they have ever experienced!'

Before daylight the next morning the entire crew had left the base. Brad had brought Rob along, even he did not want to miss this!

Kia stood in her S2, Kate was fussing over her outfit she was wearing. It was something that Sandy had researched and worked on during the night to perfect.

Checking the time on the console for the hundredth time Kia looked at Frank, 'You are sure the Chief will turn up?'

Frank nodded, 'Every day for years he comes out of his hut, meets with the elders of the village. Then, they all come down to this place, and the Chief slaughters a chicken to the mountain and dragon spirits. Unless he died overnight, he and the others will be here just as the sun rises over the top of that hill behind us. There should be eight or nine of them. Nine if his son attends.'

'Heads up people!' Brad's voice came over the coms, 'There is movement in the village. Everyone in your places, the show, is about to begin.'

The Chief and his son stood in the village centre. One by one the head of each family arrived for the morning ritual they had performed for years. Every one of them is hoping that today the spirits will accept the tribute and end the curse that they believed had fallen on the village.

Silently the procession entered the short, small path into the jungle that led to the banks of the long dry stream. In a natural clearing near the bank of the dried out stream there stood a waist-high tree stump, the top was flat and crisscrossed with hundreds of cuts. Raw testament of the years of sacrifices to the spirits.

Standing in a semicircle the elders bowed their heads to the centre and with muted voices started their prayers to the mountain spirits, the water spirits and the dragon spirits of the land.

The chief shuffled up to the stump, the chicken was thin and scrawny, and he hoped it would be good enough for the spirits.

The food was in short supply in the village and every year it was getting worse. He cursed the round eye man and the woman who had brought this to the village. He also cursed the Wildman in the jungle, for without him, they could have removed the woman and her daughter.

He lay the chicken on the stump and raise a short-handled axe, as he did so, the muttered prayers of the elders ended. Just before the axe fell on the luckless chicken, a huge boom shattered the air!

Louder and deeper than anything they had ever heard. The air seemed to hit them with a hidden force that made the entire group stagger!

The Chief looked at the sky, not a cloud in sight. His heart was pounding hard against his ribs. Suddenly, in the clearing appeared a woman, NO, a Spirt! She appeared to rise out of the ground!

Her skin was covered with scales and her headdress was woven into the face of a Dragon!

'You seek to appease me with such a scrawny offering!' She demanded of the Chief. 'I should take your life for such an insult!'

Her voice boomed around the clearing, seemingly coming from nowhere but everywhere! The elders dropped to their knees, the Chiefs son tried to run, but could not move a muscle!

'For years, this village has offended me! I sent you a girl with child! 'A girl that was born and raised here. A girl that you traded to another village for what!'

The Chief was terrified. The chicken had broken free and vanished into the undergrowth.

'The girl has brought a curse on the village! She and that demon daughter is the root of all our hardship! She offended the spirits and they took our water and let the land die!'
The Chiefs voice was shaky, and he trembled from head to toe.

'You are truly ignorant! *I* took the stream. *I* let the jungle eat your fields. *I* commanded this man to oversee the life of the unborn child, and it's mother.'

As she spoke, Frank appeared as mysteriously as the Dragon Spirit!.

'I did this as punishment for your treatment of the girl I sent to you. Your village and your son dared to hurt and abuse the girl. Ten thousand sacrifices will not appease me of your sins!
'I have in mind to take your son, all of the sons in the village and feed them to my dragons! Then you will feel like you have made the woman feel for all these years.'

The Chief dropped to his knees, 'No, please, do not take my son! He is all I have! I will do anything, anything to save him. I offer my life to you in his place.'

'Why should I not take him, and all the others? None of you have treated the woman as she should be!

'None of you have helped her or the daughter!. Your behaviour alone proves you not to be worthy.'

Her voice seemed to resonate deeply in the Chiefs head. Frank took his cue.

'Please, I beg you Great Spirit! Do not take the Chiefs son. I only wish for the women to live in peace as part of the village. No more and no less. Killing all the sons may turn the villagers against them.'

'Do you think this evil man and those behind him can ever change? I have given them many years to mend their ways and to realise the insult that they have cast on me, and the girl I sent to them for safety!'
The Dragon Spirits voice dripped with menace and vitriol.

'We did not know!' Begged one of the elders. 'We beg for your mercy, we will change!'

The Chief nodded furiously, 'We will change! We did not know you had sent her to us!'

The son was sweating buckets, he knew his life was in the balance. He looked at the Dragon Spirit. 'I pledge on my life that she and her child will be brought into the village as part of us. This protector you sent to guard her, he will know if we lie.'

Flames started dancing around the Dragon Spirit's feet. 'I will know if you lie! I know all! I give you one last chance, you are a miserable human. You will bring them into the village. You will protect and feed them both. The protector may come and go as he pleases. You will treat him with respect.'

'Yes!, We will!' came a chorus of voices from the Chief and the Elders.

A deep rumbling came from the earth. The ground swayed and cracked. Behind the Dragon Spirit, the ground erupted and a tall granite column with the head of a dragon blasted out of the ground.

Jet black, shiny granite with deep red glowing eyes, it rose to stand taller than everyone. Large granite wings grew from the side of the column! It cast a huge shadow over the delegation from the village. The chief nearly passed out from fear!

'I will leave this minder to watch your village, it sees all. No more puny sacrifices!'

With the wave of one hand, all the trees, bushes and undergrowth between the bank and the village disappeared. The villagers who had gathered after the loud boom could now see the elders clearly!

'You have this one last chance, old man. Defy me and you and your entire village will regret it!'

They just nodded, not one had the courage to speak. A low gurgling sound started to fill the air, water came cascading down the dry riverbed washing dirt and leaves in front of it. In seconds the stream was flowing with crystal clean water.

The Dragon Spirit turned to the jungle on the other bank and held both her arms high.

The jungle melted back, disappearing back to the sides of the valley. All the old planting fields from years ago were cleared and exposed again. No stick, rock or blemish marked the soil. Turning back to the Chief and elders, she stepped forward close to the Chief.

'I have restored your water and your fields, but be warned! Do not cross me again, for if I have to return, I will take everything, including your lives!'

Without waiting for a reply, the Dragon Spirit stepped back and seemed to melt into the ground.

Frank looked at where Kia had disappeared, then at the huge dragon statue.

'Holy shit!' He said under his breath! He walked over to where the Chief was staring at the statue.

'Come Chief, we have much to do and amends to make. The Chief only nodded weakly.'

Out in the newly cleared fields was one scrawny little chicken. It was pecking at the fresh soil looking for food.

Kia had got changed on the way back to the base. Sitting in the café, the air was buzzing with conversation and laughter over the morning's adventure.

'Well, Rob, what do you think? Was that good enough to scare the old man straight?'

Rob laughed, 'I think that not only did you scare him straight, but i think the whole village's elders were scared witless!

'That statue was a master touch. Tomorrow, when they get out of bed and think it was just a dream. That statue will remind them, not only was it not a dream, but that they are on notice to be well behaved. How the hell did you get that all to work?'

'That was easy Neil said, the boom was me breaking the sound barrier, far enough away not to hurt anyone. The statue was built by Kia's friend.'

'What about the stream?'

'The reason the stream had stopped in the first place was due to a landslide of rock.

High up in the valley where the water used to flow out of an underground river, a rock fall had blocked the exit. They would have lost the stream irrespective of if the girl arrived back or not. It was just coincidence that it happened when she did.

'The old men were too quick to blame the spirits for something Mother Nature had done. All I did was remove the blockage, and the water gushed out. Sandy did the maths on how long it would take the water to reach the village, so I knew when to unblock the hole.
Mel and Ray had cleared the watercourse of debris and obstacles. The rest was just timing.'

Glen stood on a chair and raised his coffee cup, 'A toast! To the Oracle Performing Troupe! Today, we saved the life of the chicken!'
That brought a roar of laughter, they all raised whatever they were drinking and joined in the toast. 'To the chicken!'

Ray came and sat with Rob and Kia. 'A question for you, what will happen to Frank now?'

'That is totally up to him Ray. I don't think he wants to go back to the States. The outside world has moved on and left him behind, and we talked about what the world was like now. He seemed overwhelmed with the progress I described. He knows his brother and father are still alive.

'I told him if he wants to go home we would make that happen, and if he wanted to stay, we would set him up with some stuff to make life easier. The choice is his to make.

'In a day or two, we can get in touch with him and find out what he wants to do. We gave him a two-way radio, and Sandy is monitoring it.'

Ray nodded, 'That sounds like a good outcome then. I was worried he would be sent back to face the brass for going AWOL.'

Kia put her hand on Ray's shoulder, 'Not in a million years would we let that happen.'

She stood and whistled, 'OK boys and girls, get fed. After lunch, we have a job to get back to. Well done one and all, but work beckons.'

<528>

Chapter Seventy Five

Two months later Rob was leaning on the 3D table. He was amazed at the amount of terrain that was now showing clear. Sandy was the only other person in the OpCen. Even Jess was out this afternoon.

'Well, young lady' he said, straightening his back, 'it looks like this will soon be over and done with.

'A magnificent achievement I must say. I will also be glad to see it end. For the first time since I set foot on this country's soil, I feel that I have helped. Albeit just a tiny bit, to correct the moral wrongs that were thrust upon the population. Just what am I going to do now? Maybe I will ask Kia for a job?'

'You any good with a broom?'

Rob looked at Sandy, but could not tell if she was joking or not!

The next two weeks flashed past, everyone had the routines down to perfection and finally the last area on the 3D table changed to clear. The main part of the job was done.

The last few weeks were the longest period since the 1970s that no reports of maiming or deceased were received. Children were playing in the fields, cattle and sheep grazed peacefully. For once the farmers could put plough to the soil and not live in fear their next step would be their last.

Four huge helicopters arrived the next morning. The Chairman and Commander in one and the other three seemed to hold an endless stream of photographers and journalists.

Quyen held a news conference with the acres of the recovered ordinance as the backdrop.

Kia had approved the visit with the caveat that she and the crew were left out of the melee. However a luckless Rob was volunteered to act as an informed source. He had all the data on a clipboard and could recite the facts and figures as necessary.

'Serves you right for learning the local lingo', Ray had offered when Rob had been told about the detail.

The news crews swarmed the recovered vehicles and equipment. They, however, were visibly subdued when walking through rows and row of munitions. Sometimes towering higher than a two story house. Hours later they piled back into the three choppers and headed back to their respective offices. Everyone trying to be the first to break the story.

Quyen and the Commander were taken through the warehouses, they were shown the rows of coffins that lined two of the warehouses. Only a selected few of the news crews had seen these, they were the ones the Commander had selected and provided a list.

'Eight hundred and seventy-one' Kia said in reply to Quyen's gaze as he entered the warehouse. 'Six hundred and eighty-eight are your countrymen, the rest are US.

'The vast majority were recovered from tunnels and burrows, some from makeshift graves. She handed a box of data discs to the commander, these hold the DNA and information on each and every one, including the exact location they were recovered from. I hope it will help you identify these lost people. We will deliver them to a place of your choosing.'

'What of the others?' Quyen asked, indicating the US side of the warehouse.

'Those we shall return to their own country. There may still be family alive there as well.'

Quyen bowed, 'Indeed, it is the time the lost sons went home. Thank you for what you have done, thank you all. You have exceeded your promises, and your reputation did you and your people a grave injustice.'

Kia smiled, 'It was our pleasure to be of service.'

They walked a few more rows together until they arrived back at the open main doors. The Chairman and the Commander reiterated their thanks and boarded the last chopper.

As it lifted off and swept from view over the tree line, Kia did a 360-degree sweep of the base compound. It was strangely quiet as if the jungle knew the end was close and that the intruders would be leaving soon.

Rob walked up and stood next to Kia. 'So that's it then, job done?'

'Not yet, there is still a lot to do. Deliver all these people back to where they came from. Remove all the garbage outside and dismantle the base, and clean up the area, Sandy tells me you may be handy with a broom so that you can help.' She walked away leaving Rob fumbling for an answer.

The Commander called with a location of where the remains were to be delivered. It took most of the day to get that done. By late afternoon all the local HR had been delivered. Sandy had scanned the US boxes out and all the munitions and wreckage outside. Only the Tower remained and the perimeter fence.

Sitting in the café, the crew were finishing an early dinner and going over everything to make sure all the boxes had been ticked.

Sandy was the last one to give a full report of the project. The figures and totals were staggering as Sandy listed off what the crew had accomplished, right at the end of her summary Sandy said everything except one last item had been taken care of.

'What's the last thing' asked Paul?

'What are we going to do with him?' Sandy pointed at Rob.

'In my opinion, he knows too much. I think that we either kill him or leave him high in the jungle' Bree said with a deadpan face.

Brad nodded, 'If he talks, he could jeopardise our entire future. Rob stared wide-eyed at Bree!' 'What!?'

Glen stood, 'Now wait just a minute, being a clean living, God fearing man, I cannot stand by and let you just kill him out of hand! At least give him a knife and an hour head start into the jungle. Then we can hunt him like that other fellow in Mexico.'

'I remember that', Ray said, 'took us hours to get the last one.'

Rob was slowly turning white! He looked pleadingly at Kia!

'Please, you have to do something!'

'I am sorry Rob, it's out of my hands. Rob made a vain attempt to dive for the door when all the girls jumped him.'

It wasn't until Miako leant over him and gave him a wet sloppy kiss on the brow that he realised he had been the victim of an impromptu prank!

'Oh, very funny, he spluttered', as they helped him to his feet, 'I damn near wet myself!'

That brought hoots of laughter from everyone, even Rob ended up grinning foolishly.

Paul wiped tears from his eyes, 'OK in all seriousness, what happens with Rob now?'

'That is up to him, we can drop him off anywhere he wants to go. We can take him stateside when we deliver the other HR.' Kia looked at the crew, 'Any other suggestions?'

'I am handy with a broom!' Interjected Rob.

'We could take him back to the island, he used to work on the docks before he took up being a journalist. I could use someone like that back there', Sandy said.

Kia turned back to Rob, 'Well, it looks like you have a lot of options Rob, 'What would you like to do?'

'Labouring on the docks isn't my scene you know.'

'Labouring! Hell no, I want someone to run the whole show. We have thousands of artefacts and items to ship around the world. I need someone with smarts to organise crews loading, unloading and things like that.'

'I currently run it remotely, but it needs a man's face in the dock office to make it work easier.' Sandy paused, 'You worked that 3D table like a pro, so I know you have the skill set to do this if you want.'

'Beats digging up explosives and risking your life everyday' added Brad.

Ray asked for a show of hands to offer a job to Rob. Everyone put their hand up including Sandy.

Rob smiled widely 'OK then, I will take the job, what's the pay like?'

Glen put his hand on Rob's shoulder, 'The pay? It's really, really shitty my friend.'

Kia stood, 'Right. I need ten minutes in the OpCen then I will be good to go.'

Out of habit, the others cleared the tables, it didn't matter the tower would be gone soon.

Up top Kia had just signed off from talking to Frank as the others arrived. They had given Frank a huge pile of equipment and supplies. Including a laptop, a Sat dish and four solar panels for power. He seemed content to stay where he was for the moment and would check in from time to time.

Kia turned from the screen, 'So people, ready to go home?' 'Lead the way boss!'

Kia led the exodus down to the S2s. Sitting in the craft she watched as the tower disappeared. The boundary fence was next, then she turned the S2 towards home and scanned one side of the receiver poles out as the others took the rest. Seconds later only lengthening shadows were left in the clearing.

Kia looked over at the small clearing, 'Come on dear, we are going home.'
With that, she turned and followed the path of the others into the darkening sky.

Chapter Seventy Six

Paul and Glen took Rob into their villa. 'Here is the spare room. You can stay here if you like or there is plenty of room in the hostel in the complex. You can have the royal tour in the morning.'
With that, Paul headed for the shower before he hit the sheets.
Glen was already dead to the world on the couch.
Rob was wide awake like a schoolboy on a field trip. He opened the fridge and found it stocked top to bottom with a huge range of beers.
He grabbed a familiar brand and walked out the front door to the table, he had seen on the way in.
He was amazed at the sight of the complex to his left and the tall OpCen on the top of the hill. 'Well, this looks like it could be a fun experience', he said out loud.
'Has to be better than digging holes in the jungle', Paul said from the front door. Paul was wearing shorts and a towel draped around his neck, he also had a beer in his hand. 'Damn shower woke me up.'
They both sat on the table, their feet on the bench.
'So what is it you do here? I know what you did back in 'Nam but not every country is an open minefield like that place was.'
Paul took a pull at his beer, 'Basically, it's all the same kind of stuff. We are all hi-tech rubbish collectors. Most we dispose of, some of it we keep. That's what the complex there is for. You will find some of the finest minds flow through that place. They look at all the stuff we collect and pick out the good things.'
'Then you sell them off?'

'No, not really. It's sorted into places of origin and then shipped off back where it came from, that's probably going to be your area.

'All this', Paul waved his bottle in a semi-circle, 'all this is not a job to us. It's a way of life. Highly interesting, we get to go all over the world, some of the things we have seen would knock your socks off.

'Everything works on a voluntary basis, you don't want to go for that day, you just don't go. If we want time off, we just take it.'

'Voluntary? So Glen was right, the pay is really shitty?'

Paul smiled, 'In all the time I have been here, I haven't been paid one cent. Everything here is free, meals, drinks. When we do go off for a break, we have a card with an obscene amount of money on it, but after two days of fun out there you get bored.

'Greedy people with greedy habits and no real ambition in life.

My background is in high finance and stock. Trust me when I say most of the population is being manipulated by higher powers and corporations.

This here, this is true freedom. I for one, could never go back.'

'You make it sound glamorous, working the docks sure isn't going to be, but it was better than being drunk in some back alley bar in Nam.'

Paul went inside and returned with a fresh pair of beers.

'I tell you what Rob, in three months, we will sit back at this table. Open a beer each, and if you still feel the same way I will personally take you anywhere you want to go and give you half a million bucks when I drop you off. Deal?'

Rob started at Paul and saw he was serious! He clinked his bottle with Paul's and said 'Deal!'

Glen woke and felt like he had been chewing on an old cat, stiff and sore from the awkward position he had been sleeping on the couch he stood and stretched.

Outside he heard Paul and Rob chatting away, he made a coffee and headed for the voices.

The early morning sun was just over the horizon and made him squint as he walked out the front door.

'Well, you aren't going to win any good look prizes' laughed Paul as he took in Glen's unshaven, dishevelled appearance.

Glen muttered something about Paul's heritage and his mother's love life. Drinking half the mug of coffee, he could feel normality starting to return.

'Morning' he said to Rob as he sat with his back to the sunlight.
Shortly Mel and Ray walked up the footpath and took a seat.

'Morning boys said Mel, where did you find the hobo?'

'OK ,OK, I get the hint' Glen said, he stood and collected the empty mug, 'All I know is you guys don't recognise awesomeness when you see it!'

Without waiting for a reply, he walked into the villa and hit the shower.

'So, any plans for today', asked Paul.

Mel said 'I am waiting for Miako and the girls we are going for a run this morning, it's good to be able to see more than 6 feet in front of you for a change. Ray is going to the range for a plink. We are just sticking close until word comes in that we are needed.

How about you?'

'Once Glen is done, I was thinking of taking Rob for a tour in the complex. Apart from that, I am in the same boat as you are. 'I don't even mind doing a flag run today, for something different.'

Glen reappeared shaved and showered, he looked a whole lot better.

Mel stood at the sound of approaching chatter. 'Girls are here, see you later, stay out of trouble.' She kissed Ray on the cheek and took off with Bree and the Coven.

Ray thought for a moment, 'Mind if I tag along? I haven't been down to the new docks as yet.'

'Sure' Paul said, 'Let me get dressed and we can go.'
He disappeared into the villa.

'How can he sit up all night and be that fresh in the morning?' asked Glen, 'It's obscene!' Paul returned shortly, and the boys headed off to the complex.

Meanwhile, up in the OpCen Kia was sitting cross-legged on a stool talking to a familiar face on the HUD. 'So, Jim, that's it in a nutshell. 'All the stories of POWs still chained in camps are just that, stories. Except for Frank, and he is there of his own free will. The ball is in your court now. You let us know when and where you want these people delivered, and it will be done.'

The President nodded, 'Thank you so much, this should clear up a lot of controversies. Although there will always be the conspiracy nuts that think everything is a lie.'
Jen came into view as she handed him a list of names Sandy had just sent him.

He gazed at the pages for a moment, 'It never really hits home until you see it in black and white.' he remarked.

Kia nodded, 'Alright then, we await further instructions and please watch your back. I don't trust those Backroom guys for one second.'

'Will do' came the reply and she cut the feed.

'So, dear Sandy, what's on the agenda today?'
'Nothing really, the flag map is clear, I reset the drones to clear everything except something extremely unusual. No outstanding requests, we had a few nibbles from a few corporations, but what they wanted was not what I would call important.

'All the new data is now listed for the HC, Historians Crew. We did not scan much off the land, but the offshore stuff was an absolute mess.

'The media are going crazy with the project news. It's all over the place! TV, Radio, Papers, the Internet is buzzing.

'Anyone that hasn't heard of us by the end of the day is either deaf, dumb and blind, or lives like Frank does.

'The only thing worth remarking on is a report I intercepted from the shipyard in Scotland. The guys there are demanding to know how the hell two subs managed to melt together and become one continuous hull without welding. Not my words, theirs.'

Brad and Neil walked into the OpCen. 'Morning ladies' Brad said, 'Anything on the agenda?'

Kia shook her head, 'Nope, looks like it's a do as you please day, and after months of solid work I don't blame you if you go fishing or something.'

'Fine with me', Brad said, 'Where is everyone?' Sandy told him.

'OK then I might find the guys', and he walked back into the elevator.

Neil just stood there, 'Yes, Neil, what have you done, this time?'
He broke into a huge grin at that. 'I would like you to see something I was working on for the last two weeks. If that's OK?'

Kia got off the chair and motioned Neil to sit, 'Show me what you have.'

'Well, before I do, I just want to say that it's something that I hope you agree is a handy thing to have.'

'Stop scaring me Neil and show me.'

Neil opened up the HUD, and for the next twenty minutes showed her his new project, the presentation ended with an 8 minute animated video. When it was done, he turned to Kia. 'So what do you think?'

Kia dragged another stool over and sat facing Neil.

'Tell me something young man. Just where the hell do you keep getting these ideas from?'
As she spoke the elevator opened, and the tribe of girls arrived, just in time to hear Kia's last comment.

Miako paled, 'What have you done now, Neil?'

He turned to her, 'Nothing! Honest, I just showed Kia an idea I have been kicking around.'

The girls looked at Kia.

She poked Neil with a finger that made him jump. 'Go on, show them what you just showed me, I will not say another word, let them decide.'

Nervously Neil repeated the presentation for the others, when the video had finished he turned to the girls. 'So what do you think?'

'Neil, you sir, are a genius!' Kate smiled. 'Where do you get these ideas from!?'

'So you like?' He turned to Kia and saw she was grinning as well. He visibly relaxed.

Bree walked over to the HUD, 'Play that video again.' He did so.

'So no tools? No, nothing and you can put one of these together?'

Neil nodded, 'Actually, you need a hammer. I have calculated that a team of six can construct one of these in about an hour.'

On the screen was a dwelling, not really a house but not a hut either.

'Play that again' asked Miako.

The video showed how the dwelling came as a flat pack unit, the animated stickmen on the screen opened the pack and laid out the components.

On a rectangular base, the figures slid interior walls into keyed slots on the base. Once the interior walls were in place the outside walls slid into place like a Chinese puzzle box, each part locking the others into place. Corner pieces locked each corner together and then a flat, sloping roof slid on tracks over the structure and was locked by driving in 10 pins. Done!

Neil showed a close up of the components, made entirely from an Oracleite material, meaning something that Sandy put together. The windows and doors were part of the structure. The walls were honeycombed for insulation.

Water and power were integrated into the walls.

'The only downside is, you have to fill the base with sand or dirt, or stake it down, or strong winds can move them. I made these dirt screws.' Neil pulled up a component. 'With a supplied key two men can screw the dwelling base to the ground. They need a pre-drilled hole 2 meters deep. One in each corner.'

'Whatever made you think of this?' asked Layla.

'I saw what those villagers were living in, not the ones close to towns, and they were pitiful.
We have so much raw material we could make hundreds, no, thousands of these and help those people. Anyone could assemble these.

'They won't leak, rot, rust or fall apart. I know they are not very big, but they are bigger and sturdier than the pitiful huts I saw people living in.'

'Neil, again, you did well' Kia said. She turned to Sandy, 'Can you put two of these in a warehouse in their flat pack form? We might have a little boys vs. girls contest later when they are finished showing Rob around.'

Chapter Seventy Six

Brad and the guys were standing in the dock managers office, it was like a mini OpCen, with windows almost all the way around, blank HUDs to show all aspects of the operation lined benches under the windows. Only one HUD was active, and Sandy was on it, explaining all the gizmos as Rob liked to call them.

There was even a small balcony. Glen was currently standing on it checking out the view. Past the docks and harbour was a magnificent view of the clear ocean and sandy beaches flanking the harbour's entrance.

He walked back inside the crowded area. 'I have seen top hotels with a view only half as good at this control tower.'

They had already been through most of the complex on the way to the dock. 'Lets go, Rob, one last place I want to show you before we go back up top.'

It took two trips in the small elevator for everyone to get back on the ground. Brad walked him past the warehouse where the now very large Norwegian team was wrapping up the remnants of their stuff. Stopping outside the historians offices Only Brad and Rob entered, the others splitting off and heading for the bar in the complex.

The HC were all there, each working away on some piece of history. They looked up when the guys walked in.
Trudy left her weird looking vessel and came over to greet them.

Brad introduced Rob and explained he was the new guy and was tasked with the shipping and dock operations.

Trudy took Rob and introduced him to each member and gave an insight into what they did.

They took an instant shine to Rob and his down-to-earth personality.

Half an hour later, Rob and Brad joined the others in the bar. Paul was just ordering their second round of drinks.

Ray turned to Rob as the drinks arrived, 'So Rob, tell us what you think?'

Rob wiped the froth from his top lip. 'I am stunned!

'That operation back there is as far from what I imagined the job would be like as you can get. Actually, I am having second thoughts on if I can even swing that kinda load! It is extremely intimidating and a bigger responsibility than I have ever shouldered before in my life. 'Don't know if I have the cahoonas to swing that.'

Glen laughed, 'BTDT! That is almost exactly what we told Kia when she approached us with the idea of forming Oracle, and giving us the job of cleaning the whole planet. Rob, you will not just be thrown in the deep end. I dare say Sandy will continue to run the operation and bit by bit train you in all the areas you need to know.

'From what I can see, there won't be that much traffic in and out so for a lot of the time you will be free to do whatever you like. You are a survivor and sort of smart, you will pick it up in no time.'

'Sort of smart!! What?'

'Well digging up live landmines for a hobby is not exactly a smart job is it?'

'Point taken. Well I did give Paul my word I would try it for three months, so I have to give it a go for at least that long.'

Paul raised his glass, 'I feel my money is safe already!'

The bar girl leant over the bar and informed the guys they were wanted in one of the warehouses.

'Good', Ray said, 'Because this beer tastes like I won't be able to work if I stay here.'

In one of the empty warehouses, the guys found Kia and the rest standing between two loaded flat packs.

On the wall was one of the biggest HUD the guys had seen. It showed two diagrams of the dwelling, one in pieces and one complete.

'OK boss, what's up?' asked Glen.

'Don't ask me, this is Neil's party, and just to be fair, Neil is excluded, and Rob can take his place. Neil, run through your presentation for the guys and then lets see how we do.'

Neil cleared the HUD and ran through the program, he played the video twice at the end and when it was over, turned to the crews.

'Girls on the left, Guys on the right' he said.

Sandy asked if she could join in, 'NO! Was the resounding answer from all.'

'OK, 10 minutes to study the manual, three for the guys as they don't read manuals and then Sandy will start the timer.'

'Ready Sandy said... a klaxon horn made them all jump! GO!'

Two hours and twenty three minutes later, there stood two dwellings in the warehouse. The guys stepped back and admired their handiwork. The fact the girls had finished half an hour before did not seem to faze their sense of achievement!

Rob walked into the dwelling and looked around, Neil came in as well, 'Wow bigger than I thought it would be!'

'It's fantastic Neil, this will save a lot of lives, you know that right?'

'Hey? How do you figure that! It is only better accommodation for the villagers!' Rob roared with laughter at Neil's confused look.

'Listen, hundreds of villagers die every year, from hypothermia, diseases, insect bites, pneumonia and a whole host of other things, most of which is directly related to the conditions they live in. Rats that chew their way into the grass and wood huts.

'This', Rob held his arms out wide, 'is a godsend to those kinda people. Neil, you are a legend!'

They walked back out the door into a wall of applause from everyone.

Neil coloured up bright red. He knew it and swore under his breath.

Paul said, 'I think once you have put 3 or 4 of these together an hour or so is a realistic time frame. Well done Neil!'

Sandy removed the dwellings and the HUD.

'Message from The President Kia, he sent some stuff through and will call in 30 minutes.'

'Thanks, Sandy. Well, I think Neil did exceptionally well. Now it's time to see what is next on the agenda, meet me in OpCen in say an hour. 'Rob, you know the Commander and have dealt with him before. Call him up and send him Neil's presentation, find out if he would be interested in some of these dwellings. I think he will be.'

Rob smiled 'I say he will be for sure!'

'Get him to send us a bunch of his engineers and we can train them how to assemble them.

'Once that is done if they send us some cargo ships we can fill the ships with the flat packs.'

'Would it not be easier to get a warehouse in Nam and build them there?' Mel asked.

'Indeed it would, but doing it this way Rob will get a lot of on job training as Harbour Master. Also, we avoid awkward questions about how they appear in a warehouse, so far away from us.'

'See Rob, that's why Kia is the boss!' Brad clapped Rob on the shoulder. 'She is sneakier than the rest of us!'

The crew dispersed in twos and threes, and Sandy blinked out.

Chapter Seventy Seven

Kia had finished reading the papers and documents when the HUD chimed an incoming call. Kia hit the receive code, and the screen burst into life.

'Hello, Mr. President.'

'Afternoon Kia. I see you are holding the permits I have sent to you.'

'Indeed, everything seems fine. Although I am a little concerned about the venue. Was that a decision on your part or suggested by the Backroom boys?'

'They suggested it, yes. Their reasoning is that your craft may not be the best thing to be seen flying over the USA. Also, they claim it to be the most secure area, and that is also in your favour. I argued against this, but was pushed into it.'

Kia nodded, 'Jim it is a trap, a wide open, teeth glaring Trap.'

'But while I am there you should be safe, they wouldn't dare do anything right in front of me, would they?'Jim frowned.

Kia smiled', I love your faith in your administration, Jim, and you're right. While you are there nothing will happen. Let me tell you how I think this is going to go.

'We arrive, give you the coffins, a bit of fanfare, a few photos that will probably never see the pages of any newspaper. After that, a friendly chat and you will then receive a phone call about something you just can't ignore and have to leave.

'After you clear out all hell is going to break loose.
That is why I asked you for, those two executive orders. If I am wrong, no harm, no foul.

'If I am right, both our asses are covered. Did you run these orders past the necessary judiciary?'

'Yes, I ran them past both of them, they are solid and airtight. I hope to god they are not necessary.'

'You and me both.'

'Given the venue, I'd like a small change in the itinerary, my people will not be staying for the duration. They will fly in the remains, meet and greet and immediately leave. I will do the rest by myself. It's safer for all concerned that way.'

'I understand, that suits me fine. Have I told you that I hate some aspects of this job today?'

'I can believe that Jim. With luck, there will be no issues, and all will be fine, I won't tell you what I really think, though. You are using the laptop I gave you?'

'Yes.'

'Good then this conversation is secure. I will see you in about six hours.'

'Roger that.' He cut the feed. Turning to Jen he looked at her for a moment, 'So Jen, what do you think?'

'Me, sir? I don't get paid to think about things like this.
But off the record, I think it is a trap. I think Kia is correct, and lastly, I think someone is going suffer a world of hurt if they try and spring the trap on her.'

He nodded sadly, 'Off the record, I think you're right'. He leant back in the chair and ran his fingers through his hair in frustration. 'Jen, if I get the recall message she thinks I will get, I won't be too concerned if you accidentally miss the flight out.'

Jen smiled, 'Understood sir.'

Kia was standing at the bottom of the steps, she was facing the crew that were sitting on the steps. 'So you all know your parts? Once we drop the HR, I will introduce you to the President and whoever is there, you then make your way back to the S2 and get the hell out of there.'

Ray growled, 'I don't like it, I don't like it one bit.'
His sentiments were echoed in the others faces.

'Look, guys, I will be fine, Jim knows I am there, they know he knows so nothing will happen, probably.'

'Probably! See, even you know this isn't good!' Paul injected.

Neil stood up, 'Kia, I will do what you ask, but I tell you now to your face, I might leave the immediate area, but I am not going home till I see you safely off the ground.'

She went to answer him, but Neil continued. 'It's either that or nothing. You would not leave us in a situation like that, and I find it kinda hurtful you would ask me, or should I say us, to do just that.'

Kia knew she had lost. 'Damn it, alright, but, no one and I mean *no one* makes a move unless Sandy clears you for it OK? In fact, if anyone of you tries, Sandy will take control of your S2 off you and bring you back here. Then when I get back, we will have words.

'Kate, you and the girls leave, irrespective of what happens, you hear me?'
The trio nodded, 'Loud and clear' they chorused.

Kia nodded, 'Now, everyone on board?'
All agreed.

'Good. I know they will want to ask me questions, in fact, I am planning on it.
'What type of questions they ask will give me an insight into what they do or do not know. Anything else?' There was perfect silence. 'OK, you mutinous mob, lets do this.'

One by one they lifted off the ground, each hovered for a moment while Sandy fitted a streamlined pod underneath with row upon row of coffins. Only Kia's S2 had no pod, she was the last to lift.

'Sandy, you heard what I said on the steps?'
'Affirmative.'
'Good, I don't want any cowboy tactics on this run.'

High in the air they made an impressive sight, two delta formations of six. One led by Kia and the other by Brad. There was very little chat over coms during the flight.

Bree had tried to break the silence twice and both times the conversation faded out.

Just before they reached the US border Neil broke the silence.

'So we really are going to Groom Lake? THE Groom Lake, Area 51?'

'Yup, that's where they wanted these people delivered', Kia replied.

'Geezus!'

They crossed the invisible border, 'Heads up people', Sandy said, 'You are now in the United States of America.'

The HUD radar in every S2 showed a lot of air traffic, but most of it was commercial. Ferrying people about on their everyday business.

They crossed the state boundary from California into Nevada. The terrain below took on a very desolate mantle, dry and arid.

Kia checked the HUD, there were eight aircraft in the area up ahead, she started to slow and descend.

Up ahead the airstrip started to take shape, a controller contacted them and asked for ID while they were 30 miles out.

Kia knew it was a stupid request. Each S2 was transmitting an IFF signal. She replied anyway and received clearance to approach and land.

Kia broke formation and headed for the airfield, the rest dropped into a holding pattern. Waiting until Kia told them to come in.

In front of one of the large hangars she could see a groundsman with the hand beacons used to guide in choppers. He stood watching the approach.

As she neared the landing zone, he raised the beacons to guide her in. Before he could move, she had landed point perfect in the centre of the zone.

Out of the window, she could see several uniforms standing in a row in the open doorway of the hangar. She also saw the President and the ever present detail standing next to him.

'OK boy and girls, they haven't shot at me yet, everyone stays focused.' With that, she stepped outside into the harsh, dry air of the Nevada desert. As she walked towards the President the door shut behind her, and it locked solid.

Kia shook the Presidents hand first and then was introduced to the brass one by one, out of the five only one seemed at ease, he was the one tasked with receiving the cargo, Captain John Hughes. Hughes shook Kia's hand and had a genuine smile that reached his eyes.

'So you're not a threat', Kia thought to herself.

'So how would you like to do this?' asked Captain Hughes. Kia took a slim folder out of an inside pocket, 'Firstly, here is a full list of the remains. You will find names where possible and DNA results so you may match what you can.'

'Anything found close to or on the remains has been bagged and is with each soldier. If you can rustle up some muscle, my people will drop the pods right here at the doorway. They have wheels so can be moved inside. The rest is then up to you.'

Hughes nodded, 'I have to ask, did you find any alive?'

'Yes, one, Frank. He is still there. The President has been fully briefed on him, and I am sure will pass the information on.'

One of the other uniforms almost snatched the file out of Hughes hand, 'You are positive you didn't miss anyone?' He asked gruffly.

Kia turned on him, 'We also picked up over 187,000 landmines alone that you just left there buried. I think we would have seen something as large as a man, don't you?

'That reminds me, where would you like me to put all the mines? I could deliver them here! Your runway is just about long enough to hold them all, six or seven deep.'

'We don't want them!', he barked.

'That's funny, neither did the civilians in Vietnam!'
He tried to bluster a reply to that and failed miserably. He spun on his heel and strode off into the hangar.

'So Captain Hughes, Mr. President, shall we bring your people home?'

At Kia's command, one S2 broke formation and Slid to a halt in front of the hangar. After dropping the pod, it then went and landed next to Kia's craft.

After the 3rd drop the groundsman gave up trying to guide the S2s in, he just stood to one side as each S2 settled next to the others, the same distance apart and in a perfectly straight line.

As each pod arrived, Hughes moved his finger down the list. Six soldiers took control of the pod and pushed it into the hangar.

As the last one dropped in front of the hangar, Hughes closed the file. '155 men and 28 women, back home at last.'

'You're welcome, ' Kia said.

Two of the other brass walked over after inspecting the contents of the pods. With a fake smile one said, 'Please invite your pilots in, we have arranged refreshments.'

Kia looked at Jim, he looked worried. 'Why thank you, Commander.' Kia gave a wave and the crew who had not left their S2s walked over to the hangar.

Starting with The President, Kia introduced him to each of the crew, then to each of the brass. Hughes being the end of the introductory line took them inside to a table with refreshments.

The brass and the President were chatting, and Kia walked over to her crew. 'OK guys, shame to eat and run, but I want you out of here. Max, five mins from now'

Ray nodded, 'With pleasure, the tension in here makes it hard to breathe.'

Miako nodded, 'I am getting very bad feelings too, I will be glad to leave.'

'OK scoot, I will let Jim know.'

Before the brass noticed the S2s lifted and left in formation. Kia met the grumpy commander halfway across the hangar. 'Sorry commander, something has come up, and they had to leave.'

She received a murderous look in return.

'That's fine', he said, trying to keep a civil tone. 'When duty calls we must answer.'

He turned and strode back to the other brass and from his body language was explaining to the other two what had just happened.

Kia walked over to the hangar door and leant against the pillar. The desert looked unfriendly and foreboding.

'You seemed to have upset them a little', spoke a female voice from behind her.

'Hi, Jen', she said not turning around. 'Nice shoes but your left one creaks just a little.'

'Yeah, damn new ones, not broke in yet.'

'So your boss been called away yet?'

'Not that I know of, hope he doesn't, sometimes I get that busy I miss the ride out.'

'Well, lets hope that call doesn't eventuate.' Kia turned and faced Jen. 'Could get sticky.'

'I like sticky.'

'Jen, "*sticky*" to your boss then. I got this covered, trust me.'

'OK, if you're sure, you still owe me a week on your island beach. I got holidays up starting tomorrow.'

Kia grinned, 'Heads up, here comes the boss.'

Jim grinned', I heard that! We are adjourning to the conference room.'

'Lead the way boss.' Kia said, she winked at Jen, 'You got a passport?'

Jen smiled.

The conference room was a huge room dominated by a single heavy timber table.

Once all seated, the President at the head, he opened a folder in front of him, reading a prepared speech of gratitude he then presented Kia with a plaque of appreciation.

Kia accepted it with grace.

The commander was fidgety, just small but definitive gestures. His body language gave it away as clear as if he was wearing a notice around his neck. The conversation around the table dropped into pleasant chat, a few questions thrown in. She was not fooled, it was the calm before the storm.

A knock on the door and a corpsman came in and handed the President a folded piece of paper. He read it and stood out of his chair. 'I am sorry, gentlemen, Kia, but I have been called away.'

'Nothing serious I hope, sir?' said the commander.

'Err, no, but I must attend to it anyway.' His gaze went around the table and settled on Kia.' He saw the slight smile on her lips. An ice cold chill ran down his spine.

'That is a shame, it has been very nice to meet you again. I am sure we will see each other in the not too distant future.'

Jim put on his best public greeting smile, 'I look forward to that.'

The brass excused themselves, and escorted the President to his chopper outside, Captain Hughes remained with Kia, again thanking her for the work they had done.

Chapter Seventy Eight

The chopper was visible in the window momentarily as it flew overhead, the door of the room opened, and the commander entered alone.

'My apologies for the rude interruption. I thought I could make it up to you with a tour, not many people get an opportunity to look around the fabled area 51!' His laugh was false and hollow.

Kia smiled, 'Why not, I need to be going really, but maybe a quick peek at the control room or something?'

'Sure! Follow me.' He turned to Hughes, 'Sort out those crates, and I will take the lady for a tour around.'

Hughes nodded, obviously displeased with the reference of the coffins as crates.

Kia followed the Commander around several sections while he explained what each area was for. Most of it was run of the mill operations. The most interesting was a SR-71A Blackbird.

Once a closely guarded secret, but now most aviation enthusiasts could quote most of its specifications off by heart.

Kia was growing impatient with the charade. She decided to push the envelope a bit. 'This is quite an impressive place you have commander. I really need to get back to work. Thank you so kindly for showing me around.'

'Not a problem, if you would just indulge me a few moments more, there are two gentlemen who would like to meet you before you leave.'

The commander guided them down a hallway and into an elevator that descended a level.

When the doors opened Kia saw what she was looking for, a huge screen covered the far wall and rows of terminals were arranged in front of the screen. To the left were three offices with frosted windows. The commander guided her into the centre office. He asked her to sit at the end of the large table in the office. She took the offered chair.

Sitting at the other end of the table were six people. Two she recognised from the hangar, two more in uniform, and the last two were dressed in suits.

The commander closed the door to the office, and Kia noted the shadows of three guards take up station outside the door.

'The two gentlemen', the commander indicated the ones in suits, 'Work in our research and development section. We have been following your work for a few months now and are very impressed with your results.'

'Why thank you', commander, 'I am surprised a small team like mine would generate so much interest.' she replied sweetly.

The commander smiled as he sat at the other end of the table, his mannerisms were now deft and sure. Here in this room, he felt in charge. He picked up a sheet off the table, she recognised it as the list she had sent to Jim with the totals of munitions that they had collected and removed. Jim had said he had not shared the list, so that meant there was definitely a leak in his office.

'I have a list of the stuff you say you collected on your trip in Vietnam. I must say that it's a very impressive list for such a short time span. That is of course if the list is accurate.'

'Oh, it's accurate Commander, I can assure you of that. As for the time frame, we were in no hurry. It was more important we didn't miss anything, and we achieved our goal.'

One of the suits stirred in his seat, 'We are just curious how you managed to collect so much stuff. I mean we get that it's possible to locate all that's listed here, but you didn't dig all the mines up for example.'

'Well, you know what curiosity did to the cat. However, I do find it interesting that you understand the location ability, yet no one applied anything to do so. You do know that for years your landmines have been killing and maiming men women and children?

'Just like you, here in this place, we also have our methods and secrets. However, there is no need for concern.'

'Actually, we are quite concerned. One of the uniforms spoke for the first time. We are concerned that if your new technology can do what everyone says it can, then if that falls into the wrong hands, terrorists, for example, then anyone could be targeted with it.'

He pointed a finger at the suit that had said nothing so far. 'Hank here just came back from Scotland where he examined those Subs you assisted in the North Sea.'

'Yes, I remember them, they had run into each other playing war games.' She made it sound like something two small kids would do in a playground.

Hank spoke, 'I was intrigued by the way you joined them together.'

'It was the only way to float them both off the seabed, welding them to each other provided enough lift to save both crews.'

Hank smiled, 'Yes indeed, a very smart move! But, you didn't weld them together, did you? I saw them with my own eyes. They had been fused together, the metal looked like it had been made in one piece!'

'The result was still the same Hank. Everyone got out alive did they not?'

'That's not what Hank meant', said the commander, 'What we want to know is how you managed to do that! An impossible task on land, never mind on the seabed!'

Kia lent forward in her chair and rested her forearms on the table.

'Instead of me telling you how we managed that, or how we removed all your surplus explosives.

'Why don't you tell me how you think we did it and I can tell you if you are right or wrong. How about you Hank, you're obviously a scientist of some sort. How do you think we did it?'

'His opinion doesn't matter', said the commander before Hank could reply.

'Well, it must matter to someone to send him all the way to Scotland to look at two foreign submarines don't you think?' Kia countered.

'Please just answer the question. How did you manage to perfectly flow the hulls of two subs together?'

'I am sorry, Commander, that information is classified. Now if you don't mind, I would like to leave now.'

'Please, to avoid any unnecessary unpleasantness, just answer our questions and you will be free to leave.'

The oldest, the high ranking guy finally said something.

Now Kia knew who was really in charge.

'Why would I want to divulge our technology to you? Was I to share this with you, all you would do is weaponise it and add it to your already overflowing arsenal of killing methods.
I am sorry, but that just is not going to happen. Our Tech, is exactly that, ours.'

'Why would we do that? As you have said, we have enough in our arsenal now.'

'Why?' Kia laughed. 'Because you just can't help yourselves, that's why. Anything that would help you gain a stranglehold on other countries is too good a thing not to have. Obviously, you have theories of how we do what we do, but that's all they are, theories.

'Now, gentlemen, and I use the term loosely, to quote your own words, to avoid any unnecessary unpleasantness I am now leaving.'

'You are not going anywhere but to a holding cell. A few days without food and a lot of water and you will tell us everything we want to know.' The old guy said.

'You do realise that the President himself knows I am here.'

'I can handle that fool easily enough. We have for the last few years. A push here, a prod there, a memo or two telling him what we want him to think.'

'For you to admit that, means you have no intention of letting me walk out of here. I am so sorry for that. That is a mistake on your part and one that is going to cost you more than you could possibly imagine.'

'Listen, dear, you are here alone, no one to help you, your disappearance will not even make the news. Many have tried to break in here over the years, none has succeeded. What on earth makes you believe you could get out? You have the balls to threaten us! Tell me what I want to know, and your stay here might not be so... unpleasant.'

Kia stood and leant her hands on the table.

'Pay attention, little man, I will tell you one last time, I am leaving. Now you can just cut your losses right now and be happy. Or you can start something you cannot possibly win. The choice is yours.'

'Commander, throw this stupid bitch in a cell!' The commander went to rise from his seat. A steel bolt thundered through the concrete ceiling. Entering through the top of his skull it stopped a good 5 inches into the concrete floor under his chair. He never even knew he died.

'Guards! Screamed the old guy. The door burst open, and three marines burst in with rifles at the ready.

As the bolt had ended the commander, Kia had felt the weight of her two guns arrive in her thigh holsters. That is one of the reasons she had stood at the table. Turning to the guards, she shot the first and the third guard, ignoring the second.

The slugs tore through the body armour as if it wasn't even there. Slugs from the first guard carried through to the second one behind him.

Movement drew her attention back to the table, the old man had pulled a revolver from a hidden drawer. Two rounds perforated his heart before he could bring the gun into line. Alarms were now sporadically springing to life.

Kia still took the time to look at the two scientists. 'I would advise you guys to get out and get as far away from these people as you can. To them, you are nothing more than an expendable resource.' She focused on the other two uniforms, 'You two, well, you'er fucked, pardon the language. Maybe, just maybe if you talk to the President, he might keep you out of Guantanamo. Depends on how much you know and what you tell them.'

She strode out of the office.

The command centre was empty. Half way across the room the elevator opened and two guards bolted out, straight into a wall of Kia's gunfire. She stepped over their bodies and into the elevator. Up on the ground floor, there was total pandemonium. She holstered her guns and strode towards the exit.

A hand grabbed her arm, and she spun towards the assailant, it was Hughes, 'This way! This way!'

He led her through a maze of hallways, several guards rushed passed going in the opposite direction. Around one last corner and the pair burst through a door into the glare of the sun. Hughes fumbled with a hidden pocket, finally dragging out a thick notebook.

'Here, take this. It's a list of all the members of the Backroom and their sponsors!'

She pocketed the book, 'Who are you?'

'I am just a military lifer that stumbled across the rotten elements. I have been working on this rat pack for three years. Now go, I can get lost in the confusion. Watch out for snipers in the hills and the jets around the perimeter.'

He dived back through the door, slamming it behind him. There was no handle on the outside.

Chapter Seventy Nine

She almost made it to the S2 without attracting any attention. As she opened the door a bullet screamed off the door frame, she turned in time to see the top of a hill disappear in a huge ball of fire and earth. She slammed the door closed and dived for the command chair. Next thing she knew she was upside down. The S2 had been hit with an RPG. It was a wreck.

Suddenly the whole side of the S2 disappeared!

She saw ValKyrie arrive sideways with her door open. Taking two steps, Kia dove through the door and rolled onto her feet. 'Nice timing!'

'Thank you.'

ValKyrie spun on the spot and scanned the remains of the S2 out, she also fired a dart into the open doorway of the hangar.

Deep in the shadows a marine dropped the smoking, anti-tank launcher and stared at the large hole in the centre of his chest, then dropped with a soggy thud to the floor.

'Take a seat dear, I will be with you shortly.'

Kia swung her leg over the seat back and dropped into the command chair. 'Sandy! Where are the crew?'

'They are parked in the hills about eighty kilometers to the west. Is everything OK?'

'Yup, it's all under control, the shit hit the fan, and we are just about to leave.'

ValKyrie broke in, 'Sandy tell the others to head for home as fast as possible, I have sourced several outgoing calls, two of them are ordering US assets to your location.'

'What!!' gasped Kia. 'Go! What are you waiting for?'

'Patience, dear, we will arrive in plenty of time, I have a few things to attend to.'

'Like what?' She glanced at the radar HUD, there were eighteen incoming icons! 'Oh, Joy!'

ValKyrie slid sideways, nose facing the concrete wall, thirty feet from the door Hughes had let Kia out of ValKyrie fired six bolts through the wall.

On the other side of the wall, Hughes was standing with his hands at shoulder height. One of the officers was holding a pistol aimed at his face.

'YOU! You helped her escape, I saw it on the security cams when you opened the door. You are a traitor to the US and the organisation.'

'You and the Backroom filth are finished, I don't care if you kill me, you're done for.'

The concrete shattered inwards as the bolts came through. There was a spray of pinkish grey matter on the wall and the headless 2nd Commander dropped in unison with the four guards behind him.

Outside ValKyrie thundered into the air. She tore in a circle around the base, the ground was just a blur out of the window. Fourteen, fifteen, sixteen high explosive darts she fired before completing the circuit.

All around the base smoke rose from various parts of the landscape. Huge craters, massively disproportionate to the size of the darts, filled with twisted metal and popping munitions marked the locations of what remained of the base perimeter defence system.

Standing on her left wing tips, she did a mind-numbing turn and headed straight for the incoming fighter formation.

The HUD exploded in icons as the jets unleashed their rockets, Kia could almost swear she heard ValKyrie chuckle.

Incoming rockets look like a black dot ringed in fire so Kia found out! A high pitched screaming came from both sides as a semi-solid stream of projectiles cut each and every rocket to pieces.

ValKyrie spat out six rockets of her own, they streaked away into the sky.

Watching the HUD Kia saw six icons flash and disappear from the screen. Another four rocket launched, again four icons disappeared. Eight left. And closing fast, really fast! They were heading directly at each other, the lead fighter was exactly dead ahead.

Kia closed her eyes. The pilot of the lead jet never saw them coming, just as his brain registered something was there it was gone!

Spreading her wings slightly further apart, ValKyrie rolled 90 degrees just before she passed under the belly of the fighter. Her wings scraped down each side of the jet's fuselage shearing off both wings at the roots!

It took the pilot a few seconds for his numbed brain to realise he was now in a rocket, not a plane! He reached for the ejection handle and pulled as hard as he could.

The other seven scattered, six continued the hunt and one solitary jet ran as hard as it would go. ValKyrie was relentless, soon she was the only thing left flying.

Kia wiped her sweaty hands on her jumpsuit, 'I swear you was enjoying that.'

'It had its moments', came her reply.

'Well, if you have finished flittering about, shall we go home?'

'Certainly, home it is.'

Kia took the notebook out of her pocket and started to flick through the pages. It was explosive what it contained! Names, dates, descriptions of black ops, descriptions of assassinations, rogue programs. Some pages detailed bribes and vast amounts of money paid for information. The further she read, the more amazed she was.

'Can you scan this notebook for me?'
'Done.'
'I need to talk to the President urgently!'
'I will see what I can do.'
Kia went back to studying the pages.

A chime made her look up, 'OH, Hello, Jim.'

The President smiled', I am glad to see you are in one piece! I take it that they didn't try anything after I left.'

'Actually, it pretty well went to hell after you left, you will hear about it, I am sure, but the reason I called is I want to send you something for your eyes only.'

'That sounds ominous.'

'Wait till you read it. It's now on your laptop. Get Jen to make you a coffee, lock your door and have a read. Call me back when you have.'

'OK, will do.'

'Oh, one last thing, can I talk to Jen a second?'
Jim got out of his chair, and she could hear the sound of the door opening, a few seconds later Jen was on screen.

'Hi, I see you are in one piece.'

Kia smiled, 'Are you alone?'

'Yes.'

'Steve works for the Backroom, he is your mole.'

'Are you sure?' Jen said wide eyed.

'According to the notebook. Don't turn your back on him, or leave him alone with Jim.'

Jen nodded 'Will do, Steve is outside, I will keep an eye on him.'

'Jen, I am not kidding, he is as black as they get.'

'Got to go, the President is coming back.'

Kia killed the feed. She dropped the notebook into a pocket of the chair like it was contaminated. 'I am so glad I don't get involved in politics!'

ValKyrie stopped level with the balcony railing, and Kia jumped from the rail onto the balcony. Walking into the OpCen, she surprised everyone who was watching for news on several HUDs.

<u>Chapter Eighty</u>

'So this is what you get up to when the boss is away!'

'Hey, you're in one piece!'

'Of course, I am! Kate I want you to look at something.' She handed her the notebook. 'Can you analyse this and give me a general idea of what it all means please, all three of you on it, urgent.'

'Glen can I have a coffee please.'

He headed for the café, 'OK, but no stories until I get back!'

'Deal. Sandy increase our scanning perimeter, I want all traffic scanned. Be on your toes.'

'On it now', Sandy said.

Deep under the tower, banks of CPUs burst into life. Overhead satellites fired small thrusters that changed their orbits.

Glen returned, almost running from the elevator. 'OK, let me get a chair', he grabbed the closest stool. 'So tell us what happened!'

More chairs arrived, Kia sat with her back to the wall and Started from the beginning. When she was finished, there was only the sound of frantic typing coming from the Coven over the other side of the room.

'Man, I would have loved to see that dogfight!' Neil said enthusiastically! 'We never get to see the good bits!'

The main HUD flashed clear, then a video started playing, it was a video taken from somewhere on ValKyrie tail section. When it was over the HUD reverted to its previous displays.

For nearly three seconds the crew continued to stare at the HUD.

'Holy mother of god!' breathed Ray, 'She really gets the job done, doesn't she.'

Bree grinned, 'Hell hath no fury like a woman scorned, and I think I just saw the epitome of that.'

Kate walked over, 'Just on the first look through, and checking what little we can without digging deeper, I would say this notebook is the mother lode, whoever wrote this was close to the main artery of the organisation, but not actually part of it. If this ever went public, there would be war. I mean a real war.'

'There are only two people who know what's in this notepad outside of us. The guy who wrote it, and the President. Now, my next question Kate is very important. Do these people have the means to launch a strike against us here?'

Kate looked at Kia, 'Are you serious!'

'Indeed I am. ValKyrie said she detected several outgoing calls two of which were aimed at retaliation.'

'Hell yes, they could! Easily, but if the President knows about this, there is a high probability he would stop it. Unless..'

'Unless what?'

'Unless the orders got to mercenaries outside the US circle or there are Backroom members in places that the President can't reach in a hurry. OH thirdly, if they are not in the book, then you might have some hidden wild cards in the deck as well.'

'Thanks, Kate, go back to the book, and see what you can squeeze out of it.'

'I don't care what they try' Neil said. 'They got nothing compared to us, and on top of that we have ValKyrie!'

Brad stood and put his stool under the table. 'Just so you all know, I am not worried in the slightest either. A bully is only a bully until someone smacks him down. So as far as I am concerned, bring it on baby.'

For the next two and a half hours the Coven backed by Sandy's network power, chased, prised and sometimes used brute power to try and confirm the information listed in the Notebook.

Sandy broke into the conversation, 'The President is on the line for you, and he sounds stressed!'

'Hi Kia, I am in desperate need of help and don't know who else I can trust.'

'Calm down Jim, of course, we will help, start at the beginning. What has happened?'

'It started as soon as you sent me that information, I made a few calls to people I knew I could trust, some I have known for years. Five of them, I only gave them the information they needed. Four of the five have been killed, car accident, hit by a bus, fell down stairs, the last one is missing altogether.

'Taken one at a time, they seem innocent accidents, but all five in the same three hour period?'

Kia nodded, 'I agree. You know you have a leak?'

'Yes, I saw that in the info as I was reading. That is my next point, about an hour ago we had a situation here, there was an argument in the kitchen area, the next thing I know three of my protection detail are dead, one seriously injured, and he is not expected to survive.'

Kia stiffened 'JEN?'

'No Jen is fine, a few bruises and a small cut on her arm. She is the one that took the other four out. Including Steven. God, it looks like a massacre in there! When I got to the kitchen, Jen was standing in a pool of blood, she was covered in it. It turns out most of it wasn't hers.'

'Where is she now?'

'She has locked me in a safe room and won't let me out, dammit!'

'Smart lady, you just sit tight I will send help. Do not trust anyone Jim. You might hurt a few feelings of genuine friends, but until you can definitely sort the good from the bad, consider them all bad.'

'She turned to the crew, 'I need volunt....' That's as far as she got. Eleven hands went up.

'Kate, you and the Coven, concentrate on that notebook. Sorry girls, but it's vital we correlate that information.'

She hesitated, looking at the others. 'As I was going to say, volunteers. This could get very messy and ugly.'

'Bree stood by Brad. 'Our choice Kia, safety in numbers you know.'

'OK, so be it, two things, treat all as hostile except for Jim and Jen.

'Secondly, no IFF, no second chances and watch each other's back.'

The President was still on the line and saw and heard the entire thing. 'I can't put you people in harms way! There has to be a better way.'

Ray approached the HUD, 'Mr. President, sir, don't worry about us, you just keep your ass covered till we get there.'
A very grim and determined crew strode out of the OpCen.
In the elevator going down, Mel kissed Ray on the cheek.

'Did you tell the President to cover his ass!'

Ray grinned, 'Guess I did hon!'

Although the crew were smiling as the elevator stopped and they raced for the S2s, there was no change in their determination.
Kia was still talking to the President.

'They won't be long.'

'They are not armed are they? 'Isn't that dangerous?'

'No, they are not armed Jim, yes, it is dangerous, for those that go against them. You may get to see firsthand the reason we will never share the Tech we have. I have told you, we are a peaceful organisation.'

Despite his dire predicament, Jim still managed a grin. 'Tell that to the guys at Groom Lake!'

'They started that. That was the result of their own game plan.

'We are peaceful, but don't mistake peaceful for either weak or submissive. It would be a fatal error in judgment. I have a friend I think we can trust and rely on for assistance. Also, we, and I mean WE, need to find the core hiding place of the Backroom guys. After what has happened, I would expect most of them to congregate together. That's the nest we need to find and eradicate.'

'You want to eradicate them! What about bringing them to justice and the courts.'

'Jim, each and every one has committed treason against your country. 'Yes, you might nail the little ones, but the real players will tie up your courts for years, just to cut deals and walk free. 'The Notebook I gave you proves there are those on the fringe who will fill in the picture. There is only one cure for this kind of disease, and that's surgically removing it.'

A door behind Jim opened, and Kia tensed up, Jim turned in his chair. Jen entered carrying two steaming mugs. The door shut and bolted behind her. Her hair was still wet from a recent shower, and she was not wearing her normal suit.
Dressed in jeans and a shirt she looked more like Jim's daughter than a highly trained agent. That is, if you ignored the two shoulder holsters she was wearing.

'Jen! Nice to see you in one piece.'

'Hi Kia, yup, all bits still attached and functioning, small scratch on the arm that might leave a scar, though.'

'I knew you were trouble since I first met you.'

'Uh-uh, and you had nothing to do with my boss losing eighteen perfectly good and expensive aircraft this morning?'

'You have a valid point. Now, while my people are on the way to you, can you please go over the information you have, any hint or any clue where they are based will be helpful.'

'How many are you sending?' Jen asked?

'Eight.'

'Eight! Is that going to be enough! God knows how deep this Backroom crud reaches!'

'Jen, there was just me at Groom Lake, well a friend and me.'

'Point taken. Eight should be fine then.'

Kia signed off and asked Sandy to put her next call through.
The call connected, Ron Baker's smiling face filled the HUD.

'Kia so nice of you to call it's been a while, I have been reading about your activities in Vietnam! Well done!'

'Thank you, Ron, I wish I could say this is a social call, but I have someone with a bit of trouble and thought you might lend me a couple of your assets to help him out.'

Ron's smile faded slightly, 'What kind of assets?'

'Oh, half a dozen choppers full of armed to the teeth Marines would suffice.'

'What! Are you joking, yes? I can see you're not. What's going on?'

Kia told Ron the entire story, omitting a little here and there. Although he didn't need to know the bits she left out. Before she had even finished speaking, Ron had hit the alarms.

'I am sorry that you only have my word for it Ron, but trust me everything I have said is the truth.'

He nodded, 'I believe you. If it had been anyone else I would be laughing at them. You sure I can't clear this upstairs?'

'You can if you want to take the risk, we just don't know how far the reach of the Backroom is.'

'I have heard rumours over the years about them. Now it seems they were more than rumours. OK, I have six choppers spooling up, they will be at the manor in less than 60 minutes. We are not that far from shore. Tell your people we are coming. You took toys off me before!'

Kia smiled, 'I will, and thank you.'

'Not a problem.'

Sandy put a call through to the crew, they were not too far away from the manor either but were moving much, much, faster.

An hour later Jen let the President out of the safe room.

Six huge navy choppers were parked in the back courtyard of the mansion. Every window had at least two hard-faced marines manning it. The crew was dispersed in a circle around the estate. Their role was to pre-warn of any incoming traffic and to either stop or delay anything that tried to get in.

Brad and Bree were the only exceptions, they were sitting in the office with the President and Jen.

'I think you are safe now, Mr. President.'

'Indeed. Now my focus has turned to what needs to be done next. I don't know who to trust and who not to!'

'Can't you call the NSA, or CIA to help out?' Bree asked.

'I could, but if they are as smart as they keep assuring me they are, I cannot believe they did not know what was happening behind the scenes, and that means either they were involved somehow, or they knew and did not care.'

'I see your predicament. I have to say you have an unenviable job.'

'At the moment I have to agree with you, I don't mind fighting for this country when I can clearly see and define who the enemy are! This is totally a different situation. I know all the top guys from the army, navy, and air force. They are the people I meet with all the time. I do not have a clue who is further down the command chain.'

'Even if you did, until we get more Intel you would not know how far down this crap goes Jim.'

Bree noticed the tired look in Jens eyes. 'You need to get some sleep young lady.'

'I tried before, but it sounds like rogue elephants upstairs with all those military boots.'

Bree stood, 'Come with me dear, I can fix that for you.'

Jen looked at the President, he nodded, 'You have been through hell, go, I am safe now.'

Bree led Jen outside into an enclosed private garden. She took a remote out of her pocket and hit a button. The S2 ned its Camo off and opened the door.

Jen was stunned! 'Wow, that's different! I did not see it here.'

Bree grinned, 'That's the point, you didn't see Brad's that we walked past either. Come on, you can sight see later.'

Jen followed into the S2.

She dropped the cot into position, showed Jen the small coffee bar and food dispenser.

Jen stripped of her gun harnesses, kicked off her runners and laid down on the cot.

'Sandy this is Jen.'

'Hi, Jen' came Sandy's voice.

Jen sat up 'A talking ship?'

'No dear, I am an AI unit on the island.'

Bree laughed, 'she never gives herself credit, Sandy is our organiser and mother hen. She will watch over you while you sleep. Only me or she can open this door, you are safe here, if anything comes up Sandy will wake you.'

Jen had laid back down, Bree doubted she had heard the last sentence as Jen was fast asleep. 'Take care of her Sandy.'

'She is safe.'

The door closed, and the Camo cut back in as Bree mounted the stairs back into the mansion.

Chapter Eighty One

Kia was pacing the OpCen thinking hard. She had been for a meal and a shower. She even tried grabbing some sleep, after tossing and turning for nearly an hour she had yet another shower and was back in the tower.

A barrage of chimes sounded, she looked at the screen. A mass of windows were popping open showing delivery and transport receipts, and a whole load of other data.

'What's this Sandy?'

'I have no idea, it's not me putting them up!' The pages and windows kept appearing over the top of each other.

'Kate?'

'Nope, not I' Kate said from her desk, 'But it's really interesting stuff!'

ValKyrie's voice cut in. 'In 1995, all this equipment and much more was purchased from various offshore accounts. Individually, they mean nothing of importance, however, if taken in context as a whole, all these items constitute a large operational centre.

'Most of this was shipped from warehouse to warehouse, some of it stored for months at a time. Eventually, it all gravitates to this area.'

A map showed on the HUD.

'Many subcontractors for various companies that build office networks, and fibre optic networks went missing around the time all of this equipment arrived. No pay records or contracts show for the period.

'An occasional personal purchase shows up on the cards of several employees of these contractors. Also in the same vicinity.

'Anonymous funding arrived at two local councils to allow upgrades to both rail and road infrastructure, with specific instructions to upgrade the 193 and 123 in Utah.

'Couple that with a sharp rise in sales of concrete trucks in Salt Lake, Denver and Las Vegas. Everything points to a large clandestine construction project in the area.

'A chronological mapping of the information shows the various phases that a large construction would require. I have narrowed the area down to 39°33'30.2N 110°22'27.6W approximately.'

'Two other projects almost matched the criteria, however, one was proven to be a NASA-funded construction, and the other was abandoned after a water table was breached and flooded the work area.'

'Damn, that's brilliant work' breathed Kate, 'What led you to the contractors?'

'These contractors are the same contractors that refurbished the control room at Groom Lake.'

Sandy positively beamed, 'That's my sister for you!'

Kia laughed, 'You two are nothing alike. Thank you, ValKyrie. It gives us a starting point.'
She next put a call through to the President.

'Can you ever remember hearing anything about Utah?' she asked him. 'From around 1995 onwards?'

He thought for a while, 'No, nothing comes to mind. Around 2002 there was talk of installing some deep ground missile silos, I believe they tested the area for seismic stability and rumour was they sank a few test bores.
But then that was done in quite a few locations around the country. Sorry, I can't help.'

He looked disturbed by the question, she put it down to the stress of the situation.

'We have uncovered some information that leads us to speculate that something happened in Utah. Nothing concrete, but hints from many different places all points in that direction.

'Any progress getting help your way?'
'Ron Baker has sounded out some of his colleagues and immediate superiors, but it's slow going. One word in the wrong place and who know what can go wrong. So far all we have is the Groom Lake incident and my agents proving to be working for them.

'As far as I know I have done nothing to tip anyone off, of course losing four top brass in one day may have already alerted them.' Jim sounded up tight.

'Oh, I think they know something is up, those guys Jen took out, who knows if they had a scheduled reporting roster? Now that you have Ron and his men, our involvement may no longer be required, or desirable.'

'Brad said the same thing about 30 minutes after the Marines landed. I spoke to Ron at length and told him what Brad has said. Ron's reply was blunt and to the point, he said, and I quote If Kia and the crew are on our side, we can't lose.

'So I am officially asking you to help. You are, apart from Ron and his men, the ONLY ones that I know for sure that I can depend on. If this did start way back in 95, they have had twenty years to infiltrate and position their people throughout the system.

Please, Kia! I have no one else to turn to.'

Kia looked at him. He was in over his head, and he knew it. She stared at the HUD, her mind was working overtime. He watched her think, he had nothing left to say.

'OK. Deal, but there are some things I want you to do for me, I am going to use your position as a tool to fight this problem, and I want you to know that up front. Not you personally per-se, but your office.'

Jim looked relieved, 'You just tell me what you need to be done!'

'Firstly reach out to all the senators, all of them, tell them there is something that's cropped up that you need to assemble Congress for. Don't care what you tell them, but once the shit hits the fan and it's over we need to lay it all out in the open. Let the people of America know what happened.'

'It is the only way that anyone we miss cannot spread lies. If we expose the rats nest, let everyone become a hunter. Any that get away will have nowhere to hide. Also tell them, they have to be there, no if buts or maybe. Can you do that?'

'Yes, yes, I think so, they have made me jump through hoops during my term in office, it's time for a bit of payback.'

'Good! I don't know how long it will take, but we need them ready to assemble at a moments notice. This may get dirty, we don't know how much of your military they control, so I am taking it for granted they have it all, not to underestimate them.'

'Geezus Kia, I hope you are wrong!'

'Time will tell. Tell Brad what's going on, he might be able to assist rounding up the senators. I am heading for Utah, it's a weak lead, but the only one we have right now. Lastly, the moment anything happens, tell me!'

'I will, God speed!'

__Chapter Eighty Two__

She cut the feed, 'God better be looking the other way when I find them! Sandy, protect the Coven, protect the island.' With that, she walked out onto the balcony stepped on a chair and jumped over the railing!

As she slid into Valkyrie's command chair, she took one long look at the complex. 'OK, lady, lets do this.'

During the transit flight, Kate and the girls had been feeding info back to Kia. Bit by bit they were managing to tease the information out of the mass of information. Whoever had hidden the info had done a brilliant job!

Hovering at the CoOrds ValKyrie had postulated they could both see it was going to be a mammoth task.

'Well, I can see why few people wander around this part of the country!'

Icon after Icon popped onto the HUD, nearly each and everyone was a mine. Few active, most abandoned, but nearly every one of them was a Uranium mine. That word alone would keep most people out. Also, large truck traffic would be commonplace, including concrete trucks.

'How do you wish to proceed?'

'Is the Uranium affecting your scanners?'

'Not in the slightest.'

'I suggest we scan both sides of the roads leading in, it will be faster than a grid search, somewhere there has to be an entrance.

'How many roads are there?'

'There are over 3000 miles of roads.'

'Damn!'

'May I suggest an alternative?'

'Anytime dear, I am all ears.'

ValKyrie headed for a sheer cliff face. As they approached a hole began to form in front of them, deeper and deeper until it was deep enough for them to enter and turn around.

They landed on the ultra smooth floor of the fresh cave facing the entrance.

Close enough to the edge they could see the road junction below but far enough in to be invisible from prying eyes.

'Now, what? We wait?'

'No, I am conferring with Sandy, one moment.'

A few moments later two Hives were built each side of the entrance and a wire frame Sat Dish.

Seconds later the hives started ejecting drones, alternating left and right, each drone turned Camo as it cleared the cave entrance.

'That was a hell of a lot of drones' Kia said once the hives stopped producing.

'Exactly one thousand, Sandy is running half via the Sat-Link, and I am running the other half. Now, as you said before, we wait.'

Kia watched on a HUD as the drones ran out from their position into a ten branch star pattern, then at 60 miles they all turned as one and started a spectacular spiral pattern search, perfectly in synchronisation.

The rotation of the spiral was quite slow.

'They are scanning to a 100 meter depth, which is why they are moving slowly before you ask.'

'OK, I get the hint, you and Sandy have it under control.' Kia grinned.

Brad called in to give her an update. 'Everything was quiet. They had restored some communications, The President was leaping about locating Senators and issuing recall orders. I asked him before how it was going he said some had been stubborn.

'When asking had not produced results and direct orders were being baulked at, he had reminded them just how much their particular state relied on federal funding. That had worked with the most stubborn ones.

'Jen had just woken up, and Miako had worked on her arm, quite a deep cut. Miako had put eighteen stitches in and dressed it.'

Brad also told Kia he had recalled the crew to the guest house at the back of the property. They were taking two hour turns to scout a ten kilometer perimeter.

'It sounds like you have it all in hand Brad. Sandy and ValKyrie are running a drone sweep of the area here. So far nothing has turned up, but we have only just started. Stay in touch.'

The next call went over to the Coven, 'How are we going girls?'

Kate looked up into the HUD, 'Oh Hi! There has been a funny development, we don't know if it's connected in any way, but we are checking it out.

'Way back in 1996 a tunnel in the Rocky Mountains was completed, actually several short tunnels for a new interstate highway. Anyway, normally when they are finished tunnelling the machine digs a short side tunnel, and they abandon the machine. It's cheaper to build a new one than transport the old one out.

'Some kids explored the tunnels before the road was opened and one wrote on a blog that when they looked for the drill head machine, it was missing.

'This only raised a flag because Jess had one of the many searches running with the word tunnelling in the parameters. It may be nothing.'

'Point taken, by itself it may be nothing, but in the overall picture it may find a place. Tell Jess good work for me.'

'Will do, anything over there?'

'Not so far, but you have given me an idea. Got to go.'

'ValKyrie, Sandy, analyse the drone data when they fly over the abandoned mines in this area. See if they have been backfilled. Also, include any valley areas.

The Hive machine on the left spat two more Drones out, and they took off in the direction of the highest mine concentration.

Twenty minutes later Kia had her answer. Most of the closed mines had indeed been filled in! Some of the open cut style mines were filled back to ground level. But the spoil tips next to them still were there!

'You sneaky sons of bitches!' exclaimed Kia, 'They have used the mines to hide the material they removed from tunnelling. What we are looking for has got to be close.'

Just after 3 pm they found what they were looking for. All the drones except 20 were recalled.

The remaining drones were re-tasked to ultra deep scanning. Like a flock of invisible circulating buzzards they bored deep into the rock and limestone.

Occasionally one drone would take off at a tangent following some buried structure or lines.

By midnight Kia had a 3D map on the screen of the hidden base. Sandy had recalled her drones and ValKyrie had left two of hers out.

They were now slowly boring holes into the rock heading closer to the underground structure.

Kia rubbed her tired eyes. She updated everyone in a group conference and told them she was getting some badly needed sleep, the concentration factor had been high for hours and mentally she was running on empty.

After the conference was done, she had a meal and stripped off for a shower. Still wet and naked she rolled onto the cot, said goodnight and was asleep in moments.

ValKyrie monitored all her vital signs and went back to work.

The drones had stopped boring and were relaying a vast amount of data back. Nothing was hidden from their probes.

Files in locked cabinets were read, hard drives in the computers were read. Even the contents of the peoples wallets and handbags, their DNA included!

Once that was relayed back to Sandy, she started to correlate all the information into flow charts and timelines. While everyone slept, the case against the Backroom core was being laid out, accurately and precisely.

Kia woke feeling refreshed sharp and focused. She grabbed herself a hot drink and sat in the command chair. Up on the main HUD was a huge chart, it listed every member and the associates. It listed all the companies that had backed the Backroom organisation.

Everything was there.

She looked at the information, the cup in her hand forgotten. This was huge! Not just a few rogue people, this was almost a parallel military operation!

'Can you patch me through to the President we need to discuss this new information?'

'I would highly suggest, that you put some clothing on before putting the call through.'

She looked down and noticed she was as naked as the day she was born. 'I guess you're right.'

The conference was a long one. She sent the President all the information she had, and together they walked through it section by section.

He had paled when reading the top echelon names list, 'I would have called some of these guys for help! OK, what do we do now?'

'That is totally up to you. These are the head guys that took my girls and had them beaten almost to death, they are also the ones behind my attempted kidnapping, so I personally have no love for them. It's not my call, it's yours.'

'I need time to think if this list is accurate and I believe it is, there are four people I need to read in on this. That way I have my ass politically and legally covered.'

'Makes perfect sense to me, just remember, you have a crowd of senators that will be getting restless and time is growing short.'

For a split second the President looked uncomfortable. There has been a delay getting to all the senators, so it's going slower than planned at the moment, but I hear you, give me two hours, that's all I need.'
'OK, two hours it is.'

Kia turned from the blank screen, 'So how will we clear this viper pit out?'

ValKyrie's voice filled the craft, 'I have been running several scenarios on that subject. Initially I would just detonate it, however, the proximity of so many seams of Uranium could make the area dangerous for humans for a long time. The answer depends on what the Americans want to do with it.

'If they have no interest in its contents, then destruction is easiest. If they want to inspect the complex, then a more surgical approach will be required. It also depends on your wishes as well.'

'Me! Why should I care what happens to it?'

'I would have thought that having the top five segments at hand, you may have wished to deal with them personally.'

She thought about it for a while, 'Actually being instrumental in their termination is just fine with me. I get no thrill from killing.'

'As you wish.'

Sandy broke into the conversation. 'I think we may have a developing situation. Over the last few hours, I have logged erratic behaviour of seven ships. That in itself is not, particularly of note. However, as erratic as their course may seem, I have postulated that in a few hours all of the ships will be exactly on our borders around the island.

'That I would call a noteworthy occurrence. They are out of range of my sensors, so I have dispatched drones underwater to take a closer look. I will report as soon as I have more solid data.'

of Kia's neck prickled, I don't like the
me updated every 30 minutes Sandy.'
Sandy cut the feed.
out the front window over the Utah ranges, lost
in thought.

Something about this new development nagged her, but she couldn't pin it down.

'Who is currently out on patrol at the mansion?'

'Melissa', ValKyrie replied almost instantly.

'Patch me, please.'

'Hi boss, what's happening?'

'Are you out on patrol?'

'Yes, doing a few expanding circles out to the 10km boundary, nothing to report. Everything seems like just another day down there.'

'I want you to do something for me, off the record.'

'Oh! OK, what do you need?'

Kia sent her some CoOrds, and instructions what she needed. 'This is ultra urgent Mel. Tell no one for now.'

'Hush it is! Anything else?'

'Nope, just check that for me, please.'

The line closed. She pulled the info back up that they had got from the hidden complex. Kia flicked through dozens of screens, looking for a specific answer. She was still looking when Mel called back.

'All clear there Kia, nothing happening at all. The area is almost a ghost town.'

'Thanks, Mel. Not the answer I wanted, but it was the one I suspected. That means I need to talk to Brad. Finnish your patrol and make sure Brad is the next one out. Tell him to call me when he is up.'

'Will do, I am getting the impression something isn't kosher?'

'Just for once, I am hoping I am wrong. Now get to Brad.'

'ValKyrie, any excessive activity at any military base on the west coast? Scrub that, make it any military base.'

'Searching.'
While that was happening, she pulled up the data, and wen .
over it again, this time looking for something specific.

Brad's image burst onto the HUD, 'Hey boss, Mel said you are looking for me?'

'Yes Brad, I want you to do something for me, it's just based on an itch I can't scratch. Zero facts to back it up.

'I have learnt to trust your hunches. If it is of any consolation Miako has been whispering to Bree that something feels out of alignment. 'So what is it you need doing?

'I want you to send the crew out to check military bases and ports on the West coast. Look for increased activity or anything out of the ordinary. Keep your eyes sharp.'

'OK, we can do that, I will let Ron's men know we will be out for an extended period.'

'No, don't tell anyone, not even the President. Just keep this between us for now.'

'OK, you the boss. I will get on it now.'
Kia Signed off and paced back and forth.

'As Brad just told you, your hunches have proven to be correct in the past, actually 98.7% correct. I advise you to continue to act on these hunches at this point.'

'Thanks for the vote of confidence ValKyrie.
I think you may be right, if I don't, this outcome may be worse than if I do.'

Kia typed a name into the search section on the HUD, followed by two others. 'I need to find these three men urgently.'

'Then that is what we shall do.'
Lifting off the floor of the cave they shot out into the bright sunlight and headed towards the east.

Chapter Eighty Three

During the transit time, Kia contacted everyone and got a status update. Nothing seemed to be out of the ordinary at the places that had been interrogated. There were a lot more to check as yet.
It didn't take too long, and Kia was hovering over the top of a house on the outskirts of Washington DC.
'The person you require is in the stables just to the left of the main dwelling.'
'Thanks, put me down in the yard near the door. Find the other two, and I will need an S2 temporarily. I am not letting them see you.'
'Affirmative.'
Kia walked across the yard and entered the stables. Letting her eyes adjust for a moment she could hear the sounds of horses in the stalls to the left. Quietly she moved down the passageway between the stalls. Movement to the right caught her attention, and she saw the man she had come to talk to. He had his back to her and was stacking feed bales against the rear of the empty stall he was in.
'Mr. Caswell, may I have an urgent word with you, please?' Caswell turned and looked at Kia, 'This is private property young lady, how the hell did you get past the guards at the gate?'
'That was easy, I didn't come in the gate. I need to talk to you urgently.'
'No dear, you need to leave urgently, before you find yourself in deep trouble.'

He went to take a step towards her. He stopped in surprise at the automatic that seemed to appear in Kia's hand.

'Mr. Caswell, please, we are already in deep trouble, way deeper than you imagine. Sit on that bale behind you and I will take ten minutes of your time. After that, if what I tell you does not interest you, I shall leave you in peace.' She saw his eyes flicker to the gun. 'You will be alive and well, I assure you.'

With a heavy sigh, he sat on the bale, 'OK, you have my attention.'

Kia holstered the gun, and took a tablet out of her other leg pocket, turning it on, she held it out to him. He gingerly took it, never looking away from her face. She stepped back to the stall doorway and leant against the post.

'Have a look at the information on that, then, if you want we shall talk. However, I must warn you time is running out for both of us.'

Caswell took glasses out from his top pocket and started reading, the further he read the whiter his complexion went.

'This, he tapped the screen with a shaking finger, this cannot possibly be true!'

'I am afraid it is, true in every aspect. Not only is it true, but I have to deal with this, by the end of the day. One way or another, either we, or they will lose. I can assure you, I have no intention of losing Mr. Caswell.'

'Oh, my god, Caswell uttered as he kept reading. No No No No!!! I feel sick! He looked up at her, but what can I do about this? This is way out of my league!'

'Mr. Caswell I don't want you to do anything, nothing at all. I will sort this.

What I need from you and two other gentlemen we are about to go and see. What I need from you three, is to be able to hand the remnants over to you. Once this has been removed, it will leave a power vacuum, and I am asking you three to be ready to fill it.

'That will mean continued stability for your country.'

'OK, I can do that. Who are the other two?' she told him.

'Geezus, this is big, isn't it? So when do we start? Kia walked over to him and held out her hand. Welcome aboard. Now we just need to convince the other two. Lets go.'

'Dressed like this?'

She smiled, 'Dressed like that may remind you a little of what's on the line here.'

He nodded, 'You're quite right there.'

The conversations with the others were almost identical, but with Caswell along for the second meeting, and the three of them for the third it got easier.

Kia left all three sitting under an awning, each was re-reading their Tablets. It was a lot to take in.

'Gentlemen, just before I leave I am going to play along with their game until I know who the main character is. After that...' She left the sentence unfinished.

She skipped out into the country put the S2 on the ground and walked over to ValKyrie, after scanning out the S2 they just sat there. They had done all they could, and now it was the Backroom's turn.
The President had called back exactly two hours as he promised.

He said 'I have reached my people, I am pretty sure of their loyalty, well, as much as one can be at this time.

They are going to see if it is possible to take down the base without involving any military personnel. If we can do that, we might blindside them. What do you think?'

'It's worth a shot Jim. If you think it can be done that way, then all the better. Remember, my people are not fighters. We can be when we have to, but that's not the same thing is it. So far we have been lucky, and no one has been hurt. Actually, I might send them home, that way they can be all in the same place and be safe.'

Jim nodded, 'Sounds like a good idea, the marines have got me covered and are trained for this kind of thing.'

'Is Jen still with you?'

'Yes, she is, do you want to talk to her?'

'No, it's ok. If she is ok with it, I would move the Marines to the perimeter and leave the house security to her. That way you will get a heads up if someone tries to get in.'

Jim agreed, 'OK. So what is your next move?'

'I am sitting on the mountain overlooking the base, there is a small shack up here I have been using for cover. I will stay hidden here and send the other guys home.'

Jim smiled, 'OK, good to know where you are and that you have it all under control. I will call the guys back and see how we are going with gathering men to do this. They said it might take a while.'

'I don't think time is an issue.' Kia said with a smile. 'I will call back if something happens. Otherwise, I shall make the shack a little more comfortable and wait.'

After signing off, Kia contacted the crew. 'Nothing is going on anywhere. The only thing I saw out of the ordinary was back at Groom Lake' Neil said.

'They had pulled the two SR-71A's out of the hangar while they were patching the holes in the buildings. Some techs were checking them out, obviously looking for damage. All the other places I saw was just everyday activity.'

'You saw both Blackbirds?'

'Yes, side by side, they look unharmed so we won't be getting a bill!' you could hear the smile in Neil's voice.

'Thank you', Neil, 'Now, Sandy may have an issue back at the island, I want you all back there as soon as you can. I won't be that far behind you.'

They all confirmed they were heading for home and would see her there.

She sat in the command chair, closed her eyes and let her mind run free. Scenario after scenario flash through her mind each one disregarded of one reason or another.

For nearly three and a half hours Kia was motionless. Her breathing became that slow and shallow ValKyrie increased the Oxygen ratio in the air.

Slowly she built up a picture that she could not fault. Lots of pieces started to fit way too neatly for its scenario not to be close to factual reality. When it finally solidified into a workable scenario, her eyes snapped open!

'You miserable son of a bitch!' she growled out loud.

Chapter Eighty Four

'Home dear, via Edwards AFB if you don't mind.'

They cruised at a leisurely Mark 2 following the terrain at 5000ft. As the base appeared on the horizon, they slowed and did a low pass over the buildings. Kia saw exactly what she expected to see. Absolutely nothing at all, the place looked deserted.

'Well, my dear, time for you to go hunting.'

'This is the beginning of the end for them. I would like to be over the island in, she did a quick mental calculation, in approximately 78 minutes, can you do that for me?'

'With ease, please fasten harnesses on the command chair.' Kia reached down and latched the 7 point harness. 'Ready when you are she said grimly.'

ValKyrie rolled to the left and accelerated.

Details of the terrain below became so blurred that small towns and villages were hard to spot. They climbed higher and higher. As the air thinned out, their speed increased.

Kia reached over and cycled the radar HUD, over a thousand kilometers away two blips showed on the screen.

'There are your first two targets. Sandy everything ok there?'

'Yes, all good the crew is all back safely.'

'Good, we are coming in now, things are going to get nasty shortly.' The HUD to her left opened up, she could see everyone standing in the OpCen.

'Listen boys and girls. Sandy was never designed for this. Stand by her and assist in any way you can. She got the thumbs up sign from a few of them.'

'Stay inside. If we need assistance, we will holler so be ready to jump if necessary. I will get a video feed to you so you can see what's going on.'
Brad and Ray both said 'Good luck.'
The HUD in the OpCen switched to the forward facing Tail camera on ValKyrie. As everyone watched, ValKyrie changed from Camo to an iridescent bright red. Neil dragged two stools over, and he sat next to Miako. Holding hands tightly they watched as ValKyrie went to war.
Bree put her arm around Brad. Paul crossed his arms and stood rigidly. Not one of them took their eyes off the screen.

A tiny speck in the distance was growing larger by the second, it was higher than they were. The speck split into two as they got closer. The pair of SR-71A Blackbird plane's were running at near full throttle. Unaware of what was approaching from behind.
Five kilometers out ValKyrie kicked out four high explosive steel darts. Each dart fired from an EMP launcher slashed through the air faster than lightning! Normal rockets were useless at this speed.
The SR71 on the right exploded. There was no ball of flame, just total disintegration! At mach3, whatever the darts had not destroyed the speed of the airstream itself had torn to shreds. The Blackbird on the left flipped on edge and did a hard left diving turn.
Due to the massive difference in speed. They overshot the turning plane. ValKyrie flipped upside down and headed for the sea below, she locked onto the other plane and accelerated. Within seconds she was on the tail of the other plane, but did not slow down. Lifting slightly higher than the tail of the Blackbird.
ValKyrie shot over the top, dipping her right wings as she did so, she tore the entire right wing off the Blackbird.
De-accelerating and swinging in a circle she followed the spinning carcass of the Blackbird all the way down to the sea.

Skimming the waves they went in search of the ships.

The seven blips on the radar showed a formation circling the island. They lined up on the closest ship and headed for it. 1000m away ValKyrie kicked out four rockets, follow by another four.

The first wave tore into the side of the small ship, they detonated with so much force the ship heeled over, and the bottom was exposed.

The second wave of rockets tore the bottom clean out of the ship and as it rolled upright there was no hull left to speak of. It sank in seconds.

Travelling anti-clockwise around the island they lined the next ship up. It fared no better! The next ship in line was the largest one of the seven. ValKyrie identified it as a refurbished destroyer.

It started firing surface to air missiles. ValKyrie kicked out darts, twelve at a time in eight waves. The missiles and darts met and nothing was left flying. Next came streams of high volume gunfire. Thousands of rounds tore through the air in a visible stream from four gun emplacements on the ship. With all the grace of a ballet dancer ValKyrie wove her way between the firestorm.

Kicking out sixteen darts, three of the four emplacements exploded. The last swung out of control and drilled holes into the deck of the ship.

ValKyrie dropped four torpedoes into the water and swung past the stern. Turning that low and hard, ValKyrie actually cut the surface of the sea with her left wings. Sweeping back in from the other side, she fired ten sets of eight rockets just above the height of the deck. It looked like she had missed with the Rockets!

The torpedoes detonated under the hull. The ship looked like it tried to buck like a horse, the deck arched high into the air! Then the rockets arrived! The first eight hit at the front of the hull, due to the forward momentum of the ship the next wave hit further back and the following waves even further.

The last set hit the stern of the ship. Perfectly spaced
and perfectly timed the rockets had torn the ship in two,
lengthwise!

The deck and the hull were now two separate pieces! The
combined force of the explosives had pushed the ship sideways
in the water! Without the structural support of the deck,
the hull buckled and twisted. There was only one outcome
possible. The ship's hull folded in the centre and it all sank in a
blaze of smoke and flames.

ValKyrie thundered across the top of the sea. She was
moving that fast a huge plume of water was being torn into the
air behind her. It was a blood chilling sight for the next ship in
her sights!

This ship was full of ex-military and mercenary personnel.
It seemed like every single one of them was lining the deck and
firing a massive range of weaponry at the approaching craft. If
Kia had been piloting, she would have peeled off and got clear
of the mass of firepower being launched towards them.

ValKyrie did not even hesitate.

Jinking around the larger projectiles and scanning out the
smallest ones, she rapidly closed the gap between them.
Suddenly ValKyrie released a massive amount of Hi-Ex bolts.
The air seemed solid with them! Detonation after detonation
blasted the ship. The entire structure was smashed in an ultra
violent, semi-continuous blast of high explosives. It did not
merely sink. It was literally blasted under the water. Even then
the detonations did not cease until ValKyrie thundered over
the spot the boat had entered the water.

ValKyrie sought out the remaining ships. Some fought back,
some were trying to flee. She showed them all no mercy. There
was nothing left on the surface as she did another circuit. She
slowed to a halt and was just hovering.

A cheer went up in the OpCen! 'Way to go Val!'
ValKyrie just hovered. Kia looked at the HUD radar, it was clear.

'Well, dear, you certainly cleaned them out!'

'Please remain seated.'

Kia stopped reaching for the harness buckles, 'what is it?'

'I thought I detected something.'

Three kilometers away the sea burst into the air as four missiles leapt from the ocean. ValKyrie flashed into the sky, firing eight darts, two darts apiece shattered the missiles less than 500meters into the air.

She rolled over and headed for the sea, this time, she didn't stop.Plunging under the surface. She went hunting, she picked up popping noises of a submarine doing an emergency dive off to the right. Swinging right her sonar soon picked it up as it was making a dash for a deep water trench.

She also could hear the high pitched sound of six torpedoes circling in hunting mode. She fired darts at the nearest torpedos, detonating them safely. The last two were still hunting. She ignored them. The sub was getting further away. She took off after the sub. Up ahead was a fairly deep trench that the submarine was running for.

She let it run, keeping pace behind it. Once over the trench, the sub dived deeper, levelling out just above its crush depth. As the sub levelled out, ValKyrie accelerated over the top of it and turned upwards and headed back for the hunting torps.

Behind her the sub was sinking uncontrollably, with both ballast tanks and all dive planes removed from the hull, there was simply nothing to hold it up. It reached the depth where the water pressure was just too much and imploded spectacularly.

They found the hunting torps still circling, and Kia scanned them out. Back in the air, Kia checked in with Sandy.

'Can you please get the crew out and clean up the mess we just made. There is oil and debris everywhere. It won't do our beaches any good. I will be back. This was only half the battle, now to finish it off.'

ValKyrie shifted back into Camo mode and headed for the base in Utah.

Chapter Eighty Five

Back in the OpCen Brad was talking to the others, 'Listen, ladies, I prefer you sit this one out. It's not going to be pleasant out there'

Sandy interrupted, 'Brad take Ray and just do a surface clear. I am sending drones to clear the wreckage and whatever from the bottom.'

'Thanks' Neil said, 'I didn't want to go and see what's left out there.'
Sandy relayed to Kia the plan for the cleanup and initialised the drones while outside the boys fired up their S2s and left to clean up the mess.

ValKyrie backed into the hole they had occupied before. She reported back that the base was a flurry of activity. There is a lot of traffic flowing in and out compared to our prior observations.

'It will do them no good, can you cut all communication in and out of the base?'

'Easily, do you wish me to do so?'

'Yes, they have forfeited their organisation by attacking the island. They were warned months ago not to do so. I also want you to do something for me.'
Kia explained exactly what she required. The hives released fifteen drones a piece.

'Communications have been cut. Nothing can get in or out.'

'OK, you know the topography and geology, time to place the drones.'

Thirty drones poured over the hill and dropped into the valley.

It looked to a bystander that they simply smashed into the hillside around the base. In actuality, they did not hit the rock face, but scanned holes and flew into their own tunnels. In a few moments, ValKyrie announced that all drones were in their optimum position.

Kia uttered one word. 'Detonate!'

For a few moments, everything looked as it had for years. A two-lane road twisting through a deep valley with towering rock sides, quite peaceful and somewhat picturesque.

Seconds later everything changed. The entire left side of the valley rock wall lifted upwards and blew out sideways! Huge sections of rock wall tried to move as one. Both up and outward. They shattered into thousands of pieces.

The wave of moving rock blasted into the valley, burying the road and half filling the valley. A deep rumbling boom echoed up and down what was left of the valley. Then there was just silence. There was very little dust and when even that had cleared the landscape was forever changed.
Kia stared at the massive destruction.

'I have fulfilled my promise.' She took a deep breath, 'Lets remove the hives. Then its time to see the President.'

As they left the safety of the cave, Kia glanced at where the little wooden hut used to be perched on the top of the right side of the valley. It was obliterated, just a scarred crater where it used to stand. She punched a button in the console as they flew past the remains.

'I need an S2 again before we get to the manor. No need to show you off to the President.'
Just short of the manor they made a stop at an abandoned farm. Kia swapped over to an S2 and continued towards the manor.

This time, she landed at the foot of the steps to the main doors. Walking up the stairs, she strode down the hallway to the main office at the end.

Without knocking, she opened the door and walked in. Jen was looking out the rear window, scanning the garden for any threats.

As the door opened, she spun towards the door and stopped with her gun drawn and pointed directly at Kia. She smiled and put the gun back into its shoulder holster.

'You could get shot walking in like that!'

'Only if I underestimated your abilities Jen.'

The President was sitting at the desk, he was surprised by Kia's sudden appearance. 'You made me near jump out of my skin! I thought you were guarding the base until the reinforcements got there?'

Kia stared at him for awhile. She took a picture out of her jumpsuit pocket and slid it over in front of him.

He picked it up and looked at it. 'What is this?'

'I will get to that in a second.

'The base has been obliterated. What's left of it is buried under thousands of tonnes of rock. Also, there were, seven ships and a submarine sent to attack my island and the unarmed people that live there. All those are also utterly destroyed. Two SR-71As had been sent from Edwards to coordinate the attack, neither of those exists either.'

Jim went pale, 'My god! You destroyed them all?'

'Destroyed? No, I annihilated them, right down to the last nut, bolt and rivet. There is nothing left.'

'No survivors? We could have interrogated survivors and got them to talk.'

'Nope, not even a single survivor. No one left to talk.'

Jim leant back in the chair, 'Well, that's a shame, but we have all the information you got from the base. Well done, you got them all!'

'Almost Jim, I still have to find the top man, the overall leader. He is never mentioned in any of the documents, no name, not even a code name for him.'

Both Jim and Jen were frowning. 'How do you know there is someone else? There is nothing in the documents to indicate there is' Jim asked.

'Because the top guys at the base were powerful people. Very powerful, but they didn't have the necessary bit "extra" that would be needed to cover all contingencies.

'Most of all, the thing that proves it beyond doubt, is that photo.'

Jim picked the photo back up, it was an aerial shot of a blast crater. 'I am sorry, you have lost me. How does a picture of some rocky ground prove there is a top man?'

Kia smiled, 'because Mr. President, that is not a picture of rocky ground. That is a picture of a blast crater where a little wooden hut used to stand on the top of a hill. A tiny hut, that I was supposedly hiding in.'

Jim's manner changed instantly, 'What are you saying?'

'You're an intelligent man, Mr. President, add the facts up for yourself.' She began to tick them off on her fingers. 'There are no Senators you supposedly sent for. The supposed attack on this Mansion never happened. The three guys that jumped Jen, were actually contracted from the NSA. Steven called a handler telling him the President informed him that Jenny was working for the other side.'

Jen's jaw dropped, 'What!'

'And last of all Mr. President. You and you alone was the only person I told that I was hiding in that hut.'

'You are out of your mind' snarled the President.

'Maybe, we will see. The Attorney General, the Vice President and the leader of Congress don't seem to agree with you on that. They will be arriving shortly. Let's see if you can convince them I am crazy.'

'In my opinion, Mr. top man, you are the lowest filth of the whole affair. She walked to the door and turned back to the desk, don't bother trying to run. Those marines outside, they are now facing inwards. Enjoy the rest of your day.'

'I will get you for this! I have connections and when this is all sorted out I will be coming for you bitch.You and all those do-gooders on the island. Mark my words!' his voice rose until he was screaming at her.

She smiled at him, 'You already tried that, and failed, quite miserably.'

He swept everything in reach, off the desk in a fit of anger.

'Get out!' he screamed.

Kia looked at Jen, she was staring at the raving President slam his fists on the desk.

'Come on Jen, time for that trip.'

Jen nodded and took a wide berth around the fuming President.

Kia followed Jen out of the office and closed the door behind them.

More sounds of destruction came through the door as he threw the laptop against the door. 'You motherless fucking bitch! I will get you all, I will nuke that fucking island!!'

His screaming could be heard clearly through the door as they walked side by side towards the entrance.

Jen looked at Kia, 'He always has to have the last parting shot, always did.Probably will charm his way out of this, he is slimy like that.'

Kia stopped walking and looked at Jen, 'Not this time.'

She turned in one ultra-smooth movement, Jen didn't even see her draw! One handed Kia sent a slug straight through the centre panel of the closed office door. She holstered just as swiftly and continued walking out the main entrance. Neither of them looked back.

Kia opened the door to the S2 and let Jen walk in first, with one last look around she climbed in and closed the door.

As the S2 door closed the Presidents hands dropped into his lap. His weak attempt to stop the blood spurting out of the hole in the centre of his chest had failed.

Chapter Eighty Six

Out over the ocean, Kia handed a strong hot cup of coffee to Jen. She had just finished talking to Ron Baker. She had told him to recall his men. There was nothing at the Manor worth protecting anymore.

'How are you feeling Jen?'

'Yeah OK I suppose, it's a lot to take in. I just never saw that coming, and I have spent hours every day with him. What's going to happen now?'

'That is for the incoming people to decide. I hate politics and avoid it like the plague, believe it or not. The people who need to know have been told, they also have copies of all the Backroom documentation.

'I suppose there is going to be a lot of questions asked of the CIA and NSA. Why they did not find this out, or if they were part of it. Either way, the courts are going to be very busy for a long time.'

'Oh god no, I don't want to be dragged into that shit!'

'I can't see why you would be, write up a statement and I will get Sandy to get it to the right people. Then just forget it. Look, you have been through a lot, so how about you put it away for the next week or so and get yourself back on an even keel?'

Jen nodded, 'Sounds good.'

Kia did a slow circle of the island so Jen could see it all from above, she pointed out the individual building and what purpose they served.

'Amazing! And look at that pure golden sand and blue water! This is going to be a fantastic holiday!'

Kia landed next to a line of other S2s in the parking area outside the OpCen. They were halfway across the area when a stream of people poured down the steps and met them.

'Jen!', Bree called and hugged her, 'So glad you are OK!' Lots of smiling and grinning and backslapping.

Kia broke through the babble, 'OK guys up to the café, I am starving!'

En-Mass they walked back to the stairs. Jen stopped at the top step and looked around, taking in the nine S2s of various colours.

'One question Just one of those awesome machines brought that ugly pack of traitors down, why didn't you use all of them?'

Everyone stopped on hearing the question.

'The S2s are not armed Jen, they are what we use to do what we do. I will show you later what we do here.' Kia replied.

'Contrary to popular belief we are quite nice, easy going people' Miako added.
Jen burst out laughing at the innocent pose Paul and Glen tried to strike.

'OK then, if it's not top secret, just how did you do it?'
Kia smiled', It IS top secret actually.'

Brad laughed, 'It's that top secret only Paul and Glen have ever seen Kia's friend close up, and those bums refuse to talk. Not fair really.'

Miako walked over and stood in front of Kia. 'I for one, would like to thank her personally for saving my life and the lives of the people I hold dear.'

Kia looked into her emerald green eyes and saw the pleading.
She threw her hands up in a simulated gesture of surrender.
'OK! OK, I see I am outvoted, BUT, only IF she wants to show herself.'
Kia looked at the sky. Everyone went silent and looked as well.
'ValKyrie? The crew are asking to thank you in person.'

Nothing happened. The next moment a deep female voice

appeared out of thin air.

'I shall be there momentarily, I am returning from removing the spy satellites that were positioned over the island during the minor altercation.'

'There!' pointed Neil excitedly, a tiny dot due south of the island, sunlight reflecting off her iridescent red skin. The dot grew larger at an unbelievable rate! In seconds she hovered directly in front of Kia.

'Thanks are not necessary. I was just doing my job, as do all the other members of Oracle Industries.'
Neil stepped closer and reached out to touch ValKyrie.

'Oh, my, God!', he whispered. Spacing the exclamation a second apart.

'No fingerprints please Neil'
He withdrew his hand like he had been burnt!

Paul burst out laughing. Miako walked up to ValKyrie and wrapped her arms around the sleek nose of the craft. 'Then you will have to contend with a hug-print!'
Miako let go and stepped back, 'On behalf of the crew we thank you, not only for doing your job but for protecting us and more importantly protecting Kia. I for one will sleep better knowing that you are near.'

Kia laughed at the look on Jen's face. 'A pirouette if you don't mind, dear then you may do, whatever it is you do.'
ValKyrie turned a slow 360 degrees, letting the crew take in her every detail.

'Now I have unfinished business to attend to.'

Kia waved, and ValKyrie turned towards the open sea and virtually disappeared!

'Geezus!' said Jen out loud, 'I have absolutely never seen anything more beautiful or deadly than that! But it...'

'She', Kia corrected.

'She looked unarmed!'

'That's because she makes the weaponry as she needs it.'
Jen looked confused, 'I also have no more questions.'

'Good' Kia said, 'because I am still hungry.'

With that, they headed to the café, chatting excitedly about what they had just seen.

Over the next week, Kia and Jen toured the complex, talking to nearly everyone there. Jen loved the historians and the artefacts they showed her every time she returned.

Miako and Neil had taken off a few days ago to visit Ben in Switzerland and check on the place. Now that it was converted to the main staging area for tourists and adventurers of the valley.

Paul and Glen had taken Kate back to see her aunt, but this time stayed close by her side.

Mel and Ray spent a lot of the time between the beach and the indoor range. He found she was a natural shooter, and spent hours coaching her. Brad and Bree had returned from a tour of friends and relatives on the mainland.

As the weekend rolled around, all had returned home.

The Coven had been keeping everyone updated on the massive upheaval in the States. The news had exploded over the whole world. A secret military organisation had tried to take over the US from behind the scenes and had been led by the recently deceased President.

It was reported that the President had died from a heart condition during the course of the investigation.

There was no official inclusion of Oracle's involvement, but the stories and innuendos were there that the Secret Military Order or SMO as it was being touted as having tried to attack Oracle and lost badly.

Not just lost but had been wiped off the face of the map. Lawsuits and warrants were issued in the hundreds by the newly founded committee's that were tasked with cleaning up the mess. They relentlessly chased down the ones who funded the SMO or aided it in any way. No other investigation had ever been as public as this one.

Almost everything was done with transparency.

One news by-line that made Kia smile was the promotion of a Captain Hughes to General Hughes. The promotion had jumped several ranks, but there was need of good top men.

Seated in the pub, the entire crew, including Jen and Rob and some of the historians took up a huge table. They had just finished their evening meal and were discussing any and everything that came up in conversation.

Drinks were ordered, beer arrived by the jug full for the boys. Kia leant back and looked from person to person. She reflected just how good things had turned out. She was constantly amazed by the enthusiasm each person had for what they did.

Jen leant over to Kia, 'You have an amazing bunch of people here! I have never seen such a dynamic in any organisation! They all complement each other.'

She nodded, 'Indeed, these people are just the best, and I feel privileged to work with each and every one.'

'You don't give yourself enough credit Kia! You built all this!'

'Maybe so, but without them, Oracle would not exist.'

By the end of the evening everyone had drunk just a little too much and eaten more than they should have, but all had a great time.

Kia was the first to stand and bid everyone goodnight.

'I am off for a shower and bed.' She raised her near empty wine glass, 'Here is to each and every one of you. I am proud of you all.'

A rousing cheer and shout rose from the table as everyone joined in the toast.

Jen stood as well, 'I shall also call it a night, all this fresh air and sunshine is hard to take!' That caused a round of heartfelt laughter.

Outside, as Jen and Kia walked up towards the villas, Jen was quiet.

'Penny for your thoughts.' Asked Kia.

'I was wondering if you had a job I could do here? I really love this place, and to be honest do not have anything to go back to in the States. Even if it's just as a beach bum.'

'Jen, I am sure we can find something for you to do. You told me when you were little, you always wanted to be a diver or an astronaut.'

Jen laughed, 'Yes I did. I love adventure.'

'Well then, why don't you join the main crew? That gets mighty adventurous from time to time!'

Jen stopped in her tracks! 'You have got to be joking! I am nothing like those awesome people!'

Kia looped her arm through Jens and started them walking again, 'Now who is not giving themselves enough credit. I tell you what, think about it. I will ask them tomorrow what THEY think, and we shall see what happens.'

'OK deal!', Jen said with a huge smile, impulsively she hugged Kia. 'Thank you so much!'

In the villa Kia headed for the shower, and Jen busied herself making coffee, her mind was racing. She had secretly hoped that there would be something for her to do on the island.

Kia finished her shower and wrapped in a huge towel with her hair up, she sat in the lounge drinking the coffee. On a laptop, she was flicking through the reports of the day.
Jen appeared also wrapped in a towel. 'I needed that, I think I had one glass too many and was feeling fuzzy.' Kia grinned.

Jens eyes flicked to the laptop, 'You working?'

'Nope, just checking in with Sandy, it's a habit I have.'

Jen nodded, 'I can relate to that, I always check the rosters for the next day, or I should say I used to.'
Kia closed the laptop and put her coffee cup in the sink.

'That was the old Jen, now we have a whole new Jen. I think you are perfect for the crew, you impressed me right from the start.' Jen looked directly into Kia's Tawny-Gold flecked eyes, 'And you had me awestruck the first time I saw you.'
Kia smiled back, their eyes met, their lips met and the towels hit the floor.

Chapter Eighty Seven

The sun was shining through the open balcony door into the OpCen. Jen and Kia were on the balcony watching the complex hustle and bustle. Rob had just left and was on the way down to the docks. He was nursing a hangover this morning and was the butt of a few jokes from the crew inside. Glen and Ray were not doing too much better themselves but were trying to hide it, and failing.

'Come on Jen, now Rob has gone, lets see if I was right or not.'Kia stood. They walked into the shade of the OpCen.

'OK boys and girls. Gather round, I have a question for you all. You have two minutes to think about it, and then we vote. That includes you Sandy and the Coven.'

'That's not fair' Neil said', Sandy can do a lot of thinking in two minutes.'

Mel ruffled Neil's hair, 'Foolish boy the extra time is for your slow brain!'

'Jen, has asked for a job. She suggested becoming our resident beach-bum.'

That brought giggles.

'I think she undervalues herself. So I offered her a different job, but one I want you all to vote on.'

Paul, Brad, and Bree lifted their hands and said 'Yes!'

'Hang on! I haven't told you yet.'

'You offered her a job on the crew with us, and I endorse that 100%. It's obvious that she is perfect for the job.

'Actually, I would say she is more qualified than the rest of us combined! So my vote is a resounding YES!' Paul finished with a huge grin.

Kia sighed, 'Damn your analytical mind, Paul. Yes, I think that Jen would be a great asset, her mind thinks out of the box. My personal feelings aside, I still want a vote from you. It's important to me.'

Miako smiled and hugged both Kia and Jen. 'The aura that flows between you both is very strong! It is the same aura I see between Brad and Bree, Mel and Ray and Neil and myself. In my eyes, it would be impossible to say no on so many different levels. You have my blessing.'

The vote was unanimous! On the HUD came the result 13 yes, 0 no.

Kia looked at the number wide eyed! Not only had the 11 crew voted and Sandy, but ValKyrie had cast her vote as well!

Jen teared up badly and tried her best to hide it, but after the fifth handshake and a hug, she lost it all together.

Chapter Eighty Eight

The next week rushed past quickly. Most of the crew were doing flag runs or picking areas the drones had not yet cleared. Jen had taken to the Sims like no-one else. Managing to top Neil's score on the second day. She had been out as Kia's wingman for the last few days.

There was nothing urgent on the board to do. All the mess over the previous weeks had been sorted. They had all just had a few days R&R and were relaxed and content.

All but Jen and Neil were in the OpCen. Sandy had given them an extra special task today. One of the Sats had started to malfunction and she had sent them both to go and retrieve it. Neil had been stunned when he heard of the mission. He was actually going to go into space! Jen was wide eyed when she realised where they were going. Kia had just smiled and said, 'Well, you wanted to be an astronaut, now is your chance.'

Kia sat with her back to the wall and felt all the tension ease out of her. Life was once again quiet and normal. On the HUD in front of her was a display showing two green icons heading back towards the island.

She closed her eyes and willed her brain to slow down. Even Sandy was humming some obscure tune as she went about her business.

Brad sat next to Kia. She opened her eyes.

'Problem?' he asked

'Nope, this is the first time we have had a clean task board for over a year, and I am enjoying the peace for a change.'

'Good to hear' he said, 'Well, enjoy it while you can, I am

sure something will turn up.'
    Sandy stopped humming! 'Incoming call Kia.'
She raised an eyebrow at Sandy.
    'It's the Russian President, he is asking for you personally.'